PRAISE FOR HIDING IN HIBBING

"I had never even heard of Hibbing, Minnesota. But I'm grateful David O'Malley had. It inspired him to write a totally absorbing book. For four consecutive days, his *Hiding in Hibbing* and its wonderful characters have kept me happily involved and thoroughly entertained."
~ Carl Reiner, award-winning writer, director and comedy legend
Author of *Enter Laughing* and *I Remember Me*

"This is the comedy that Garrison Keillor and Bob Dylan might have written if they had met at a party and both drank too many margaritas. *Hiding in Hibbing* has wonderfully flawed, all-too-real characters who just want a tiny sip of that elixir called fame. A deft and funny novel."
~ Pierce Gardner, screenwriter of *Dan In Real Life*

"David O'Malley has written a smart, funny page-turner full of quirky characters in a unique, colorful setting. Fans of Carl Hiaasen will love *Hiding in Hibbing*."
~ James L. Conway, author of *Dead and Not So Buried*

"*Hiding in Hibbing* is terrific! Tightly crafted, informed and funny. Absolutely on target. Great work! I'm green with envy!"
~ Jerry Bowles, author of *A Thousand Sundays*

"The flow and detail made it a pleasure to read. I loved harking back to the 1970s and revisiting characters of that era. I may have even hung out and partied with some of those dudes back in the day. A truly fun story!"
~ Barry Livingston, author of *The Importance of Being Ernie*

*Nan—
Thank you so much for everything you've done! You've made my book a success!!! —David O'Malley*

HIDING IN HIBBING

David O'Malley

CB
Crockett / Bradbury

Los Angeles

This novel is a work of fiction. Any references to real people, events, establishments, organizations, or locales are intended only to give the fiction a sense of reality and authenticity, and are used fictitiously. All other names, characters, places and incidents portrayed in this book are the product of the author's imagination.

All rights reserved. No part of this book may be reproduced or transmitted in any form or by any means, electronic or mechanical, including photocopying, recording, or any information storage and retrieval system, without permission in writing from the publisher.

Cover Design by Phillip Leftfield

HIDING IN HIBBING
Copyright © 2015 by David O'Malley
All Rights Reserved

Published March 2015
ISBN: 978-0-9909636-0-8
(Trade Paper)
ISBN: 978-0-9909636-1-5
(eBook)

For Karen

A wall of white. An empty canvas upon which—with a flurry of painterly strokes—a most unusual tale can be told. A splash of irony here, a daub of deceit there, along with a broad smear of confusion and magical misdirection ... and, unexpectedly, surprisingly, amazingly... much of it ***actually happened.***

PART ONE
HIBBING

"Some memories are realities, and are better than anything that can ever happen to one again."

Willa Cather

1

January 14, 1971
Near Hibbing, Minnesota

Within the white swirl of a winter blizzard, the towering snow banks along route 73 muffled the mechanical growl of a chugging beast, its angry rumble swallowed by a trillion tiny ice dancers cast down by darkening clouds.

A cranky snowplow emerged from the thick pallor, its angled iron nose scrapping the concrete road, shoving cascading mounds of snow and gravel into huge heaps, carving a path that was immediately filled with more snow.

Sam Huffnapf, the plow driver, squinted hard through a pitted windshield clumped with ice clods, blinded by the messy swarm of cartwheeling flakes splattering the glass. Frustrated, he shoved his head out the window, his ruddy skin blasted by the blowing snow, eyelashes quickly coated with sticky wet flakes that gummed up his vision. He could barely make out anything a few feet ahead. The snarl of exasperation deep in his throat mimicked the harsh roar of the old snowplow's straining engine. "Goddamn winter," Sam muttered. Not a curse, but a mantra.

A wavering dark shape appeared faintly in the path ahead. Sam tensed every muscle, blinking, not certain what he was seeing. Then...a thud. Not loud. Soft, as feathers against flesh, but undeniably clear and distinct. His foot stomped hard on the brake pedal, ramming it nearly to the floor, a pain shooting through his arthritic toes and the arch of his bad foot. The heavy tires locked, skidding on the icy surface, unable to find traction.

Finally stopped, Sam sat unmoving. His eyes refused to blink. There was a roar somewhere, rising and falling, but he couldn't distinguish its source. Until he realized it was his own panicked breathing, sucking and blowing through his nose and gaping mouth. His warm moist breath puffed out clouds of vapor, quickly fogging the windshield. He could feel his heart thumping in his chest—Gene Krupa bashing out an angry drum solo.

His mind whirled. Damn, he thought. Maybe a deer. Or an elk. Stupid goddamn animals. Roads are for cars and trucks. Animals got the woods. The whole forest. The whole God-dang wilderness clear to Canada. They don't need to come prancing out on the highways.

He climbed down from the snowplow cab, clumsy boots slipping on the slick hard-pack. Steadied his body against the door, then small-stepped his way toward the front of the plow, trying to keep a creeping anxiety at bay.

As he peered around the big blade, Sam came to a jarring halt. He felt the air rush from his lungs and his stomach churn with the hollow plunge of nausea. His legs buckled as he sank into the snow, staring. "Awww fer geez."

This would not be one of his better days.

2

Southeast of Hibbing, on state road 37, a VW bus crawled steadily through the deepening snow. Its headlights poked dull beams into the thick curtain of flakes, no more helpful than a couple of weak flashlights bobbing around in a bowl of pea soup. It rode low on its small tires, weighed down by the four men huddled inside. The rear seat had been stripped out, every inch now jammed with various sized boxes and metal equipment cases.

Ray Decker hunched over the steering wheel, squinting hard, trying to penetrate the persistent barrage of swirling snowflakes. They whipped at the frosted windshield with the ferocity of mad albino bees. He blinked once, twice... eyes dulled with fatigue. Brushed the long shocks of stringy hair back from his face, trying to hook the annoying strands over his ears. Damn hippy hair, he thought. You're twenty-six, Ray. What're you doing with stupid hippy hair and these bullshit tie-dyed hippy rags? Fuck the counter-culture. How about acting your age and getting some real culture. When was the last time you went out to a movie? Read a book? *Any* book. Or even a newspaper?

The front wheel abruptly caught a hard edge of the shoulder, spitting up gravel buried beneath the snow.

Tony Gallagher sat up like a rocket, steel rod tense, arms braced against the door and dash, eyes bugged out. He had been awkwardly slumped in the seat next to Ray, riding shotgun, struggling to twist himself into a semi-comfortable position to catch a few restless winks, when... whomp! The bus suddenly ricocheted around carnival style.

Ray snapped out of his self-critical reverie, jerking the wheel hard to the left, throwing them back on course.

"What the fuck!" Which was how Tony talked when startled. Under normal circumstances he had a greater facility for language. Fact was he had a genuine fascination with words.

Ray barked, "Shut up, Gallagher." Because that's what they called him. Not Tony. Or even Anthony, which was his birth name. Just Gallagher. He didn't mind too much. It had some cachet. And he liked that word..."cachet."

"Both of you knock it off. I'm trying to work on this thing here." That was Joe Studebaker. Squatting on the metal cases in the darkness behind them. Having already crept into his mid-thirties, Joe was the elder statesman of the group. Had shorter hair than the others, but it was still an unruly mop. Liked to run his fingers through it, from front to back, palm flat on his forehead, whenever he wanted to appear like he was deep in thought, anguishing over ideas.

"I think... frogs," said another voice from the darkness. After a moment, Arthur Zigmond leaned forward into the light. Just a couple months shy of twenty and boyishly handsome, Arthur—who didn't look anything at all like an Arthur—was saved from that stodgy misnomer by nearly everyone embracing the quirkiness of his unusual last name, Zigmond, which quickly mutated into simply Ziggy.

"What?" Joe said, staring at Ziggy with irritable puzzlement.

"I said, I'm thinking...frogs."

Joe shook it off dismissively. "No, no. Talking... trout."

"Trout?"

"Yeah. Trout. Bass. Crappies. Whatever. Fish. But a clever looking fish. With bright, intelligent eyes."

"For a beer commercial?"

HIDING IN HIBBING

Joe sat up straighter on the camera case, letting his imposing stature signal his authority. "This is Minnesota. It's all about fish up here."

"Frogs would be funnier."

"Ziggy, you're the camera assistant. I'm the agency producer. And the director on this damn thing, see?"

"I know, but frogs..."

Joe cut him off sharply. "Your job, carry cases... load mags... find lenses. I'm the creative one. The idea guy, see? "

"Yeah, but I got ideas too. I think..."

"Don't go there, Zig. You start thinking, you'll just get in trouble."

Ziggy looked down at the floor, chastised, and now dejected. A silence hung in the air. The steady hum of the VW engine filled the void.

Finally, Ray chimed in from the driver's seat. "It's just some stupid local brewery anyway, right?"

Ziggy looked up at Joe. "You never give me a chance."

"It's not your calling, Zig. Some people are cut out for thinking—ruminating and cogitating, and all that—it's just not your bailiwick."

Gallagher's ears perked up. *Bailiwick.* He liked the sound of it. The way the *b* rolled gently into the soft airy sigh of both the *a* and *i* followed by the tongue gently touching the back of the teeth to form the letter *l*, trailed by another *i*, only sounding like a long *e*. And then the sharp, definitive conclusion provided by *wick*. He mouthed the word silently, filled with enormous satisfaction.

Ziggy just stared blankly at Joe, flummoxed.

"You know... bailiwick."

Nothing from Ziggy.

"Bailiwick!" Joe stated firmly, intoning it even more loudly the second time to better stress its comprehension, like people do when speaking to foreigners, thinking that greater volume will somehow improve their ability to translate.

Zig gave a little shrug. Had no clue.

Gallagher stared into the blizzard, silently mouthing the word over and over, a blissful smile on his lips.

"Well it's not yours," Joe grumbled. "Trust me."

"But frogs have personality. Fish can't even smile."

Ray belched like a frog. "What is it? Weasel Piss Ale or some shit like that? Who cares?"

Gallagher entered the roundelay with enthusiasm. "How about dancing weasels?"

"If it ain't Blatz," Ray offered, "it ain't beer."

"Knock it off," Joe barked. "This is not a brainstorming session. You're the camera team. I'm handling creative on this. I'll decide what's what. So can it!"

The heavy silence returned. Hum of the engine. Tires crunching softly in the snow. Ziggy squirmed restlessly on the hard camera case. "I just feel in my gut that frogs can be very funny."

Joe lowered his voice to make a pronouncement with weighty finality. "Listen to me, Zigmond. I know what I'm talking about. Nobody will ever—*ever!*—buy beer from a talking frog."

This hung in the hushed, cold air without challenge. You could almost hear the sound of flakes dive-bombing the windshield over the drone of the small engine. Then, suddenly, Ray slammed the brakes. The VW bus slid to a jarring stop, catapulting Ziggy from his tenuous perch on the metal camera case. He landed on his back between the two front seats, head lodged between the passenger seat and gearshift handle.

Joe scrambled forward to get a look through the windshield, straddling Ziggy, one knee digging into Zig's stomach.

Through the blizzard Joe saw a Minnesota State Trooper push the door of his cruiser open, planting his fur-lined boots into the calf-deep snow.

He gave Ray's shoulder an urgent nudge. "Where's your grass?"

"In the Arri case I think." But there was no time to dig through the cases to find it and nowhere to dump it anyway.

The Trooper tromped toward them, pulling the flashlight off his utility belt with professional proficiency.

"I'll handle this," Joe said. Ziggy groaned under the weight, the persistent pressure of Joe's knee pushing down against his stomach and rib cage.

The Trooper stood outside the driver's side window, staring at them through the frosted glass. He clicked the flashlight on and shined it through the thick rime.

Twirled his finger, motioning for them to open the car window.

Ray slowly rolled the glass pane down. A sharp gust sprayed a blast of freezing ice crystals into his face.

The Trooper peered inside, playing the flashlight beam over the scruffy collection of characters, scowling at their long, unkempt hair. He squinted with suspicion at the cases piled high in the back of the V-dub. Then, abruptly shined the bright light in Ray's eyes.

"Where ya off to there?"

Ray turned away, blinded by the light, eyelids squeezed tight,

"Bemidji, sir," Joe said with uncustomary politeness.

The trooper clicked the light off. "Golly, not tonight. The road, she's closed. Situation up ahead on route seven-three. Plus add to it the flurries. Had ta shut 'er down."

"Flurries?" Ray said. Then, once again, with a different emphasis, as if he hadn't heard right the first time. "Flurries?"

Joe pushed forward, hoping to intercede before Ray said something stupid. "When's it gonna open up?"

"Might tomorrow. Might not. Couple days. Who knows, eh?"

Joe nodded, keeping it friendly. "Big storm, huh?"

"It'll do. Buried my brother-in-law's Buick. Ain't found her yet. LeSabre. Darn tall car, that one."

"You don't say. Buick, huh?" Joe shifted around and pushed forward so he could engage the officer directly with a forced grin, working hard to keep things amiable. Ziggy groaned under the knee shoved like a pile driver into his gut.

Looking out into the blinding storm, Joe asked, "Where exactly are we?"

The trooper scrunched his face up in a pained grimace at the sight of Ziggy cringing in agony on the floor between the seats. "What's his problem there?"

Joe and Gallagher looked down at Ziggy in dumb silence, as if seeing him for the first time. Ray stared straight ahead, biting his tongue, attempting to see if he could somehow make himself invisible.

The trooper clicked the flashlight back on. Shined it in Ziggy's eyes, blinding him. Ziggy groaned.

"He on dope?"

"No, sir," Joe came back quick as a bunny. "Got a hernia."

Ziggy opened his mouth. "I was... ummmmph!" Gave out a moan as Joe dug his knee in harder against Zig's rib cage.

"Easy, kid. We'll get you to a doctor."

Still skeptical, the trooper ventured, "So... it's not one of them LDS hallucination type deals then?"

Gallagher stifled a disdainful snort. He wanted to straighten out this yokel on the obvious difference between the psychedelic properties of LSD and the Mormon Church, but wisely reconsidered.

Joe shook his head with certainty. "Nah. Standard hernia is all. We should probably find a motel."

Reluctantly clicking off his inquisitor's torch, the trooper said flat out, "No sir. Not a good idea. Better you go on back, is what."

"Back?"

"Where ya come in from."

"We drove in from Chicago."

"Never been there. Heard it gets cold."

They all looked out at the frigid swirling snow. Bursts of surly flakes blasted in through the open window on a harsh wind.

Ray couldn't help himself. "Colder than this?" Ray said.

The trooper shrugged. "Couldn't say. Never made me a trip down there."

"Can you point us to a motel?" Joe said, tired of small talk.

Leaning in a bit, the officer squinted hard at the metal equipment cases, his eyes drifting across the four travelers with obvious suspicion. "Last year some of them radical Wisconsin students holed up in a motel room, don'tcha know. Hatched a plan to wreak havoc and mayhem up the state capitol."

"Well, we're not from Wisconsin," Joe said with a smile, hoping that would put the subject to rest.

"Uh-huh..." the trooper replied, using every bit of his thirteen and a half years' experience as a law enforcement officer to scrutinize the potential suspects. Then, with a dismissive sniff, his investigation was complete.

"Well, okay then. Mind ya now, these folks hereabouts are a touch irritable, what with the taconite mines closed down an' stuff. Everybody outta work, ya catch my drift."

Joe nodded. "Not really...but thanks for the tip." He reached across Ray and rolled the window up, keeping an amiable smile plastered on his face.

The trooper just stood there in the weather, his dull dark shape barely visible through the frost-covered window. After a moment, he tapped the glass with his flashlight.

Ray and Gallagher exchanged nervous glances. Ray threw a quick, uncertain look back at Joe, who gave a nearly imperceptible nod.

DAVID O'MALLEY

Ray rolled the window down part way, just a cautious crack. The frigid air bit at his face again, stinging his eyes. The trooper leaned down.

"My brother-in-law... with the LeSabre. Had a hernia. Dint kill him. But walks stooped over now. Pert'near a hunchback." He looked down at Ziggy's pained face. "You ought get somebody check that out soon's ya can."

3

They didn't go back to Chicago. That wasn't even in the cards. Night was closing in and the storm was getting worse. They'd already driven sixteen hours in that cramped German sardine can, so taking orders from some small town Barney Fife was just not an option.

Instead, they doubled-back to route 169 and right smack into the outskirts of Hibbing. When the neon lights of Carl's Front Range Restaurant poked through the curtain of falling snow, Ray made a beeline for the parking lot. The warm glow from inside the hardwood-framed diner was a welcoming sight.

As they stepped through the door, all eyes turned their way. Conversation stopped. The air grew heavy with mute expectation. They may as well have been draft dodgers walking into a VFW convention. Their unkempt clothes and long hair were bad enough; the fact they were strangers made things even worse.

A neatly hand-lettered cardboard sign mounted in a metal frame rested on a makeshift easel next to the cash register just inside the door.

It read: ***What are you waiting for? SIT YOUR BUTT DOWN.***

Joe nudged them, nodding toward an empty booth. They headed for it, sliding easily into the slippery tuck-n-roll Naugahyde bench seats. Ziggy trailed after them, eyes scanning the other customers uneasily, feeling out of place.

At a two-top along the back wall, Sam Huffnapf hung his head over a cup of coffee, wallowing in sorrow and guilt. Ziggy stood by the booth gazing down the aisle at Sam with concern. Impatient, Joe grabbed Ziggy's arm and pulled him into the booth.

"Sit down, Zig." He dropped a menu in front of him.

Ziggy looked back over his shoulder at Sam. Then, ignoring the menu, let his eyes drift around the spacious room, taking in the locals. Most had already turned their attention back to their food, apparently deciding that the trashy strangers, though reprehensible in appearance, were probably harmless.

Next to the order window, Carl, the middle-aged owner, hovered over Janey Olsen, a young waitress who appeared emotionally wrung out, her face flushed with tears. Both hung their heads in silent, brooding contemplation of either the floor or their feet.

"Janey...go on home," Carl told her in a hushed voice, trying not to attract undue attention or embarrass her. "You shouldn't have to be here, what with the tragedy and all."

"It's okay," she said, even though it wasn't.

"Oughta be home. Your granny woulda wanted..."

"I'm fine. Really. I want to, okay? Just, ya know... okay?"

Ziggy watched them, peering over the top of his menu.

They looked like a couple of unlikely baseball umpires huddled in a concentrated effort to sort out a disputed rundown between first and second.

Joe checked his wallet, quickly counting his cash. "Order small, fellahs. Gotta stretch this. Didn't count on us getting stuck by a goddamn blizzard."

Ziggy folded his arms across his stomach, rocking forward a bit, wincing in pain. Didn't make a big deal out of it. But Joe noticed.

"S'matter? Ribs achin'? "

"Well, jeez...you think?"

"Couldn't let you talk, Zig. Ya got this honesty problem. Open your mouth and the truth slobbers out like baby drool."

Gallagher blurted a laugh, enjoying the drool imagery.

Down the aisle, Ziggy saw Janey drop off an order. She started toward them, a vision of vulnerable loveliness torn by emotional distress. Ziggy blinked; slid straight up in the seat, nervously checking the menu for something that might spark a question, anything that would give him an opportunity to speak to her.

She paused at their table, glancing back at Sam with sincere concern. He continued to peer into the depths of his coffee cup, sobbing quietly. Janey's hand trembled as she pulled the pencil and pad from the pocket of her waitress apron. She paled, lips mashed together, fighting back more tears.

Ziggy stared openly, captivated. She's so fragile, he thought. Fragile...and delicate. Those were the very words that floated through his mind, though he'd rarely, if ever, spoken either of them aloud in his entire life. Watching her, he felt certain that she might suddenly shatter like crystal.

Janey fumbled with her pad. "Okay, uh...can I, uh... would any of you like some...coff..."

She stopped, biting hard on her bottom lip. The word choked in the back of her throat, hanging in limbo, trapped. "...coff..." she repeated.

Ray and Gallagher looked up at her with mouths agape, wondering what her problem was. Meanwhile, Ziggy was riding every sharp surge of Janey's emotional roller coaster, suffering right along with her. He leaned toward her slightly, head bobbing softly with encouragement. Her face began to twist into a mask of great sorrow. "...coff..."

Ziggy hunched forward tensely, straining inside, trying to use his mind to help her push the elusive word out. Joe turned his eye to Ziggy, watching him with wary puzzlement, sensing the pressure building.

Finally, Ziggy couldn't take it anymore. "...fee?" he said as gently as he could manage.

And Janey lost it. An eruption of sobs poured forth. Tears gushed. Mortified, she rushed toward the restrooms.

The customers turned to glare with disgust at the long-haired reprobates. A hushed buzz of guarded speculation rolled through the room. Carl looked toward the ladies room where Janey had dashed to take refuge. He strode toward them with a scowl of rage.

"What'd ya say to Janey?" he demanded, his neck getting flushed a bright red that nearly matched the slippery Naugahyde of the booth.

Joe shrugged sincerely. "Nothing. Not a thing."

"I don't tolerate instigatin' my hourly employees to squirt tears!"

Sam Huffnapf buried his face deeper into his crossed arms on the table, causing a loud clatter of cup, saucer and spoon.

"Look there. Now you're upsettin' Sam!"

Ray muttered, "I knew this was a bad idea." Gallagher nodded silently.

"I'm not gonna kick you outta the darn place," Carl said, trying hard to keep his cool. "This is America. Even jerks got rights. Just order your food. Eat it. Get out. And no more insurrective behavior." He started to leave, then came back. "I'm not one to argue politics, but Woodstock... and that Kent State fiasco...now, see, we got a problem here... while these decent, hard-workin' folks are tryin' to drink their coffee, eat their pie and all."

"Pie! Yeah," Gallagher blurted out, a glint of inspiration flashing in his eyes.

Carl rolled his cold gaze toward Gallagher.

"I love apple pie," he shrugged with a big dumb grin and no sense of context. "It's my fave."

Carl's lip twitched. He wanted to cuss this goofy little bastard up, down and sideways. But deep inside he knew he served up the best damn apple pie within a hundred miles of Hibbing and didn't want to get into a pissing match over something he agreed with, even if it was coming from the mouth of a commie-loving street slug. He stifled his irate sneer and turned instead to Joe

"So you follow my track here? Where I'm going with this?"

"Yes sir." Joe nodded politely, knowing when to call it quits and leave his cards face down.

"Well, okay then," Carl said. He let his stern gaze sweep across the bunch. Then marched toward the kitchen, jaw jutted out, giving his customers a bold look of confidence that shouted *situation under control.*

Gallagher slammed his menu shut. "Yep. Apple pie it is."

Joe ignored the pie lover and turned his attention to Ziggy, summoning a scolding tone. "What's the matter with you? You don't go jumpin' in like that to finish what somebody's saying."

"I was just trying to..."

"Help. I know. It's not polite."

"I didn't mean to..."

"Upset her. I got it. Just don't."

At the two-top against the back wall, Sam cut loose with a keening sob followed by a heartbreaking moan that plumbed the depths of his despair. Joe glared accusingly at Ziggy, who shrugged with sincere innocence. "I didn't do anything. Honest."

"Big, big mistake comin' here," said Ray.

"Why do you always look at the negative side?"

Ray shrugged. "Just being realistic."

"You're being negative." Joe turned to Ziggy. "He's being negative, right?"

"I try not to judge people."

"Well, I do. He's an idiot," Gallagher said, puckering up to puff on an improvised plastic straw blowgun, shooting the straw wrapper at Ray, hitting him in the face. Ray wadded the paper wrapper into a tight ball and fired it right back at Gallagher's head.

Joe heaved a leaden sigh. Shook his head at their adolescent behavior. "That kind of attitude doesn't help things. It's replete with negativity."

Gallagher grinned at the word *replete*. "Ye-e-e-ah."

Ray shrugged it off. "Just being realistic, man. And reality is we're stuck here 'cause of the goddamn snow."

During this heated exchange, Ziggy watched Carl console Janey by the cigarette machine next to the restrooms. She nodded several times, pulling her tear-dampened hair back from reddened eyes, trying hard to compose herself. Then, unexpectedly, she looked their way. Ziggy quickly averted his eyes, snapping his head around so fast he wrenched his neck.

Drawn to the sudden movement, Gallagher gaped at Ziggy's pained expression, trying to decipher its source.

Flustered, Ziggy grabbed the wrong edge of his menu, struggling vainly to open it. "You guys ready? Know what you want?"

"Pie pie pie," Gallagher chanted like a mantra. "Apple pie."

"What's this pie fixation you got?" Ray said. "It's probably crap!"

"Negative," Joe muttered low. "Negative...negative..."

"Well, yeah, Joe. What do ya expect? We're stuck here in friggin' Hibbing, Minnesota with some wacko waitress..."

"She's just upset," Ziggy shot back, but nobody paid any attention.

Suddenly, Janey reappeared at the table, her lips pressed in a tight, straight line, straining to keep her emotions in check, securely trapped inside. A faint crooked ribbon of tears clung to the soft skin of her cheeks and a small droplet of moisture was already beginning to form under the tip of her nose. Still, she forced a pained smile.

"Sorry for the...I'm just...uh, I'm..."

Her blue eyes met Ziggy's gaze. She detected a look of genuine empathy and trembled, clutching her order pad and pencil. Took a deep breath. "Okay then...would any of you like some..."

Emotion welled up inside her chest and then moved up into her throat. "Coff..." Trapped again, the half-word just hung there, floating in the air, incomplete and meaningless, crying out for resolution. Her lips quivered uncontrollably. Tiny, tight sounds emanated from deep in Janey's throat, competing with small gasps and halting breaths.

They all watched her with tense anticipation. Ziggy ached to jump in and scream the word to end her suffering and provide everyone at the table respite from this cruel embarrassment.

"...coff..."

Ziggy turned to Joe, eyes pleading. But Joe shot him a warning look that proclaimed, "don't...say...anything."

"...coff..."

Pushed over the line by wild impatience, Ray leaned forward, nearly lunging, brittle eyes the intense grey orbs of a charging wolf. "Coffee! Yes! We'll all have fucking coffee!"

A brief inundation of roaring silence; an emptiness so profound that an actual void was created, sucking everything natural from the room. And then, to fill the horrible vacuum, Janey burst into a storm of tears and sobs, rushing away.

"And I want pie," Gallagher called after her.

Joe slammed his menu shut and slid from the booth, shoving Ziggy aside. "That's it. We're gone."

On his feet, Ziggy started to follow after Janey. But Joe hooked his arm and spun him back around.

"I want to see if she's okay."

"No you don't," Joe said, pushing Ziggy toward the door. Ray and Gallagher dragged themselves sluggishly from the booth in protest, disgruntled and mouthing curses, hesitant to look up at all the accusing eyes that were surely on them.

As the four fools shuffled out the door, Maggie Thorson shouldered in past them, barely aware of their presence. She stomped the snow off her boots and tossed back her parka's fur hood. Scanned the room with predatory concentration until she caught a glimpse of Sam seated in the back, his face planted in cupped hands, elbows braced on the table. Maggie smiled.

4

Hunched over, hands crammed deep in his parka pockets, Joe tromped with resolute purpose toward the VW, leaning hard into the frigid wind. The others had to double-step to keep up, feet skittering this way and that on the slick hard-pack.

"Now we gotta find a damn motel," Ray said.

"There goes all our expense money," Gallagher moaned.

Ziggy did a tipsy pirouette in the snow so he could glance back at the café windows, neck craning to catch a glimpse of what might be unfolding inside. "Don't we have to get up to Bemidji?" he said. Even though preoccupied with Janey and her emotional crisis, Ziggy seemed to be the only one still thinking rationally.

"We're not gonna make squat on these damn beer commercials now," Ray said. "I knew this was a mistake."

"Why don't we, just, you know...?" Gallagher was rarely at a loss for words, but he didn't want to be the one to voice the obvious.

"Fuck it! Yeah. I agree with the pinhead," Ray said, loud enough to be sure Joe heard him. "Let's blow this pop stand and head back to Chi-town. Go down to Casey's for a few beers."

Joe whirled around to face Ray. "Because...we can't." That stopped all of them in their tracks. "This is..." He searched for a word that would somehow convince them. But instead, all he could come up with was, "This is important."

"A lame beer commercial for some rinky-dink tank town brewery? Yeah, right, life and death. Who gives a rat's ass?"

Joe turned to the VW, shivering now, fumbling with the keys. "It's a favor for Murray McCloud at Y and R. We're doing a favor for him as a favor for this other guy at BBDO who needed a favor. And if we do these couple of favors, Murray's gonna throw some very big accounts our way. You guys'll make out like bandits."

"What you mean is, you're gonna snag a cushy account at Y and R, then jump to J. Walter Thompson or Leo Burnett and throw us a stiffie." Ray felt free to talk tough like this because, in his mind, he and Joe went way back. But if you actually counted up the days and weeks and months, it wasn't really all that long. The only reason Joe put up with Ray's crap was because he was a halfway decent cameraman and the only shooter willing to do a gimme for chump change.

Joe crunched up his face into a hard scowl, jabbing a finger at Ray. "You guys'll make out too. Down the line. There's a derivative effect."

"Derivative..." Ray said, his voice thick with cynicism.

"Accruing therefrom," Gallagher said. "As a result of."

"I...know...what... it means." Ray said, pronouncing each word separately, glaring at Gallagher. "It means we get the shaft... and maybe, MAYBE, sometime in the future we'll get to work for half-rate on more bullshit beer commercials somewhere out in the boonies." He flapped his arms at the inclement conditions, "In bullshit weather!"

"We'd be working," Ziggy said. "That's a good thing."

"Shut up, Zig. *You* won't be working. *We* will be working."

Gallagher brightened. "Great! Right? Nothing wrong with that. Work is work."

"Yeah, but while we're bustin' our butts for peanuts, Joe will be head of creative bullshit at Burnett," Ray said. "He'll be rakin' in the dough..."

"And hiring all you guys to work at full-rate, on commercials for top tier clients like Ford and Kelloggs and maybe even McDonalds." Joe let that little carrot hang in the air for them to consider.

"See? Derivative effect," Gallagher said, nodding.

They stood in the whirling snowflakes, the silent space between them filled with a smoke-like cloud of breathy vapor. Nobody said a thing.

"Or," Joe said, "we could drive eighteen hours all the way back to Chicago and have a bunch of beers at Casey's, spending all that money that none of us is gonna be paid because we didn't do the job we came to do."

That rendered an even greater silence. After a moment, Joe pulled open the door of the V-dub. It squeaked; a metallic whine of pained acquiescence. They all climbed inside.

5

Inside Carl's, Maggie sat across from Sam at the small table, watching him sob, his face buried in the folds of his grimy parka sleeve. She waited patiently, unmoved by his pain and torment. A faint smile lurked behind her blank expression.

She reached into her big purse and pulled out a clunky audio cassette tape recorder about the size of a Michener hardback. Brushed Sam's coffee cup and saucer aside with her arm, ignoring the spill, efficiently setting up the recorder, plugging in a small plastic microphone and bracing it against the saucer. Using two fingers, she hit the PLAY and RECORD buttons simultaneously. The cassette began to whir softly.

She looked at the top of Sam's head as if gazing right into his eyes. "Okay, then, so what went through your mind when you seen she was pulverized?"

Sam shuddered in misery, his pathetic weeping growing louder. Maggie gave a little grin and a cock of the head. "Yah, sure," she said, as if excusing someone who had simply sneezed, "Take a sec to pull yourself together."

She slid her own coffee cup toward her. Stirred in some cream and way too much sugar, then sipped the warm brew casually, gazing around, masking her impatience with professional nonchalance.

Maggie had done plenty of interviews in her three and a half years with KHIB-AM, the Voice of the North Woods. When she first started with the station, just two weeks out of Hibbing Community College, she spent a good ten minutes of air time quizzing the local fire chief, Dick Jacobson, about the size of his fire hose, sparking a good deal of sly chuckling among the male listeners down at Bob's Main Street Barber Shop. Oblivious to the coarse joke inherent in her persistent queries, any potential embarrassment eluded her.

She soon followed that questionable achievement by launching a scandalous journalistic interrogation of the stock boys at the local Kroger store regarding their intentional mislabeling of sale prices on the tuna cans. It got no laughs from listeners, but it did stir up quite a bit of anger among the loyal Kroger shoppers.

But her biggest scoop had come just the previous summer when actor Frankie Avalon stopped in town to buy gas on his way up to Lake Pokegama for a visit with his cousin. When Maggie spotted him at the gas pump, she breathlessly grabbed her cassette tape recorder from the trunk of her car and backed poor Frankie up against the soda machine, grilling him about what the heck it was like to work with Annette Funicello in *Beach Blanket Bingo* and do all that kissing and hanky-panky stuff while the whole crew was watching. It caused such a stir and the demand was so great that Wayne Brawley, the station manager, had to run repeats of the interview a dozen times a day for the rest of the week. That was when Maggie started carrying the tape recorder with her everywhere she went.

Three years in the trenches had taught her that broadcast news offered many incredible opportunities and she didn't want to miss a single one. She had touched greatness and was not about to settle for covering bake sales and mislabeled tuna cans anymore. There was a world shimmering with sophistication and seductive fame waiting out there. KHIB-AM was no longer an elusive goal to Maggie. It was now the escape hatch to an amazing future.

This epiphany left her blessed with a confident calm, knowing that her big chance resided just around the corner. All she had to do was keep her eyes and ears open and leap on that horse when it came galloping past. And if it meant sitting here patiently drinking coffee across from a snowplow driver bent by misery, waiting for him to suck it up and pull himself together, then so be it.

She casually raised her empty cup toward a waitress, summoning a refill.

6

The snow clung to the Ramada Inn sign like gooey cake frosting. Red and green neon lettering cast a soft colorful glow that permeated the thick white fluff lending the entire scene a sparkling festive appearance.

"Looks alright," Joe said with undaunted confidence, ignoring the bitter cold that slapped his face.

They shuffled across the motel parking lot through the knee-deep snow, laden with metal equipment cases. Ziggy struggled in the rear, burdened by more than his share of the load.

Joe paused, heaving an irritated sigh, looking back. "Grab the mag cases and film boxes, Zig," he shouted. "We're not leaving all that raw stock out here in the V-dub." He dug in his parka and pulled out the keys, tossing them in a high arc.

Ziggy dropped the cases at his feet and frantically scrambled to snag the keys from the air before they disappeared forever in a deep drift. He hung his head, and then, with a disheartened shiver, turned slowly to lumber back toward the VW.

The metal-framed glass doors of the Ramada Inn swung open with a crash as Ray and Gallagher awkwardly stumbled inside, arms loaded with camera cases and duffle bags. They dropped everything on the spot with a thunderous clatter, grateful to be out of the cold.

Joe pushed in behind them, eyes flitting around the lobby for a pay phone. He spotted one on the wall in the corner by the cigarette machine.

Pete Peterson, groggy and running fingers through his thinning disheveled hair, shuffled out of the doorway behind the check-in desk, obviously awakened from a slumber by the racket. He scrunched up his eyes, blinking, trying to clear the fog of sleep.

When it was first proposed, the idea of becoming Night Manager had sounded like a highly regarded move up the professional ladder to Pete and he had happily leaped at the opportunity. It only took a few nights of nodding through endlessly long stretches of darkened emptiness, minimal paperwork and a parade of random guests slinking silently through the lobby like ghosts for him to realize why they called it the *graveyard shift*.

But before long he embraced the opportunity to peacefully snooze through each night, feet up on the office desk, tilted back in a comfortable chair, snoring blissfully until the alarm went off at 5:55 a.m., when he had to start making wakeup calls to guests.

The fake smile he had forced through his lethargy quickly faded when he saw Ray and Gallagher, looking like a couple of vagrant refugees from Haight-Ashbury. Pete threw his hands out to stop them from approaching the front desk. "Whoa! Hold up there! Forty-ninth parallel. Mason-Dixon line." But they just kept coming, throwing themselves heavily against the registration desk, exhausted and not in the mood for corny metaphors of protest.

Joe jiggled the switch hook on the pay phone, trying to get a dial tone. That's when he found himself looking up at a huge blow-up of Bob Dylan, framed and neatly hung on the wall in front of him. He glanced around. The sparsely furnished lobby walls were cluttered with photos, all of them Dylan; publicity shots of him performing before adoring crowds, portraits of him strumming his guitar, wheezing like an angry cat on his trademark harmonica, along with a few candid shots from national magazines.

Joe jiggled the useless switch hook again, then slammed the receiver down and marched toward the desk. Pete took a nervous step back, not used to being encroached upon by so many people at this late hour.

"Phone's not working," Joe grumbled.

"Yah, lines're down. Toucha snow."

"Toucha snow," Ray repeated with a dry laugh, tossing his long hair back over his shoulder, raising his eyebrows sarcastically at Joe. "And no rooms, I bet."

Pete nodded. "Yah, full up." He glowered at the jumble of metal cases and boxes. "Some set of luggage got yourself there. What's in them jobbies?"

"Pips and turks," Joe said, without missing a beat. "Mandibles and cataclysms."

Ray rolled his eyes. Gallagher grinned. They'd both heard Joe's straight-faced bullshit many times before. He was an expert at conjuring fantastical improvisations that left the heads of the uninitiated spinning.

"Don't spoze I'm familiar with them," Pete said, squinting curiously.

The door swept wide open, sucking air through the gaping portal, spinning snowflakes with it as Ziggy recklessly shoved his way inside with overloaded arms. They all watched as he let the cases and boxes drop to the floor with a series of crashing thuds.

"He's with us," Joe said, sensing Pete's discomfort.

Pete nodded, more than uncomfortable. He continued to eye the pile of metal cases with distinct suspicion.

"Don'tcha know we had these here radical Wisconsin boys stood over at the Holiday Inn down Squaw Lake. Was gonna turn a mess of angry wolverines loose up the state legislature." He tried to force an ironic smile, but it came off more like a pained grimace. "Kept 'em in boxes right in their room." After a long awkward pause, he added offhandedly, "Ornery wolverine'll chew your leg clean off."

"Well, we're not from Wisconsin," Joe said.

"Uh-huh. Pips and what, ya say?"

"Turks, etcetera."

While they sorted this bit of nonsense out, Ray's eyes did a quick 360 around the lobby, checking out all the Bob Dylan images. "You seem to have a thing for Bob Dylan?"

Pete straightened up, buoyed by an abrupt surge of pride. "Hibbing boy. Played in the Golden Chords '56 to '58. Cut that one there outta Life Magazine myself," he declared, raising a thumb over his shoulder at the wall behind him. "Glued it in a frame boughten down at the five-and-dime."

"He from Hibbing?" Ray asked in disbelief.

"I hope ta shout. Grew up here, ya. Stopped in one time to use the facilities, back in '60 it was." He pointed proudly to the men's room off the lobby. A big poster of Dylan was taped to the door. "I seen him go in. Seen him come out. Was the day he left town." Then a solemn cloud seemed to form over Pete's head, tinged with sadness and regret. "Never looked back. Drove him away, far as that goes. What with Happ pullin' the plug and all..."

His words drifted off as he stared down at the floor, not wanting to revisit that time any further.

Joe felt the door to opportunity swing open. "Sir, could I speak with you privately for a moment?"

That knocked Pete a tad off balance. "Oh yah, sure. Spose. If ya hafta." Nobody had ever asked if they could speak to him alone, in private. That is, except for his wife, Giselle; and those odd times never resulted in anything that he cared to dwell on. It usually led to some kind of scolding that he had to patiently suffer through, nodding, agreeing, then humbly tucking his bruised ego back into an old box where it belonged.

Pete moved hesitantly to the end of the check-in desk. Joe matched his pace, ambling down to meet him. Suddenly,

HIDING IN HIBBING

Joe swung his arm around Pete's bony shoulders with uncharacteristic amiability and a curious secrecy, guiding him to the far side of the lobby where they huddled next to a cheap contraption that dribbled out lukewarm coffee in the morning for drowsy guests.

Ziggy turned to Ray and Gallagher with a look of genuine perplexity, wondering just how much he had actually missed while wrestling camera gear and film stock from the bus. Ray shrugged indifferently, while Gallagher plastered on a sanguine grin that just made him look goofy.

Over the several months they had traveled around with Joe shooting slipshod regional television commercials, they had seen him pull this kind of stuff many times. Despite his rants and grumbling, Joe liked nothing more than to have his back flat up against the wall, caught between a rock and a hard place. It was where he shined. When forced to twist reality in some cleverly creative way, he dug the hole deeper, making the challenge tougher. The greater the stakes, the more alive he felt.

He leaned in toward Pete, hand now resting on his shoulder with a familiar ease, his voice all folksy and softly confidential, as if he was about to share a great family secret. "You see, truth is... we are actually... musicians." Pulled that one right out of the dark night sky, with an assist from Bobby Dylan winking down at him from a poster over Pete's left shoulder.

Pete cast a critical eye toward Ray, Gallagher and Ziggy. "Soooo that's it," he said with a tone of enlightened discovery.

"Those cases got all our instruments, amps, speakers, what not..."

"The pips, etcetera..." Pete confirmed, demonstrating his quickly acquired knowledge.

"Yep. You nailed it."

"I used to play banjo," Pete confided, his eyes brightening.

"So you're a fellow musician then?"

29

"Not official. Think I stuck her down in the cellar couple summers back."

Joe looked off toward Ziggy, giving a little nod his way. "See that guy in the middle?"

Pete turned to look. "Short, funny-lookin' one?"

"Yeah," Joe said. "That there is...Ziggy Jett."

He enunciated the name with respectful emphasis and the exaggerated arch of one eyebrow.

Pete stared at Ziggy, squinting with even greater intensity. "Well I'll be." Then he paused uneasily as a wave of uncertainty and puzzlement washed over him. "Now... where would I know him from?"

"Might not heard of him yet, but you will," Joe said with conviction. "Gonna be the biggest thing since Elvis."

"Yah? Oh-fer-geez..." Gaping off at Ziggy.

"Bigger than the Beatles."

"Aw, them, yeah," not so impressed. "What about Bobby Dylan?"

"With all due respect, sir... even bigger than Dylan."

Pete studied Ziggy prudently. "Don't look like much."

"Who does, before they're famous?"

"Yah, that's sure true enough," Pete agreed. Then, his mind started to click on all cylinders. "What the holy heck ya doin' here in Hibbing?"

Joe firmly gripped both of Pete's shoulders and moved him back toward the wall, lowering his voice to a confidential whisper. "Okay now..." He raised a finger up between them that, somehow, in the mysterious physical language of human gestures, indicated that he was about to share a secret that must not be shared with anyone else. "In two weeks, Ziggy Jett is scheduled to make his world debut on Ed Sullivan."

Pete's eyes widened. "Sullivan? No kiddin'?"

"Live on TV. Ziggy's gonna be the biggest show biz phenomenon to ever hit America. And Mr. Sullivan does not want anybody to steal him away."

"Steal him?"

HIDING IN HIBBING

"Ed likes to be the first to introduce a new star to the world," Joe said, talking out of the side of his twisted mouth like some wiseass racetrack tout sharing an inside tip on a hot horse. "Doesn't like anybody else to steal his thunder."

Pete tugged his ear and scratched the side of his head with great concentration. All this complicated political show business manipulation was starting to make his brain throb. "Guess he wouldn't want that."

Over by the check-in desk, Ray and Gallagher amused themselves by nailing Ziggy's arm with playful, but painful, knuckle-punches. Ziggy pulled his fists in tight to his chest, flapping his elbows like a put-upon chicken, fending them off. Pete watched their horseplay, clearly not grasping the vagaries of showbiz types and their odd entertainments.

"Oh-fer-geez...It's Ziggy, ya say?"

"Ziggy Jett," Joe said, then added with an air of prestige, "...and the Jetstream."

"That's some moniker alright."

"We're hiding him and the band right here in Hibbing, keeping a lid on so to speak, until his big debut on Ed's show." Then, Joe heaved a despondent, world-weary sigh worthy of Brando. "But, hey, you got no rooms left. So..."

"Hold on now," Pete said, pretending to wrack his brain. Only he was no Brando; he came off more like a flustered Wally Cox trying to remember where he'd left his glasses "We, uh, ya know, I think maybe we do keep a coupla rooms set aside, just for celebrity types and such that come through, like yourselves." .

He scampered behind the front desk, flipping through the guest register and juggling random papers. Stopped, gazing off in deep deliberation, lightly tapping his cheek thoughtfully, then his upper lip, with a finger. "Geez...yah, okay then." Grabbed some keys out of the key slots. "Yah, looka there. How about that. I got four rooms available."

Joe dug into his coat pocket for his wallet. A hand shot up in front of him, fingers fluttering around bird-like. "No,

31

no, no..." Pete said. "No sir. There's no charge for our celebrity guests. Gotcha the best rooms here. Telephone in each and all of that." Motioned at the drinking fountain. "Bubbler there in the corner, if ya got a thirst. Ice machine and whatnot down the hall."

Joe smiled graciously and tucked his wallet away, giving the guys a quick wink of complicity. Leaned in toward Pete, resuming his clandestine pose. "We'd prefer it if no word of this got out. You know..."

Pete nodded slyly, all hush-hush and secretive. Felt he was in some kind of James Bond movie, only without all the beautiful women. "Oh yah, you bet. Got my lips zipped up tighter'n a beaver trap." He pinched two fingers together and made a zip-up-my-lips move across his mouth to seal the deal. Then turned to Ziggy with a knowing wink. "And since you're the star, I'll give you the room that's got two towels."

Pete hustled down the corridor to the guest rooms, motioning for them to follow. Ziggy stared after him, baffled by the *star* reference, beginning to feel strangely uneasy. Ray and Gallagher were so happy to learn they had rooms—and free rooms to boot—that they completely ignored Pete's towel remark to Ziggy, scrambling to grab as much of their gear as they could carry between them.

Ziggy quickly hoisted a couple camera cases, and struggled to corral a third, but Joe grabbed them away. "I'll get those, Zigmond. You just go on ahead. Make yourself comfortable."

Ziggy gawked at Joe in stunned silence, disoriented by this odd breach of personal reality. Joe looped his fingers through multiple handles and straps, awkwardly hoisting the remaining cases up and heading off behind the others like a packhorse. After a moment of dull stupefaction, Ziggy trailed after him, feeling naked, vulnerable and weirdly incomplete with nothing to carry. Pete's words echoed back to him in his head. "Since you're the star..."

7

Gallagher bounced around on Joe's bed, laughing hysterically. "Ziggy JETT," he yelped between his breathless snorts.

"Hey! Feet off my pillows! Get off my damn bed." Even though Joe was enormously pleased by the shrewdness of his own scam, he kept it bottled up, not wanting to further incite his motley crew.

Even Ray had to admit Joe had pulled off an admirable con job, cadging free rooms for everybody. He loved that about the guy; Joe had an uncanny ability to squeeze out of tight spots by coughing up brilliant loads of bullshit.

Gallagher let loose a rat-a-tat barrage of machine gun laughter, jumping to his feet and sweeping his arm in a wide arc, as if imagining a marquee illuminated by spotlights. "Ziggy Jett, rock star!"

"Now there's a stretch for ya," Ray said, choking back a derisive snicker.

In the corner, Ziggy sat slouched in a chair, feet planted on a metal case, arms folded tight across his chest. "Why me?"

"You were griping I never give you a chance," Joe said. "Well, here's your big chance."

"Not exactly what I meant."

Gallagher stopped laughing long enough to drum up a straight-faced request. "Sing something for us, Zig." He couldn't resist lacing it with a sour note of mocking sarcasm.

"Yeah, come on, Zigmond" Ray said. "Let's hear what ya got."

Ziggy sat up, chin out, challenging. "What? I can sing."

"In the shower maybe," Ray said.

"I was in the high school choir," Ziggy said.

And he had been, back at William Howard Taft High School in northwest Chicago. He and two of his pals had signed up for choir because they figured it would be an easy "A" and a great way to meet girls. None of the three could sing a lick, except in the locker room off the gym where the concrete block walls created a great echo effect that vastly improved their painfully off-key doo-wop harmonies.

Given their unmistakable lack of talent, they simply resorted to rampant flirting with the girls, soundlessly miming the lyrics of insipid choral arrangements chosen by Mrs. Staples, the antiquated choir director. Problem was, choir class was scheduled immediately after lunch, during fourth period, when the urge to sleep would descend on everyone like a warm, comforting quilt.

That was when Ziggy and his pals discovered the incredible subconscious impact they could have on their female classmates as they stood in a semi-circle, facing nearly half of the choir. When they yawned, the girls yawned. It was clearly cause-and-effect. The heady power of suggestion rendered their impressionable victims totally helpless.

Within moments of the boys beginning their gape-mouthed charade, the entire choir was tottering with drowsiness, unable to bring forth voices from those yawning chasms filled with darling white teeth, ugly braces and bright pink tongues awkwardly shielded behind dainty fingers splayed in tittering embarrassment.

During this almost daily charade, Ziggy became particularly fixated on a fresh-faced cutie named Suzy, her delicately perfect features framed by an adorable pixie cut with come-hither bangs that neatly emphasized her deep

HIDING IN HIBBING

blue eyes. Each time the pseudo yawn fest would begin, her eyes focused directly on Ziggy, not fooled for a minute by his humorous ruse. He loved her for that, feeling they shared a profound personal secret; it was an unspoken link, private and unassailable.

This juvenile subterfuge lasted two weeks. Until the nearsighted Mrs. Staples finally caught on to the gag and unceremoniously kicked the boys out of class.

"Oh yeah, sure, high school choir," Gallagher said, swaggering around on half-bent knees, arms akimbo. "Then let's hear you sing something."

Just the thought of it made Gallagher collapse in another spasm of staccato hiccupping giggles. He tumbled headlong into Ray, who shoved him back onto Joe's bed.

"Hey! Hey!" Joe leaped to his feet, pissed. "You numbnuts got your own rooms. Quit messing mine up."

For some reason, Joe's sharply brusque proclamation propelled them into an absurdly surreal exchange.

Gallagher led off with, "So what kind of guitars we play?"

"You don't," Joe said.

"We're not musicians, man," Ray said.

"But we're still a band."

Joe stared at him in disbelief. "Jesus! Are you a dunce? I just told that guy we we're a band to score us some rooms."

"Right. So if we're a band, we gotta play guitars."

"Or pianos," Ray said, trying to be funny.

"Not if we're a rock band."

"Billy Joel," Ray shot back.

"He's just one guy. Not a band."

Ziggy tried to inject a note of logic. "Pianos wouldn't fit in the cases."

"Maybe horns then," Ray said, not letting it go. Still thinking he was funny.

"Rockers don't play brass," Gallagher said.

35

"Blood Sweat and Tears," Ziggy offered.

Joe couldn't take it anymore. "You don't play *anything*, for Christ's sake. No musical instruments."

Ray looked at him straight-faced, "You saying we perform archipelago?"

"You mean *a cappella*," Gallagher said.

Ziggy nodded. "Yeah...it's *a cappella*."

"See, even choir boy knows that."

"Alright! Christ! Stop!" Joe yelled, gesticulating wildly. "You're a rock and roll band. You guys are the band. Ziggy's the lead singer."

"I can't sing," Ziggy said.

"See. He admits it," Gallagher said. "He can't sing."

Ray grinned. "He's no Sinatra, that's for sure."

"I like Sinatra." Gallagher said.

"Everybody likes Sinatra. But he's not rock and roll."

Ziggy tried to jump in again. "Yeah, neither is James Taylor, but..."

"Yeah, you singing James Taylor, that's a good one..."

Joe's eyes bugged out. "Nobody has to sing. You're not a real band."

The silence lasted only a moment, when Gallagher abruptly breached it.

"So... what kind of guitars we play?"

"We don't!" Joe, Ray and Ziggy all blurted in unison.

"Then what the hell's in the cases we dragged in?"

"Alright, alright, stop, stop. Lemme see if I can follow your idiotic train of thought here," Joe said, turning to Gallagher. "You're asking me...What kind of guitars are *not* in the cases." Pointing at them. "The cases that do *not* have any instruments in them."

Gallagher nodded. "Correct."

"That *nobody* here knows how to play?"

"Pretty much, yeah. Theoretically."

"Okay," Joe said. "Then...theoretically...electric."

"Electric?"

"Yeah. You're a rock band, right...so, yeah. Obviously. Electric. Guitars...amps...the whole meghilla."

"The pips and turks," Ray said.

"Exactly," Joe said. "Which are also *not* in the cases."

They let that soak in for a moment.

Gallagher looked straight at Joe, serious as a cancer diagnosis: "So...what do I play?"

"I don't know," Joe said, unfazed. "Uh, let's say...bass guitar."

"Like a Fender?"

"Yeah, sure. Whatever that is."

Gallagher looked off, slumped, rolling his shoulders uncomfortably. "Ehhhh... "

"What?"

"I don't know if I want to play guitar."

"Then drums!" Joe shouted. "You're fucking drums."

Gallagher brightened at that, throwing his arms up triumphantly. "Alright! Yeah! Ringo!"

"You're not Ringo."

"Not even close," Ray muttered.

"You guys are not the Beatles."

"The Beatles broke up," Ziggy pointed out.

"Yeah, Zig," Ray said softly. "We know."

But Gallagher was undaunted. "Then... we're the New Beatles."

Fretting over this, Ziggy said, "I don't think we're allowed to use their..."

Joe exploded. "Okay. Listen up, you friggin' morons. You're Ziggy Jett and the Jetstream. Ziggy's lead singer, Gallagher's on drums and Ray is lead guitar."

Gallagher contemplated this with a furrowed brow: "So who plays bass guitar?"

"Me," Joe said without hesitation.

"You can't. You're too old."

"Old? I'm thirty-six."

37

"That's his point," Ray said. "For rock and roll, you know, that's ancient. You can't be in the band."

"Wait," Ziggy said, confused. "The band's breaking up already?"

"You could be our road manager," Ray suggested.

"I'll be road manager <u>and</u> I'll play bass."

"How come you get to do both?"

"Because I'm the oldest and I said so."

"And it was his idea," Ziggy said. "And he's the boss."

Joe cut him off. "Shut up, Zig."

"So who plays rhythm guitar?" Gallagher asked

"Nobody." Joe kept his voice amazingly steady and poised amidst this nonsensical gibberish.

"You gotta have a rhythm guitar or there's no rhythm."

"Okay. So Ray plays both rhythm and lead."

Ray looked doubtful. "I don't think I can do both."

That ignited Joe's fuse again. He leaped to his feet. "You don't have to do anything! Nobody does. You're all *not* playing what I said you're *not* playing. And that's the end of it."

"Except me," Ziggy said. "I'm not singing."

Gallagher jumped up, still energized by the crazy image of Ziggy as a rock star. He hammered out mock *Satisfaction* chords on an imaginary guitar, strutting across the room like a loose-limbed Jagger.

"Duhhh-duhhh-da-da-duhhh-da-da-duhh! And now! Direct from Podunk High School Choir...ZIGGY JETT!" He mimicked the roar of the crowd with a hollow-mouthed hiss.

Even Ray was amused by this goofiness, hand cupping his chin, concealing a smirk behind fingers resting easy on his lips. "Sure as hell looks the part."

"Yeah. Buddy Holly was a dork too," Gallagher said. He did a Chuck Berry duck-walk imitation, bouncing bent-legged on one foot across the room, his other leg stuck straight out, crashing into a lamp.

HIDING IN HIBBING

All the way down the hall and out in the lobby, Pete reacted to the noise of the crashing lamp and the burst of laughter that followed. He looked up from his copy of Field & Stream magazine, wondering what kind of lunacy those darn hippy musicians were up to. Trashing their room, no doubt, like *The Who* and that crazy bastard Keith Moon did at the Holiday Inn over in Flint, Michigan.

That incident was legendary among hotel/motel professionals.

His eyes went to the phone behind the desk, giving a tempting thought some serious contemplation. It wasn't a new thought. It had been granted birth the moment he promised to keep his lips zipped.

Some secrets are just too good to keep tucked inside. And the effort to do so was exhausting.

8

Ziggy had a rough time sleeping that night. He tossed and flailed restlessly between clean sheets that smelled vaguely of ammonia and mothballs. Nothing had actually changed. He was still the subject of continual derision and mockery from the guys; an endless running joke without a punch line. But something felt different. There had been a seismic shift in his world that defied interpretation, leaving him feeling both oddly exhilarated and deeply troubled. He couldn't wait for morning, yet at the same time he dreaded its approach.

A thick blanket of snow muted the world outside. But through the haze of sleep that had finally claimed him shortly before dawn, Ziggy sensed dull sounds of car doors closing and motors running. Indistinct voices, high-pitched with excitement and strangely counter-balanced by intermittent hushed mumbling, created a distant symphony of sounds that gradually drew him from his exhausted slumber.

He peered out from beneath the twisted covers, blinking at the thin line of daylight that squeezed into the room around the perimeter of thick curtains that reeked of stale cigarette smoke and cold pizza. A croaking groan escaped as he stretched, rubbing his face to get the blood flowing. He dragged himself from the bed, shuffling toward the window in his boxer shorts, pausing to look down at the sock on his left foot. It was half-off and half-on, draped crookedly off his toes like a limp hand puppet. The other sock was nowhere to be seen.

HIDING IN HIBBING

He fumbled around trying to locate a pull-cord for the curtains but couldn't find one. Giving up, he gripped the curtains in the center and yanked them wide apart, revealing a Cinemascope panorama of the motel parking lot covered with glistening snow. Squinting into the harsh splash of light, it took him a moment to focus on the dozen or so teenaged girls standing vigil outside his window.

Casting aside their trembling shivers, the girls abruptly exploded in a chorus of shrieks and screams upon seeing Ziggy. They pointed and squealed, jumping up and down with youthful abandon, wildly inspired by the image of him totally naked except for his ridiculous boxers. One of the girls, overwhelmed by an uncontrollable hormonal surge, rushed toward the window and threw her wadded-up A-cup bra at the glass.

Startled, Ziggy yanked the curtains shut. He pressed his body against the wall, shaken by a rush of adrenaline. Trembling in the semi-darkness, a rampant profusion of emotions surged through his veins, leaving him alternately astonished, scared, and then thrilled. A helpless grin spread across his face, stretching as wide as a hot desert landscape shimmering with exotic promise and lusty potential. The tantalizing phrase *"this is so cool"* raced through his mind over and over. And then a chill of sheer terror gripped him by the throat.

9

Joe grinned with private delight as he steered the VW bus out of the parking lot an hour later, maneuvering cautiously through a swelling crowd of frantic teenaged girls. He loved the feat of pulling a hopeless situation out of the toilet and turning it into waffles and whipped cream. It was his *forte*.

"Shove over, I'm driving," he had announced as they scrambled to the VW. Ray hesitated at the door, confused by the sudden shift of responsibility and seating positions. Joe forcefully elbowed him aside, jumping in behind the wheel. Hearing the shrieking pack of teens on their heels, Ray threw himself into the rear seat beside Gallagher. That left Ziggy with no choice but to grab the *shotgun* position next to Joe, slamming the lock button down with his palm.

Joe didn't have to justify his decision; he was, after all, the producer, director and creative head of this makeshift fiasco. But he did it anyway, just to keep things straight. "I have experience with crowd control," he announced with authority. And he did, if you counted out-maneuvering six brothers and sisters for a position at the family's modest-sized breakfast table, and, more critically, access to the only bathroom.

The panting girls pounded the side of the VW bus, desperately clawing at the windows. They wailed Ziggy's name with plaintive devotion, despite their total lack of familiarity with who he even was. After all, they had only heard his name for the very first time late the night before when it was excitedly whispered in a roundelay of clandestine midnight phone calls initiated from within cramped closets, or under bedcovers, muffled by piles of pillows so as not to disturb or alert sleeping parents.

A secret well-kept is a secret not worth telling. This one had the potential for exploding the dull, mind-numbing despondency of a frigid small-town winter into a panoply of overheated adolescent opportunities.

Ziggy peered out the window in an unfocused trance, as if still a small boy watching frenetic puppies playing in a pet store cage. He placed an open hand on the frosty pane. A rosy-cheeked girl with bouncy spirals of hair pressed her own fingers and palm hard against the glass, matching his hand perfectly on her side. When his eyes drifted over to meet hers, she screeched with orgasmic delight, jumping up and down, tumbling back helplessly into the snow, writhing.

Ray and Gallagher were bedazzled by this wild display of unbridled adoration, both of them wondering if this was how the Beatles must have felt.

Because he was older and clearly more experienced, Joe had a much more nuanced impression of the unruly crowd of clamoring teenaged girls. To him they were chattering seagulls, flocking madly for whatever crumbs might be tossed their way. And, being the wiser one of the bunch, Joe had come prepared with a whole loaf of bread.

10

Having eluded the hysterical hordes at the Ramada Inn, Joe pulled the VW into a Standard station a couple miles down the road to fill the tank. The snow had been falling steadily all night and the station had not yet been shoveled out. Ziggy sat in silence, numb, watching the grizzled owner, Max Poznick, struggle through knee-deep drifts. He was bundled in a bulging parka with fur-lined hood, feet clad in huge, ridiculously heavy insulated pea-green boots.

Ziggy had shoveled out a million gas stations just like this during a dozen bitter Chicago winters. Dragged his body out of bed before dawn, hiking a mile in the deep freeze just to get to the Gulf or Phillips 66 or Standard. Then scraped foot-deep, hard-packed, brick-heavy wet snow for fifty cents an hour, until he had to race off to school where he sat all day with an aching back trying to focus on whatever dumb stuff the teacher was droning on and on about. The memory of it made him feel small and solitary, trapped in a cycle of meaningless effort. Even on this day, with all the screaming girls throwing themselves at him, Ziggy didn't feel like a star. Not even a fake one.

Once the tank was topped off, Max hunched over and shuffled back toward the service station office, sucking in icy damp air through his clenched dentures. As Ziggy watched him, a new thought crept up. He turned to gaze at the gas pump. Stared a hole right through it. "They oughta put computers inside the gas pumps," Ziggy said.

"What?" Ray said, not getting it.

"Computers. They oughta put computers inside the gas pumps. And some kind of automatic thingamajigs that can read credit cards too so nobody has to go out in this crappy weather."

Gallagher perked up, tickled by the thought. Laughed to himself, turning it over in his percolating brain.

"Oh, that's brilliant, Zig," Ray said. "You know how big a computer is? Big as a freakin' house! How you gonna fit that inside a gas pump?"

Joe was listening now, curious what Ziggy's response would be.

"So, make it smaller," Ziggy said.

Gallagher jumped in. "Jeez, ya know how much stuff they gotta jam inside one of those gigantic computers? Words, numbers and facts and stuff. Massive enumerations."

Ray winced. "Enumerations? Shit, Gallagher. Will you speak English?"

"I'm supporting your position, man. I'm just saying, they can't make 'em any smaller."

"That's right," Ray said. "They can't."

"Sure they can," said Ziggy.

"Can't."

"Negative, negative..." Joe said.

"Factual," Ray came back.

"Or they could just connect the computers together." Ziggy stopped them cold with that one. Nothing but silence... and whatever sound four brains make when they are all going at it, trying to work through a puzzle with no apparent solution.

"You know, link them all up," Ziggy went on. "So you could take advantage of their combined capacity."

Another silence took root.

"Like that's gonna happen," Ray finally said.

"Hey, what'd I tell you?" Joe snapped. "Knock off all that shit, Zig. You're gonna give Gallagher a headache. And it just pisses Ray off and makes him get negative about everything."

Max Poznick reappeared, shuffling around the front of the car with his arms loaded down.

Ignoring him, Joe said, "Look at the good side, we got free rooms."

"Still gotta pay for gas," Ray said.

Joe heaved a sigh, sensing Max at the window. Rolled it down. Pulled his wallet out, fingers flipping reluctantly through the thin stack of bills inside.

"Gosh, no. All set. No charge," Max said, waving off the money, bright and cheery despite the bitter cold. "We're hunky-dory."

"Aw, no, we can't let you..." Joe started.

But Max cut him off, pushing two quart-sized cans through the open window. "Couple cans'a 10-W-30," he said. "Cold weather stuff. I can check your battree you want, make sure the 'lectric ain't edging up on kaput." Then right away, not waiting for an answer, shoved in a yellow strip of cardboard with a string loop attached to it. "And better yet, here ya go, a free lemon smelly strip to hang from your rear view. Springtime-like in January."

Joe let the oilcans tumble out of his arms into Ziggy's lap, then took the smelly strip, giving it a polite little sniff and an appreciative nod.

"And best of all," Max said, grinning slyly, "a Bettie Page calendar." He raised a cardboard calendar into view. An image of pinup queen Bettie Page adorned the front, her perky perfection decked out in the skimpiest nurse's uniform imaginable.

The VW bus squeaked on its struts as the weight shifted in the vehicle, everybody leaning forward to get a good look.

"Got our name on it and everything," he said proudly. "Right there under her, uh, ya know..." And indeed, there it was. *Max Poznick's Standard Service and Auto Repair,*

HIDING IN HIBBING

Hibbing, Minnesota... spelled out in bright blue letters right under her *"ya knows."*

Max bent his knees and scrunched down low so he could see across Joe to Ziggy in the passenger seat. He grinned slyly and wiggled his eyebrows at him with a salaciousness that somehow lacked vulgarity. Ziggy flashed on the crowd of eager girls gathered outside his motel room window, feeling a surge of queasiness in his stomach. But it was a good queasiness, tinged with the purity of butterflies and the welcome stirrings of raw lust.

11

It was with some measure of trepidation that they ventured back to Carl's Front Range Restaurant. When they left the night before it hadn't been on the best of terms, so returning now didn't seem like the wisest of decisions. But wisdom has no place interfering with a truly serendipitous adventure, so when Joe turned left into the parking lot of Carl's, no one in the VW raised any objection.

Besides, as far as they knew, the only other decent place to eat was the orange-roofed Howard Johnson's they'd spotted way back down the highway in Duluth. And it was common knowledge that, aside from the excellent clam strips, most the other stuff on HoJo's menu was nowhere near worth the inflated premium you paid.

For a brief instant, as they entered Carl's, they felt as if they'd made a serious misjudgment. All eyes flashed their way with prickly recognition as a towering young hostess charged toward them, a dark twisted mound of beehive hair accentuating her already imposing height. Joe tensed, bracing, ready to protect his crew from this Amazonian aggressor.

"Right this way, gentlemen," she gushed sweetly, grinning so expansively it nearly cracked her ruby lipstick.

She grabbed a clutch of menus and spun on her heels with a gravity defying grace that seemed impossible given her lofty stature, guiding them to a large corner booth near the front. "This here's the best seat in the house," she proclaimed with the proud wave of her hand. "Got a straight bee-line back to the men's room and cigarette machine." Swung around, really selling it. "And as you can see, it affords an excellent view of our parking lot."

Joe struggled to muster a courteous smile, glancing out at the drift-covered expanse; scattered cars, like big fat marshmallows, seemed to grow plumper by the moment.

Already fired up by the prospect of apple pie, Gallagher wasted no time, diving straight into the booth, ready to dig in. Ray glanced at the tight cluster of waitresses giggling and fidgeting excitedly near the kitchen pass-through. As he lowered himself into the seat, he sized up the situation; there appeared to be considerably more young women on-duty than reasonably required. And their whispered huddle, humming with a furious buzz of excitement, almost seemed threatening. The phrase "come back to bite us" bolted through his mind.

"One of our super friendly waitresses will be with you in a jiff," the hostess purred, giving Ziggy a flirtatious nudge and obvious wink. He began to glow with the warm rush of embarrassment.

The tall-haired hostess skittered away, hips rocking with an exaggerated gait, all eyes fixed on her pendulum swing. Gallagher gave a little bark of approval under his breath, his persistent visions of apple pie momentarily replaced by more carnal thoughts.

Ziggy searched the room for any sign of Janey, finally spotting her at a corner booth in the back languidly taking a food order from a family of rowdy kids and two put-upon parents. She seemed sad and deeply preoccupied, snapping back into focus only when one of the kids let out a raspy shriek or unintentionally kicked her shins with flailing little feet.

His view of Janey was abruptly blocked when a chubby waitress with a million freckles and bright red hair descended on them carrying a big platter of Vienna sausages wrapped in dough. "Complimentary pigs-in-a-blanket for ya," she said. They looked more like pudgy worms in stiff overcoats.

She hurled a flirtatious smile at Ziggy, gnawing voraciously at the inside of her cheek, then hurried away, doubling over with a giddy giggle.

Sally, a fresh-faced blond with a bouncy ponytail, immediately replaced her at the table, clutching two steaming coffee pots. Her eyes went straight to Gallagher and when he returned the gaze, she looked away shyly.

"Can I warm ya up...?" She caught herself, choking back an embarrassed laugh, blushing. "I mean...what I'm sayin' is...oh, gosh...coffee, ya know?"

Gallagher slid his empty cup toward her with a big grin. "Hit me with your best shot."

Her face reddened as she poured, eyes dancing between the cup and Gallagher's gaze. When the cup started to overflow, she emitted a sharp little squeak of distress before moving quickly on to the others, filling their cups without bothering to ask. "Bottomless cup," she said. "All ya want."

Despite a knowing demeanor, hinting that she had a couple years on her flighty teen co-workers, Sally remained readily vulnerable to the many provocative fascinations of girlhood.

Connie, a solidly imposing girl with a sassy smirk, elbowed Sally aside, flipping out her order pad. "We got two specials," she said, nudging Sally further from the table with her thick arms. "Beanie-weenies... they're reeeal good... or meat loaf. Got the buffet too. All-you-can-eat with a bunch of flavors of Jell-O. And there's regular menu. So... need more time I bet."

Joe eyed the beanie-weenies, then his watch. "It's not even eleven. What about breakfast?"

"Oh, we got breakfast anytime. All day, all night. Fact we got everything alla time. We don't discriminate betwixt our meals. Food is food. Time is the devil."

"Guess we better look then," Joe said, flipping the menu open.

"Spiffy-cool. Just give a yell. I'll be back in a shake." She hustled away, all swivel-hips and cracking gum.

Sally hesitated, shifting on her feet, continuing to eye Gallagher. Splashed a few more drops into his still-full cup. Buttoned it up with a pert smile and reluctantly ambled off, already hatching her return.

Ziggy, unaware of this potent exchange, was busy tracking Janey as she moved across the room. But then his eyes fell on four hulking north-country *good ol' boys*, all in their early twenties, slouching in a nearby booth. One of them, a tall, lanky, chiseled-jawed ballbuster named George, spouted off with cocky bravado.

"Over in Chisholm at the Sip 'n' Nip I catch this creep checkin' out my pumpkin and I tell 'im, 'hey buddy, ya want a piece of this?' and he shivers like a little baby, backs right down. Crawls away off like some dumb fuckin' chicken, crappin' in his pants." The pals around him bellowed with clamorous laughter, pounding the table; a rowdy form of north woods applause.

George caught Ziggy staring at him and stared right back, turning on the tough, his upper lip twitching with an overplayed Elvis-like sneer. Ziggy quickly averted his gaze, studying his untouched coffee cup intently like it was a crystal ball.

Sally abruptly reappeared at their table without the coffee pots, clutching another big platter instead. "Free smoked walleye on toothpicks," she said, pushing their coffee cups aside to make a space for the overstuffed plate of fishy tidbits, maneuvering it into place right in front of Gallagher.

"While ya hunt for your entrée," she said, making a gun with her forefinger and thumb, pointing it at Gallagher. He stiffened. She cocked her thumb back and fired. A squishy gunshot sound squeezed out between pursed lips. She mimed blowing gun smoke away from the end of her finger, gave him a suggestive wink and sauntered away.

Gallagher slapped the table. "Now that's the way we *should* be treated."

"It'll just come back to bite us," Ray muttered, giving voice to the thought that had been simmering. "Always does."

"Don't go layin' your negatory trip on us," Joe said, dipping a quick nod toward Ziggy. "It'll just mess with his mojo."

But Zig was oblivious to all this mojo talk. He wasn't much of a lady's man; they all knew that. Back in high school, his idea of a date was cornering a girl at her locker to ask if he could borrow a pencil. Getting up to bat wasn't anywhere in his repertoire, much less making it to first base.

Joe said, "So how about it, Zig?"

Still not hearing him, Zig couldn't take his eyes off Janey across the room.

Joe lowered his head, making like an ornery bull. Leaned toward him, voice booming. "Ziggy!"

Startled out of his reverie, Ziggy shuddered, whipped his boggled face back to Joe. "Huh?"

"How's it feel to be a big rock star?"

Ziggy didn't answer, gazing blankly, as if Joe had asked him a question in some foreign tongue. After a moment, he swiveled to look toward the big front window. A growing horde of teenaged girls had gathered outside, their faces pressed hard against the glass, gazing inside with crazed adolescent eagerness.

Arthur Zigmond was not one to dive into the pool without testing the water. He found females to be puzzling creatures, mysterious in their demeanor and capricious in their preferences. Like a curious visitor to the zoo, he hung back, an invisible observer, carefully dissecting the quirks and ticks of these strange beasts, attempting to discern patterns that made sense. From this safe perch on the periphery, he never found comfort in what he witnessed. And the swirl of frenzied female swarming he had experienced during the past several hours did nothing to calm his growing anxiety.

"Yeah, how does it feel?" Ray said, egging him on.

"Like puking," Ziggy said, pale and dead serious. They all laughed.

Out on route 169, Maggie hunched over the steering wheel of her Chevy, straining to peer through the windshield as she passed Carl's. The surging crowd of curious groupies grew larger by the minute, becoming its own strange animal with dozens of skittering legs and bobbing heads. She slowed the car, stretching across the passenger seat to frantically scratch with her fingernails at the speckled white frost on the side window.

"Oh yaaaah," she muttered to herself. "Somethin' cooking alright."

12

Winters in Hibbing were always disagreeable. But this storm was setting a record snowfall that hadn't been matched since 1950 when a hundred and seventy inches were dumped on the state. Or as far back as 1888 when the bitter cold froze more than two-hundred souls; the kind of weather that laid a silence on the land, killing all joy and enthusiasm, smothering everything in a frigid tomb. It made the already stoic residents feel even more reclusive, hopelessly isolated from the world and each other.

Hibbing was set smack-dab in the middle of the Mesabi Range, a ruggedly foreboding landscape that was originally home to the largest vein of viable iron ore in the nation. By 1895 it had become a hardscrabble frontier town invaded by desperados and speculators who ravaged the terrain with ruthless abandon. The first wave of settlers swarmed in from the distant shores of Finland, Sweden, Norway and Italy, followed by a colossal rush of Slavic immigrants - Croatians, Serbs, Slovenians - then a steady flow of Austrians, Germans, Jews, Russians, Armenians, Bulgarians, Poles, French and, finally, the Irish.

Stubbornly maintaining their own unique European identities, the new arrivals also coalesced into a new amalgam of hardy pioneer. All those strong enough to survive the incredibly brutal elements and heartless strife—proudly obstinate enough to call the vast Mesabi Range their home—became known simply as *Rangers*.

HIDING IN HIBBING

Mayor Happ Grunwald, dressed in a heavy parka and hunter's cap with earflaps, stood before his house in the thigh-deep snow, holding a shovel. The end of the handle rested on the frozen ground, hidden within a drift, the big metal scoop pointed skyward. He looked like a bundled up male-half of Grant Wood's painting *American Gothic*, only with a snow shovel instead of a pitchfork; motionless, gazing blankly at the white tableau, daydreaming of earlier times, embraced by the vacuum, consoled by the hushed emptiness. Someone passing by might have thought he was a marble statue, placed there by the some local civic group to represent the spirit of Hibbing. And in many ways, that's exactly what he was.

His wife, Barbara Grunwald, opened the front door and poked her head out, a puff of crystalized breath floating ahead of her. "Happ! Ya got Pete on the phone."

He blinked, but nothing else. His cone of silence had been rudely breached; his sacred peace, disturbed. If he waited, perhaps she would disappear back into the house and he could pretend the intrusion had never occurred.

"Happ!"

His head slumped imperceptibly, maybe an eighth of an inch. But to him it was a grand gesture of surrender. There was no way he could perpetuate the illusion any longer. The sanctity of his bliss had been stabbed by a shrill cry from the present, allowing the world to rush back in and wake him.

"Who is it?" he asked.

"Pete."

"Pete?"

"Pete from the Ramada."

"Oh. Pete."

A wonderful silence returned. He listened to it, still not moving. Thinking maybe he had just dreamed all the words that went before. And now the blessed quiet, soft against his ears, would cradle him again.

"Happ! He's waiting."

"What's he want?" Happ finally asked, moving only his mouth, watching the misty cloud float away.

"How would I know? He didn't elucidate."

His chin dropped lower, his head truly slumped forward now and cocked to the side. A chuckle gurgled from his throat. He shook his head. "Elucidate," he muttered so quietly that even he could barely hear it. Barbara had been reading her darn Reader's Digest again, he mused to himself; that *More Colorful Speech* section with those long fancy words to replace all the normal short ones that already worked just fine.

"Okey-doke," he said, turning slowly with great difficulty, his boots pretty much frozen in place. "Maybe I can get him to *elucidate* what the heck he wants."

13

The Record Rack on Howard Street was the only place to buy recorded music in Hibbing, unless you count Bert Stinchcomb's Melody Chest, a musty hole-in-the-wall sandwiched between the Quitting Time Bar and Ratner's Pharmacy on the south end. But all Bert stocked were some ancient 78s of big bands from the forties and a limited inventory of the newer stereophonic 33 rpm recordings of familiar classical pieces that might be purchased by a grieving widow looking for something appropriate to play at her husband's funeral.

Teenagers rarely ventured into Bert's dismal cave. Although, a couple of high school boys did come in once to order The Fugs' newest LP and Bert threatened to shoot them both on the spot for talking filthy.

But at the Record Rack, giggling teen girls were already clustered around the stacks of record albums, pawing frantically through the vinyl treasures. Freddy, a nervous young clerk, hovered over them, awkwardly pretending to offer assistance, but hoping more than anything to simply be noticed.

"Where are all of Ziggy's albums?" a wildly quivering girl of fifteen demanded. Her high voice squeaked with an urgency that suggested a raging blaze was about to consume her if the fire department didn't arrive immediately.

Freddy had no idea who she was talking about, but he was staunchly determined not to let this opportunity pass him by. "Ziggy, uh...that's, uh...is he...?

"Jeez-o-Pete, you're in the record business, Freddy," the girl squeaked with tremulous angst.

"You know my name?" he uttered softly, staring at her in awe.

"Well, yeah...of course. You're Freddy the record guy." Another girl chimed in. "Oh come on. You gotta know Ziggy Jett and the Jetstream."

Freddy rocked his head side-to-side and rolled his eyes, winding himself up to fake his way through this pretense. "Oh yeah, sure. 'Course I know them. I was just pulling your, ya know...I mean, c'mon, they are really hot stuff." He flipped randomly through some albums. "They musta got moved around or filed wrong or something."

He continued digging, not exactly sure what he should be looking for. "They are big, man. I mean, I'm talkin' super big, ya know. I hear they're really hot over in Europe and all."

"Wow!" the squeaky girl squeaked. "You mean like England Europe?"

A girl in the back of the store suddenly let out a piercing shriek. "I found one! I found one!" she shouted, her ponytail bouncing as she spasmodically jumped up and down. A rush of girls scrambled to the back, surrounding her.

"That's Jefferson Airplane, ya dumb dip," someone said, gazing over her shoulder.

A chorus of disappointed groans erupted.

14

Gallagher was slumped down casually in the booth, one foot up on the seat, gazing at Ziggy across the litter of empty plates and crumpled paper napkins.

"You look pale, man."

"They make him nervous," Ray said, nodding at the crush of girls outside the window. "He's never seen female animals in heat."

"I've seen lots more stuff than you know," Ziggy said.

"Pictures in Playboy don't count."

Ziggy watched the frenetic hamsters clambering against the window, their expulsions of chilled breath appearing fiercely hot. Fire-breathing sirens, Ziggy thought. "I don't read Playboy," he said flatly.

A scoffing laugh from Gallagher. "Who said *read*?"

Joe squirmed, irritated. "Quit picking on the kid. That's my job."

"Yeah, leave him alone, he's a big rock star," Ray said, not bothering to hide his resentment.

Another waitress, next in the rotation that had been steadily servicing their table, suddenly appeared bearing yet another platter crammed with tiny sausages wrapped in tasteless dough. "Can I refresh your weenies?" she blurted with a broad beaming grin, twinkling eyes and deep-set dimples.

They flashed uncertain looks back and forth. Gallagher puffed out his cheeks, signaling that he was about to explode.

Carl pressed his way in, nudging the waitress aside. "Wrap 'em up to go, Sheila," he told her with a dismissive wink. "They can munch on 'em later."

DAVID O'MALLEY

He brushed the dirty dishes aside and dropped a stack of white paper napkins and a couple ballpoint pens on the table. "I was wondering maybe you might autograph a few napkins for the cooks working back in the kitchen."

Ray glanced toward the kitchen pass-through. The giggling waitresses flocked together, watching with excited expectation. Ray smirked. Cooks, huh?

Gallagher grabbed several napkins and a pen, making quick doodles followed by a broadly flourished signature.

Joe grabbed one. Looked at it, head tilted, face scrunched up. "What's this? Tits?"

"Yeah," Gallagher shrugged, grabbing his fourth napkin. "It's the only thing I know how to draw."

Joe shook it off dismissively, tossing the napkin to Ray, who studied it, grimaced, turned it, cocked his head. "Looks like ice cream cones." Rotated it again. "Or clown hats."

"I didn't say I could draw 'em good," Gallagher said.

"Then don't draw 'em," Joe said. "Show some respect."

Carl peered over their shoulders, trying to get a look at the ice cream cone, clown hat tits. "I was, uh, sorta hoping maybe Ziggy could sign a few."

A disturbance drew Ziggy's eyes to the crowd of lookie-loos outside the window. Several of them shrieked when they saw him look their way. A phalanx of girls surged toward the front door.

"Oh jeez. They're coming in!" Ziggy leaped up and hastily beat a panicked retreat to the men's room.

Just as quickly, Carl dashed toward the front entrance, arms spread wide, fingers splayed, knees bent and braced for the onslaught. "Whoa whoa whoa! I said ya could gawk through the window. Ya can't come inside 'less ya buy an official entrée item. Not just Cherry Cokes."

But they hardly heard his admonitions, eager eyes peering past him, desperately searching for any sign of their elusive rock idol.

Fortunately, Ziggy had picked the one safe haven available, and further increased his ostensible security by crouching next to a toilet in the cramped restroom stall. Ziggy tensed when, a moment later, he heard the door woosh open and the momentary buzz of voices and clattering dishes flowed in, then quickly faded to silence. He pulled his arms in hard against his chest, fists clenched, his thighs and calves squeezed tight, ready to spring forward through the adoring hordes and batter his way to freedom.

The stall door moved slightly. It slowly swung open with an agonizingly elongated creaking borne of rust, age and never having received a drop of lubrication. Gallagher gazed down at Ziggy with wry amusement. He tossed Ziggy's parka at him.

"The owner guy chased 'em all back outside. We're ready to split."

Ziggy wadded the parka up in his lap. "I'm not a rock-and-roll star."

"No shit. We know that, Zig."

"I don't like being something that I'm not."

"Better'n being the nothin' that you definitely are," Gallagher said with a cocky certainty. "C'mon. We're going back to the motel. Hang out there."

Ziggy hesitated, glancing toward the door with trepidation. "Think I'll just stay here awhile. Catch a ride back later."

"Whatever," Gallagher shrugged. "Freeze your ass. Change your mind in the next ten seconds, we're sneakin' out the back way, making a run for the v-dub."

He started to turn when Ziggy stopped him with, "Maybe if they see you guys drive away... they'll follow you."

"Yeah," Gallagher said, letting this thought knock around in his brain like a pinball. Then, an inspired grin lit up his face. "YEEAAAAHHHH!"

He spun around and barreled out the restroom door.

DAVID O'MALLEY

Ziggy carefully uncrumpled the wadded parka. Looked up at the pathetic schlub reflected in the restroom mirror. "You're just a dork, Zigmond. Get used to it."

In the front of Carl's Restaurant, the exiled mob of hyperventilating girls jostled for prime positions at the plate glass window, tightly cupping hands around the sides of their faces to block annoying reflections. They squinted through the frosted glass, eagerly straining to catch a glimpse of their celebrity prey.

Meanwhile, Joe quickly led Ray and Gallagher through the kitchen with confident strides, nodding amiably at the puzzled cooks. Slipping through the back exit and quietly shutting the door behind them, they dashed around the trash dumpsters along the south side of the diner and scrambled toward the VW in the side parking lot, ducking behind parked cars on their circuitous path.

Gallagher was the first to reach the vehicle. He whirled around to Joe, hands out in desperate supplication. Joe tossed him the keys on the run. With one quick twist, Gallagher unlocked the door and leaped into the driver's seat. Joe hooked his arm through the open driver's door and pulled the back door lock button up.

Without hesitation, Ray yanked the rear door open and threw his body onto the back seat, causing Joe to slip on the slick hard-pack, going down in a flurry of pinwheeling arms and legs. While Gallagher fumbled to fit the key into the ignition, Ray thrust his arm back toward Joe, offering a hand up. But as Joe rose on one knee to grasp the five-fingered lifeline, Gallagher began to swing the driver's door shut, slamming Joe in the back, knocking him face-first into the snow.

Joe scrambled to his feet spitting clumps of crusty snow and heaved himself into the back seat with the crazed power of a quarterback diving over a crush of tacklers into the end zone. As the cold starter began to churn arduously, Ray stretched across Joe to slide the door shut. Their heads collided with a dull thud, followed by a strange harmonizing groan from both of them.

The Three Stooges, in their prime, couldn't have executed the operation with greater antic finesse.

A moment later, the primitive, but always reliable, little German engine roared to life, punctuating its confident growl with a few stuttering coughs. Gallagher gazed back toward the restaurant, waiting.

"What're you doing?" Joe asked. "Punch the fuckin' gas. Let's get out of here!"

"Hang on, hang on." Gallagher said in a soothing tone, leaving the gear in neutral and revving the engine loudly.

"Come on," Ray said. He kicked the back of the seat. "Move it!"

Gallagher just grinned like a fool, still staring into the rear view, his foot bouncing briskly on the accelerator until it finally produced a loud backfire. Ray and Joe whirled around, eyes wide, as the churning crowd of teen girls dashed around the corner of the building, spotted the VW idling and hurtled toward it, slipping and sliding and stumbling.

Shoving the gear into first, Gallagher gunned it and the clunky bus started to rumble away. A wailing cry of dismay rose up from the herd of stampeding girls as they lumbered to a deflated stop, some of them falling to their knees, gasping in the cold air.

Gallagher glimpsed them in the rear view mirror as they gave up the chase. He stomped hard on the brake pedal, bringing the VW bus to a sharp halt at the edge of the parking lot. Then, popping it into neutral, he softly pumped the accelerator, causing the engine to alternately purr like a cat and growl like a tiger.

The throng of disheartened girls stood staring in disbelief, their chests heaving, clouds of crystalline breath pumping from their mouths. They could hear the taunting rise and fall of the engine revving in the distance, as if calling

63

to them with a seductive challenge. They hesitated, silently watchful, bewildered by this oddly unfamiliar development. Then, as if the pulsing multitude had made an instant decision as a single being, the entire pack shrieked and rushed toward the VW.

Gallagher looked back at Ray and Joe with a cocky smirk, a sly click of his tongue and a confident wink. He slammed the gearshift into first, crushed the accelerator with his boot and they plowed off down the road, fishtailing wildly in the deep snow.

The frenetic females scattered in every direction to jump in their cars and follow.

15

Ziggy cautiously pushed the men's room door open, slowly poking his head out, listening intently, hearing only the faint tinkling of utensils, clatter of plates and the muted hum of conversation from the remaining customers. He slid along the wall, past the pay phone and cigarette machine, peeking with one eye around the corner.

An irascible geezer was bent over his patty melt at the short counter, chewing with great concentration to keep his uppers from falling out and landing in his coleslaw. A dour middle-aged couple sat at a two-top; she dug into a heaping mound of mac and cheese while he picked at the broiled whitefish special, both muttering softly, debating the validity of the latest local gossip and, no doubt, analyzing the veracity of this wacky new rumor about some big music star being somewhere around town.

Ziggy leaned out an inch further to catch a glimpse of the big front window. He exhaled, relieved. Not a single girl anywhere in sight. All that remained was smudged glass and the remnants of a thick mottled frost from their lusty gasping.

This felt more than puzzling. It was as though none of what went before had really happened. Ziggy felt painfully discombobulated, searching his mind for some reasonable explanation. Was it all a dream? Or was he dreaming it right then, still asleep and lost in the confusing maelstrom of conflicting shreds of logic and illogic, trying desperately to wake himself up?

Legs weak, Ziggy edged around the corner of the restroom alcove and quickly slipped into a secluded booth in the back, his eyes remaining focused on the room, scanning back and forth vigilantly.

He heard a small gasp to his left and turned abruptly to see Janey sitting in the booth directly across the table from him tabulating the stack of receipts from her shift. They stared at each other for an uncommonly long moment, neither knowing what to say.

"Can...I...uh..." Janey began, without a clue what would follow next. She cleared her throat, sensing a great dryness, wishing she had a tall glass of cool water to drink. "Can I get you anything?"

"Uhhhhhhhh..." he said, glancing around randomly, wondering if he might discover any sign of impending rescue or a possible route of escape. Their eyes met again. "Yeah, um...No. I'm just...I was...I wanted to, um, apologize..."

"Apologize?" She cocked her head. "For what?"

"For, you know...last night. I didn't mean to finish your word."

"My word?"

"Coffee."

"Oh. That." She looked down at the table, at nothing, just away from his eyes. "It's okay. It was my fault."

"No. I shouldn't have done that."

She shook her head, still averting her gaze from his, embarrassed. "I was just upset."

"Why?"

"Uhhhh...I can't talk about that." Her cheeks flushed and a patchy redness appeared around her eyes.

"Oh..." Ziggy said softly, struggling to let it go. "Okay." But it just hung there between them, making the silence even more pronounced.

"My grandma Dagne died," Janey said abruptly.

"Was she sick?"

Janey shook her head, finally looking up at him, forcing herself to seek solace in his eyes.

"She got clobbered by a snowplow out on Route 73."

Janey looked off toward Sam sitting alone in a booth now, slumped down low, head resting back against the smooth, cool tuck-and-roll plastic surface, staring mournfully up at the ceiling, crooked tracks of dried tears on his ruddy cheeks.

"He didn't mean to do it."

Ziggy looked at Sam, finally putting the pieces of Janey's misery together.

"She wanders. Gets all confused. Goes out looking for French fries. She likes fries, the skinny kind, ya know, done crisp. Sam didn't see her, what with the storm and all. She..."

As before, her voice became trapped deep in her throat, choked by painfully acute emotions. Ziggy squirmed in his seat, not knowing what to do. He looked at her small fingers resting on the table, just inches away, easily within reach. He could touch them. Lightly. Gently. Just so she'd know that it would be all right and that, even though he didn't know her at all, he cared. He hesitated, playing various possible scenarios over and over in his mind.

Janey looked up through her tears. "My granny...she taught me everything." She sniffled, catching the droplet of moisture that had formed on the tip of her nose. "How to sew...how to make aebleskivers...how to sing..."

"You actually sing?" Ziggy said, cutting her off sharply.

She sucked in a startled breath. "Not for real. But my grandma Dagne, she sang like an angel."

"Sing something," Ziggy said excitedly, leaning closer.

"Uh-uh. No. I can't," she said, looking away shyly, a faint, nearly invisible smile the only indication of how flattered she felt by his abrupt and unexpected request.

Ziggy studied her. "I just figured, if a guy is having his birthday..."

Her head snapped up. She wiped away the tears with the back of her wrist. "It's your birthday?"

His mouth fell open, poised to speak, but nothing came out. He felt strangely detached from his body.

"Wait right here," Janey said, brightening. "Don't go anywhere, okay?"

"What?"

"Just...wait. Okay? Stay right...I'll be..."

Without completing the thought, she scurried out of the booth and disappeared around the corner.

Ziggy swallowed hard, his throat burning from the lie he had just expelled. "Why'd you say that?" he thought, chastising himself with an inner voice that sounded exactly like his father's. He buried his face in his hands, then rocked back, his eyes rolling heavenward, and groaned. The harsh agony of regret.

The seconds ticked away like small eternities. "Did she leave?" he wondered, draining his glass of confidence, a half-full vessel he had carried since childhood, always too readily emptied upon the slightest provocation.

Maybe it was just a pretext to flee the restaurant and hide from him forever? He leaned slowly out of the booth, turning to peer back over his shoulder toward the kitchen. Maybe she was going to get the owner and have him tossed out in the cold. Or call the police and have him arrested for stalking her. "Negative, negative" he thought, hearing the echo of Joe's persistent admonition to Ray.

As he pondered a host of other radical, and clearly unlikely, possibilities, Janey suddenly reappeared with a slice of apple pie on a small plate, a candle stuck in the middle. The words *Gallagher's pie* flashed through his mind. Great, he thought, now I'm going to betray my friend by eating *his* apple pie.

Janey was smiling in a truly winning way that Ziggy had never experienced. Her hand shook with excited anticipation as she struck a match and lit the small candle.

"Go ahead," she said, beaming. "Make a wish."

Ziggy couldn't take his eyes off her, enchanted by the sweetness of her generosity.

Mystified by his expression, she tilted her head slightly. "What?" she asked.

"Aren't you gonna sing Happy Birthday?" Those words had just tumbled from his mouth. He didn't even think them first. "I can't really blow out the candle unless someone sings."

Janey felt a warm flush of blood surge in her head, making her scalp itch. The soft skin on the back of her neck tingled. She experienced a loopy dizziness, the whole room spinning slowly. She hadn't felt such a crazy sensation since *that time*—so long ago, it seemed—when it had all gone horribly wrong.

Then, surprisingly, as if possessed by something greater than fear, she began to sing *Happy Birthday* with a soft, satiny voice.

Ziggy was transfixed, swallowed whole by the pure innocence of her. When she reached that part of the song extolling the birthday boy's name, she paused, raising her arched eyebrows with curious expectation.

He leaned forward, whispering "Arthur."

"Ar-thuuurrr," she sang softly, rendering his name with such stunning elegance and graceful reverence that, to him, it sounded more like the joyful ascendancy of *hallelujah*. For all he knew, there could have been real angels singing backup harmony.

He was so captivated by her delicate voice, her eyes, her perfect mouth, that he didn't even hear the repetition of the chorus that invoked a final happy birthday.

She bit her lip shyly. "Did you make a wish?"

"Yeah."

"Better blow out the candle or it won't come true."

"It already did," he said.

She stared into his eyes, not blinking, not moving. Afraid to read too much into his few words; frozen like a bird cornered by a cat. If she didn't move, maybe the world would stay just as it was and never change, locked in time.

Ziggy pursed his lips and blew the candle flame out with a tiny puff of breath. He saw her smile grow into a radiant wave of bliss and, just as quickly, felt a rush of guilt consume him, averting his eyes to conceal his ache of remorse. But she sensed his unease instantly, realizing the sad truth. Her smile melted, hardening into a cold glare of hurt.

"Not really your birthday, is it?"

"No." The word dropped from his mouth softly, a silent bomb of regret that destroyed all that had come before.

"You lied to me." Her words filled with disappointment and sadness, not anger.

"I didn't exactly say..."

"That was cruel."

"But I didn't mean to..."

Then, a release of tears brought the anger out. "I don't like being tricked." Janey sprang from the booth and rushed away.

16

Ziggy's long frozen walk to the Ramada Inn felt like a trek across the Himalayas. The few cars that rumbled past never slowed for the lone figure huddled deep within his parka. No one recognized the fabricated celebrity trudging through the knee-deep snow. Like most heavily bundled and grandly anonymous Minnesotans, he was but a tiny island amid a vast white sea.

Ziggy had messed up badly. A precious opportunity—one that comes along so rarely in life—had been instantly extinguished by rash hubris and a desire to be something he was not. He gave himself a mental kick in the ass, followed by a swift kick to the head. But no self-inflicted punishment, imaginary or real, would change the situation. He had blown his opportunity and there was no going back. Being an adult sucked that way.

Junior High School had been a lot easier. Back in sixth and seventh grade Ziggy stirred up a foul kettle of fish numerous times and still managed to come out on top, floating high and dry on a Ritz cracker and smelling just fine. Like the day of the big assembly, when a popular music group—a perky girl quartet, the Chordettes—had made a special appearance in the gym. Their propulsive career, which had blasted off with *Mr. Sandman*, a number one hit in 1958, was now in precipitous decline. They had been reduced to performing a medley of their past chart toppers for a grinding circuit of school assemblies.

Their other big hit, a frivolous rock ditty called *Lollipop*, always proved to be a crowd pleaser. On the original recording, a champagne cork "pop" sound effect had been added at the appropriate moment—during a palpable silent pause without melody or lyrics—instantly turning an unremarkable tune into a smash novelty hit. But when it was performed live, this signature sound effect was to be eliminated. Nervous school administrators felt it would somehow prove disruptive. The very idea of four young women plunging wet fingers into their mouths—to snap their cheeks in a sloppy attempt at recreating the widely anticipated "pop" noise—would be extremely inappropriate, unladylike and flagrantly suggestive. This critical decision, however, had not been made known to the student body.

When the Chordettes began singing, the entire crowd bobbed and bounced excitedly. They were thrilled to have genuine stars actually performing live in the middle of their own crummy gymnasium, a dreary venue normally associated with lethargic after-school sock hops and losing basketball games. As the song neared its notorious high point, Ziggy instinctively slipped a finger into his mouth, pulled outward on his cheek and, right on cue—"POP!"

It echoed through the gym like the shot heard 'round the world.

The entire crowd of students erupted in delighted laughter, jumping in their seats and applauding wildly. The flustered singers lost the tempo, stumbled to a halt and wandered off the stage amid a chaotic clamor.

Teachers leaped to their feet and glared at the crowd, angry eyes searching for the perpetrator. The assembly was immediately cancelled and students were sent tromping back to their classrooms.

The echo effect created by the cavernous gymnasium made it difficult to determine from where the offending sound had emanated. But Carl Betts, the Vice Principal, was certain it originated in the block of students from Miss Stouffer's class.

He entered the classroom, hands on hips, head bent low accentuating his high forehead, steely gray eyes peering from beneath dark fuzzy brows, sweat glistening on his floppy jowls; one day in the future he could have easily been seen as the perfect caricature of Richard Nixon on the verge of declaring "I am not a crook."

But on that day he launched into a growling, self-righteous diatribe touting the critical responsibility of proper student behavior, eventually getting to his point. "I want whoever made that disgustingly absurd noise to step forward and take their punishment."

Of course, everyone in the class knew it was Ziggy. He had been sitting smack dab in the middle of them when it happened. But no one was ratting on him. He looked down at his desk, torn by guilt, knowing that if he confessed it probably meant suspension, a tortuous lecture from his dad, a loss of privileges at home, and his mom piling a ton more vegetables on his plate every night.

"Come on," Mr. Betts grumbled, surveying the blank faces. "You're not going to get away with this. Either stand up and admit your guilt or I promise I will punish this entire class."

Ziggy knew he couldn't let that happen. It wouldn't be right if they all suffered for his stupid mistake. He heaved a sigh, slid higher in his chair, tensing his thighs, hands shaking, sweat creeping in around the back of his collar, an ache deep in his gut. He quickly rehearsed the simple and straightforward admission in his mind; "I did it," he would proclaim with succinct clarity and conviction.

He rose to his feet. Opened his mouth to speak. But before any sound could emerge, the student beside him, Brian Doyle, also stood suddenly and announced, "It was me." Then a girl in the third row, Sandy Hotten, stood and brightly stated, "I did it. I'm the one." Followed by another kid in the back, and then another and another, until the entire class was standing, willing confessors all.

What Mr. Betts didn't know was that nearly everyone in the class had been downtown at the Bijou Theater the previous Friday night to see Kirk Douglas in "Spartacus." In the pivotal scene, a Roman officer tells a group of captured slaves that he will set them free if someone among them will simply identify Spartacus, the rebellious slave who led the revolt against him. When Douglas boldly rises up to confess that *he* is Spartacus, each of the other slaves around him, led first by Tony Curtis, rises also, and then one by one professes loudly, "I am Spartacus."

Ziggy's loyal friends and classmates had saved him. And for a brief time, like so many other rebels and clowns who have gone before, he was even thought to be somewhat heroic among his peers. It was the first time in his life that he felt genuinely alive.

But on this particular winter's day of miscalculated behavior, with a young girl's precious trust at risk, there would be no last minute rescue. This time the full weight of Ziggy's actions fell squarely on his shoulders alone.

17

Pete Peterson looked up from his new copy of True Magazine when Ziggy pushed through the door of the Ramada lobby and trudged inside, pausing to stomp the caked snow off his boots.

"Anything I can get you Mister, uh...Ziggy?"

Ziggy ignored him, never even casting a quick glance Pete's way as he pulled his parka open and headed toward the guest rooms.

"Well okay then, I'll just get back to my..."

Pete let the thought dangle in the air, waving the True Magazine with a photo of Howard Hughes on the cover.

Joe leaped up when he heard Ziggy's timid knock, yanking the door open wide and dragging Ziggy inside by the arm. Ray and Gallagher sat stiffly in chairs, each doing his uncharacteristic best to portray an impression of professional, polite demeanor.

Mayor Happ Grunwald sat across from them on the corner of the bed. His ill-fitting business suit reeked of mothballs and attic dust. The bulky parka he wore over it puffed him out like a bulbous wine barrel incongruously combined with a goofy hunter's cap dangling furry earflaps. When he turned to see Ziggy being led in by Joe, he sprang to his feet, a broad meandering smile on his flushed face.

"Yah, so this is him, eh?" he said, capping it off with a hearty laugh. He rocked on his feet, looking Ziggy up and down, his colossal grin fading a bit as he felt a flutter of disappointment course through him.

"Funny how they're always smaller than ya think they are," he said to Joe. "Famous people, ya know." Then quickly turned to Ziggy, raising his pudgy palms. "No offense. You're a good size fellah and all."

Anxious to take the edge off his inadvertent slight, he grabbed Ziggy's hand and pumped it with enthusiasm. "Mayor Happ Grunwald. I'm pleased as a pool of punch to meet ya."

"Mayor came to welcome us," Joe said, giving Ziggy a quick encouraging nod and weak smile, covertly raising his eyebrows to signal a desire for polite compliance.

"Yah, like I was sayin', we're proud as a peck o' peaches to have you fellahs select our town." Happ shot Ziggy another uncertain glance, working hard to find something positive to latch onto. "So ya sing and play the guitar there?"

Ziggy gulped and shrugged. "Well, I, uh..."

"I used to toot a bit on the saxophone myself. But the wife stuck it in a garage sale. Soooo...that was the end of that." His voice trailed off, eyes wandering the room in search of a decent conversational transition. Inspired, he gave Ziggy a wink. "Let's hear a little tune, eh?"

Ziggy's eyes flashed to Joe, trapped, helpless. Both Ray and Gallagher stiffened in their chairs, jaws working like marionettes but their brains not coming up with anything coherent to spit out.

"Naahhhh!" Happ blurted with a chuckle. "I'm just yankin' yer antlers. I know yer busy and what not. Hoped to give you fellahs a key to the city, but we don't have one. Nobody locks up. Nothin' to steal. Mines closed up and all."

He looked down, his brisk manner turning somber and reflective. "Hard times. Yep. Real hard." Squinted at Ziggy and cocked his head, as if suddenly recognizing an affinity for the lad. "Ya know, a time back, we had our very own celebrity right under our darn noses and didn't even know it 'til he was gone. Yes sir. Bob Dylan. Ya seen the lobby, I bet. Course he was Bobby Zimmerman way back then. Probably changed it so he wouldn't be last in the phone book."

He let loose another burst of hearty laughter and jostled Ziggy's shoulder. "Was 'bout yer size too. Skinny little Jewish fellah. Played in the Golden Chords. That was the name of his group...band or whatever."

Pulling more 180's than a tennis ball, he reversed his disposition yet again, tumbling back into another solemn funk.

"Then he, uh...he up'n left us. Went off...New York. Back east. Got hisself all famous." He bowed his head, as if to start praying. Instead, he just stared down at his hands, plumbing the depths of regret. "Yep. Left us high and dry."

The protracted silence that followed was crushingly uncomfortable. Gallagher got a wise-ass grin on his face. Joe knew he was about to say something incredibly stupid, so he aimed a squint-eyed scowl his way to shut him up.

Thankfully, the tennis ball bounced back the other direction and Happ broke the spell with a sly chortle and an unexpected twinkle in his eye. "Ya know that song of his, that *Lay Lady Lay*? My wife's young cousin, Marjorie, cute little thing with brown hair, she was the 'lady' from that. Swears she was. Back just out of high school. Knew Bob. Might even of dated. That's the story anyway. Her story."

Joe jumped in, attempting to push the conversation in another direction. "You know, we'd like to keep our being here kind of..."

"Oh, yah, sure," Happ said, nodding his head with that sly intimacy politicians become adept at projecting. "Gotcha. Hush-hush. I fully understand. We'll put the kibosh on it. Keep the lid on. Hibbing's a real good spot to hole up if ya don't want folks to know ya even exist." His shoulders rolled back proudly. "We're practically invisible, ya know."

"Thanks," Joe said.

"You betcha. I always say, keep your ear to the ground, listen what's blowin' in the wind. Now, I don't know if Bob stole that from me—blowin' in the wind—but I used ta say it alla time. That's okay. I don't mind. He can have it. No charge."

Happ zipped up his parka and tugged his earflaps down tight. "I best be goin' then." He moved toward the door, then abruptly turned back. "Oh...you boys want to take anything I said, make a song out of it, that's swell by me. Have at it."

The moment Happ closed the door Gallagher fell onto the bed in a fit of giddy laughter.

"Yeah, real funny," Ray said. "I told you...come back to bite us."

Gallagher rolled off the bed, casually waving him away. "Nobody's getting bit. Doesn't matter. We'll be gone."

"Right," Ziggy said, "we need to get moving. We got a commercial to shoot."

Joe scratched his neck, reluctant to share bad news. "I tried calling over to Bemidji. Lines are down. Both 169 and route 2 are still closed."

"So what's that mean?" Ray said, pissed. "Now we're stuck here?"

"It's no big deal," Gallagher said. "They're treating us like kings. Free food. Free beds. Girls chasing us. What's the problem?"

Ziggy felt an awkward chasm of silence fall open. He recklessly jumped in.

"Maybe we should just tell them we're not really a..."

But an abrupt knock at the door interrupted his naive suggestion. They all froze, suddenly feeling like criminals trapped in their lair. After a lengthy exchange of overly concerned glances, and a palpable sweaty silence, Joe finally heaved a labored sigh, marched to the door and yanked it open.

A curly-haired eighteen-year-old kid stood there with four pizza boxes. He shoved them into Joe's arms, stepped back and started snapping his fingers rhythmically, doing a dismal imitation of a hip lounge singer as he launched into a painfully off-key rendition of Dion's *The Wanderer*.

Ziggy silently mouthed the words to himself, feeling an odd rush of pleasure and gratitude that the spotlight had shifted away from him and onto someone else for a change.

Banging home a big finish, the pizza delivery kid awkwardly spun on one foot and struck a jazzy pose. Dion had nothing to worry about.

18

It seemed impossible that the wind could ever be any colder, the snow any deeper, the night any darker. But it was. The angry storm that battered Hibbing had grown considerably angrier, lending the normally soft snowflakes razor sharp edges that stung the skin.

Maggie's Chevy barreled through the squall and nosed into a big drift in front of the Ramada Inn, heaving to a wrenching stop with a dull thud, the headlights buried. There was no telling where the parking lot stopped and the sidewalk began, but with a winter blanket this thick, it didn't much matter.

"Got some new guests, eh?" That's what she said to Pete as he stood gloating behind the desk at the Ramada.

"Oh yah, maybe, might be." Not hiding much with his goofy crooked smile. Then, bent over the top of the registration desk, grinning like a cat that had gobbled up a whole flock of canaries, he whispered, "Gonna be on Ed Sullivan." Eyebrows wiggling like worms, head bouncing like one of those bobblehead dolls people put in the back window of their cars to annoy other drivers.

"Ya don't say," Maggie whispered back, honoring his confidential tone.

"Didn't hear it from me. I never said it."

"Got ya," she confirmed with a wink. Gazed toward the corridor leading off to the rooms. "They down there, are they?"

"Oh, shoot, I don't know. Couldn't really say, could I?" Rocking on his rubber legs. Wiping away the sweat on his upper lip with a jittery finger. Nervously scratching the hair behind his left ear, then his right.

"You like the Winter Ice Carnival, don't cha Pete?"

His eyes lit up. "Oh gosh, yah. Who doesn't? Big ice blocks and chainsaws, ya know."

It was his favorite event of the whole year.

Maggie rambled the broad corridor from side to side, searching for the room numbers Pete had so easily volunteered once she offered him ten free tickets to the Hibbing Ice Carnival, the popular February event that was conveniently sponsored by WHIB-AM.

Turns out she didn't even need the room numbers. Rabid female fans had already deposited homemade food dishes, personalized gifts, intimate lingerie items and a host of other esoteric offerings outside the doors of their newly discovered idols.

She paused to dig through the bounty of aluminum foil covered Midwestern epicurean delights that cluttered the hallway: tuna casseroles, fresh baked chocolate chip cookies, canned tomatoes, jars of plump pickles, hastily prepared mostaccioli burned around the edges, cakes dripping with gobs of lovingly applied frosting and numerous six-packs of Pabst Blue Ribbon.

She surveyed the stash, pausing to pick up a baking dish, carefully lifting the crinkled foil wrapping for a quick peek at the meatball casserole within. The door suddenly swung open with a whoosh of air, startling her.

It was Ray, wearing jeans, no shirt, barefoot, hair a messy mop that somehow managed to look wildly attractive.

"Oh, hi," she blurted, flashing a smile with lots of teeth.

He glared back at her with a stone cold flatness. "Yeah. What?"

She gulped for air, feeling her lungs tighten up with the crazy excitement that always accompanied the pursuit of a good news story. "Yah, um... I'm Maggie, uh... just Maggie, and... whew!" She fanned herself with her long fingers, tugging at the loose scoop neckline of the blatantly sexy blouse she'd picked up on sale at Sears.

"Oh goodness, it gets so warm in here when you come right in from the weather. I, uh...." She held up the meatball casserole. "I brought ya a hot dish." She gazed around at the stacks of Tupperware treasures. "But I see you already have, uh..."

Ray looked at the offerings scattered at his feet. Leaned down to grab a six-pack of beer, cradled it protectively, then met her eyes with a long silent stare, considering a host of options.

"So'd ya like me to come in?" she asked, working hard to maintain the toothy smile. "Dish it up for ya?"

Ray couldn't stop his gaze from dropping lower, exploring the soft cleavage on display courtesy of Sears & Roebuck. After a moment, he stepped back and held the door wide open.

In the room next to Ray's, Ziggy sat cross-legged on his bed, sampling the array of homemade dishes he'd discovered outside his own door when he wandered out earlier in search of the ice machine.

A loud thumping emanated from the wall he shared with Ray, startling him so badly that he dropped a half-eaten chocolate chip cookie into an open Tupperware tub filled with some kind of unidentifiable goo that smelled a lot like lasagna but looked more like gray chow mein.

He froze for a long moment, listening to the persistent thump-thump-thump-thump slamming with fierce rhythmic regularity into the other side of the wall, finally deciding to just ignore it and dig the cookie out of the Italian/Chinese concoction. Ray must really be pissed off, Ziggy thought.

Probably kicking the hell out of the wall to relieve all that pent up cynicism.

Ray and Maggie were actually engaged in a bout of earth-rattling sex. The bed's cheap pressed-wood headboard was about to crack from the relentless slamming and the wall was taking the full brunt of it, a deep concave impression left in its wake.

Ray's overwhelming sense of suspicion and negativity had been instantly overcome the moment Maggie removed her long down-filled coat, revealing an unseasonably short skirt. As she turned to put the casserole on the flimsy coffee table, Ray was further treated to the sight of lovely sculpted calves and soft creamy thighs, neither of which were diminished in the least by the pair of goofy fur-lined winter boots on her feet. In fact, the strangely anomalous contrast of smooth sultry legs and clunky waffle-stompers only seemed to enhance the attraction that swept over him.

Once their cacophonous intercourse had fully concluded and the furniture settled back into place, splintered but basically whole, Maggie used the stiff bed sheet—emanating that disturbingly pungent aroma of both detergent and bleach—to wipe the perspiration from her face and body, proud of her journalistic dedication. Getting the big story was always the primary goal to Maggie, despite whatever difficult sacrifices she might be required to make.

"So it's really true then?" she said, not hesitating to leap right to the point. "You're all gonna be on Ed Sullivan?"

Ray's suspicion swiftly returned, the hair on his neck, and chest standing up with an unpleasant prickly sensation. "Can't talk about that," he said flatly, not looking up.

Maggie smirked to herself, taking his reluctance as a definite "yes." She was well schooled in the vagaries of human behavior and knew full well that when a person says they can't talk about something, it's a solid confirmation the thing they can't talk about is most certainly true.

She flipped onto her back, the splendid nipples of her naked breasts pointing heavenward. "Wanna go again?" She didn't wait for an answer, rolling over on top of him. She was starting to feel this could be more fun than she'd anticipated.

While round two of Ray and Maggie's table-rattling, bed-shaking, wall-thumping revelry got underway, Joe tossed and turned restlessly in his room just down the hall, his mind wracked by dreadful anxiety. The solemn promise he'd made to Saul Johnson at Young & Rubicam was at great risk of blowing up.

These were heady times in the advertising game. Every move was precise and carefully calculated, strongly dependent on a complex matrix of personal relationships governed by a delicately quixotic balance of tantalizing elements generally consisting of power, money, liquor, clandestine affairs and heavily guarded secrets, both personal and professional. Taken individually, these elements were often innocuous blips on the radar screen of daily life. But when combined in certain sequences, impacted by a variety of unpredictable external and internal influences, with the precious—though usually shortsighted—ambitions of big business at stake, the results could be explosive.

So when Saul Johnson took advantage of his access to certain vulnerable financial accounts, carelessly spending the agency's money on champagne and hotels in order to arrange a series of trysts between a highly prized client and Sheila, the blond bombshell who ran the Y&R secretarial pool, he found himself in the crosshairs of potential controversy.

How was Saul to know that Sheila was already the undisclosed mistress of Harvey Benson, owner of a couple of small breweries in upstate Minnesota? Which wouldn't have been a problem either if not for the fact that Harvey was also an old school chum of Murray McCloud, senior partner at Y&R.

HIDING IN HIBBING

This delicately volatile state of affairs is what ultimately triggered the ridiculous arrangement that now burdened Joe, robbing him of precious sleep.

Saul had screwed up. Harvey was upset. Which made Murray angry, threatening Saul's position. To calm the waters, Saul promised Murray that he would somehow placate Harvey.

But how?

It was Harvey's wife, Florence, who came up with the solution, and she didn't even know about her husband's predilection for the luscious hussy, Sheila. All she knew was that her husband was very cranky and some hotshot advertising guy down in Chicago owed him a big favor.

"Tell him he should make you some commercials for the brewery," she said.

"I can't afford that." Sometimes Harvey was slow. He didn't get it right off.

"For cryin' out loud, Harv, you're not gonna pay him," she said in her big voice, a potent burst of compulsion ribboned with strident shrieks. "He's owes you a favor, right? He can do it for free."

She was a smart cookie. But, on the other hand, here she was unknowingly enabling her husband's illicit dalliances.

So Harvey told Murray what he wanted and Murray told Saul that he needed him to do a favor and shoot a couple of quickie regional commercials out-of-pocket and off the books.

Which is where Joe came into the picture.

Saul teased him with the *almost absolutely certain* signing of a highly-prizèd Kelloggs account, plus some off-handed mentions of both Ford and McDonalds—which Joe knew was total bullshit but bought into anyway—implying that Joe would be handed the creative reins on all three ephemeral accounts if he did this itty-bitty favor for him.

So when broken down into a mathematical formula, it all seemed pretty straightforward; a big screw up (plus)

85

embarrassment (plus) anger (multiplied by) fear of further repercussions (plus) an idea, naively offered (plus) another favor couched in a veiled threat (plus) the request of a favor seductively linked to the promise of career advancement (plus) a hellacious snowstorm (minus) any common sense whatsoever (equaled) Joe in purgatory. Albert Einstein, of course, would have used clever acronyms and the formula would have looked extremely cool when scribbled on a blackboard.

The whole mess plagued Joe's mind. A cavalcade of disconnected words and phrases raced through his addled brain tissue, tires squealing, engines roaring:

...*diverse circumstances... dangerously unstable... infinite and erratic variability... perilously compounded... predictability virtually impossible...*

Meaningless multi-syllabic sheep crashed themselves into the rock walls of his dark consciousness with sacrificial despair until—ravaged and exhausted—he finally fell into a pit of fitful slumber.

Joe woke up, left hand numb, fingers curled into a tight ball. No feeling at all. As if it wasn't there. He wondered if he might be fading away, dying one piece at a time until his body would finally just vanish, leaving nothing but a wisp of vapor in place of his pathetically thin hopes and ruptured spirit, all of his effusive dreams unfulfilled and withered.

To feel regret for eternity—was this the fate of all men?

In this moment of dull waking he began to fear that he might be even more deeply cynical than Ray. Perhaps Ray was smarter...wiser. Expect the worst, then, if something—*anything*—good happens, it just might provide a pleasantly flickering flame that could inspire him to carry on for yet another day. *I guess*, he rationalized, *it can't get any worse.*

Then he remembered. He was stranded in Minnesota.

19

The snow had continued to fall steadily all night. As the first faint light of day began to appear, a snowplow made a labored pass at clearing the blanketed road, offering just enough adequate access to allow the intermittent arrival of cars laden with dedicated Ziggy Jett groupies; puffs of their fresh Colgate morning breath fogged the windshields, their chattering chipmunk squeals of anticipation muted by the steel and glass encasing them.

In his room, Ray sat upright in bed, a stack of pillows behind him, digging into the cold casserole with two fingers. He watched Maggie, who stood before the dresser mirror, fiddling with her hair, fluffing it out in the back where the pillow had mashed it down.

"This is pretty good stuff," Ray said, scooping up more. "What is it?"

Maggie eyed his reflection; she had no idea. She resisted the instinct to openly shrug and instead simply said, "Homemade."

"You a professional cook?"

"I do Tupperware part time," she improvised with ease. "You know, the parties where the women come to your house, eat cookies and buy stuff." She sifted her hair with twirling fingers. "And hairdresser part time."

"Well, you should be cooking full time."

She smiled at him in the mirror, tickled by the clever web of creative deception she had just spun. God, she loved her job.

87

"My mother was a really good cook," Ray said, swiping a finger around the edge of the casserole dish. "But she never made anything this good."

"But good enough to keep your dad happy, I bet."

Ray paused, letting his finger go un-licked. "Wasn't much made him happy." The corners of his mouth turned down, eyes boring a blank stare through his feet sticking out from the end of the blanket. "I can hear him now. 'How long it take ya to cook this shit?' "

Maggie quit fussing with her hair. There were times when she tried to recall her own parents, straining to remember what their voices sounded like. In her mind, she would try to evoke the tone, pitch and cadence of their words when they would tell her "You're not working up to your potential, Margaret. You need to try harder."

But she could never manage to find the key; the precise intonation skipped away like a disobedient child, hiding in a dark closet, mute and brooding. Funny how the voices you hear every day—from the time you're born until the day you slam the door behind you—can so easily vanish with such consummate finality. As if they were never there.

Her mother was an elusive ghost, thin and wispy, turning away, always turning away, with a dismissive wave of her hand, nothing worth saying above a discontented whisper. And the only sound she could vaguely imagine coming from her father was a throaty, unintelligible grumble, perfectly in keeping with his coarse informality and notoriously irascible demeanor.

The one voice that did echo clearly in her memory was that of Aunt Rosalind, scalding and pinched, striking like a poison-tipped arrow as she bitterly warned, "That girl is trouble." Always making certain that Maggie was well within earshot.

Who knows, Maggie mused in the cold stillness of the motel room, maybe all their efforts to demean and belittle her had paid off nicely in the end, driving her to relentlessly pursue unreasonable goals, heedless of consequences, regardless of the collateral damage.

She rarely saw her parents anymore and never called. But, then, they never called her either. They existed in their own world of dusty illusion, sipping cocktails and playing cards with like-minded neighbors in the prosaic burbs of Minneapolis. That was fine. It was what they called life. But when they had neglected to even acknowledge Maggie's graduation from community college, she had written them off. If they ever wanted to elicit any further expression of familial affection from her, they would have to try much, much harder. They would have to work up to their potential.

20

Gallagher slowly opened his eyes and stared at the chalky ceiling, enjoying that delicious brief moment when the brain has not yet registered where you are, giving rise to any flight of fancy the imagination might want to conjure.

Words flitted rashly through the gray soup of his mind, where they were brusquely severed, casually disjointed, then reassembled randomly to create strange new terms, prefixes mashed with disassociated suffixes, pumping out a mutating aggregate of incoherent jargon, untested and unsanctioned.

Oddly enough, Gallagher had no particular interest in language or word forms when he was a child. School was a ponderous drag, an interminable confinement only briefly suspended by the glorious liberation of recess. What he craved most was the true emancipation afforded by the 3:30 bell and, better yet, the arrival of summer.

His junior year in high school was particularly difficult. He found the very existence of words to be an irritating audible distraction, a recurring verbal annoyance that interrupted his ability to focus on the meaningless trivia of adolescence. That is, until the day he started his summer job at the Island Green Country Club, a private golf course on the outskirts of Philadelphia.

He was joined by four other young men who possessed varying degrees of enthusiasm that tended to diminish precipitously with the daily rise of heat and humidity. Their first project was to re-sod all of the greens on the sprawling 36-hole course, delivering stacks of fresh turf, ripe with the smell of the earth, to the site each morning. The squares of sod were piled high on a flatbed wagon with rubber tires and pulled by a tractor. Once the old grass—dry, withered and past its prime—had been dug up and removed, the young men would unload the fresh chunks of turf from the wagon, cutting and placing it carefully in the pre-defined circle, oval, ring or other irregular shape to create a smooth new green carpet on which golfers could elegantly tap their tiny balls with pride.

Cloygene, a blocky clump of sweaty skin, antediluvian hormones and matted hair that smelled faintly of cow manure, leaped up onto the tractor seat, raising his arms as if leading the warriors of Sparta.

"Everybody get offen the wagon!"

Gallagher and the other three young men just stared at him.

"Do what?" Gallagher said.

"Git offen the wagon," he said back, "I'm gonna pull it outta here."

Gallagher stood where he was. The other three slid on their butts down over the edge.

"That's not a word, you know," Gallagher said. It's surprising the stuff you learn in school when you're not even paying attention.

"What's not?"

"Offen," Gallagher said. "You said 'get offen the wagon' and 'offen' isn't a word."

"Hell if it isn't."

Gallagher wasn't absolutely sure why he had decided to challenge this meathead. Although the creep did have a mouth on him that he'd been running all afternoon. And his loutish demeanor and brainless assertions were quite clearly provocation enough.

"I think what you meant to say was get *off of* the wagon."

"No asshole, I said what I meant to say. Get offen the wagon. Now get your ass offen it."

"What's it mean?"

"Move your butt is what. It's right in the 'cyclopedia."

"You mean the dictionary."

"Both of 'em probably," Cloygene said. "Look it up."

"I'll do that."

"Bet ya twenty bucks it's in there."

"How do you spell it?"

"You're a dumb fucker, aren't ya?" Big old smirk creasing the dirty sweat on his face. "O-F-F-E-N. Wanna write that down?"

"No. I got it."

That night, Gallagher dug out his older sister's dictionary, the one she'd been awarded by the National Honor Society in her senior year. A Merriam-Webster Unabridged and Unexpurgated Dictionary. It was massive and weighty; the kind of book rarely consulted but traditionally hauled out every Thanksgiving and plopped on a chair so your three-year-old cousin could sit at the table with the big people. Occasionally someone stood on it to reach the box of chocolate creams stashed on the top shelf of the kitchen cupboard. If the house blew away in a tornado, this majestic volume would be the only thing remaining on the shattered foundation, undisturbed and immortal.

As he expected, there was no *offen*. It went directly from *offcut* to *offend*. Still, he heaved a long sigh of relief. There was no way he could have afforded to cough up twenty bucks, especially to pay off some Neanderthal blockhead.

He carried the dictionary to the golf course in his mother's old hard-sided Samsonite suitcase, heaving it onto the sod wagon with an impressive crash. Opened it with a bold flourish and flipped to the page he'd marked with a wooden ruler.

"No *offen*. Pay up," he told Cloygene.

HIDING IN HIBBING

The hulk screwed up a sour face, jabbing the heel of his shoe into the soft turf, burning with mortification. "Bullshit. You prob'ly ripped the page out."

Gallagher pushed his finger into the dictionary. "Right there, between offcut and offend. That's where it'd be. No such word."

Cloygene gave it a sidelong glance, then sputtered, "What the hell they know anyways." Then grabbed a pitchfork and angrily plunged it into the ground next to Gallagher's foot to scare him. But his careless aim was as far off as his vocabulary skills. Two of the tines pierced Gallagher's leather boot, stabbing his big piggy - the one that went to market - and nicking the small toe - the one that went wee-wee-wee all the way home.

Abashed at his own clumsiness, Cloygene stomped away with the grace and gait of a petulant gorilla, neglecting to apologize and completely forgetting to pay off the bet. Gallagher didn't mind. The big toe only required three stitches and the little one was good-to-go with a Band-Aid. Besides, sometimes being right is its own reward... even when you bleed.

From that day forward, Gallagher became best friends with his sister's dictionary, combing its pages with the manic compulsion of a biblical scholar searching for details of Jesus Christ's teenage years. His fascination with words grew into an obsession. The contradictions of linguistics, the mysteries of meaning, the breadth of vocabulary, the untangling of word derivation; all captured his imagination like nothing had before. Suddenly the annoyance he previously found so intrusive was like a salve... and his salvation.

When he grew weary of toting the cumbersome volume around in the Samsonite, he sprang for a lighter soft-cover edition. He read it by lamp light far into the night, consuming it like a beloved novel, studying each entry as if it alone contained the mystical key that would unlock the true meaning of life. Delighting in the pure structure of each word, letter by letter, tasting the sweet sound of diverse pronunciations on his tongue and deep in his throat.

Three relevant events flowed from this new awakening.

First, in the late autumn, he developed agonizing hand cramps from scribbling lengthy lists of words that had captured his fancy. With five spiral notebooks already filled and fingers aching, he finally gave in to the notion of purchasing one of the hot new Phillips Compact Cassette Recorders everyone was talking about. The size of a book, it could be easily carried anywhere. He could whip it out instantly and notate whatever new word might pop up in conversation or be overheard in clandestinely observed public discourse.

Second, while sitting in a coffee shop near Temple University, casually eavesdropping on nearby students earnestly discussing transcendentalism and Heidegger, he was circumspectly scrutinized by a neatly bearded man with John Lennon glasses. Each time Gallagher overheard a new word that sparked his interest, his eyes lit up and he covertly muttered a notation into his recorder.

The bearded man turned out to be a forward-thinking English professor seeking someone to do an audio recording of his new textbook—*Faulkner versus Hemingway: Too Many Words or Too Few?*—hoping to peddle cassette tapes of the tedious tome to his gullible students, turning a nifty little profit each semester.

"I'd record it mythelf," he said with a slight lisp, "but that would theeem terribly crath, wouldn't it?"

What he was really looking for was a relationship—a *liason* in professorial lingo—but Gallagher was completely oblivious to this veiled motivation. Ever hopeful that the young man's naïveté might eventually evaporate, Professor Hotchkiss—a truly unfortunate name for a man with a lisp—offered Gallagher twenty-five dollars to read his book on audio tape at the university media center. Never one to turn down the opportunity to put more cash in his pocket, Gallagher readily agreed to do it.

The third event occurred at the campus studio while recording the book. Noticing Gallagher's ease at the microphone and his affinity for working with recording equipment, the studio manager offered him a part-time position maintaining and repairing the university's collection of consistently abused Ampex recorders, which had the unfortunate habit of breaking down with irritating regularity. This ultimately transitioned into a full-time job after graduation from high school. Five days a week he schlepped all the way across Philly by bus to work as an assistant recording engineer at the university language lab.

After that, each step forward transpired with the crushing rapidity of an Olympic marathon. Before he knew it, he was working as a full-fledged sound recordist on generally amateurish local TV commercials, wielding a Nagra recorder with deft professional ease, all the while taking special note of colorful and quirky industry terms like *gaffer* and *scrim* and *apple box*.

Within a few months he had moved to Chicago, rented a cheap flat and began checking out colleges. But his flirtation with academia was cut short when he caught the attention of ad agency producer Joe Studebaker on the set of a regional commercial for Alpo. Gallagher was there to beg a part time gig to help pay his rent when one of the unruly dogs snatched a tape reel from the production's Nagra recorder and scampered away, leaving a ribbon of acetate scattered in all directions. The pissed-off sound recording engineer let loose a litany of vile expletives and walked off the job. Meanwhile, Gallagher tackled the dog, retrieved the reel and gingerly rewound the tape, saving the day. Joe fired the dog and hired Gallagher.

His employment trajectory was notable. Within two short years of graduating from East Philly High School he was recording sound on a national TV commercial for Nabisco, delighted to be taking home more than two-dozen promotional boxes of saltine crackers that would easily last him the winter.

Sometimes at night his big toe would ache. He'd laugh to himself, recalling the lummox named Cloygene and his ignorant insistence that *offen* was an actual word. But he never truly grasped the profound connection between that odd incident on the golf course and the circuitous path he had ultimately taken. That non-existent word... *offen*... was the true origin of the road he now traveled. All else that lay before him would derive from that.

Hearing the faint intruding sounds echoing distantly through the motel walls, he turned his head to the side, staring at a pie tin filled with the remains of crumbled crust and glops of cherry filling, an empty beer bottle dissecting the circular pan like a compass needle.

He untangled his legs from the sheets and covers, swinging them out, planting his feet on the floor. A scattering of Pyrex baking dishes, grease-stained pizza boxes and hastily conceived gift baskets surrounded him like an obstacle course, the various remnants of stale foodstuffs coalescing into an unidentifiable aroma that was at once sweetly enticing and sharply repellent.

Standing and stretching, he adjusted the boxer shorts on his slim hips, leveling them in a straight line just below his belly button. Caught his image in the dresser mirror. Struck a rock star pose, raking an imaginary guitar.

When he flung the curtains aside, the pulsating cluster of female fans gathered outside in the snow erupted in a fit of squealing and chaotic jumping, casting off any sense of dignity or self-control they might have summoned during the course of their frigid vigil. A raven-haired girl whipped her tattered parka open and, without a smidgen of shame, pressed her naked breasts against the window, mashing her soft lips on the frosty surface, rocking her head from side to side with dramatically calculated exaggeration.

Gallagher laughed, stepping forward with swaggering bliss to plant a kiss on his side of the glass.

This was clearly a wagon he did not want to get *offen*.

21

Joe's languid eyes peered into his coffee cup, exploring the murky liquid as if it held some precious key to the future. But the java at Carl's Restaurant had no magical qualities. It consisted of nothing more than a surfeit of caffeine and a complex blend of other substances that could only be unkindly described as unpalatable sludge. He raised his cup, allowing a bitter rivulet to wash over his tongue, wincing with disgust. This questionable north woods brew was clearly made for intense observation—and possibly the removal of rust and tarnish—but not for appreciative consumption.

Across the table, Ray gripped his cup with both hands, enjoying the warmth that radiated through his fingers and up his arms, recapturing the sensation of touching Maggie's skin. It compelled a euphoric smile to play upon his lips, a perfect accompaniment for his heavy-lidded vacant gaze.

Ziggy returned from his third trip to the men's room, brought on by the potent collision of too many conflicting food groups and the gastric revolution arising within. He flopped heavily into the booth, jostling both Ray and Joe out of their exclusively personal reveries.

"Where the hell's Gallagher?" Joe growled, pushing the coffee cup away.

Ziggy shrugged. Then made a convoluted gesture with his hands and fingers that was apparently meant to represent some kind of nefarious sexual activity, but looked more like a

HIDING IN HIBBING

third base coach signaling a runner to either go low and slide, return to second base or change his underwear.

Joe and Ray gaped at Ziggy, slack-jawed. "What's that?" Joe asked, dumbfounded.

"You know..."

"No. I don't."

"Sure. You know..." Ziggy said, waggling his head, as if that would somehow aid Joe's comprehension.

"No. I really don't. What is it, some kinda deaf talk, sign language mumbo jumbo?"

"No, it's..." He lightly punched his open palm with his fist, then entwined his fingers and twisted them back and forth. "Ya know."

"What? What's this?" Joe's hands flew up, making similar crazy gestures, wiggling his fingers around madly. "Lassie, Timmy's in trouble!"

"Maybe Gallagher's sick," Ray said.

"How the hell you get 'sick' from that?"

"Or still asleep?" Ray ventured.

Joe smacked his forehead. Barked at Ray, "What're you, *guessing* now? Playing charades?"

"I'm trying to interpret."

"He's at the motel," Ziggy finally announced flatly.

"See. I told you," Ray said, slapping his chest with one hand. "He's still in the sack."

Joe looked at Ziggy. "How do you get 'he's at the motel' from this?" He interlocked his fingers, holding them up in front of Ziggy. "It's like an Indian teepee or something." He wiggled his fingers, fluttering them like scattering birds. "Flying fucking teepees! What's that supposed to mean?"

A waitress named Darlene swooped in with a coffee pot and made a move on Joe's cup. He slid his hand over it to block her, shaking his head rapidly.

Ray held his cup out for a refill, craving a renewal of fantasy-inducing warmth.

99

Ziggy leaned toward Darlene, speaking in a hushed confidential tone, even though Joe and Ray were sitting right there. "Is, uh, Janey around?"

"Janey Olsen?" Darlene said, brightly cheerful and not at all hushed. "She's probably up to the Methodist Church, just past the stop-and-go light on 9th Street. Some kinda memorial thing for her grandma." She slid her top lip to the right, her bottom lip to the left, creating a bizarre expression of twisted anguish. "Got smacked by a snowplow out on 169." She crossed her eyes, tongue dangling grotesquely from the side of her mouth.

A palpable silence descended on the table as Joe and Ray looked down and away, pretending they weren't even there. Darlene shattered the uncomfortable void with a breezy, "Hey, how about some of them little weenies or a platter of elk meatballs?"

"Nothing," Joe said.

"Slice of toast," Ray mumbled. "No butter."

Ziggy just shook his head, cringing at the disturbing rumble he felt building again in his gut.

Darlene skittered away for the toast, her cheerfulness unbroken. Right on her heels a woman in a fleece jacket wrapped tight around two layers of sweaters suddenly appeared. She dragged two young children behind her. A five-year-old boy tenaciously gripped his mother's hand and a seven-year-old girl clung to her jacket with a tight little fist. Both kids looked shell-shocked, as if their mother had shaken them awake from a deep slumber, stuffed their limp bodies into whatever clothes were handy and hauled them through the bitter cold to Carl's.

It's amazing how a truly dedicated stage mother can so accurately conjure the image of a fiercely grinning Satan, red eyes glowing with unstoppable resolve, lips drawn back into an obsessive smile that promises no room for compromise or surrender. It can make a grown man shudder.

"My two," she announced, ignoring any pretense of introduction, "they both got four years of tap. And the little one here juggles. Store-bought oranges now, but working his way up to apples come summer. Lemme tell ya, they are both real ready for the show business."

She pulled the two stunned kids closer, ripped their unzipped parkas off and unceremoniously tossed them aside, chattering away as she roughly executed the task. "They're perfect for television. It's got that little screen, ya know. And they're both little ones too, so they fit just perfect. 'Course, as time goes by, they'll get bigger...the screens. And my two will grow right along with it, see."

She began to snap her fingers, rhythmically bobbing her head, humming some unidentifiable melody. The kids stared up at the three grown men in the booth, their tiny mouths hanging open, nervous eyes wide and unblinking. The woman gave the boy a hard nudge with her hip, snapping her fingers louder.

The two numbed kids started tap dancing like stiff little robots, way off the woefully un-rhythmic beat and awkwardly out of step with each other.

Joe seriously began to wonder what evil thing he had done in his life to deserve this. He tumbled deeply within himself, the finger-snapping off-key humming and clickety-clack tapping swallowed up by the hollow nothingness of an imagined snowdrift in a deep forest.

22

KHIB-AM was located on Howard Street, the town's main drag, in a brick building constructed in 1884 to house one of the first banks to serve Hibbing. When the bank was moved to new quarters two blocks away in 1921, Grover's Hardware set up shop until, at the end of the Korean War, it was eventually replaced by the radio station. KHIB quickly became the number one source for news and music in the vast Range. A day didn't pass without every Ranger on the slope tuning in at some point; it was how they took the pulse of the community and felt a connection with the notably diverse melting pot of neighbors.

Maggie spun slowly in the chair at her desk, still feeling the glow of her randy escapade in the sheets with Ray. It had been months since she had indulged in the exhilaration of physical intimacy. She didn't count Ernest Benson, the dreary realtor who helped her find the house she was buying on the north end of town. They had gone out to dinner only once, to celebrate signing the mortgage documents and his ridiculously piddling commission. They drank way too much wine, laughed at too many things that weren't funny, and then, floating on a cloud of good will and relief, tumbled into bed at his newly constructed tract house for a meaningless session of celebratory sex.

It was a perfunctory encounter, concluding swiftly, before the ink was barely dry on the mortgage docs. Ernest had climaxed almost instantly, his white boxers still wrapped around his spindly thighs, a meek groan signaling the culmination of his involvement. Maggie hadn't even found her way past the spinning room, the saggy bed, the wrinkled sheets tangled up with her twisted skirt, when his gaunt body stiffened and the pathetic sound escaped his lips, wafting in her ear on the damp breeze of a harsh sigh. Everything went cold at that moment and Maggie withdrew into her well-ordered world of professional concerns, relegating the very concept of orgasmic release to some future moment of private indulgence.

Ernest draped his limp arm across her hip, snuggling himself along the contour of her body, falling into a steady pattern of guttural breathing. Maggie stared at the ceiling. In her head, she ticked off a list of all the mundane tasks facing her prior to the move. It was in this random mental inventory that she discovered a spark of inspiration, an excuse that would afford her an immediate escape.

"Oh gosh," she exclaimed, throwing Ernest's arm off and sitting bolt upright. "I think I forgot to turn off the gas burner on my stove!" She leaped from the bed, untwisting her skirt and primly pulling it down to cover her knees. "I gotta go. My house could be burning to the ground."

All beautifully conceived and quite convincingly played, but totally unnecessary and lost beneath the steady rumble of snoring from Ernest. However, it did save her the embarrassment of explaining how she could possibly forget to turn off a *gas* burner on her *electric* stove. Such are the unforeseen traps of desperate improvisation.

But Ray was definitely no Ernest. He possessed an aura of real danger, his long unruly hair boldly flaunting the stuffy conventions of small town life, his brooding nature and dark eyes hiding terrible secrets. Amidst their tempestuous tumble in the sack, Maggie had found herself inexorably drawn to his taut body, simultaneously relishing both his edgy impatience and seeming contradictory lack of interest.

He was a true mystery, a puzzle, a conundrum that demanded further exploration and ultimately, revelation. Her clever reporter's ruse to gain access to the exploitable facts behind a story had opened a rusted door to something within her that she hadn't allowed herself to experience since her freshman year in college. It was deeply unsettling, yet incredibly exciting.

She looked up at the clock above the control room window. 10:15 a.m. It was only an hour later in New York. The enticing images of Ray abruptly grew fuzzy and muddled as her journalistic instincts once again assumed control. She felt the blood in her veins stir, cranking up a notch, wrapping her thumping heart in the embrace of pure ambition, making it beat faster, harder. In an instant, she had flown directly from the caressing comfort of that sweaty motel bed into a maelstrom of unbridled resolve.

Maggie rummaged through the scraps of paper on her desk finally coming up with the one she had scribbled a number on earlier. She pulled the phone closer, clutching the receiver to her chest like a baby, pausing to compose a coherent inquiry in her head. Then, she dialed.

23

"Yah, this Ed Sullivan?"

After being circuitously transferred through a maze of switchboards at CBS Studio 50, Maggie's call had finally been routed to a small, musty, smoke-filled room without windows, where an impatiently brusque voice responded with a labored sigh. "It's the Ed Sullivan *Show*, yes ma'am."

Paul Rafferty did not suffer fools easily, even though his position as talent coordinator required him to do so more often than any human being deserved. He stood, slouched forward, leaning heavily, one arm on the battered conference table stained with coffee rings and branded with cigarette burns, shoulders hunched forward as if the entire burden of civilization rested squarely on his back. This world-weary posture had developed slowly over his long journey from mailroom runner to cue card flipper and glorified production assistant, ultimately landing him in the thankless and unheralded position of talent coordinator.

"So you're not him yourself, then?" Maggie pressed, making sure to get her facts straight.

"No, I'm not him," Paul said, droning flatly, making no pretense at amiability. "Ed...Mr. Sullivan...doesn't answer the phone."

"Oh, yah, sure. Why would he? Must be plenty of folks there to do that for him," she said with an awkward laugh. "Like yourself."

"Right," he muttered. Then, a disturbing thought pushed at him. "Why? Do I sound like Ed Sullivan?"

An awkward pause ensued on Maggie's end as she weighed the potential consequences of her response. "Well, ya know, not on the phone, no, uh-uh."
"Who is this?"
"Oh, uh, sure, yah. This is Maggie Thorson up Hibbing, Minnesota. WHIB-AM. Just wanted to confirm you got this singer and his band up here, Ziggy Jett and the Jetstream, gonna be on your show in a couple weeks."
"I don't know what you're talking about, lady."
Another pause on Maggie's end. A gently sighing hiss on the line established its own breathy voice, until Maggie interrupted it. "Sooooo, you don't have this famous rock star, then? Hiding out up here 'til he's on your program? Big Elvis debut kinda deal?"
"Absolutely not," he stated flatly. Christ, another loony, Paul thought, slouching even lower in deflated frustration. He made a mental note to tell the switchboard to stop routing these crank calls to their room.
"That your final statement on the issue?"
"Dammit! What'd I say, lady?"
"Well, okay then," Maggie said, keeping it cheerful. "Thanks a bunch." She gently placed the receiver in its cradle, smiling to herself, bathed in the glow of professional pride and, now, certainty.
Paul slammed the receiver down and flopped into the tattered leather chair that was normally used for napping whenever Ed was safely off the premises, working alone at his apartment/office for Sullivan Enterprises in the Delmonico Hotel. The call had deeply troubled him, but he couldn't determine precisely why. It wasn't just Maggie's pesky insistence. There was a sly sincerity in her voice that hinted she was privy to some highly confidential knowledge beyond the scope of others.
He tried to erase his unease by focusing on the talent roster that dominated the opposite wall; an imposing framed rectangular corkboard with a clutter of 3x5 cards randomly

stuck to it with multi-colored pushpins. But this only increased his agitation.

After twenty-six successful years on the air, the Ed Sullivan show was beginning to feel the strain of an over-exposed talent pool and the viewing audience's capriciously unpredictable taste in entertainment. A glut of variety shows had already satiated the American public's desire for tuning in to a potpourri of unrelated performers. Finding a faithful weekly audience for a mish-mash of jugglers, ballet dancers, performing dogs, Borsch Belt comics, and opera singers was just not making it anymore. Keeping things fresh and current was becoming an exhausting race with no finish line in sight, short of cancellation.

Paul's depressive angst was interrupted when Marty, a dedicated young intern, ambled into the room with an armload of papers, carefully stuffing each of them into its appropriate folder in a tall metal file cabinet. Marty politely ignored Paul, figuring he was catching a few quick winks in the "snooze throne", as the large chair had been christened by the rest of the envious staff.

"Hey, Marty," Paul said, startling him. "You know Ziggy Jett and the Airplanes?"

Marty stared at him with a blank look. "Airplanes?"

"Uh, no no, not airplanes." He conjured up Maggie's voice in his head, replaying their strange conversation. "Ziggy Jett and the, uh... Jetstream."

Marty opened his mouth, as if about to speak, staring silently at the file cabinet. He'd been on the job for more than two months and this was the first time anybody had asked him anything, except the time the floor director demanded to know why the hell he was standing right in the middle of the shot during a final dress rehearsal. Now he was being put on the spot by a talent coordinator. Maybe it was a test to see if he might deserve a promotion. He fearfully reconsidered; perhaps he was being assessed for possible elimination. This could be a critical turning point in his

nascent career. He squinted intensely at the file cabinet drawer, enacting his own youthful interpretation of deep thought and solemn concentration.
"Ziggy Jett," Paul reiterated, enunciating clearly. "Rock star. And his band, the Jetstream. Ring a bell?"
"Ohhhhh yeah, sure," he said with squeaky confidence, his voice quavering. "They're hot, man. The best. "
"So you know them?"
Gulp. Marty froze. "Uh, me? No, not personally, no..."
"I mean, you know who they are, right?"
Marty's grand sigh of relief fluttered the papers in his hand. "Oh yeah. 'Course I do. They're great. They got a beat and, uh, you can dance to it...and stuff." His voice trailed off as he continued to nod confirmation of his enthusiasm for the, until now, completely unknown Ziggy and company.

An hour later, Paul Rafferty paced the stuffy office, crisscrossing the cramped space, restlessly circling the table, trying to describe the strange conversation he'd had with this Maggie person calling from some jerkwater radio station in Minnesota.

Johnny Stromberg, stood quietly, arms folded, listening with great patience. He was a seasoned veteran of the TV talent game, having already been in the trenches with the crazies at *Laugh-In*, as well as surviving several seasons at the Tonight Show, servicing the contrasting proclivities of both Carson and Jack Paar. When he was recruited for the Sullivan show, he was known as "Mr. Unshakeable" because of his rock-steady calm in the face of any crisis. But the recent downturn in the show's customarily consistent ratings had begun to reveal small cracks in his cool demeanor. His arms were folded tighter, jaw clenched with a more determined sense of purpose. His steady eyes seemed to gaze just beyond the person who was speaking, perhaps peering off into the distance at a vast spectrum of possible future employment options.

"Run that by again." That was Ann Darling, a tightly knit package of soft curves and velvety voice that could easily distract anyone from her prickly obstinate, uncompromising spirit. She leaned languorously against the doorjamb, one elbow resting lightly in the hand of the arm that lay across her slim waist, a cigarette locked between two delicate fingers of the other upraised hand. A silky coil of smoke drifted toward the ceiling like an undulating question mark. In a 40's film noir she could have been easily mistaken for a sultry femme fatale.

"Okay," Rafferty said, looking down, hands on hips, taking a long moment to gather his thoughts. He wanted to condense the gist of it into a more concise clarification; something that would make a solid impression, so they would truly believe that he wasn't just cooking up some cockeyed baloney. "This big rock star...from Minnesota...is supposed to be on the show in two weeks."

"Our show?" Ann said, brows knit, head cocked.

"Yeah. Our show. This show. The Ed Sullivan Show."

Ann stepped into the room. "Who is it?" Ann was a woman of few words, but they were always to the point. As the junior talent coordinator, not to mention being a woman in a business dominated by males, she needed to hold her own by making every word count.

"Ziggy Jett and the Jetstream."

"Oh puh-leeeeeeze," Ann said, tapping her cigarette dismissively. A clump of ash fell to the table, where it smoldered, eventually burning a scar into the worn surface, memorializing this moment in time forever.

Bob Brenneman, the show's longtime producer, had been seated calmly in the corner, listening to all this unfold. It wasn't the craziest thing he'd heard. In the early days of the show, rumors about who was going to appear next week on the Sullivan stage were constantly flying about. Wild reports of the Beatle's imminent appearance were running rampant long before the British lads even considered breaching American shores.

"Who we got scheduled?" Brenneman asked in his deep, sonorous tone.

"The Flying Banzinis," Stromberg said with a shrug, not even bothering to glance at the schedule board.

"Banzinis cancelled," Ann said. "They dropped the tall guy on his head."

"With the mustache?" Brenneman asked.

"The other one."

"With the ears?"

"The other other one," Ann said. "With the hair and feet."

"They all have hair and feet, for Christ's sake."

"Curly hair. Big feet."

"Oh, yeah. Him. I don't like him."

"Guy with the mustache is bald," Stromberg interjected.

Brenneman stared at him, trying to make sense of his comment. "Yeah? So?"

"You said they all have hair and feet. He doesn't. Not the hair anyway."

"That's right," Rafferty said. "He's totally bald."

Brenneman blinked this digression away like a bad dream, jumping back to the point. "Who else we got?"

Rafferty checked the board. "Wayne and Shuster."

"Myron Cohen," Stromberg offered. "Bobby Darin."

"Darin cancelled too," Ann said, flipping more ash.

Brenneman smacked his hand on the table. "Jesus, guys! We could use a break here. Neilsens are in the toilet. And Senor Wences just ain't gonna pull us out of the crapper anymore."

"S'alright," Stomberg uttered in guttural imitation of the classic but seriously threadbare routine that featured a disembodied head in a box that always responded *S'alright* to Senor Wences whenever he asked, *S'alright*? Truly lame, but to most Americans incredibly funny, until you'd seen it played out a thousand times.

"You think this is amusing, Johnny?" Brenneman growled, making the most of his commanding voice.

"That's the problem, Bob. It's not funny anymore. The kids think it's stupid and their parents are asleep on the couch."

A loud crash rumbled down the hallway, causing everyone except *Mr. Unshakeable* to stiffen slightly. Ann recovered first, taking a long, shaky drag on her nearly expired cigarette.

A booming voice echoed down the corridor. "I said BIG, dammit! Really big!"

A door slammed, rattling the very core of the building, vibrating the ancient wood frames within the walls. The blurry image of a man in a gray suit flashed past their open door, hunched over, head lowered, a charging bull. An instant later, another door slammed, loudly punctuating the outburst. A tense silence followed, much like the haunting quiet that arises immediately after a passing tornado.

"Ed's still pissed over that Doors fiasco," Rafferty muttered softly, nearly a whisper.

Ann made an incredulous face. "That was like three years ago."

"Morrison never should have said what he said." Stromberg glanced at the open doorway. "Not to Ed."

"What was he gonna do?" Ann said, sharply invoking her usual directness. "Ed told him 'you'll never play the Ed Sullivan Show' and Jim said..."

"Yeah, I know...'We just *played* the Sullivan show'...but he shouldn't have said it. Out of respect."

"But it was true, Johnny," Ann said with an obvious shrug. "They'd already played the damn show."

"True doesn't matter. It was a challenge to Ed's authority. He deserves better than that."

Rafferty slipped back into the fray, trying to smooth things over. "If they just hadn't sung that line about 'couldn't get much higher' there wouldn't have been any problem."

"But that's the song," Ann said, heating up, cheeks flushed. "It's a funeral pyre. The flames 'couldn't get much higher.' It's about the flames."

"The line was '*girl* we couldn't get much higher'," Stromberg said with certainty. "It wasn't flames. He was talking about him and some girl getting high."

Ann folded her arms, crushing her lips together. "So what if he was? What about artistic freedom?"

"Christ, Ann!" Brenneman stood up like a shot, shoving his chair back with a loud scrape to remind everyone who was in charge. "You're not seriously defending those schmucks, are you?" He let his eyes sweep across all of them, bracketing them as a group so no one could ignore his words. "Bottom line, if you can't come up with somebody who can pull in some younger eyeballs and kick the ratings right off the charts, right into the stratosphere, Ed's gonna pink-slip all of you." Poking holes in the air with a rigid finger. "Not me. You!"

Another round of booming voices erupted in a room down the hall putting an emphatic button on Bob Brenneman's rant. He lowered his chin, cocked his head slightly to the side and widened his eyes at them, as if to ask, "Need I say more?"

He turned to leave, then paused in the doorway to look at Rafferty and drop a hemlock-laced cherry on the cake. "And as for that fuckin' Hendrix fiasco... I'm not even gonna go there." With that, he vanished down the hall.

Rafferty lowered his head, trying to muster a viable defense. Then peered up at Ann and Stromberg with a humbled and helpless shrug. "He was alive when I booked him."

This prompted an awkward hush that could easily have been misinterpreted as a respectful "moment of silence" in memory of Jimi. Actually, it was a terribly embarrassing reminder of the many booking blunders they had all perpetrated over the years. After a long gloomy pause, the phone abruptly jangled, shattering the self-conscious stillness and startling all of them.

Rafferty grabbed the phone. "What?" he snapped. Then eased off, his face going slack, eyes shifting to Stromberg and Ann. "From *where*?"

He hesitated, and then hit the third blinking button, taking the call.

A thousand miles away, a throng of teen girls crammed into, and clustered all around, a phone booth outside the Record Rack in Hibbing. They giggled with breathless abandon, periodically filling the air with sharp, helpless squeals, followed by even more giggles. Sarah Rehborg, the dedicated self-appointed leader of the fanatical groupies, clutched the receiver tightly with both hands, refusing to relinquish control.

When she heard a voice on the other end, she lost all pretense of restraint, maturity or discipline. "Oh God! They are sooooo hot! We luuuuve them! When are they gonna be on the show?"

"Wait wait wait..." Rafferty interjected on his end, trying to capture control of the exchange. "You're not talking about Ziggy Jett..."

A piercing wail of high-pitched teen girl voices completed his inquiry with "And the Jetstream!" Followed by a chaotic chorus of shrieks and screams that forced him to pull the phone away from his ear.

Rafferty slowly rotated the receiver toward Ann and Stromberg, eyes wide. A fervent chant—*Zig-gy Jett... Zig-gy Jett... Zig-gy Jett*—penetrated the stale air of the small room. Not even a thousand miles of telephone lines could compress, filter or diminish the intensity of their fanatical adolescent plea.

24

Joe's eyes, glazed over like two sugary doughnuts, stared listlessly into a deep pit of remorse, his caffeine-addled mind a whirligig of second-guesses and doubts. This whole crazy scheme had been his loony brainstorm—a desperate attempt to scam a couple motel rooms until the blizzard blew itself out—but now they were being sucked deeper into a complicated scenario of deceit, burdened by the inevitable payback that comes with it.

For more than an hour, he'd been trapped in a booth at Carl's with Ray and Ziggy, besieged by a parade of hopeful locals eager to show off the shallow depth and narrow breadth of their questionable talents.

Four doddering gents in Rotary Club red blazers serenaded them with seemingly endless barbershop quartet renditions of *Camptown Ladies* and *Goodnight Irene*.

Three perpetually grinning waitresses followed them, warbling a dreadful a cappella version of *Mister Sandman* while clutching coffee pots, apparently unaware of the irony in their choice of song and props. And then, keeping a local vibe going, a skinny, pimply-faced kid floundered through a nasally, whining Bob Dylan impression, slaughtering *Like a Rolling Stone* and blowing tortured cat noises on the harmonica precariously suspended from his neck on a bent coat hanger.

Just when the excruciating parade of hapless wannabes appeared to be finally, mercifully, near its end, a uniformed city police officer with an accordion strapped to his chest stepped over to their table with painfully polite hesitancy. He offered a timid nod, as if this small silent gesture provided sufficient introduction requiring no further explanation, then launched into an ear-popping performance of the flat-footed toe-tapper *Lady of Spain*.

As everyone in northern Minnesota was well aware *"Da person who plays a kor-deen is the most important one in da polka band."* But the goofy jollity of polka music combined with the flowery romance of Spain made for a disconcerting mixture that precipitously tipped the scale into a realm of the unbearable.

Ray made a dive for freedom, miming intense physical anguish, declaring, "Gotta hit the head. Coffee catching up with me."

Ziggy scrambled after him, hurriedly muttering a series of seemingly random words—"Me too...bathroom...gotta... men's, ya know...need to, uh...don't stop... sorry"—all spewed without the benefit of conjunctions to logically knit them together.

This flurry of desperate avoidance didn't faze the musical cop, having already felt the harsh sting of rejection many times before at family picnics and amateur talent shows down at the American Legion hall. He happily plowed his way through the unrelenting melody, rocking on his hips, fingers dancing on the keys, a chipper grin aimed directly at Joe, tickled pink to see that at least one-third of his audience still remained.

Joe plastered the mindless, brightly contented smile of a beauty pageant winner on his face, swaying slightly to the numbing rhythm, while his mind retreated once again to that wonderfully serene mystical forest of silence; it was a place he was beginning to like more and more. Besides, he rationalized, it couldn't hurt to keep a member of the local police force on their side given the escalating nature of the deceptive frauds they were perpetrating on the community, and the unpleasant consequences that could likely result at any moment.

At the rear of the diner, Ray made a sharp right turn outside the restroom door and vanished into the kitchen. The cooks greeted him enthusiastically, waving and grinning broadly with giddy shouts of "Ray! Ray!"—pretending to wildly strum invisible guitars and beat on imaginary drums.

Ziggy hesitated at the kitchen entrance, looking toward the men's room door, confused by Ray's unexpected detour. Then, propelled by the momentum of his originally announced intent, he pushed his way into the men's room, gave a quick blink at the unattended urinals, spun around like a wobbly dreidel, and exited right back outside.

He stood there fidgeting, torn by conflicting impulses. Should he live up to his blurted declaration of desperately needing the men's room or follow Ray on some unknown adventure? The wheezing sound of the cop's accordion drummed on his ears, making the decision easy. He burst into the kitchen, caught a glimpse of Ray exiting through the back door, literally seeing nothing more than the heel of his left shoe as the door closed behind him. Ziggy muttered unintelligibly to the cooks, helplessly miming with a flurry of confusing gestures as he made a quick dash to catch up to Ray.

Hunched over, hands stuffed into the pockets of his jeans, Ray made his way around the dumpsters, leaning hard into the blowing snow. Ziggy appeared behind him, suddenly chilled by the sight of translucent flakes clinging to Ray's hair like tiny desperate ghosts.

Ray spun around, glaring at Ziggy. "Where you think you're going?"

"Where *you* going?" Ziggy shot back, biting crunchy ice crystals whipped into his mouth by the wind.

"Jesus it's cold," Ray said, glancing back at the warm light glowing in the diner windows.

HIDING IN HIBBING

Both of them were trembling. "And we don't have our coats," Ziggy said.

"No shit, man. You just pick up on that?"

They were both rocking, swaying, shaking. Hands tucked into their armpits. Cheeks burnished red.

"So go get 'em," Ray said. No debate. No discussion. Just flat out.

"Why me? Why don't you go get 'em?"

Ray stared at him. "Because you're the big superstar, Zig."

"If I'm such a big deal, why do I have to be the one to get the coats?"

"Because we do everything else. All you gotta do is be the stupid star. You get off easy. So get the coats! Christ!"

Ziggy stared into the whirling flakes. He couldn't believe what he was hearing. "That makes no sense."

"Course it doesn't," Ray bellowed, little shards of angry spittle turning instantly into crystal spires at the sides of his mouth. "Now go get the fuckin' coats."

Ziggy slipped in through the front door of the diner unnoticed. He winced as the aching wheeze of the accordion assaulted his ears. The musical cop was now plowing through a lively polka version of *Surfin' Safari*, bouncing and swaying gaily.

Ziggy grabbed their two down jackets from the wooden pegs by the door.

As he turned, his eyes met Joe's unblinking gaze. Though at least thirty feet lay between them, Ziggy felt as if they were nose-to-nose, Joe twisting his shirt collar with tightly clutched fingers, holding him close enough to feel the heat of angry breath on his skin.

But then Joe's eyes softened and his lids dropped shut as he tilted his head, tossing a dim nod toward the door. *Go ahead, make your escape. I'll take the bullet, kid.* It was a profoundly delicate gesture by Joe, projecting an array of conflicting emotions: resentment, envy, resignation and then selfless acceptance.

Ziggy felt all these surge through him at once as he retreated back into the cold.

Outside, Ray grabbed the coat away from Zig, pulled it on and zipped it without a word of thanks. A big red Buick Skylark swerved up beside them, tires crunching the snow. Gallagher leaped from the back seat. A retinue of squealing girls stuck their arms out the windows, wiggling fingers at him. He touched each hand lightly, quickly, making as perfunctory an exit as possible.

"I love you all," he shouted with a growling enthusiasm that any 16-year-old girl would interpret as absolutely genuine. They all shrieked instinctively and the car sped away, fishtailing on the slick icy surface. The fresh blanket of snow muted a sputtering punctuation of wild horn honks as the car disappeared.

"Every girl loves a drummer," Gallagher announced proudly to Ray and Ziggy.

"So you're still the drummer then?" Ray said.

"Yeah, yeah. Why not? I can beat on stuff with sticks. Who can't? Right?" Then caught himself, eyes shifting. "Well, maybe not you, Zig. But you got your deal already. The fake singer star guy."

Gallagher gave Ziggy a teeth-rattling slap on the shoulder, fortunately padded by the heavy down jacket. Then he caught a glimpse of Ray's dour expression.

"Oh man. Did you want to be the drummer? I didn't even think about that, Ray. I'm sorry, man. That was truly thoughtless on my part. Maybe you could be like a back-up drummer. Get some mileage out of that."

"I don't want to be the drummer."

"Oh, okay. Good, good. But if you ever do, you could easily be the second drummer. These girls don't know how many drummers a band has. And our band can..."

HIDING IN HIBBING

"We're not a real band, Gallagher. Did you forget?"

Boom. Silence. So quiet you could hear the snow falling. Gallagher chewed on this for a moment. "Okay, well, *fake* band then. They don't know how many drummers a *fake* band has."

"Joe wants to see you inside," Ray said, curtly ending the fake band discussion. "Said it was important."

"Okay. That's cool. I need some pie. I been burnin' up the calories. These girls. Jeez, they're runnin' me ragged."

"Yeah, we heard you."

"They're insatiable. Like animals."

Ray, unimpressed, repeated, "Animals."

"But good animals, ya know. Friendly." Then pushing it with a lascivious eyebrow wiggle. "Very, very friendly."

"That's groovy," Ray muttered flatly. Raised his arm toward Carl's. "Pie. Get your pie."

"Yeah! Pie!" Gallagher spun around. Charged into the restaurant, nearly colliding with the musical cop shambling toward the exit, grinning like a big kid, clutching his accordion, bathed in the glow of some kind of personal victory.

Gallagher checked their usual booth. Joe stared down at the table, steeped in a welcome silence. Gallagher slid into the booth across from him. "This is so freakin' great."

"Where you been?"

"Signing autographs and stuff. This one chick, man, she..."

"Today's the day we shoulda been shooting the beer spot."

Gallagher said, "Oh...yeah." Then blinked it away. His face lit up. "But this is way better."

"We're here to work. You get that, right?"

"Supposed to, yeah. Then, the snow, roads closed and shit. What're you gonna do? But it's all good. Turned out great."

"Turned out, huh?" Joe said.

119

"Yeah."

"Just turned out. So I didn't have anything to do with it?"

Gallagher let that penetrate. "Well, yeah. You did. The doofus over at the motel, ya got him to comp us rooms. Otherwise we'd be sleeping in the bus freezin' our asses off."

"You're welcome."

"Yeah, thanks."

Joe took a mindless sip of his cold coffee. Winced with distaste. Looked at Gallagher. "These girls. Be careful. Or you open up a miasma of trouble."

Gallagher smiled. "Miasma. Nice." He liked the sound of it. Mimed it, his lips gently touching on the *m's*, the soft hiss of the *s* between them. "What's that? A mess?"

"I don't know. A cloud. Fog. Something like that."

"Sounds like a mess."

"Okay, a mess then. Whatever. Steer clear of it."

"Miasma." Gallagher said it slowly again, feeling it in his mouth.

"Paul Harvey says it a lot."

"The news guy?"

"On the radio. You know, 'This is Paul Har-vey...good day!' "

"Cool." Then, gave it more thought. "A stink, maybe."

"Could be."

"A stinking mess."

"Just avoid it."

Carl ambled over. Flashed a toothy grin. He clutched a shiny saxophone in his hands. "Picked her up in a garage sale. Was Happ's but he let 'er go, so I grabbed her. His loss, eh?" Cleared his throat. "Give this a listen," he said, and began to blow.

Gallagher cringed at the mournful wail.

Feel the pain, Joe thought, watching Gallagher squirm uncomfortably. *Feel the pain, my friend.*

HIDING IN HIBBING

Ray trudged along the roadside. Ziggy followed behind, struggling to keep his footing in the gnarls of plowed snow and gravel, now frozen into crunchy rock-hard burrs.

Over his shoulder, Ray grumbled, "Where you think you're goin'?"

"Into town."

"You following me?"

"I'm just walking into town."

"Feels like you're following me."

Slipping and stumbling, Ziggy said, "This snow, jeez, you can't even..."

"I don't like being followed."

"I'm walking in your footsteps so I don't slip."

"You walkin' in my footsteps, you're following the wrong guy."

"It's easier."

"Dumber, I'd say."

One of Ziggy's feet snagged an ice clod, slid sideways. He whirled his arms to keep his balance, trying not to stumble headlong into a drift.

"Christ, Zig. You're like a pathetic little dog back there. Walk up here."

Ziggy hustled to catch up, plodding awkwardly on the snowplowed mound heaped up along the shoulder.

Ray grabbed his arm. "Not there!" He swung him out onto the roadway. "Walk on the road. Keep cars from hitting us."

"Now they're going to hit me."

"They're not gonna hit you. You're the big rock star, remember?"

Ziggy studied Ray with sidelong glances.

"You jealous?"

"Right. I'm jealous of you. That'll be the day."

"Then why don't *you* walk in the road?"

"You got it, numb nuts."

121

Ray grabbed Ziggy, flung him back on the inside track. But you fall on your face, I'm not picking your useless ass up."

They walked on in silence, wet snow whipping their skin.

"You don't like me much, do you?"

"I love ya, Zigmond. You're the fuckin' love of my life. I want us to get married and grow old together. Now shut up."

25

They didn't speak the rest of the way into Hibbing, trudging along, shoes clomping in the thick layer of fresh snow, occasional cars rumbling slowly past them on clinking tire chains.

Ray's father had always told him he wouldn't amount to anything. "You want to be a pile of dog shit, so be it." And Ray believed him. But that didn't stop him from trying to prove his father wrong.

Just out of high school, he joined the Navy. He and a few of his pals had bought into the cornball *"Join the Navy, See the World!"* hype being pushed by recruiters, imagining themselves scampering around Paris like Gene Kelly in sailor suits or prancing down 5th Avenue with luscious babes on each arm. Viet Nam was heating up and looking dicey, so a few years in the Navy seemed like a reasonable alternative to risking the draft. And it would certainly show his old man he could amount to something.

"Dog shit with a stupid looking hat," was the send-off his father gave him. "Real men carry M1's and protect the country. They don't go sailin' around in little toy boats like Popeye." His dad said it with a crooked grin, but he wasn't joking.

After two months scrubbing latrines and buffing floors in Philadelphia while waiting assignment, Ray was finally shipped off to the Naval Amphibious Base at Little Creek, Virginia. Not exactly Paris, but at least no one would be shooting at him.

DAVID O'MALLEY

At his check-in interview, a bored clerk asked him what kind of experience he had. Determined to avoid anything involving a mop or buffer or latrine, Ray had mockingly joked that he was a pornographer. But the indifferent clerk misheard his sardonic wisecrack and scribbled down *photographer*. Ray was assigned to an open slot in the base public information office, handed a battered Nikon SLR and told to go shoot pictures of Navy Seals running exercises on the beach. Such were the peculiar quirks of an undiscerning military bureaucracy.

Ray got an *early out* after an upsurge of ground troops in Nam precipitated cutbacks in Naval personnel, shuttled unceremoniously right back into the civilian circus with two years of snapping humdrum photos under his belt.

He tried to find work as a photographer, but everybody wanted to see his portfolio.

"My what?"

"You know, your portfolio. Photographs. Your work. Your best shots."

Were they yanking his chain? He hadn't even saved old copies of the base paper where his photos occasionally appeared—guys getting medals while shaking some bored officer's hand, ships being deployed to Nam, clean-up after a fire at the base administration building—real exciting stuff.

But he caught a break when the portrait photographer at Sears was fired for drinking on the job. Ray was hired on the spot to replace him. But it only took three weeks of trying to snap decent shots of squirmy kids, crying babies and scowling parents for Ray to quit. "I get why he was drinking," was all he said to the floor manager as he walked out mid-shift.

If he was going to get anywhere, he knew he had to take a big step up the ladder. He borrowed a suit from his cousin, came up with a crazy story about his portfolio having been stolen by an envious competitor, and walked into

HIDING IN HIBBING

BBD&O, the biggest ad agency in Chicago at the time. That's when he met Joe.

"Stolen, huh?" Joe said, seeing right through Ray's cockamamie tale but appreciating his chutzpah. "That's a bitch, man."

"Yeah. But I get knocked down, I get right back up."

Joe was a low-level manager for creative accounts at the agency. Had his own dreams, his own chutzpah. He really liked this brash kid who thought he could be a big time photographer simply by willing it to be.

He told Ray he needed to have an education.

"What? In photography?"

"That'd be helpful, yeah."

"I'm intuitive."

"Yeah, and I'm Presbyterian on occasion, but you still need some professional credentials to work here. This is the big leagues, pal."

Ray liked Joe's no bullshit approach. It gave him comfort to stand on solid ground for a change.

"So where do I do that?"

"Lots of good schools out there. Where you want to go?"

"What's the best one?"

"The best?" Joe scratched his ear, stalling, trying to figure a direction to go. Wanting to keep it real. "The Art Center College of Design is top of the heap. But expensive. And I won't lie, hard to get into."

"What about just...good, but not so, you know..."

"Costly?"

"Yeah. Cheaper. But decent."

Joe shifted around in his chair. Didn't want to steer him wrong.

"Brooks, I'd say."

"Brooks?"

"Brooks Institute."

"That nearby?"

Joe smiled. He knew he'd see this guy again. "Santa Barbara. California."

"Shit," Ray said.

The next week Ray arranged with a drive-away company to deliver a car to its owner on the west coast—a freaking Cadillac no less—driving straight through with only a few stops to crash in rest areas and parking lots. Walked into Brooks Institute two days later and told them he wanted to enroll as a student. Hadn't even given a thought to calling the school first or sending in an application.

The GI Bill and an abundance of charm got him in. But then he learned that every student was required to own an expensive 4x5 large format camera. Most students opted for the Calumet, but it still cost a pretty penny. After the Sears debacle and his floundering job search, Ray was already short on ready cash.

The only course of study that didn't require having your own camera gear was cinematography. The 16mm film cameras—Arriflex, Beaulieu, even the spring-loaded Bolex Rex 5—were too pricey for most students, so the school provided them. Without a blink or a balk, Ray announced his desire to become a cinema student. Then groused about it for the next three days.

It's hard to pinpoint precisely when Ray first developed his deeply cynical view of life. Certainly, the constancy of his father's caustic sarcasm played a part in it. But there were other, more obscure and intangible, factors as well.

Ray viewed everything with deep skepticism and caution, complaining about the raw deal he'd always been handed. He often cited his father's verbal abuse, not realizing it had been a major motivation, inspiring in him the resolve to seek his own path. He griped about the Navy shuttling him off into a line of work he hadn't sought, forgetting it had opened the door to an exciting career. He even bitched about not being able to get a job and having to move all the way to California, where he was forced by limited finances to ultimately enroll in a course of study he had no interest in pursuing, seemingly unaware that in the process he had grown incredibly passionate about the art of cinematography.

Each blow had caused him to be knocked in another direction, thrown through a different window, shoved off another cliff. From each insult or bitter disappointment a greater opportunity had arisen, yet cynicism and suspicion festered in his bones.

His mother's words had flown past his ears. "Good things happen and bad things happen; they tumble down on us like hailstones," she told him. "Some leave the sting of regret; others melt as they fall, never reaching us, never touching us. Life is a magnificent and unpredictable storm. Surviving with clear eyes and an open mind, that's what is important." He had nodded, looking off, pleased with the soothing, certain sound of her voice. But the meaning in her wisdom eluded him.

Two years and six goofy, self-indulgent short films later he was ready to return east and take Chicago by storm. While hanging out in L.A. for a few days before catching a flight to O'Hare, he encountered a filmmaker with a jet black beard named Francis zealously talking up a project of his—something called *The Rain People*—that he was going to shoot while rambling across the country in a couple of motorhomes and a caravan of cars. It sounded crazy to Ray and, naturally, he was skeptical. Francis offered Ray a job shooting second camera on the film. Or production stills. His choice. He had this other friend, a guy named George, who could go either way too, so whichever position he wanted was his.

Ray shuffled around, unsure, then fell victim to his dark side and turned down the gig. He flew to Chicago the next morning and went straight to Joe's office with the 16MM reel of the shorts he'd made at Brooks.

DAVID O'MALLEY

Sometimes the hailstones hit you smack on the head and you don't even realize it. So you just walk away and stick your head in another cloud.

26

The Donut Palace in Hibbing was far from palatial. Seven wobbly tables against one wall, opposite a smudged glass case filled with doughnuts, bear claws, and other gooey delights. A sharp tingle of sweetness wafted from the kitchen, stirring a rush of sexual longing in the stomach tempered by the overwhelming weight of buttery guilt. It was a distinctly American Sodom and Gomorrah, the perfect blend of passion and punishment.

Wayne Evenson sat across from Maggie, gently pulling apart a big sugary cruller, his eyes watering with lust. "Good crullers," Wayne said, sounding like the end of a prayer. The *amen* was silent.

"The fellah in New York, he said 'no, definitely not'." Maggie leaned forward. "Even used profanity. So I'd say that clinches it, don'tcha think?"

"But he said 'no'...yah?"

"Sure, but 'no' means 'yah', don't ya see?"

Wayne looked up from his cruller. "How ya figure?"

Maggie fixed her eyes on Wayne, scrutinizing the lumpy man huddled over his half-devoured cruller, bakery flakes dangling in his fuzzy mustache. She wondered just how deep she should go with her explanation. *Keep it simple.* That's what her journalism professor had told her.

"He wouldn'ta been so definite if it wasn't so."

Wayne gave her a dubious look.

"You do the news long enough, ya pick up on the subtleties, Wayne."

"Uh-huh," he said, still not sure he understood her point.

"They're in on it, see. Keepin' it all buttoned up."

"Buttoned up."

"On the QT. A conspiracy like thing."

"So you want to run it?"

"On the noon." Maggie checked her watch, tapping it. "About twelve minutes."

"Think you will then?"

"Well, gosh Wayne, you're news director. Your call."

"Oh, yah. Well, okay then. It's news, I guess. If yer sure."

"Okay." She grabbed her purse, scooted up in the chair. "You comin'?"

Wayne looked at the remains of his flaky pastry. "Think I'll set awhile. Ponder the vicissitudes of life."

She nodded. "Read the paper, eat your cruller."

"Yep."

Ray and Ziggy plodded up Main Street, hands in their pockets, heads bent against the blowing snow.

"Think we're doing the right thing?" Ziggy said.

Ray stopped short; backed himself up against the brick building, out of the wind, chewing the inside of his cheek, a touch irritated. "What thing?"

"Letting people think we're a band."

Pondering this, feeling the bite of snow beads pelting his skin, Ray finally ventured, "Like they say, every day is a thread. You can tie it in a noose, hang yourself, or crack it like a bullwhip, show 'em who's boss."

Ziggy considered this run of gibberish, trying to bestow it with an earnest response, but could only manage, "Who said that, one of your Navy buddies?"

"No." Ray blinked away the snow bits caught on his eyelashes. "My mom."

Ziggy pictured the noose, heard the crack of the whip in his head. Tried to imagine what Ray's mom looked like.

"You got all these threads, see, and you weave them together," Ray said. "That's your life."

"Huh," Ziggy said, thinking it over.

"Yeah. Huh. That's about it."

Ray saw Maggie come out of the Donut Palace down the block and turn up the street away from them. He felt the disturbing contradiction of a hot chill.

"So where you going?" Ray said, emphasizing the 'you.'

"Going?"

"Yeah. I got things to do." He looked after Maggie, keeping her in sight. "You're not gonna follow me around all day."

"I...well, no." Ziggy looked up and down the street. "I'm just gonna, ya know, check out the town and..."

"Yeah. Good idea. Be a rock star, man."

Ray whacked Ziggy's shoulder blade, making him cringe in pain. Zig was growing tired of the guys constantly pounding on him like a punching bag, even if it was in the manly guise of good-natured fun.

"Keep out of trouble," Ray called back as he hustled away.

Ziggy watched him go, then shuffled across the street. He may have looked lost, but he already knew where he was headed.

Squinting through the curtain of flakes, Ray caught sight of Maggie again as she entered the squat brick building with a block-lettered sign above the door: *WHIB-AM Voice of the Range.* He paused, gripped by a tight fist of confusion in his gut.

Inside, Maggie hurtled past the studio control room window on her way to the newsroom. Donnie, the DJ, clicked the P.A. switch. "Two minutes, Maggie."

"I know, I know," she said. "Under control, Donnie."

The cramped excuse for a newsroom barely allowed enough space for a clunky teletype machine, a small desk and a wooden file cabinet. Maggie ripped a long spewing sheet off the chattering Associated Press wire, quickly scanned the stories. Tore off a few possibles.

Donnie stood in the doorway watching her. She felt him there, but was too excited, too focused to care.

"Got a real hot one this time. Gonna blow the lid off, make some waves. Leave this tank town in the slush. Could be my ticket to an anchor spot in St. Paul. Maybe even Chicago."

Donnie said, "Oh yeah. What is it?"

His voice took her by surprise. She turned to him with a blank stare, suddenly realizing she'd been thinking out loud.

"None of your beeswax."

"Chicago...?"

"Was I talkin' to you?"

"You quitting?"

"Didn't say that."

"Yah, you said..."

"No I didn't."

"But I heard..."

She abruptly moved toward Donnie, crowding him in the doorway, her voice tight and serious, almost a whisper now. "Donnie, ya think maybe it's about time I tell Beth that you and me been dancin' in the sheets?"

"Doing what?"

"You know what. Doin' it."

"Huh?" He still hadn't caught the ball she'd thrown.

"Sleeping together."

"But that's not... we... we haven't."

"Yah, that's right. And if I was to tell her that we have been, I'm sure she'd believe you instead of me."

Donnie played that back in his head, parsing it like a dirty song lyric. "Is this a blackmail sorta deal?"

"You know what coercion is?"

"Like when your car gets all rusted out?"

She closed her eyes, overwhelmed at how dense he was. Then, let it go. Eyes back open, she gave him a hard glare. "It's a 'keep your yap shut about me quitting or I tell your wife we been humping' sorta deal."

Maggie tapped his chest lightly with the rolled up news copy in her hand, confident that he'd finally get her meaning.

She went into the sparse broadcast booth next to the studio. Nothing but a small table the size of a chess board, folding chair and a microphone, but it did the job. A window opposite the table looked into the studio where Donnie spun his records between bouts of senseless patter and badly produced local commercials. A smaller window in the booth door offered a tight view of the station lobby.

Maggie sat down with the AP copy and flipped open her trusty reporter's notebook. Normally, on a big story like this, she would have taken the time to write the piece first, judiciously selecting the most effective words and phrasing. But she'd been composing this one in her head since the night before, from the very instant she first heard the words *Ed Sullivan Show* come tumbling out of Pete's mouth at the Ramada.

All Maggie needed now were the meager notes she'd jotted down. The rest, heck, she could just wing it. Lay it all out in a breaking news story that would turn the town upside down with excitement. It'd make the state news, no doubt, then the national wire. Put Hibbing on the map, and with any luck, land her a prime position with a big city station.

Everybody in town knowing something is one thing, but going public with it on the airwaves was quite another. It could mean the difference between her withering away in obscurity or seizing the future.

Donnie slid behind the console in the studio. Checked the clock. Adjusted his microphone. Maggie could see the troubled creases in his forehead as he continued to digest her dire warning. On the turntable, Dave Brubeck's *Take Five* bounced through the last few syncopated chords of its jaunty jazz melody. But to Maggie it felt like the soundtrack overture of her imminent rise to fame.

A flash of daylight caught her eye in the small window that looked out to the lobby. Someone had entered from outside. Ray's face suddenly appeared in the glass frame, peering into the broadcast booth. Maggie stared at him.

"That's it for this hour," Donnie's voice echoed shakily over the lobby monitor. "Maggie Thorson is next with the News at Noon here on WHIB-AM, the Voice of North Range." The pre-recorded Noon News intro began to play.

Maggie looked down at her notebook, unexpected emotions churning in her chest. She turned her gaze back to the small window. Ray's face was gone. She exhaled. So, maybe it was just an illusion. A trick elicited by the tension and excitement coursing through her.

The red *ON AIR* light popped on in the booth as Donnie opened her mike.

Abruptly, Ray's face reappeared in the small window. He pushed a small fragment of hastily torn paper against the glass. On it, the scribbled words: *Dinner? Tonight?*

Donnie looked into the broadcast booth, alarmed by the hollow roar of dead air. He saw Maggie, gazing to the side, as still as stone. Donnie flipped the mike switch off and on, the red light blinking anxiously in the booth.

Maggie snapped out of her stunned daze. Next to the scribbled note, she saw Ray's eyebrow arch questioningly. She nodded to him with a sharp snap of her neck, feeling a burn run down the nerves in her back.

It was not what you'd call a carefully considered decision. More like an instinctive reaction from somewhere deep inside. There was no thought process involved. No calculation. No manipulation. For Maggie, this was a whole new experience. And it unnerved her. As did Ray's pleased smile as he moved away from the window.

Her big breaking news story evaporated.

She closed her notebook, sliding it into her lap, letting it fall to the floor. Maggie quickly shuffled through the AP copy as the red light continued to flash. She shot a look at Donnie through the glass, signaling reluctant assent with a blink of her eyes. The red light stopped flashing. Locked *ON AIR*, glowing.

"In the headlines this afternoon, sources in Washington report that Saigon may collapse in days." Her voice betrayed only a slight quaver. "That snowplow fatality out on 169 is under further investigation by local police." Then, slipping into the groove with an unexpected and puzzling surge of mindless elation, "...And how about those darn Vikings, eh?"

27

Ziggy stood outside the Methodist Church on Oak Street. Inside, amid the angelic harmonies of a choir, a solitary female voice rang out above the others.

The cottony flakes had become puffier; they glommed onto each other, picking up weight and density as the wind died down and the temperature began to drop. Ziggy looked like a snowman, white icing stacked atop his parka hood and shoulders. His motionless body was beginning to suffer the first numbing effects of hypothermia, but he was unaware of the discomfort, caught up in the mesmerizing chorus of voices seeping out into the dimming light of late afternoon.

When the music finally stopped, it took him several long moments to even become aware of its absence. The choir members began to emerge from the church, fanning out in different directions after hasty waves and brief, but amiable, farewells. Ziggy had become so fully absorbed into the winter setting, that no one passing by gave him a second look. Perhaps they thought he actually *was* a snowman. Or, he began to fret, maybe he really was just an inconsequential shadow, a meaningless cipher, always invisible to everyone.

When the last of the choir members had departed, Ziggy walked to the church entrance. The clumps of snow fell from his shoulders and hood as he shed his unintentional camouflage. He tugged the double doors open very slowly, cautiously peering inside. The church was empty. Muted voices came from a cloakroom to the right.

HIDING IN HIBBING

He felt like an intruder, skulking along the long wall toward the half-open cloakroom door. The voices grew louder, clearer now. He looked through the gap, catching a glimpse of Janey and the portly minister, Reverend Dawson, as they carefully draped the choir robes on wood hangers and hung them in a dark oak wardrobe closet.

Ziggy ducked back into the shadows, pressing himself hard against the wall beside the doorway. Now was no time to get caught slinking around like a prowler. That kind of behavior would certainly seal his fate in her eyes.

"Your grandmother would be very proud of you," Reverend Dawson told Janey in a soothingly ethereal tone that only clergymen can summon with easy consistency.

Ziggy couldn't see Janey now, but he could easily imagine her squeezing out a sad little smile, appreciative of the generous compliment, but not believing for a moment that she deserved it.

"Janey, would you consider performing a solo with the choir this coming Sunday?"

"I'm sorry. I can't. You know why," she said, her voice tiny and meek.

"Aw, that's a bunch of caca-doody," Reverend Dawson exclaimed. "Aw, dammit! I'm sorry. 'Scuse my filthy mouth."

Janey muttered something low and faint. Probably "That's okay." But Ziggy couldn't tell for sure.

Reverend Dawson abruptly segued into a different voice, a distinctly righteous intonation that signaled he was directly channeling God or, at the very least, someone who knew the Supreme Being personally and was comfortable quoting him. "In Leviticus, Simon says... 'thou must chuck out all that which burdens us from the past and move the heck on'."

Are you kidding me? Ziggy thought. *Simon sez?* What kind of clergyman is this guy?

137

"You made that up, didn't you?" Janey said, her voice suggesting a broad smile that Ziggy couldn't see, but could definitely feel.

And then, in his real person voice, the Reverend said contritely, "I believe I did."

Ziggy huddled outside the church, waiting for Janey to eventually emerge. The surrounding pine trees nodded under the weight of wet snow, hulking white-hooded nuns bowing to the god of winter. When she finally appeared, his nervous intake of breath chilled his lungs.

He felt her eyes quickly take him in, then flash away. At least he wouldn't startle her. She had seen him.

As she made a quick turn onto the recently shoveled sidewalk, already deep in a layer of fresh snow, he cut across on an angle and fell into step beside her. She continued looking straight ahead, acknowledging him only with her obviously intentional lack of awareness. They walked side-by-side for close to a minute, their carefully measured footsteps seeming to go on forever.

Finally, Ziggy said, "Sorry about yesterday."

"You seem to apologize a lot."

"Only when I screw up."

"You screw up a lot?"

"When it helps justify my apologies."

She smiled at his clever self-deprecation. "How human of you."

That didn't make any sense to him, but it was better than a bruising slug in the arm from Ray. After a few more steps he self-consciously steered the subject away from him.

"When is your grandmother's funeral?"

"Not until Spring."

"Spring? Really? Why?"

"Ground's too hard."

"Oh," Ziggy said. "Right. Yeah. Makes sense."

"It's Minnesota. High water table. Really cold. Not even a John Deere 460 backhoe with a claw scoop can make a dent."

"My uncle in Michigan had a dog that died one winter. He was going to bury it in a hole in his backyard, but instead he had him cremated."

Janey didn't respond, thinking there might be more.

Ziggy suddenly felt a sharp twinge of regret. "I didn't mean... that was, jeez, really stupid. What I was trying..."

"I know what you meant. It's okay."

"Sorry."

"There you go again."

"Jeez!" Clenched his fists at his side, growling in aggravation. "Urrrrrrhh. What's wrong with me? Sorry."

She laughed. "Can't help yourself, can you?"

"It's like I have all these words in my head and they keep falling out of my mouth."

Janey stopped abruptly and turned to him, a serious expression on her pretty face. "You have nothing to feel sorry about. Nothing. So if you have a lot of words in your head, just make 'sorry' not one of them."

They walked on. Ziggy felt like a giant weight had been lifted. This girl is capable of magic, he thought. She has this crazy mojo thing happening.

"My granny wouldn't go for cremation at all," Janey said. "She'd think she had ended up in hell and freak out."

Now it was Ziggy's turn to laugh. He felt light and surprisingly buoyant in her presence. It was as if everything she said was perfect for the moment. And within the circle of her bold confidence, he began to feel infected by a strange freedom to be reckless.

"So, what do people do around here for fun?"

"The usual," she said. "Hunting, ice fishing, skating, tobogganing." She paused, obviously at the end of her list. "Ice fishing," she repeated

"Oh..."

"And, there's always...ice fishing."

He chuckled softly at this. "I was thinking more like something , you know...indoors."

"Bowling."

"Mmmm," he said, clearly devoid of enthusiasm. "I don't bowl."

"Sure you do."

"No, really. I don't. Never have."

She laughed again. "Come on...everybody bowls."

28

Ray and Maggie met at the Pastie Hut for dinner. It was primarily a casual lunch joint where locals gathered to consume hot greasy crust pouches filled with an assortment of meats and cheeses. But in the evening the dozen or so tables were empty and the short countertop attended only by a few solitary souls seeking shelter from the storm. It was the perfect place for Maggie to meet Ray, free from prying eyes and gossip mongering ears.

"About not tellin' you I'm in radio news, no harm done I hope. Ya know, thinking I was tryin' to squeeze a story outta ya because of the celebrity deal and all. Don't want you worrying that I had any inferior motives. "

Even Ray knew she had meant to say *ulterior* motives, but he refrained from the urge to correct her. He fiddled with the pastie on the plate in front of him and simply said, "It crossed my mind."

"Oh, well sure. You'd expect that, wouldn't ya, what with the circumstance."

"I'm just naturally cynical," Ray said.

"Oh yah, sure, with the show biz and all. No doubt, eh?" She let that sit for a long moment, sipping her coffee. "So, he's the main singer and you're in the band, right?"

Ray's eyes tightened. He shifted in his chair, the leg scraping the floor with a short raw screech.

Maggie shook her head, issuing a grumble of self-deprecating disgust. "Darn. There I go again. It's that 'nose for news' deal. I just can't stop with the questions see. But

I'm sincere as all get out when I tell ya I couldn't give a holy hoot. I like you for you, not because of all the celebrity stuff; I've seen plenty of those in my time, let me tell ya. Frankie Avalon sat down for an interview once. Real nice young man. Polite. Had nice teeth, good breath and all. Curly hair. Short, but real curly."

Maggie eyed Ray's long hair with its dangerous sweep and threatening tangles. A tightness gripped her chest. She felt as if she wasn't getting enough oxygen to her brain. "So... you like those pasties."

"They're good," he said, with a transparent lack of enthusiasm. "Don't think I ever heard of 'em before."

"Oh, they're real big up here. And up there in northern Michigan. Northern Wisconsin. North Dakota. I guess *up north* would be what the heck connects 'em." She pushed out a weak laugh, feeling flushed, a salty moisture forming at the corners of her mouth. "Their defining nature, so to speak."

He poked at the flaky crust with a fork, taking a peek inside. "They're kind of like...some kind of a..."

"Meat pie," she said. "Only wrapped in a blanket, so you can pick 'em up easy."

"Yeah. Mexicans have this taco thing. Just like this, only different. Cold, not hot. I had 'em once at a bar out in California."

"These here are Norwegian. Swedish or something. Been around forever." She was beginning to feel lighter, breathing easier. "Don't need a fork. You can just grab one and eat it on the run. Driving or whatever."

"Are you from here? Hibbing?"

"Me?" Knocked off balance by this. "Yah. Yep, born and bred."

"So, tell me about yourself."

"Uh...well, uh..." Maggie looked around helplessly, cast overboard and set adrift on an unfamiliar sea. "You want to know about *me*?"

"Where you went to school. Your family. How you got into radio."

Her mind went blank. She stared at the table.

"You alright?"

She slowly raised her eyes to his. Cheeks pale. Fingers trembling, her bright red nails, with the polish so carefully applied, tapping nervously on the table surface. "I'm just not used to being the one being interviewed is all."

29

Hibbing's only bowling alley, Bob's Pin Spot, was located on the south edge of town. It took nearly a half-hour for Ziggy and Janey to trudge there through the deepening snow. The parking lot was empty. The big fluorescent bowling pin glowed faintly in the gathering dusk, several bulbs that traced its outline having burned out and never been replaced.

Bob Koenen, the amiable owner, looked up from his battered floor buffer as Janey and Ziggy entered the door at the far end of the building. They paused by the counter in front of the multi-slotted shoe rack. There were only ten lanes, just enough for a town the size of Hibbing, except on some Saturday nights when high school kids swarmed the alleys. But on that night, with the blizzard in its sixth straight day, things were dead.

Bob finished wrapping the cord around the handle and rolled the buffer up the alley. "Ohfergeez, we're closed up, Janey."

"Could we bowl just one game?"

He looked Ziggy up and down. Smiled at Janey like a kind uncle, unable to deny a youngster's wish. "Oh, yah. Sure." Stepped behind the counter and flipped the switch for the alley lights. The lanes lit up with a jittery flicker.

"I was so sorry to hear about your granny."

"Thanks," she said, looking away to avoid the twinge of sadness that always produced a small tear.

"She was a real peach, ya know." He sensed her fragility and let it go at that. Grabbed his parka from the hook on the wall. "When you're through, just close da light, eh - this switch here - lock the door up behind you. Okay then?"

He slipped on his parka and gloves, giving Ziggy a steely look with squinty eyes that sent out a plethora of fatherly warnings. Then turned to Janey with a wink and a grin. "Go easy on him." He pulled his hood up and headed out into the cold night.

Janey threw her coat off, grabbed a ball from the rack at the end of the counter and spun around on her toes like a pixie. "Come on."

"I don't really, uh..."

"Sure ya do," Janey said, scampering off toward the lanes. Ziggy followed, hands in his pockets.

Janey kicked her shoes off and slid onto the slick wooden surface of the lane, peering down at the pins, tiny soldiers in formation, poised and ready to resist assault.

"Don't you need bowling shoes?" Ziggy asked reluctantly, struggling to remain uninvolved.

"Not really," she said, without turning. "I like socks. I can feel the floor under me. It's comforting." She raised the ball, focused on the pins.

"I like the way you sing," Ziggy said. It came from nowhere, crisp and clear and much louder than he intended, hanging in the air like a giant neon sign. He hadn't let the words out. They had escaped.

Janey smiled to herself, feeling warm around the shoulders. She rolled the ball, splattering the pins with a thunderous crack. They all went down, flipping wildly and spinning. Strike!

Ziggy stared, startled by the sudden power of it. Janey spun around, perched on her toes like a ballerina. "Your turn."

145

"No, no." Hands out of his pockets, palms raised in refusal. "You go again. Bet you can't get two strikes in a row."

"Ahh, *strike*, huh? So you do know how to bowl."

"No, I... it's just, everybody knows it's called a strike."

"Uh-huh." Smirking cutely.

"I bet you can't get another one."

She took the challenge, snatching the ball from the return rack. Did a perky pirouette to face the pins. Raised the ball, tipping her head forward slightly, getting the head pin in her sights.

"You ever sing in public?"

An emphatic silence followed. Once again, he had surprised himself. And her, as well.

Janey held her position. "Not really. I mean, once... almost..."

She took two quick, slippery steps and rolled the ball. The pins exploded. Another easy strike.

She whirled around and struck an adorable, triumphant pose. Ziggy nodded his approval, impressed.

"Beat that," she challenged.

"I can't."

"You could try."

"Almost? How does that work?"

"What?"

"You said that you '*almost*' sang in public once." Emboldened now, he pressed her further. "Kinda, sorta, almost. How does that work?"

She was cornered and knew it. When you open the door a crack, the light comes in. If you close it, the room may grow dark again, but the light doesn't retreat back outside. It's already been allowed inside and it stays there, hiding, anxiously waiting to shine once more. It wasn't exactly physics, but she knew it was true. She couldn't avoid his question.

"It was dumb. I mean, you know, embarrassing. God, I..." She turned, looked off, not wanting to see his eyes. "Let's talk about something else, okay?"

"I'd like to know," he said. "I really would."

"You'll think I'm..."

"No I won't."

"What...?"

"Whatever you thought I would think...I won't think it. Honest."

She wanted to trust him.

The ball was spewed out onto the return rack with a dull thud. She grabbed it nervously, clutching it to her chest, grateful for its return. She looked down the lane at the pins, rigid reminders of all those heartless, faceless pinheads who had mocked and taunted her. They stood in compact array, a wooden brigade of insensitive judges.

She wound herself up tight, pivoted on the balls of her feet and took two mighty steps, heaving the black orb down the alley with the power of a cannon. Strike!

"Yeah!" Ziggy yelled, leaping more than a foot off the floor, flailing his arms crazily. Janey could feel him grinning with admiration behind her. She turned slowly with a cocky, lopsided grin, delighted by the momentary victory over all things uncontrollable.

She sat back against the edge of the ball return rack, looking down at her legs, crossed at the ankles. Wiggled her toes. Heaved a long sigh filled with ironic longing. Then looked up at Ziggy, her brave smile hinting at a willingness to finally let something go; to empty the dank cellar of regret and purge her soul.

"In high school I rehearsed with this band—just some guys fooling around. They were supposed to play the Winter Escapades. Ya know, the annual school talent show." She raised her eyebrows dismissively, shrugged her shoulders with sweet disregard. "Called themselves the Fish Hooks.

Started out as the Del-Tones, then changed it to the Elk Humpers, then the Fish Hooks."

"Sounds like a logical progression."

"You think so? They could never agree. They're still around. Only now they're The Brewskies."

"Lemme guess. Because they drink a lot of beer."

She nodded, rolling her eyes. Her bowling ball clunked onto the return rack behind her. She grabbed it instinctively and quickly executed another effortless strike.

"Nice," Ziggy said, dragging the word out to emphasize his genuine admiration.

Janey waved it off casually. "Lucky throw."

"Four strikes in a row, are you kidding? You've got a real talent."

"Nah. I'm a spot bowler. Pick my spot. Roll it exactly the same every time. Stuff falls down. It's not a talent. I'm just consistent." She punched the button on the air blower, hands floating over the blast of warm dryness.

"Says you."

"Uh-huh." Rubbing her hands together.

"Well, I think you have a lot of talent."

"Well, you'd be wrong."

He locked his eyes on her. She refused to look at him.

"But that's pretty cool, you being in the school show."

She had hoped he'd forgotten and moved on, distracted by her bowling prowess and clever chatter. "No big deal," she said quietly, trying to end it there, but at the same time not wanting him to stop.

"Well, I'm impressed."

"Don't be. When I came out on the stage and saw all those faces staring at me... I just froze. Opened my mouth to sing and nothing came out. Nothing at all. I was like some kind of stupid statue, only even dumber looking. You know what that's like?"

He gave a little nod. Yeah, he did know. He got up in the morning to that feeling and tried to forget it at night, so he could sleep. He wore stupid and dumb like a long heavy coat that he couldn't shake off.

Ziggy asked, "What happened?"

"Nothing. I just stood there. Dumb deer in the dumb headlights. Then I walked off. Band played without me. I went down to the girls' locker room and cried for about three stupid hours."

She sneaked a quick look at him, hoping that he wasn't watching her, certain that her face was turning bright red. But he *was* watching. Staring right at her with a dull, blank expression. No forced sympathy or harsh judgment, like the others. And because he appeared so clearly disconnected, so totally lost in another world, what he said next startled her.

"Sing something now."

"Ha!" she blurted, loud enough to echo off the walls. "I don't think so."

She snatched the ball from the rack and turned away to face the pins, her face flushed, hands trembling.

"It's just me," Ziggy said. "Sing anything. Something from the radio."

"Why?"

"Because...I like it when you sing."

Janey closed her eyes. The warmth she felt rising through her body was not like anything she had experienced before. She was a bit dizzy and her tongue felt strangely numb. But the butterflies dancing in her stomach didn't bite like before. They caressed her inside with the beating of soft wings.

"You don't have to do a whole song," he said.

Janey couldn't open her eyes. It would bring the real world crashing in and destroy this sweet moment of release. She squeezed her eyelids tighter, bringing in the darkest night. Lying in her bed, the Zenith radio reaching through the static to pull in the thrilling sounds of another world on WMIN in Minneapolis.

Her lips parted and she began to softly sing *All Alone Am I*, Brenda Lee's wrenching anthem of isolation. Her pure voice tenderly reverberated off the bowling alley walls, filling in gaps of silence with echoing harmonies.

A chill ran down Ziggy's spine, ten times better than the false chill that the kids at school replicated by sharply squeezing the back of your neck, tapping each shoulder blade, then raking fingers down your backbone. This was the real thing.

As she finished the chorus, her enchanting voice holding the word *heart* for what seemed like an eternity, Ziggy imagined hearing that voice in the early morning as he awoke, floating to him amid the mountain of blankets, sheets and pillows. And in the evening before he slept, chasing dark dreams away, opening his world to innocence and endless possibility, wallowing in the comfort it would bring,

Afraid to turn around, Janey slowly opened her eyes, feeling the tears glistening on her cheeks. There was only one way to escape the weight of this moment. She compelled a sudden surge of energy through her still quivering limbs and charged up to the release line, stomping her foot down hard as her arm swung in a powerful arc, launching the ball toward the pin soldiers. The sphere spun and skidded, but never lost its powerful track, smashing through the pins, exploding them; a hand grenade tossed into the middle of a woodpile. Just enough distraction for Janey to rake her sleeve across her eyes, unnoticed, wiping away all trace of tears.

She whirled around to Ziggy, a pert smile creasing her face, dimples and shiny cheeks aglow.

"Okay. Now you."

Not yet recovered, Ziggy managed, "I'm not much of a bowler."

"I mean...sing."

"Me?"

"Yeah. You're the star."

HIDING IN HIBBING

Trapped now, he wanted to explain. He opened his mouth and released the hollow sound of nothing. There was not any breath to exhale. His brain had purged itself of all rational thought. His body had shut down. His tank was empty.

"Come on," Janey prodded teasingly. "I did it for you. Twice, if you count 'Happy Birthday' at Carl's. Now it's your turn."

"I, uh... "

"You're the professional. You're a *real* singer."

"Janey, listen, about my singing..." he said, half-deciding to come clean. Only half, because the words in his head didn't match the ones coming out of his mouth. "See, I gotta save my voice, uh..."

"Yes, I know," she said, disappointed. "For Ed Sullivan."

Ziggy was surprised. "How did you know?"

"This is Hibbing. Not exactly some big city, ya know. Crazy rumors spread like a bad rash. But I just thought it was..." Her voice caught in her throat. She studied his face as it washed pale.

"Oh my gosh. It's really true. The Ed Sullivan Show?"

Ziggy spun around and grabbed the bowling ball from the return rack. Heaved it awkwardly down the lane. It bounced from one side to the other and back again, clunking into the gutter and rolling into the darkness at the end of the alley with a dull thud.

30

Night came early with leaden clouds and a thick drape of cascading snow. Gallagher was already happily ensconced in his hotel room bed with Sally, the fresh-faced waitress from Carl's who had refilled his coffee cup so many times that she became a permanent fixture at their table.

She sat astride Gallagher, half-naked, breasts glowing in the warm lamplight. She enthusiastically warbled the Stone's *Satisfaction*, off-key and breathless, her ponytail bouncing spiritedly.

An insistent tapping at the door finally drove Gallagher to distraction. With an annoyed grumble, he leaped from the bed, causing Sally to tumble off with a high-pitched yelp. She instantly collapsed into a fit of delirious giggles.

Gallagher unlocked the door and pulled it open a crack. A clutch of rabid young groupies pressed against the door making excited noises.

"Listen, listen, listen...LISTEN," he whispered harshly, attempting to quiet them. "I'm engaged in some very serious negotiations at the moment. So right now...is just not...this isn't...could we, uh..." He puffed his cheeks out, releasing an exasperated breath.

Dealing with a tidal wave of good fortune was not as easily manageable as he would have imagined. Slowly, firmly, he pushed the door shut. Then, quickly reopened it a crack.

"But don't go away."

Wound the golden goose, if you must, he reasoned...but don't kill it.

Janey and Ziggy dutifully clicked off the lights and locked the bowling alley doors. After his calamitous display of physical inelegance, Ziggy had simply looked at her with a humble shrug. "Like I said, I'm a terrible bowler." Janey had to agree. His dexterity was abysmal, making him a danger to both himself and others, not to mention a viable threat to the physical integrity of Bob's Pin Spot.

At Main and Oak, they paused under the amber glow of a streetlight watching in silence as the flakes tumbled down. It seemed to be a new normal; white fluff incessantly descending, a form of benevolent dandruff that clung to clothing and skin. Ziggy couldn't remember a time when it hadn't been snowing. But now, even the sharp cold air released its spiteful grip on him, the warmth spreading from his insides outward. The secret to this felt undeniably clear; the warmth was warmer when Janey was in his presence. It had nothing at all to do with climatology or meteorology, but everything to do with chemistry.

There was comfort in their awkward silence, a welcome and unexpected gift. Their eyes met, without a need to speak. Faint shared smiles glimmered, giving them both enough space to just *be*. Free of the compulsion to impress or dazzle each other, they felt no need to justify themselves.

"Well," Janey said finally, "I should be getting home."

"Yeah. I need to get back to the motel."

"And the band."

"Yeah, them too..."

"Okay."

"So... guess I'll see you tomorrow then."

"Maybe." She touched his forearm lightly. He could barely feel it through the heavy parka.

Janey turned away and, as she did, he thought he saw a bittersweet smile on her lips, a slight sadness in her eyes. She walked away from him, up Elm Street.

Ziggy turned and headed out Main Street toward Route 169. The word *maybe* resonated in his brain. What did she mean by that? It left room for *maybe not*. A sudden rush of insecurity drenched him with damp sweat under his parka. He turned to look back at Janey, but she was already gone.

The Ramada parking lot was littered with cars, most of them drifted over and randomly parked askew between raggedly plowed piles.

Inside the lobby, Ziggy gave Pete a half-hearted wave as he trudged past. Pete quickly improvised a little drum solo on the registration desk with his fingers, then summoned Zig over with a wiggling crooked digit.

"There's a bunch of 'em down there, swarming like flies," he warned ominously, nodding toward the corridor leading off the lobby, as if it was the entrance to a mine shaft in imminent danger of collapsing.

"Thought you chased them all out."

"Did. Like a bad leak in your cellar wall, they just keep seeping back in."

Ziggy looked off toward the corridor with trepidation.

"You don't wanna run that gamut," Pete said.

Ziggy pondered that, unsure. "You mean gauntlet?"

"Where folks line up on each side and beat the willies outta ya while ya run through 'em?"

"Yeah, that's gauntlet."

"Some Indians do that. And I think Romans back in ancient times. Read that in the National Geographic," Pete boasted, doing his very best to approximate a demeanor of legitimately acquired wisdom.

Ziggy nodded. "Guess I'll take my chances."

"I know, they're just girls, but you get enough of 'em together in one place, squealing like a bunch of wild banshees and it's terrible scary. Make your hair stand right up."

"I'll just make a run for it."

"Or you could go 'round back, take that fire exit door at the other end. Get to your room that way."

"Isn't that locked?"

"The little buggers jimmied it so now it's always open. That's the leak."

Ziggy tromped through the snow around the side of the motel, following the scattered tracks of the migrating girl herd and, sure enough, the fire exit door had been irreparably busted to allow easy access. He pulled it open slowly and peeked around the doorjamb down the long corridor. An encampment of the young faithful sprawled outside Gallagher's room at the end of the hallway.

He heard the rumble of an engine behind him. Turned to recognize the four hooligans from Carl's Restaurant climb out of a Chevy pickup. They all wore the traditional North Country winter uniform; hunting caps with earflaps, fur-lined logging boots and bloated down-filled jackets. And they all carried rifles.

It didn't take Ziggy long to figure out these were not a bunch of characters he'd want to hang around with. He hastily slipped inside the door and made a beeline for his room, awkwardly fumbling his key into the lock and vanishing inside.

Ziggy locked the door, leaning against it, breathing hard. He heard the emergency fire exit squeak open, a hollow whoosh of air sucked out through the crack under his room door. The menacing murmur of deep voices rolled past his room. He backed away from the door, listening tensely as the grumbling sound of the good ol' boys moved away, down the corridor toward the girls.

That's when it occurred to him; these guys were there because of the *girls*. Probably pissed off that an invasive bunch of rock-and-rollers were making them look bad by stealing their women. Or maybe they knew this was where all the young girls in town would be gathered and had simply come by to harvest the crop.

Ziggy sat on the corner of the bed, staring at the wall. A darker thought consumed him; w*hy were they carrying guns?*

He listened intently. But it was dead silent. Then, the distant sound of female voices arose—two or three, talking at once—interrupted by a deep baritone murmur that was unquestionably male. He strained to hear them, remaining perfectly still so the rustle of his clothes did not compete with the faraway voices.

Suddenly, the door crashed open, revealing the four bruisers. The one named George had kicked the door in with his big logger boot, leaving pieces of splintered wood hanging from the doorjamb. Ziggy had flinched convulsively in that moment when the door burst open, but then instantly froze in abject terror.

He told himself, just sit still—don't move, don't breathe, don't make eye contact—maybe they'll sniff around and go away. Like a pack of wild dogs who find a possum crouching in the woods, then wander off, thinking it's dead already.

"Guess ya didn't hear us knockin'," the one named George said, as all four of them squeezed through the open doorway, filling the room with their rangy bodies cloaked in parka padding, the smell of gun oil and metal emanating from their clutched weapons.

The possum act was clearly not going to buy Ziggy salvation. He elected to break the ruse and move, scooting back along the end of the mattress, giving them room to wander.

"You're the one's after my pumpkin, aren't ya?"

Ziggy summoned enough breath to whisper, "What?"

George stepped closer, cradling the rifle. "Figure you can just take whatever you want?"

"Me? No." Ziggy said, trying to scoot further away. But he'd come to the far corner of the mattress. Sitting on the floor didn't seem like an appropriate option.

"Oh yeah, I know what you're looking for. You want a taste of my pumpkin."

The other men snickered at this, finding humor where there didn't seem to be any. George shot them a cold look and they canned it.

"No, no, no..." Ziggy sputtered, unable to elaborate further, since he had no idea what George was talking about.

"Think you're some kind of goddamn long-haired Elvis, don't' ya? HUH!" George slammed the rifle butt on the table. Ziggy jumped and recoiled, staring wide-eyed at their weapons.

"Whatsa matter?" George asked, holding the rifle up. It was an impressive Remington 30:06 with a scope and hand-carved stock. "You lookin' at this?"

Ziggy gulped. "Uh, no...well, yeah, I guess."

"Curious, huh?"

"Just wondered why, you know..."

"Why the hell do you think, punk?"

Ziggy rolled his eyes upward, as if searching the air above for a reason. "Oh, uhhmm, I don't...I guess...maybe, protection. And stuff."

George leveled a cold, silent stare at Ziggy, milking it for every bit of intimidation he could squeeze out. "Deer hunting season."

"Oh..." was all Ziggy could say.

George's lips folded into a caustic grin, filled with the dark promise of bodily harm. He motioned to his buddies with the snap of his head. That was their cue to meander around the room with casual menace; backwoods marauders, knocking over lamps, smashing bedside tables, crushing a flimsy motel chair with stomping boots while emitting theatrical macho growls.

"It's deer hunting season, pal," George told Ziggy again. Then, dropping an octave to give his warning weight, he added, "Better watch yourself."

Ziggy caught a glance of his image in the cheap wall mirror, surprised to see how small he looked. With startling suddenness, George shattered the glass with the butt of his rifle, a shower of bright shards cascading to the floor. Before he dragged the battered door shut, he leered at Ziggy with a creepy smile.

After waiting what seemed an eternity—actually less than a minute—Ziggy raced on trembling legs to the broken door, jerked it open and peered down the hall.

The cluster of faithful groupies outside Gallagher's door huddled in hushed apprehension, gazing toward Ziggy, mouths agape. Ignoring them, he made a dash for Ray's adjacent room.

An insistent rapping brought Ray to the door, pausing only to tuck his shirt in and swiftly run splayed fingers through the stubborn snarls in his hair. The door was barely open a crack when Ziggy shouldered his way inside, spinning in circles, a whirling dervish. "Shut the door!"

He paced, quaking with the charge of adrenaline. Ray gave a quick look out, then shut the door.

"Some guys busted into my room."

"Guys?"

"Guys with GUNS!"

"Gallagher's got a dozen babes lined up outside his room... and you've got guys?"

"With shotguns!" Ziggy said, his voice keening.

Ray rolled his eyes dismissively. "Guys with shotguns. Right."

In less than a minute, they were standing in the doorway of Ziggy's room scrutinizing the devastation.

"Whoa," Ray said. "What happened, man? You go balls out rock-and-roll on us?"

HIDING IN HIBBING

"I told you..."

"Think you're Keith Moon or something, trashing your hotel room? That's some crazy shit, you know?"

"These guys, they threatened me."

Ignoring Ziggy's plea, Ray shook his head at the damage. "And here I thought you'd be down collecting Gallagher's overflow."

"Right. Me. I wish."

"Quit wishin', buddy. Gather ye rosebuds..."

"That's what they thought I was doing."

"What? Gathering rosebuds?"

"Told me to keep my hands off some girl."

It suddenly dawned on Ray, maybe Ziggy hadn't flipped out, gone ego addled rock star and nuked his room. Maybe it was worse. "She married?"

"I don't know."

"What's her name?"

"I don't know! Pumpkin, I guess."

"Pumpkin? Like the pie?"

"I guess."

"You're puttin' it to some chick named Pumpkin?"

"No," Ziggy said. "That's what they *think*. But I'm not. I was with somebody else."

Ray ran a quick replay of the past few days. "The freaky waitress, right?"

"She's got a name," Ziggy said. "Janey Olsen."

"Sure it's not Pumpkin?"

"It's Janey."

"You're absolutely sure?"

"Yes, I'm sure. And get this, Ray...unlike us, she can actually sing."

Ray felt a flush of deflation that always accompanies the cruel heartbreak of experience. "Oh, I bet she can," he said, his bleak skepticism cutting through like a razor blade.

"Got a voice like you wouldn't believe," Ziggy said, brimming with ardent enthusiasm. "I'm telling you, she could be a star. A real star."

Ziggy's words floated right over Ray's head. "She's just using you, man."

"Jeeeez, you're always so cynical."

"Bet she asked ya..." falling into the mocking imitation of a young girl's sweet high-pitched voice, " 'How do I make a rec-cord?' "

"She never said that."

Then, again as a young girl, " 'Do I need a manager?' " Followed by a sonorous warning, "She's a fuckin' opportunist, Zig."

Ziggy refused to look at Ray, afraid he would hypnotize him into seeing things his way. "She likes me."

"Of course she likes you. She thinks you're her ticket into show biz, man. Fame, fortune, fuckin' freedom; she wants out of this dump."

"You're wrong."

"Yeah, right." Ray pointed off. "Those girls down the hall, they're chasin' after you 'cause they just all of a sudden realized what a stud you are. 'Oh, look, Arthur Zigmond's not a freakin' dork like we thought. He's really cool.' "

Ziggy folded in on himself, feeling even smaller than he'd looked in the reflection just before George smashed the mirror with his rifle butt.

He hated to admit it. Maybe Ray was right.

31

By morning the storm had subsided. But a new one was already brewing.

At Carl's Diner, Ziggy and Ray had abandoned their corner booth up front and retreated to the seclusion of a table near the kitchen. When Gallagher found them, he dragged a chair out, legs scraping the floor loudly, and threw himself into it with an exasperated grumble. "What's with this?"

Ziggy didn't look up. Ray fixed Gallagher with a hard glare.

"They can't even see us back here?" Gallagher said, head whipping around. "We're invisible."

"That's the idea," Ray said.

"Are you nuts? We can't hide. This situation is just too good, man. We've got it made. It's like a bodacious buffet of beautiful babes out there."

Ray ignored his babbling, coming at him head on. "You screwin' some girl named Pumpkin?"

Ziggy's head snapped up, eyes on Gallagher who just stared dumbly at Ray with his mouth open.

"What? Like the pie?"

"Yeah," Ray said. "Like the pie."

"Oh Ye-e-e-ah," Gallagher oozed, suddenly inspired, searching for a waitress. "Pumpkin pie."

Ray plunged the tips of four fingers and a thumb into his water glass, flicked the droplets of icy liquid in Gallagher's face.

"Yo, Mick Jagger. Pay attention. You bangin' a chick named Pumpkin?'

"No!" he barked back, face glistening, jagged rivulets running down his neck and dripping off his nose. "What kinda name is that?"

Ray threw a crumpled paper napkin at him. "It's a nickname, stupid. Like Honey or Pookie."

"I don't know their names," Gallagher said, swabbing the water off his face with a napkin.

Ray leaned back, his fingers interlaced behind his head. He threw a cocky smirk at Ziggy. Nodded sharply toward Gallagher. "It's him."

"What? I don't know anybody named Pumpkin."

"Well, some bastards with great big fuckin' guns are looking to kick Ziggy's ass." Ray said, poking Gallagher's shoulder with a stiff finger. "Because of *you*."

Gallagher's eyes flashed between Ray and Ziggy. His drastically furrowed brow and incredibly blank expression made it clear he still didn't get it.

"Because *you* are nailin' some chick named Pumpkin," Ray said, measuring his words slowly as if talking to a 3-year old. "They think it's Ziggy humpin' her. And they're pissed."

A long pause ensued as Gallagher juggled these pieces in his mental tumble-dry. "How come he gets the credit?"

"Cuz he's the big rock star, dipshit." Ray whapped Gallagher's forehead with the palm of his hand. "And you're gonna get him killed."

Joe wandered back from the front of the restaurant. Pulled out a chair, sat down, arms folded. "What's with this? We hiding out back here or something?"

"Exactly," Ray said.

"Snowplows are on the move," Joe said. "Road's finally opening up."

"Good. Now we can split."

"Not yet."

Gallagher perked up, hopeful. "Yeah, what's the rush?"

"You shut up," Ray warned, aiming a sharp finger at him. Then, to Joe, "Nah nah, man, we gotta go."

"Just sit tight. Relax. Enjoy your situation."

"Precisely...our situation," Gallagher chimed in. "That's what I'm saying."

"I got a meeting today with the guy, Harvey something, from the Brewery in Bemidji. He's driving over. Don't worry. I'm gonna work everything out."

"Work what out?" Ray said. "Let's just shoot the beer commercial. Get it over with and go home."

Ziggy stirred from his hibernation. "I agree with Joe. We can wait a little longer."

Ray fixed him with a hard stare. "He wants to bang the waitress."

"What waitress?" Gallagher said.

Ziggy straightened in his chair. "I'm just saying... Joe's our boss. The leader. We should do what he says."

Joe smiled. "So you *were* payin' attention."

"Suck up," Ray muttered.

"I'm impressed, Zigmond," Joe said, nodding proudly.

Ray, still muttering..."Yeah? Wait'll you see his room."

Only catching part of that, Joe turned to Ray. "What?"

"I told you, Zig, this girl is a user."

"She can use me anytime," Gallagher said.

"Shut up, Gallagher." Ziggy said, threatening to come up out of his chair.

"Yeah! Shut up!" Ray shouted. "And no more Pumpkin' for you, man."

Joe rocked forward, interceding, "Hey, hey, hey. If he wants pie, let him get the damn pie. It's his friggin' stomach."

That brought the heated exchange to a dead stop. They stared at Joe. It was all too complicated to explain and nobody wanted to go there.

"Jesus. Where the hell's the coffee?" Joe rubbernecked with marked impatience. "They can't even see us back in this hole"

32

A dark green Chevy Chevelle; not the trendiest car on the road, but the only thing still available when Rafferty and Stromberg deplaned at Duluth International Airport. They had managed to snag a last minute flight out of LaGuardia but had no time to call ahead to reserve a rental car.

The apple cheeked girl at the Hertz desk, with sassy lips that smiled too broadly and way too often, explained that they did have a bright red Corvair, but the heater was iffy. So they wisely opted for the Chevelle. It came outfitted with snow tires and the color was much more suited to the stealth nature of their incognito mission.

"What shade of green is it?" Stromberg had inquired.

"Oh, you know," the cute clerk responded, pushing her shiny apple cheeks to new heights of vivacity, "sorta like trees."

"Perfect," Stromberg said.

They set out on a northwest trajectory, desperately in search of a miraculous new talent they imagined would somehow save the show and their jobs, plodding steadily on snow-cushioned route 169, their thick-treaded snow tires crunching.

"What a dumb name for a company," Rafferty said with a testy scowl, already bored, thumbing through the rental paperwork. "Hertz. Why not just call it Pain and Suffering?"

Stromberg, behind the wheel, rocked his head side-to-side, annoyed.

"Not gonna move any cars with a name like that."

"That's what I'm saying." Rafferty thought about it some more. "Or Agony Car Rental. 'We make you suffer in the driver's seat.' I got enough misery in life without having to pay for it."

"We fly all night, then drive all the way from Duluth on ice, for cryin' out loud, and this is what I gotta put up with from you?"

"But, I mean, c'mon...Hertz? It's a downer, no?"

"They're number one."

"What does that say?" Rafferty continued, refusing to let it go. "We got a nation of masochists?"

"Maybe the guy's name was Hertz."

"What guy?"

"The guy who started the company."

Rafferty watched in silence as small clapboard houses came into view along the road on the outskirts of town. Their grim plainness reflected the bleak austerity of hardscrabble life in the North Country.

"Christ, this is Hibbing?"

"Why am I having serious doubts we're gonna find the next Elvis here?" Stromberg mused, an unpleasant ache in his chest.

"Elvis would never put up with this weather." Rafferty said.

Stromberg thought about it. "All the movies he made, I don't think he ever made one with snow in it."

That's what a long drive will do. Force you to talk about things that you'd never think of discussing under normal conditions.

After a lengthy pause drenched in solemn reflection, mentally scanning every title he could think of, from *Love Me Tender* through *Blue Hawaii* and the little-seen *Change of Habit*, Rafferty finally said, "I believe you're right."

Rolling down Howard Street, sucked into their loony vortex of esoterica, they completely missed seeing Ray and Gallagher hunched against the cold, hands dug into their pockets, being followed at a distance by a flock of giddy young girls.

"Seriously, pal, you gotta cool it with the babes." Ray said, trying a little too hard not to sound like Gallagher's father, feathering the nest with guy slang.

The Buick Skylark filled with teen girls rumbled past, swerving and honking, arms flailing out open windows. Gallagher perked up, spinning on the sidewalk ice to flash a wink and a wave.

"No way, man. This is like a dream come true."

Ray poked Gallagher's shoulder hard with three stiff fingers. "What's the matter with you? Ziggy's gonna get the shit kicked out of him because of you. Maybe even killed."

He riveted him with another quick series of jarring pokes to emphasize each syllable. "So...lay...off...the chicks."

"No."

"NO?"

"No."

"Are you even hearing me?" Ray yelled.

"I hear ya!" Gallagher yelled back. Then fell into a more restrained voice, calm and assured. "But I'm not gonna stop."

"Shit! You're a selfish prick. You know that? A stupid little selfish prick. I should put my fist right through your face." Ray stomped a mad circle around Gallagher, frustrated, trying to hold it in and not come undone.

But Gallagher stayed centered, looking down. When Ray finally dropped anchor, ending his reckless rambling, Gallagher said, "I may not be the smartest guy in the world, Ray. But I know enough to know that this is the best thing that's ever happened to me. And it's not gonna get any better."

"You're a fucking' idiot then. You got your whole life to chase women," Ray shouted.

"You think I can't see past my own nose, man," Gallagher said. "Twenty years from now I'm probably gonna be working some crappy job I can't stand, married to some perfectly nice boring-as-hell woman who spends every day wondering what the fuck she's doing stuck with me. And she'll be right. 'Cause I'll be all pissed off, sitting in front of the tube, drinkin' a beer, trying to figure out what it's all about. Just like my old man did his whole pathetic life."

Gallagher chewed at the air, sucking in enough breath to fill his lungs. "But at least I'll be able to look back and say 'man, that was some time I had in Hibbing.' So don't tell me to give it up, Ray, 'cause it's all I've got right now. And it's probably all I'm ever gonna have to hang onto."

Gallagher felt the cold sting of a tear threatening to expose an even darker fear deep inside him. He turned abruptly and walked away.

Ray watched him go. Opened his mouth, as if he was about to shout something at Gallagher's retreating figure—something harsh and hurtful—then thought better of it.

33

Stromberg parked the Chevelle up against a pile of chunky plowed snow on Main Street, blocking the passenger door, forcing Rafferty to crawl across the driver's seat to get out.

They wandered up the block, stomping their feet every few steps to keep the snow from clumping on their city shoes.

"I didn't think there was anything worse than winter in Manhattan," Rafferty grumbled, pulling his wool overcoat tighter.

"You don't get out much," Stromberg said. He could feel the frost on his teeth.

"Au contraire. Went down to the Village last week. Froze my ass off."

"Out of the city, I'm saying. Into the real world."

At the corner of Decker Street they ducked into Dag Gunderson's Pharmacy. If nothing else, it looked warm inside. Coming through the door, all eyes shifted as the locals at the short lunch counter initiated a curious appraisal of the strangers before finally turning back to their inky coffee and fritters.

Louise, behind the register, rotated her hefty girth and gave them a distasteful examination, from hat to shoe laces. Clearly out-of-towners. Not rumpled enough for Chicago, too clean for Detroit. Way back east, she figured. And her confident speculation proved accurate when Stromberg spoke up with that corny New Yoikish way of bending his words.

HIDING IN HIBBING

"I was wondering maybe you got the Times?" he said, searching for a news rack.

"Times?" Louise said.

"New York Times. The paper."

"Got the Duluth Monitor. Hibbing Herald."

"No Times?"

She shrugged. "Just what I said."

Rafferty cut to the chase. "You don't by chance have any celebrities here in Hibbing, do ya?"

Louise gave him a hard stare, smacking her lips together slowly, as if tasting something bitter in her mouth. "That's a sore point."

This stopped Rafferty short. But he decided not to pursue it; letting it go with a thoughtful nod.

"Okay," said Stromberg. "Thanks anyway." He nudged Rafferty toward the door. They could feel the watchful eyes of the Hibbingites pushing the door closed behind them as they exited.

Louise squeezed one lid partially shut, giving them a final *stink eye* through the plate glass window. Grabbed the coffee pot and plodded around the end of the counter to refill the empty cups.

Daryl Mitchell, a crusty native who'd worked the mines longer than most folks had been alive, fiddled with his brown-stained coffee spoon, tapping it restlessly against the saucer under his cup. "So what're those slickers in here for?"

Louise looked toward the door. "New York Times."

"Don't say."

"Wouldn't lie, Mitch." She poured a sloppy cup, then moved on.

The septuagenarian busybody beside him stirred with prickly interest. Annie Sootsman, Hibbing's most thorough purveyor of public opinion and grandiose analyzer of unsubstantiated rumor, loosened the ragged wool scarf tied around her head, wiggling with pent up anticipation on the counter stool. "What's that she say?"

169

"Those fellahs, the slick Willy ones just left. They're from New York Times."

"Naaah," Annie brayed in disbelief.

"Yep."

"Goddamn greasy reporters. Stirring trouble."

"Ya think?"

Annie cocked an ear, tugging the scarf back. "What?"

"Reporters. Out for something?"

"Don't care," Annie said, waving him away with a wrinkled, veiny hand. "None of my business."

"S'pect me ta believe that, eh?" Chuckling in his cup.

"Far as dat goes. Said so, din't I?"

34

The VW bus was parked outside Helstrom's Buffett, the best place in town to eat too much and still spend as little as possible. You couldn't argue with an establishment that offered twelve flavors of Jello every day, and that's not even counting the special Jello salads with fruit floating magically inside, a wiggly rainbow of bright shades and tangy flavors. Kids loved it and the grownups secretly lusted after it. Along with the savory brisket and cheesy scalloped potatoes.

Joe sat opposite Harv Benson, a too-serious man in a too-tight sport coat under his bulky parka. Neither one of them had Jello. Just black coffee. Jiggly incandescent food seemed out of place at a business meeting.

Joe pushed a shaky smile, hoping to get things off on the right foot. "Thanks for driving over to see me. Murray said that..."

"Murray said you'd be in Tuesday." No smile, just a tiny nervous tick in his left eye. Blink blink. Then nothing. Then, blink blink.

"I know. I'm sorry. We had a..."

"Yah, but Tuesday we was all set, see."

"This storm just came up sudden," Joe said.

"Uh-huh, but the deal was Tuesday. Had six college girls — cheerleaders from up the Twin Cities — all set to go. Had the darn bottle outfits and everything."

"Bottle outfits?" Joe said.

"For the dancin' beer bottles."

Joe gave it a moment. This was going to be tougher than he had anticipated. "Remember we talked on the phone about the, uh... the fish?"

"The talkin' fish? Yah. Thought about it. Didn't float. Nobody's gonna buy beer from a talkin' fish when ya got a big bottle with a good set o' legs."

"I promised Murray we'd do this for you..."

"Yah, but Tuesday was the deal, see." Harv thumped the table hard with a stiff, demanding finger. "We were ready Tuesday."

"But the road was closed. The blizzard..."

"Happens alla time up here. Coulda gone around. Up 73, then west on Route 1 over to State 71, and drop right down into Bemidji. Or, if 73 was plugged, like today with the plow mess, go up 169 and snag 53, go over that way ta come down."

"Didn't know that..." Joe said, looking down at his hands, feeling thoroughly chastised.

"Yah, well you tell that to six cheerleaders freezin' their tails off in beer bottle suits waitin' down by the squirt line all day to film the darn commercial."

"We're ready. We can shoot it now," Joe said, cranking up a veneer of enthusiasm.

"No sir," Harv said, looking off. "Girls are gone. Skedaddled outta Bemidji. Had cheerin' ta do back in Minneapolis."

"We can re-cast."

"Ya think it's easy to get good legs around these parts? Most are like ham hocks. Nobody's gonna buy beer from girls with those."

A bleach-blond mother sidled over to their table with humble caution, tugging the wrist of a 7-year-old girl dressed in a spangled leotard, a cheap plastic tiara on her head.

"Excuse me there. Don't mean to interrupt your meal. This is my Lolly." She pulled her daughter closer. "Go ahead, honey."

HIDING IN HIBBING

As if turned on by an invisible switch, the little girl abruptly popped bright eyes and a fake smile, bursting into a piercing, and thankfully short, rendition of *Twist and Shout*, wiggling her hips with awkward kid-like jerks. Her final screeching high note made them both wince. Joe hid his reaction pretty well, having grown accustomed to these strange intrusions by now. But Harv appeared distinctly uncomfortable.

The mom, who Joe now noticed was actually quite attractive when viewed close up, slapped a scribbled paper napkin down on the table. "Got my name, number, address, all the necessaries right there in pencil. Okay, then. Sorry. Letcha get back to your java."

She winked slyly at Joe, holding his gaze about three seconds longer than appropriate. "You can call whenever. Won't disturb us. And her daddy won't care because he ain't in the picture." Then, tugging the skinny little wrist, "Come on, honey."

They both watched as she quickly led her daughter away. Joe found himself staring openly at the bleach-blond's shapely hips swaying under her pleated skirt, momentarily distracted from the crisis at hand. He turned back to Harv forcing an amused smile.

"See there. Auditioning for the commercial."

"Way too small for the bottle suit," Harv said, his tone flat and brittle as a burned pancake. He stood up, scowling. "You tell Murray I'm not happy. And he still owes me. Big time."

Joe listened for the door of Helstrom's Buffet to thump shut, staring at the hasty scribbles on the napkin, picturing those soft hips swaying under the skirt.

35

Patterson's Market offered the usual assortment of grocery items, plus a vast and variable stock of clothing, a few assorted household tools and an unusually large array of flashlight batteries long past their date of usefulness. Whatever didn't manage to sell—whether it was Corn Flakes, hammers or Elmer's Glue—remained on the shelves until falling out of fashion or drying up, awaiting either the second coming of Christ or someone dumb enough to take the stagnating business off Luther Patterson's hands.

It was less a store than a gathering spot for locals who wandered the long aisles like affable zombies, exchanging muttered greetings and bits of rumor spun wildly into more palatable slices of intrigue. *Comin' for the groshrees* they called it, but it was really fishing for the latest juicy gossip.

Annie was a regular, stopping in three or four times a day when the weather permitted, picking up this and that, whether she needed it or not, driven by boredom rather than necessity. Which is why she stacked two-dozen cans of cat food on the checkout stand when she already had at least twice that many at home for her dappled, butt-ugly cat, Tony Curtis.

Charlene, the cashier, rang up the cans and bagged them, leaning toward Annie with a cagey cock of her head, muttering low, "Did I hear you tell Mrs. Caswell about some men over at Gunderson's?"

"Two of 'em."

"That right? And they were what, cops?"

HIDING IN HIBBING

"Reporters it looks. New York Times."

"Oh yah? The newspaper?"

Annie nodded.

"Oh fer gosh sake," Charlene said, wobbling her head, intrigued.

"Probably looking for our Ziggy Jett," Annie said. "So's they can steal him away from us."

Charlene nodded firmly, catching on. "Make us look bad."

"Just like when them heathens back east lured young Bobby Zimmerman away to Sodom and Gomorrah. Made Hibbing out a joke."

"Who cares?" It was grizzled old Gunnar Stout, a cranky curmudgeon, bundled in a checkered hunting jacket and John Deere cap, biting his smelly pipe with a sour sneer. "Goddamn bunch of no-good, lazy, long-haired hippy bums. Oughta rot in hell, is what."

"A good stair-step up from you, Gunnar," said Annie. "They're musicians and that takes real talent."

"Bull pucky! They're 'bout as talented as that filthy cat of yours."

"Don't you besmirch my Tony Curtis."

"What the hell is bee-smirch?"

Charlene laughed. "Got a twist in your shorts, do ya, Gunnar?" It was this sort of lively exchange that made her day sail right by.

Only twenty minutes later Donnie drifted back into KHIB-AM from his lunch break, chewing on a stale Three Musketeers that he'd picked up at Patterson's.

Maggie looked up from the chattering teletype. Called out to him, "Better get your butt in there. Less than two minutes left on that Percy Faith crap." It was *Theme From A Summer Place*, the enticing melody dripping with irony, what with all the snow outside.

Donnie stuck his head into the newsroom. "Where the heck's Roger at? His shift's not over yet."

"Far as he's concerned it is. Just left. Said he had a doctor thing or something. Said he told you."

"Well he didn't," Donnie huffed, pulling his coat off. Then, as he headed for the broadcast studio he tossed back, "Couple reporters in town from New York."

That caught Maggie's attention. She hustled after him. "What the heck ya talkin' about?"

"Yep. Word at the Donut Palace. Heard it over at Patterson's too."

"Oh yah? From New York you say?"

"New York Times."

"I'll be darned," Maggie said.

36

Two long folding tables had been set up in the private banquet room of the Front Range Hotel for the weekly meeting of the Hibbing Civic Action Committee. In the early days it been attended only by Mayor Grunwald and five officially elected members of City Council. But as the savage winter beast settled in, interest waned. The meeting was soon opened up to whoever might be suckered in by the huge platter of day-old pastries contributed by the Donut Palace.

Carl had arrived early, followed in quick order by Pete, from the Ramada, and then Wayne Everson, who used any handy excuse to avoid slouching around the radio station listening to Maggie's convoluted gibberish.

Making an uncustomary appearance was old Daryl Mitchell, who had given up his coveted counter spot down at Gunderson's to seek out fresh baked goods while looking to spread the word on the two suspicious new arrivals in town.

Bob Koenen popped in next; since nobody was bowling midday, he had just shut the lights and left the doors to the Pin Spot unlocked in case somebody got the itch to toss a few balls.

Bob wasted no time, launching an exploratory poking of the pastries on the platter. Wayne nudged him aside, gazing at the pile of sweet delights.

"Got a bear claw in there ya think?" Wayne said.

"Not conspicuous," Bob surmised.

"Down in maybe."

"Gotta dig."

Ronald Von Ahlen, the Minnesota State Trooper, straggled in, cheeks all ruddy from the cold. Gave the Mayor a quick wave. Pulled off his furry earflap hat and big insulated gloves, like baseball mitts. He'd been first on the scene after the snowplow smacked Janey's grandma, making him a treasured source of grisly detail for curious inquisitors over the past few days.

"How's she look?" Pete said.

"Could be another flurry pullin' up," Trooper Ron said. "I miss the start?"

"Not a tick," Carl said. "Just jawin'."

Daryl piped up. "I seen em down at Lou's, dem two..."

Pete said, "Oh yah?"

"Overcoats. Clean shoes."

"Don't trust that," Bob said, looking up from the heap of donuts.

"Lookin' for Ziggy then?" Carl said.

"I hope to shout."

Hearing this exchange, Happ shouldered his way into their circle, shadows of deep concern carved into his cheeks. "We gotta keep the lid on. Gave my word."

"Maybe those fellahs just wanna print a story is all," Trooper Ron said.

"Sure they do," said Carl. "That's the gad dern point. They run a big story, give away where the band is hid at, then Ziggy and them'll hafta skeedaddle outta here, lay low in some other town 'til Ed Sullivan." He cast an accusing gaze at the Mayor. "And we end up losin' out, just like before."

"Aw fried moose flop," said Wayne, "youse all know same as me, hard times and greed's what shut the mines. Had nothin' ta do with chasing young Bob away."

"Matter of opinion," Carl grumbled.

"Up for discussion, that's sure," said Pete.

"Got one!" Bob Koenen shouted, pulling a bear claw out of the heap.

"Oh yah?" Wayne said, eyes ablaze. "Slide 'er down."

Bob dropped the bear claw on a napkin and slid it down the table toward Wayne, who snatched it up, an eager goalie nailing a sugary puck.

"Then some other place'll get the spotlight," Carl said, "and we get the short end of the stick again."

Trooper Ron pondered this, brows knit tight, having lost the tangled thread of the discussion. "Oh-fer-geez...how ya figure?"

"Well, 'cause then that other town'll be the town where Ziggy and the boys hid out before their big world debut," Pete said.

Carl jumped back in. "It'll be all over the news, see."

"That's how she goes with headlines and such. Wayne'll tell ya."

"Oh yah..." Wayne mumbled, mouth full of bear claw. "Way she goes."

"Whereas, we keep it all under wraps from those newspaper fellahs, it'll be 'Tonight on Ed Sullivan, Ziggy and the boys, direct from Hibbing, Minnesota.' Right out of Ed Sullivan's own mouth to the whole country."

"It'll be big, don'tcha know" Carl concurred. "Real big.

"Historical, even," Happ said with authority.

"Then, all a'sudden, everybody's talkin' Hibbing."

Pete nodded with enthusiasm. "Must be a good place to live, they say."

"Folks move in..."

"New companies. Factories and such."

"More bowlers," Bob Koenen added with a self-serving twinkle.

"Put us on the map," Pete said. "That's how she works. Wayne'll tell ya."

"Oh yah," said Wayne, nodding. "How she works."

179

Carl grinned to himself. "And I kinda like that bunch, no matter the long hair."

"They're good boys," Pete said, casting aside the vivid image of Ziggy's trashed motel room.

"Jeez, real good," Happ concurred, feeling the tide turning in his favor. "We need to put the word out. Nobody gives these New York slickers a dern-tootin' thing. Not a whisper."

"So..." Bob said. "We need a resolution then?"

"I second it," Daryl shouted, raising a half-eaten donut, his beard awash in powdered sugar.

"Call it unanimous," Happ said. "Whatcha say?"

"YAH," they all chimed in with gusto.

37

Rafferty and Stromberg huddled over their menus at Carl's, while Sherry, a new waitress, stood by anxiously. She shifted from foot to foot, straightening her plastic nametag. Tapped her pencil restlessly on the order pad. Wondered if she should stay or go.

"Maybe I oughta give you a minute," she finally said, disturbed by Rafferty's intense scowl.

"What are abel...skiv...?"

"Oh, abelskivers," Sherry said, doing her perky best. "Yah, they're good."

"What are they?"

"Did ya ever have a muffin or a, you know, a bready type baked thing with, uh..." She made an undecipherable wiggly wave motion with both hands, looping them around and back again. "It's sort of like that, only kinda different, but really, really good and everybody eats them. Want some of them?"

"Is there any entertainment in town?" Stromberg interjected sharply, his impatience mounting.

"Just me," she said with a giggle, striking her gawky version of a fashion model pose. Then, flashing an uneasy look to the front, "That's just a joke. Don't say anything to Carl, okay? He doesn't like us making jokes on the job."

Stromberg stares passively, waiting. "So, is there?"

"What was the question?"

"Entertainment. Do you have any entertainment in town?"

"Uhhh, entertainment. You mean like moving pictures and such?"

"Singers," he said. "Performers. Local talent."

She shot another shaky glance toward the register, where Carl was now surveying incoming customers with serious deliberation.

Sherry pretended to ponder the question, hoping for rescue. "Uh, golly...lemme uh, hmmm. I'm not...I'll just, um... okay, hold your horses a sec..."

She scurried away.

Stromberg rolled his eyes. "Is that a hard one?"

But Rafferty didn't hear him, still engrossed in the provincial mysteries of the menu.

"Got something here called a pasty," he said, only pronouncing it *pace-tee*. "Isn't that what strippers cover their nipples with?"

"Somehow I don't think they serve nipple covers here."

"Maybe it just looks like one, but it really is food."

"That'd be a good guess, since they supposedly serve food here."

"Wouldn't want to eat it though," Rafferty said. "I'd keep thinking of, ya know..."

"Tits, yeah."

That was the moment Carl appeared at their table.

"There's a question?"

"I was just inquiring where a person might find some of your local talent," Stromberg said.

"No talent here. Everybody works for a living."

"There must be musicians...singers...like that."

"You putting up a show?"

"No, no. I was just curious."

After a long pause, Carl said, "Well, Jeb Hankey plays the saw. Big cross-cut deal. Gets a nice sound out of it."

Stromberg looked at Rafferty, widening his eyes. "Uh-huh. Saw."

HIDING IN HIBBING

"And Nancy Gustafson, she's been practicing her opera. To records, you know. Pair of lungs won't quit."

"I was thinking, what about bands? Maybe rock-and-roll."

"Not a one," Carl said. "Unless you count the marching band over at the high school. Took two trophies downstate."

This dancing around was making Stromberg antsy.

"Ever hear of Ziggy Jett and the Jetstream?" he said, jumping right to the point.

Carl's response came out flat and final. "Can't say I have."

It felt like that would end it. Carl stood there, looking down at them with a stony visage, waiting to see if they had any more dead-end inquiries.

Rafferty saw his chance. "What the heck is a pasty?"

"It's a pass-tee," Carl said, emphasizing it phonetically. "Not pace-tee. It's a meat pie. No stripper tits involved."

An hour later, after consuming three abelskivers and cautiously poking and prodding a single pasty with their forks until it was mush, they stopped by the Ramada Inn to see if they might uncover some useful leads. While Stromberg grilled Pete with a laundry list of questions designed to elicit a confession regarding any big stars hiding in Hibbing, Rafferty casually surveyed the reverential gallery of Bob Dylan photos plastered all around the lobby.

"Mmmmmm, nope," was the extent of Pete's reiterated replies. Given his notorious loose-lipped proclivity for babbling more information than anyone needed to know, Pete had been duly warned by Happ and the others to keep his responses to a single word.

"And don't blink," Happ had warned him. "That there is a dead giveaway you're lying through your dentures."

"Mmmm, nope," he said over and over, eyes frozen wide until they ached.

DAVID O'MALLEY

They didn't do much better at Bob Koenen's Pin Spot Bowling Alley. Bob revived his long-abandoned high school ambitions to tread the Broadway stage, giving them a full-fledged dramatic performance, half James Dean posing, half Marlon Brando meandering and mumbling, as he denied any knowledge of celebrities in their midst.

He squinted at Stromberg, head lowered and cocked at a rakish angle, thumbs hooked casually in his back pockets. "Jett, you say? Heck, fellahs, we don't even have a real airport. Just takes them small prop jobbies."

Pulling the wool over the eyes of these New York goombahs was a snap.

38

Joe watched Ziggy climb into the VW bus and start the engine. He felt like a nervous father giving his son the keys to the family car for the first time. Ziggy shut the door and rolled down the frosty window.

"Bring her back in one piece," Joe said. "We don't have insurance."

Ziggy nodded, shoved in the clutch and turned the key. The engine stuttered, then growled, then purred, the normal VW choral progression. But when he shifted into first, gears grinding harshly, Joe grimaced, a disturbing gorge of regret rising in his throat. Ziggy shrugged sheepishly.

"Watch the ice patches and keep it slow," Joe said, straining to remain even and unruffled.

Ziggy released the clutch carefully. The VW heaved and lurched toward the road, spitting back bits of snow with what little tire tread remained.

Ziggy had spotted a notice in the local paper and it prompted a reckless inspiration, which in turn triggered the necessary courage for him to pick up the phone and call Janey. He didn't use the actual word *date* while fumbling around for a way to ask her out, but that's what it was, a date; definitely a rendezvous of sorts, with all the attendant social implications. If it had simply been a casual plan to hang out, unexpectedly blurted forth on impulse, the air would have hung more lightly over his head. But the weight of his intentions created a cloud of acute anticipation.

After driving in loopy circles through a depressing sprawl of dilapidated houses, many abandoned, Ziggy finally found the street he was looking for. Janey's house was a small, weathered cracker box sitting back from the ice-caked dirt road in a cluster of stark trees, naked of leaves, jagged limbs grasping toward the gray clouds with skeletal hands. It was an austere setting, distinctly lacking any romantic atmosphere.

Standing at the front door after his tentative knock, he noticed a spread of rimy crystals clinging to the warped wood like frigid mold. It mesmerized him, seeming a disconcerting portent. The door abruptly swung open with a sharp squeak, jolting him to the welcome vision of Janey and her irresistible smile.

She stepped back in the doorway, welcoming him into the musty warmth with a blithe wave of her hand. The dark, cramped foyer opened to an equally small living room. A muted glow from two dim lamps barely illuminated the gloom. Janey's mother, a large woman with the countenance of a grumpy bullfrog sat on a tattered fabric sofa, her pasty girth cascading over the cushions.

"Um, you can sit or...I'll just go grab my coat," Janey said, a bit flustered. She disappeared into a tiny bedroom down the hall.

Ziggy couldn't take his eyes off Janey's mother. A large dark mole on her upper cheek gave the impression of a sleeping fly. He felt a strange urge to swat it away, but wisely resisted, shuffling nervously in place.

Her indolent gaze traveled downward to his crotch. He looked down at himself, afraid he may have forgotten to zip his fly, then back up to her eyes. She squinted hard at him, sending a stern warning that required no words. He stopped breathing.

Janey abruptly reappeared, pulling on her coat. "Okay. Ready."

"Great," Ziggy said, awash with relief, air rushing back into his lungs.

"Bye mom. I won't be late."

Janey's mom stared at the closing door without a word. The ash fell from her cigarette onto the floor.

Their warm moist breath clouded the windshield. Ziggy wiped the glass with his hand and smeared it with his coat sleeve as he drove.

"The, uh, heater doesn't work all that well," he said. "Sometimes it does, but then, for no reason, it just doesn't."

The spongy muffled purr of the engine filled their uncomfortable silence. "My mom doesn't talk much," Janey said.

"Yeah? I didn't notice."

"She ran out of things to say about six years ago. When my dad left."

"Your dad left?"

"Uh-huh."

Ziggy wanted to ask her why he'd left and where he went, but the questions seemed intrusive, so he swallowed them. If she wanted to tell him, she would. There was no reason to jeopardize their tentative bond with indelicate inquiries that might create an insurmountable wall between them.

She sensed his discomfort, turning to him brightly. "So, where are we going?"

Ziggy smiled then, keeping his eyes on the road. "Surprise."

She felt a tingle in her stomach, not knowing why. Then realized, it was the very mystery of not knowing, the excitement of an undefined adventure, that stirred her.

They drove on for twenty minutes, mostly in silence, until they approached the outskirts of Chisholm, a small town northeast of Hibbing. The glow of a large neon sign came into view. Holiday Inn. Ziggy turned into the mostly empty parking lot and steered toward a space.

Janey stiffened, the tingle in her stomach replaced by a sickening fear. Had she gotten in over her head? She looked at Ziggy, but he simply stared out through the windshield, a faint smile on his lips.

"What are we...?" she started to ask.

"You'll see," he said, turning to her with an enigmatic grin.

They crossed the empty lobby, Janey's legs weak with anticipation, fingers prickly and cold. Ziggy guided her past the registration desk, lightly touching her elbow, turning her toward the darkened lounge.

A printed sign on a wooden easel materialized before them.

APPEARING TONIGHT!
THE BREWSKIS
(formerly The Elk Humpers)

A surge of surprise washed over Janey, followed quickly by the exultation of relief. "I can't believe that...are we?...did you...?" she babbled, trying to piece together the rush of thoughts into a coherent sentence.

"Heard on the radio they were gonna be here," he said. "Uh, actually, I read it in the paper. I don't know why I said radio. I guess, I don't know..." But then he let it drop since Janey wasn't even hearing him. She was laughing at the sign.

"Danny...he'll be an Elk Humper to the end. He can't get past it."

They stopped in the entrance to the lounge. Ziggy's heart fell into his shoes. The room was nearly empty. Just a couple stiffs in cheap sport coats, ties loosened sloppily, eyes already glazed over from the booze; accountants from Minneapolis in town to sort out the books for the recent Chisholm Glass Company bankruptcy. They yakked it up at a

HIDING IN HIBBING

small table, laughing boisterously at their own lame jokes, completely ignoring the band on the triangular wooden riser in the corner that served as a stage.

The Brewskis, three loose-limbed guys in faded jeans and plaid woolen shirts, cuffs rolled up, plodded through an appropriately somnambulant rendition of Santo & Johnny's instrumental hit *Sleepwalk*. Their unit was a familiar one; two guitars and Ludwig drum kit, disheveled hair in modified Beatles-cuts, and a dazed, distant look in their eyes that envisioned much more than they had yet experienced.

Janey sensed Ziggy's keen disappointment with the empty room. "It's Bingo Night at the Elks Lodge in Hibbing," she said. "Nobody goes anywhere else on Bingo Night."

Danny, the lead guitar player, spied Janey. He shot her a big goofy grin, pleased to see her, but seemingly not all that surprised. As if he expected her to be there, she thought. But the slippery feeling darted away; she gave him a shy wave.

The band finished the drowsy song. The two stiffs at the small table didn't even take notice, their stream of rude jabbering flowing unabated.

"Heeeey, Janey," Danny said, stashing his Rickenbacker and stepping off the riser to greet her. "Long time, girl. We missed you." He gave her a quick, tentative hug.

"Danny, hi." Her voice was milky warm, but she kept him at arm's length.

"She speaks," said Mike, the bass player, like it was a big deal, his sly sarcasm baldly transparent.

"Very funny," she said.

"Ignore him," Danny told her. "He's an idiot."

Mike plucked a drooping bass note in response.

Janey swiveled toward Ziggy, telling Danny, "This is my friend, Zig..."

"Arthur," Ziggy said, cutting her off. He extended his hand to Danny.

They shook hands with a reserved hint of familiarity. But Janey didn't catch it, still distracted by the swirl of surprise.

"You guys sounded great," Ziggy said.

"Thanks. You know Janey here used to sing with us."

Hal, the drummer, hit a wise-ass rim-shot, smirking.

"So I've heard," Ziggy said.

Danny exchanged a quick sidelong glance with Ziggy. Gave Janey a nudge. "Why don't you, ya know, do a number with us?"

Janey blushed. "Oh no, I can't." Her face went from crimson red to pale white as the blood rushed downward in an attempt to rescue her quivering legs.

"Yeah. You should," Ziggy said. "That would be great." Calling on every ounce of sincere enthusiasm, striving to make it sound spontaneous and uncalculated.

Danny jumped back up on the riser. Mike fingered a rumbling bass riff, snickering.

Janey turned to Ziggy, feeling a stab of helplessness. "Uh-uh, I can't do it."

Ziggy flashed her an encouraging grin. She glanced nervously at the two sport-coat jerks downing their drinks.

"Those two schmoes?" Ziggy said. "You don't know them. They don't know you. You'll never see 'em again."

"How do you do it?" Janey whispered.

"What?"

"With all those big crowds of screaming girls..." She hesitated. Then, in a voice so soft it was barely audible, "People judging you."

Ziggy moved between Janey and the band, his back to them, his words only for her. "I don't look at the people out there. I look way out over their heads. And I get a glimpse of the future...my future...and I just hold onto that. It's all I see. Like this bright light glowing off in the distance."

"But I'm not you." She peered past him, toward the stage; the frightened eyes of a small child. Then shifted to the side until the stage fell from her line of sight. "I just know if I go up there, I'll always regret it."

Ziggy grasped her slender shoulders with a calm firmness, so she couldn't turn from him. "Regrets are a waste of time. They stop you from living."

He had read that somewhere. Or heard it. Didn't even know if it was true. But there it was.

She looked into his eyes, searching; she could find no reason not to believe him.

Danny adjusted the microphone, restless. Tapped on it. "Come on, Janey. For old times."

Ziggy took her hand, holding it gently, pointing it toward the stage. She inhaled deeply, steeling herself, and gave in. Stepped up on the riser.

Danny gave Ziggy a nod, then looked to Hal, who leaned back languidly on his stool, furtively switching on a big Ampex reel-to-reel tape recorder connected to the soundboard by a snarl of cables.

Janey stepped reluctantly to the microphone, gripping it tightly — a precious anchor of security. Hal bent toward Mike and muttered, "This oughta be good for a laugh."

Back in high school, Janey had consistently been an impressive vocalist in their afternoon garage band rehearsals, but inevitably collapsed whenever they tried to perform in public. The infamous Winter Escapades debacle had been the final straw; a wrenching humiliation that threw the band into chaotic dissension, causing them to nearly break up for good. The only solution had been to drop Janey. But they were saved from delivering that cruel *coup de grâce* when Janey tearfully told them she had to leave the band because her grades were suffering. They knew it wasn't true. But they were so relieved at being spared the pain of giving her the ax, they gratefully let it slide and moved on.

That was two years before. The intervening span of time sent the band into a spiral of beer-fueled disagreements, breakups and name changes. A month of doing nothing but smoking grass in Mike's garage finally afforded them the clarity they needed; big time rock-and-roll success was not in their future. But if they applied themselves, they calculated they could probably eke out a passable living on the hotel lounge circuit doing four-chord covers, picking up random barroom gigs in between.

Danny launched into the four bar intro of *It's Too Late*, the Carly Simon rocker that they'd played around with in rehearsals many times. Janey closed her eyes, felt the familiar beat, shifting from one foot to the other, rocking slowly side-to-side. Lost in the music, she missed the first vocal cue. The guitars and drums stumbled to a clumsy halt.

Mike and Hal twisted their faces away to conceal their looks of cruel derision. It's exactly what they figured would happen. Crash and burn, like before. Danny snapped them a flat glare and started over from the top. The bass guitar and drums caught up.

Janey began to sing, her voice barely a whisper. The band gnashed to a rough stop, Hal's drumsticks hitting an angry snare shot. "You gotta turn the mike on."

Janey squeezed her eyes shut, ashamed. Her trembling fingers fumbled for the off/on switch.

Mike buried his chin against his chest, stifling a rude smirk, craning his neck around to roll his eyes at Hal. The tension congealed as Janey's flustered fingers searched awkwardly for the switch

Ziggy couldn't abide her helplessness another moment. He leaped to the riser. "Here, I'll get it," he said softly, sliding his hand along the base of the mike, faking momentary confusion to ease her embarrassment, then flipping the switch.

A grating snarl of raw feedback screeched from the speakers. The musicians groaned in agony, sardonically exaggerating their reactions with twisted body contortions. Even the two oblivious creeps by the stage were wrenched from their self-indulgent revelry to shout curses and hoots of scorn at the shrill discordance. Mike stretched back toward the amp, twisting a knob to kill the unwelcome yowl.

Danny saved things from descending into further chaos by raking the opening chord of an entirely different song, weaving his way through an extended instrumental intro. The sporadic traces of melody sounded familiar to Ziggy, but he couldn't place it. Mike and Hal knew it very well however, instinctively falling into line with the throbbing beat, riding high on the shot of adrenaline injected by the bone-rattling feedback.

Janey was still shaken. She looked at Ziggy, expecting to see him glaring at her with harsh disappointment. But instead she saw his broad sunny grin and heard him laugh with ridiculous glee at the cacophonous craziness of the moment.

That was when she realized which song they were building up to, swept into the addictive rush of music that enveloped her, startled to feel her fear swiftly drain away. She synched herself with the insistent beat, grabbing the microphone to wail *come on...come on...come on...come on....*

Ziggy was blown away by the power of her voice, tottering back on his heels until his calves struck a chair and he tumbled into it. Janey's vocal plunged precipitously into a valley of soul-searing pain as the band decelerated through a throbbing bluesy riff for the opening verse.

Ziggy recognized the song now. It was unmistakably *Piece of My Heart*. Not Janis Joplin's hard-driving, gut-wrenching, throat-ripping version; this was the much more, provocatively powerful interpretation recorded first by Erma Franklin, Aretha's older sister. It was soulful and gritty, with a tough jazzy pulse driving its inexorable message of feminine resilience.

This was a far cry from the softly dulcet vocal Janey revealed to him earlier, barely whispering *Happy Birthday* at Carl's, then nakedly exposing her vulnerability with *All Alone Am I* at Bob's Pin Spot.

Danny and Mike flashed surprised looks at each other, unable to hide their astonishment. Invigorated by Janey's spirited vocalizing, Hal spiked his drum kit with renewed enthusiasm. Even the two drunks were sucked into the excitement, banging on the table wildly, twisting in their chairs, bobbing their heads with intoxicated abandon as Janey cried out for someone to *break off another piece of her heart*.

She charged ferociously toward the final chorus, ascending to a high place, aiming for a crescendo and quick conclusion. But Danny and Mike were psyched now, in a sweaty groove and not wanting to slow it down. They pumped their heads at Hal, hunched over their guitars, Danny raking chords, Mike thumping the heavy bass line. Hal took their cue and tossed away the climactic crescendo, shrugging it off with a flurry of whipping hair, thrashing an even more intensified beat into a repeat of the chorus.

This shift caught Janey by surprise, but she instantly adjusted, hurtling into the final chorus once more. Ziggy took all of this in with proud exhilaration, eyes riveted on Janey, enthralled by the seductive urgency in her delivery.

That's when the two drunks went berserk, pounding on the table with flat hands, ice-melt bourbon sloshing in squat glasses, their animal howls interspersed with bellowing laughter. The beasts had been unleashed.

Janey faltered, losing the rhythm, distracted by their unrestrained display. The surge of pandemonium pulled her out of the song, her voice wavering and cracking, lyrics whipped away like wind-spun leaves. A drink glass vibrated off their bouncing table, shattering on the floor. Janey crumbled.

She rushed from the stage, past Ziggy and out into the lobby as the band, propelled by sheer momentum, flung itself headlong into a rousing finish.

39

Ziggy found Janey sitting in the VW bus, fighting back tears, shivering.

"I brought your coat." He handed it to her. Then, as she struggled to find the sleeve openings, helped her pull it on. She huddled deeply into the coat, warmer now, both inside and out.

He wanted to take her in his arms, hold her, tell her everything would be okay. If he could just summon the words he'd heard movie stars say a hundred times before. Those perfectly constructed phrases that magically unlocked a woman's heart and gave her comfort, made her swoon, and solved the crisis-at-hand within five seconds. But that stuff didn't really come from Steve McQueen and Paul Newman. It was crap made up by movie writers. Probably a bunch of old, fat guys with thinning hair and hemorrhoids who sat around in their underwear and ratty slippers, making it up, pounding it out on their clunky typewriters, never even leaving home. They didn't know anything about women. Not from experience. They probably stole all those brilliant gems of emotional insight from other old movies. And who knows where those movies got them? Probably Shakespeare. Or poems. Yeah, love poems. He cursed himself for not reading more poetry when he was in high school. But he could never get into it; most of it didn't even rhyme. What was the point?

Janey sniffled. He turned to her. The warm light from the Holiday Inn sign made her face glow with a radiant softness. She looked like Katherine Ross in *The Graduate*, all soft edges, vulnerable and lovely, a youthful goddess caught up in the disorienting whirlwind of Benjamin Braddock's confusion. He flashed on the ending; Benjamin and Elaine sitting in the back of a bus, the look of helpless trepidation on their faces as they stared into the future—that void of the *unknown*. He quickly purged the disturbing image from his mind. It was not helping. .

"Janey..." he said. And that was all. He hoped that if he said her name, the rest would quickly follow, shoved out of his mouth by a brilliant subconscious. Jesus, he thought, what would Elvis say in this situation? Then it hit him. He wouldn't say anything. He would sing. One of those cornball schmaltzy ballads. And the luminous Ann Margaret would instantly dry her glistening tears and collapse into his arms. It hit him like a cold slap. That's where they got all those cool romantic lines. From songs. Those fat, dorky movie writers stole them from songs.

He wracked his brain for musical inspiration. A rush of random lyrics stampeded wildly through his tortured mind.

Come on baby, let's do the twist.

Jesus! Where did that come from?

I can't get no...

No, no, no. Wrong on so many levels. You need something truly romantic. Something from a love song, you doofus.

You've lost that loving feeling...

Damn. No. Sounds like Ray. Keep it positive. Wait! Elvis. Yeah. Stick with Elvis, the King. He was the ultimate romantic; bedroom eyes, curled upper lip, the promise of both sweet seduction and exciting danger. That guy could even melt the heart of a Nazi torture queen like Ilsa, She Wolf of the S.S..

He conjured up a mental playlist. The honey smooth voice of Elvis wafted through his mind.

Wise men say...

HIDING IN HIBBING

Now where's this going?
Only fools rush in...
Well, that's not gonna work.

The tiny hardened crystals of sugar snow began to pelt the windshield, skittering across the glassy surface to form gracefully rounded white mini-drifts at the corners.

"Sorry," Janey said, brushing away the moisture clinging to her eyelid with a quivering fingertip.

"No, no... you sounded great." It erupted from him without a wisp of conscious thought or consideration, a far cry from the melodious poetry he was seeking. He winced at his bland declaration, stabbed in the heart by his own tongue.

"I sounded awful," she said, looking into her lap to avoid his eyes.

"I think you were amazing up there."

She squirmed, hiding the glimmer of a smile.

"It was a beautiful performance. I mean it. I liked everything about it." Elvis had vanished; the fat bald movie writers and musical poets, forgotten. These were his words now. Simple and direct. "It was really incredible."

"Until I fell apart at the end," she said.

"Aw, those two creeps. They should have been tossed out on their asses." Then catching himself, "Sorry, I mean their butts...or whatever."

"No. You were right. Out on their asses," she said. "That's what they were, a couple of asses."

He smiled. Liked hearing her say *asses*. It made her feel real to him.

"I got a surprise for you."

"Not another surprise," she said, squirming a little. "Surprises make me nervous."

"It's not a bad surprise." He pulled a plastic audiotape reel from his coat pocket, holding it up. Her eyes widened.

"What's that?" She gulped audibly, feeling a twinge of anticipation.

"They taped your song."

She stared at it, letting the pieces of the evening fall together. "You planned all this," she said. It wasn't an accusation, but not exactly a question either.

"I wanted you to hear what you sound like."

"I don't have to. I know I was awful." A dark cloud of dread filled her eyes. "Oh God, they didn't record the beginning, did they? When I messed it all up and made such a fool of myself."

"They cut that part out," Ziggy said. Then added, "I asked them to cut it out." They hadn't really. There wasn't time. They'd just handed him the tape. But he could do it later. So it wasn't really a lie, just a benign time shift in reality.

She felt a wave of grateful relief. "Thank you," she said with a tiny voice, pulling her cold hands up into the sleeves of the coat.

"I think I know a place where I can get this transferred to vinyl—you know, a record—so you can listen to it."

"Really?"

"Yeah. I'll do it."

"You don't have to."

"Yes I do. You have a beautiful voice."

She smiled at this, certain of his sincerity. "It really means something special, you saying it."

"I don't know about that."

"You're a professional. A star. You've been around all kinds of really famous people. I mean really, really talented people."

He averted his gaze from her, looking out at the pebbly sugar-snow pelting the glass, afraid his eyes would reveal he was a fraud.

"You've been to the mountain," she said.

"The mountain?"

"Yeah. Like Muhammad."

His face was a blank. "Muhammad?"

"You know the saying...'If you can't get the mountain to come to Muhammad, then Muhammad has to go to the mountain.'"

"Oh, yeah. He's like the religious guy, from Arabia."

She nodded. "I don't know for sure if I understand what it means, but sometimes I *feel* like I understand it."

"I know *The Bear Went Over the Mountain*," Ziggy said. "We used to sing it on the bus driving to camp."

"You went to camp?" Her eyes widened, excited by this prospect.

"Just for like a weekend. Maybe three days in fourth grade. We roasted weenies and marshmallows. Paddled canoes around the lake. Had water balloon fights. Sang the stupid bear song."

"I remember it. The bear went over the mountain to see what he could see."

"Yep. That's it." Ziggy chuckled to himself. "Dumb song."

Janey smiled. "Maybe the bear is Muhammad."

They both gazed out into the darkness, mesmerized by the bony fingers of frost creeping up from beneath the wiper blades.

"Wonder what he saw. You know...when he went over the mountain."

"That's probably one of the great mysteries of life," she said with a wry twinkle.

"Yeah," Ziggy said. "I guess it is."

40

Stromberg and Rafferty had checked into the Androy Hotel, a prominent four-story brick structure on Howard Street that dated back to the days when the mining industry was at its peak in Hibbing. The town center had originally been located farther north, but in 1914 when the Oliver Ore Mining Company decided to spread its arms, widening its voracious influence, the whole town was forced to pack up and move. They jacked entire houses onto wheels and rolled them four miles down the road, creaking through the night, cumbersome and sluggish, a herd of wooden elephants seeking a new watering hole. The resettlement cost more than 16 million dollars, a pretty penny in those days.

To help compensate aggrieved citizens for the merciless upheaval, the company launched a massive civic project, constructing an impressive city hall, the stately Androy Hotel and, in 1921, an opulent high school that featured massive murals and friezes, elegant mosaics, beveled glass and a palatial auditorium fashioned after New York City's acclaimed Capitol Theater. The school alone cost 4 million dollars, an unimaginable expenditure for a small town.

Throughout the early forties, the ore produced in the Misabi Range's massive open pit operation provided the grist for the war machine that was ravenously consuming the world's resources. But by the early 1950s, the best iron ore had been depleted. A taconite process was introduced, using giant magnets and sifters to squeeze out the remaining, barely usable, ore. The former run of golden prosperity had evaporated, creating an erosion of hope in the once vibrant town.

By 1971, the Androy itself had fallen victim to the dull ennui that infected the region. The rooms had lost their former sheen, shrouded in the dust of neglect and declining occupancy. The hotel's Crystal Lounge, once touted as Hibbing's finest supper club, had ceased to draw the well-heeled sophisticates that populated the town when it was known as *the richest village in the world*. Their numbers had dwindled along with the diminishing quality of iron ore. And the number of guests crossing the Androy's impressive threshold, a marvel of Italianate terrazzo floors, had faded to a depressing trickle.

On their arrival, Stromberg immediately placed a long-distance call to Ann Darling from the lobby phone booth, anxious to get some assurance that their absence had, so far, gone unnoticed. She calmly reassured him that no one was the wiser. She had neatly covered their tracks, explaining to Bob Brenneman they had dashed off in pursuit of a major talent to plug the unexpected hole in the booking schedule. She had shrewdly avoided the subject of *where* they had gone, *who* they were pursuing, and *why* they might be operating in such a strangely surreptitious fashion. Ann was a fast-talking dynamo when she put her mind to it, using the slow burn and heavy lids to draw you in, then dancing circles around you with a crazed tango of dazzling elocution that left your mind spinning in directions you didn't see coming.

Ed avoided Ann at all costs. He possessed such genuine sincerity and linear thinking that less than a minute in the chaotic pandemonium of her presence left him reeling in a disorienting fog. So Bob, as the show's producer, became Ed's protective intermediary, dealing with Ann's oblique explanations by simply accepting them at face value, assuming that her trippy elucidations would somehow make sense once they had finally settled and aged a bit.

"So everything's good then?" Stromberg said, angling for further confirmation to soothe his nerves.

"Oh sure, it's all great," Ann said, hollow as a wet cardboard box.

But he was open to whatever meager carrot she'd offer. "Thanks, Darling."

"Seriously?" she said with smoky sarcasm. "You went there?"

"I couldn't resist."

"It wasn't funny the first time somebody said it. It's even less so now."

"You love it."

"Want me to throw some cold water on your jaunty spirit?"

"No thanks."

"Ed got the ratings for last week's show."

"Bad?"

"In the crapper. He's flipping out. And the network is shitting bricks."

"Trying to cheer me up?"

"Not in the least. But you better get back here soon. Or come up with something really huge."

They listened to each other's silence. The soft spitting clicks and static sliding up and down the line.

"So... how's that going?" Ann finally said.

"Consider me chastised. I won't make that dumb joke anymore."

"I couldn't care less, Johnny. You know I love it," she said. Then, with an opaque huskiness that she saved for the really serious stuff, "I got you covered for another day. Two tops. After that it's your ass. Probably mine too. Could mean all our jobs. But no pressure, Johnny. Enjoy yourself."

At dinner in the hotel dining room, Stromberg and Rafferty ate the prime rib special in silence, pushing the lumpy mashed potatoes around their plates, creating little snow drifts covered with slushy gravy.

"So, everything's cool?" Rafferty said.

"You know Annie. She's got it buttoned up."

"She's a real darling," Rafferty said with a snarky smirk.

Stromberg let it go. He'd done that dance already.

The broad hotel dining room was dark and musty with a prevailing aroma of old carpet, the moldy pad beneath it compressed flat as a crepe. There were only a couple other patrons seated at scattered tables, eating with slow precision, silver utensils tinkling faintly against the very old fine china, some of it chipped. The rest of the hotel seemed equally vacant, apparently occupied by only a few guests.

The deadpan waiter was one of those unobtrusive older gents; the guy who trails you around the hardware store to help you find mislabeled paint cans, the right sized nail or a quarter-inch nut. In his late sixties and should have been retired but still at it because it's what he does, he's good at it and you need him.

"Enjoy your meal," he said with a slow dusty flatness, shuffling away.

"I don't know about this band, this Ziggy Jett thing." Rafferty made the observation while slicing a hunk of knotty gristle off his slab of prime rib that wasn't so prime. "Could be a wash."

"Or maybe not."

"I don't get it. Why don't we just cut straight to the chase? Come right out and ask somebody?"

"Might be exactly what they want."

"Well, there you go."

"But that's not what we want."

"How you figure?" Rafferty said, dropping his knife, giving up on the gristle.

Stromberg continued smoothly, "We don't want to tip them off who we are until we know for sure if this guy and his band are the real deal or not." He paused, then added with a folksy lilt and knowing wink, "We need to know if the fish is worth catching before we drop a worm on the hook."

Rafferty's shoulders twitched. "What're you getting' all Minnesota on me now? Since when do you fish? You gonna go hunting mooses next?"

"I don't think that's the plural of moose."

"Meese then."

"I think it's just moose. Whether you got one or two or a dozen. Just moose. Like deer. One deer, two deer...ya know."

Rafferty contemplated that. "What about goose and geese? How do you explain that?"

"I don't. Look, point is we gotta blend in. Not show our cards while we're poking around."

Rafferty leaned back, both palms up, "Like we don't stick out already."

"They don't know who we are. We could be mine company reps from Monsanto. Businessmen looking to open a paper mill. Whatever."

Rafferty nodded slowly, starting to see it. "So then they don't suspect we're specifically trying to find this Ziggy Jett character."

"Exactly. We're just a couple guys on a business trip looking for some entertainment."

"But not hookers."

"*Musical* entertainment."

"I was just kidding."

"I can never tell with you."

"I'm slippery that way," Rafferty said with a cockeyed grin. He liked to yank Stromberg's chain occasionally, just to break his confident rhythm.

"If this Ziggy guy and his band turn out to be garbage, we gotta hightail our asses back to the city before we get canned."

"And if they're good?"

HIDING IN HIBBING

"Not just good. Gotta be great. Fantastic. Blow-the-lid-off *amazing*. We need to find an act that'll shake up the whole country. Elvis big. *Beatles* big. Snag ratings that'll fucking resuscitate the show from the brink of death. Give it a whole new purpose, instead of all that recycled Senor Wences shit. We need to make Ed Sullivan synonymous with a new age of discovery."

"Like Columbus, only discovering new talent instead of America."

Stromberg blinked, stone faced. "Sorta, yeah, sorta. Revolutionary."

"George Washington..."

"That's old. We wanna go opposite of old."

"Mao tse Tung..."

"No, no..."

"Castro..."

"Reel it in, Paul. Forget all that for now. First we need to find out if these guys are even worth a crap."

Rafferty snapped his fingers, inspired. "Teen girls."

"What about 'em?"

"If these guys are great, who would be their audience? Teenaged girls. Right? Right? Remember the phone call? Screaming like banshees. We talk to them. We ask them."

Stromberg heaved a long sigh, letting it out slowly. "You ever talk to a teenaged girl?"

Rafferty thought about it. "Well, yeah. When I was a teenager."

"You remember anything they said? Anything you understood? That made any sense at all?"

Rafferty gave it serious consideration, scanning his memory for a viable example or anecdote, coming up empty. Now it was his turn to sigh. "You got a point."

"And how's it gonna look, two old farts like us, in overcoats, walking around town, strangers, chasing after young girls, hanging out talking with them."

"Like perverts."

"Bingo."

"We gotta keep a low profile."

They both fell into a silent funk, thinking.

"You know Bob Dylan's from Hibbing?" Rafferty said.

"Yeah, I heard that."

"Was a really big deal here, until he left, went to New York."

"I saw all those pictures at the Ramada. Local hero." Stromberg crooked his neck, looking down, as if searching for something on the floor. "When was it he was going to be on the show?"

"On Sullivan?"

"Well, yeah. That's the show we're talking about."

"Aw, hell, that was back, Christ, I don't know," Rafferty calculating, eyes flitting. "Maybe '63 I guess. Something like that."

"And he blew up, stomped out because Ed wouldn't let him play."

"Nah, that's not what happened."

"Ed wanted to throttle the little bastard."

Rafferty shook his head. "Nope."

"It was in all the papers."

"When the legend becomes fact, print the legend."

"That one of your dumb movie quotes?"

"*The Man Who Shot Liberty Valance.*"

"John Wayne, right?"

"Yeah, but somebody else said it."

"Jimmy Stewart."

"Nah. Another guy. One of the no-names."

"All I know is Ed hit the ceiling." Stromberg said, twisting his shoulders side-to-side to crack his back, tired of sitting. "I heard from everybody he went berserk."

Rafferty folded his arms, shaking his head. "I was there. You didn't even come on the show until fall of '65."

Stromberg scowled, squinting down at his plate of cold meat. Realized Rafferty was right. He'd left the Tonight

HIDING IN HIBBING

Show in September when Ed had called on him to join their staff. But that didn't mean he was wrong about what had happened. "Way I heard it, Dylan said he was going to sing some crazy ass..."

"*Talkin' John Birch Society Blues.*"

"Yeah, that thing. Made the Birchers out to be a bunch of lunatic Nazis."

"Not exactly," Rafferty said. "But the network censor... you remember Thorn Hammond... wanted Dylan to change to another song. The CBS lawyers were all in a big panic they'd get sued."

"What, by the wacko Birchers? Who cares? They're nuts."

Rafferty shrugged. "Yeah, go figure. But Dylan stuck to his principals, very polite about it, said if he couldn't do his song, he'd prefer not to do the show."

Stromberg just glared at him across the table. "So you're telling me there was no big blow up? Dylan didn't throw a crazy-ass tantrum, storm out? Ed didn't go ballistic?"

"All a crock of baloney. Ed actually liked the song. Thought it was funny. Fully supported Dylan's decision. Even came out and said so to the press. But, hey, they were looking for conflict, not cooperation. Nice-nice doesn't make as good a news story, so..." He shrugged again.

"And you know all this because...?"

"I was right there. Fly on the wall."

"I'll be damned," a tinge of disappointment in his voice.

"Gotta remember though, Dylan wasn't at his peak yet and we already had a full line-up for the show that night, so Ed wasn't really feeling the pinch. He didn't break a sweat making that call."

When Rafferty had first casually dropped Bob Dylan into the conversation, only minutes earlier, an entire scenario had instantly flashed through Stromberg's calculating mind. But that was when he still believed Ed was royally pissed off at Dylan. He figured if the hometown Hibbing boy had the brazen audacity to walk away from a spot on the most famous television show in America — callously rejecting an invitation from the uncontested toastmaster of the century — then Ed would be chomping at the bit to get his revenge and stick it to Dylan. And what better way to shove it in his face than to simply reach into the stew pot of Hibbing and pull out someone who was better, hotter, more talented than the recalcitrant and unappreciative Bobby Zimmerman.

But now that his expectations had been totally flipped, he envisioned a new approach. Ed Sullivan had always been an avid supporter of discovering new talent. He embraced the time-honored mantle of a showbiz Svengali, magically pulling unheralded stars from thin air and debuting them on his stage to an awed American audience. But if, as Rafferty indicated, he had famously lost his battle with the CBS censors and the network's lawyers, as well as the collective media, he might now crave an opportunity to strike back by reaching into Bob Dylan's own Minnesota backyard, pulling another shining star—indeed, a cluster of stars—into the American spotlight. Both retribution and redemption would be at hand. He would show the network that now threatened his very existence how an old dog could learn some new tricks—how a limping beast could reinvent itself on the run—capturing big ratings in the process.

Stromberg leaned back in his chair with a labored sigh. "These guys better be fucking great."

41

Joe stood in knee-deep snow outside a boxy clapboard house, sheets of rusted metal, cut in squares of various sizes, nailed to the front, concealing the damaged and rotted wood siding. On closer examination, the entire structure appeared in dire need of serious rehabilitation. A glow of muted yellow light seeped out from behind cheap curtains in the windows neatly framed by the surrounding pristine white drifts.

He looked at the folded paper napkin in his hand to confirm that the address scribbled there matched the badly oxidized metal numbers nailed beside the front door. His prolonged hesitation had nothing to do with indecision. He definitely intended to knock on the door. But in this extended moment he found himself enthralled by the strangely peaceful setting, consumed by the deeply muffled silence and bathed in a soothing light. It provided a respite from the contradictions that plagued his life.

Finally, when his legs began to shudder from the bitter cold, he stepped to the door and knocked. After a chill eternity, marked by the indecipherable murmur of voices from within, the bolt clicked and the door swung open. The bleach-blond woman, whose name was Marjorie, stood in the doorway. She was dressed in a pink bathrobe, a long tress of hair coiled around a large plastic roller atop her head. A wispy curlicue of smoke snaked upward from the cigarette she held at her side. She appeared somewhat stunned, but not unhappy to see him.

Behind her in the house, *Gunsmoke* played on the TV. Marshall Dillon was telling someone to go fetch Doc and have him meet him at the Long Branch in fifteen minutes.

Without saying a word, Marjorie raked the roller from her hair with a smooth stroke of her hand—the one without the cigarette—and pulled the door open wider to make room for him to enter. Joe stepped inside.

On the other side of Hibbing, the perpetually ponytailed Sally Johansson cornered Gallagher in the small kitchen of her second floor apartment, hands all over him, giggling with giddy abandon while the unattended Chef Boyardee spaghetti sauce bubbled over on the stove.

"You sure do get ebullient," he said, letting her plant wildly enthusiastic kisses up and down his neck. She pulled back abruptly, not sure if she'd just been insulted. Gave him a look, eyebrows pinched.

"You know...excited," he said, doing his best to clarify. "Amorous."

She continued to drill him with skeptical eyes.

"I love weird words. Like ebullient. Efficacy. Sanguine. Amorphous. I think my all-time favorite is rubberneck. And, of course, rumpus. That's a real...ummph!"

Sally shut him up by mashing her lips against his, practically devouring him on the spot. She reached behind him to flip off the gas burner, then dragged him toward the bedroom. Gallagher thought...*Who knew mere words could have such a powerful effect?*

She kicked her shoes off coming through the doorway, whirling around to nail him with a head-twisting soul kiss, her tongue darting around like a jittery minnow. Gallagher backed off, gasping for air, while Sally urgently tugged her blouse out of her jeans and pulled it over her head, snagging her ponytail in the jumble. She shrieked and giggled, yanking harder, helplessly unhinged. He was laughing now too, delighted by her comical struggle.

HIDING IN HIBBING

When she collided with the closet door, he finally dove to her rescue, plunging his arm into the tangle of sleeves and hair to wrench the blouse upward. Sally laughed dizzily, her face shimmering red, freckles glowing with exuberance. She popped the snaps on her jeans, stripping them off.

Gallagher stepped back, unbuttoning his shirt, starting to undo his belt. But then, stopped. Watching Sally wrestle with her jeans, he was abruptly struck by an ominous surge of apprehension. As she reached behind her back to unfasten her bra, he cautiously ventured, "Pumpkin?"

The frilly bra dropped at her feet. She paused, looking at him in deep puzzlement, nose wrinkled.

"What?"

"I said...pumpkin?"

"Why?"

"No reason." He shrugged. "Nothing."

"You mean like on Halloween?"

"Sure. I guess. Yeah."

"But it's winter. Halloween's over."

"Oh...yeah, right," he said with another wobbly shrug, as if just now realizing the seasonal discrepancy.

He gave her a beguiling grin, secretly driven by a dose of intense personal relief. Then whipped off his shirt with comical macho flair, throwing it across the room. Crooked his leg and grabbed his left shoe with two hands, hopping around on his right foot, trying to pull the shoe off, crashing into the dresser. His display of unbridled lunacy somehow stoked Sally's passions to unimagined new heights.

Things were much quieter at Maggie Thorsen's modest bungalow in the new housing development on 4th Street. Maggie was cuddled up against Ray on the couch in front of a crackling fireplace. She kissed Ray's cheek, a soft peck, absent any overriding passion, but not without guile.

"You like playing music?" she said. Then waited a long time for his answer, the fire flickering its steady warmth.

"It's alright."

She pulled her face back to study him, searching his eyes for more than his words were revealing. "Just... alright?"

"Has its ups and downs," he said, draining his beer bottle.

"Want another?"

"Sure," he said, leaning forward to carefully set the bottle on the oak and glass coffee table.

Maggie headed for the fridge. "Strohs? Pabst? Blatz?"

He shrugged. "You choose."

She returned with three bottles. "Got 'em all." Lined them up in a row on the coffee table.

"A regular beer buffet," he said, grabbing a Blatz.

She snuggled in next to him again. "This must be pretty tame for you, I betcha. Sitting around by the fire with a few beers."

"I like it," Ray said. "I like it with you."

Maggie let a half-smile play on her lips, careful to avoid eye contact.

"Not very exciting though, what with your usual wild parties. Girls bustin' down your door'n such."

"Yeah, well, that's overrated."

"You say. I've read all about the Stones...Beatles... Kinks. The groupies and all. Hard to be immune to that."

"Not my cup of tea," he said, sucking down another gulp of Blatz.

"You drink tea?"

"No."

She studied him with a cocked head, admiring his profile and feral mane. The dancing light from the fire made him appear untamed and fierce, despite his meditative stillness.

"You're a funny kind of musician."

"Oh yeah? How's that?"

"Ones I've seen, can't stop 'em. They always gotta be performing. It's like a sickness."

"Well, there's more to life."

"Uh-huh," Maggie said, not bothering to hide her skepticism.

"You know a lot of musicians?"

"My share, I'd say." Then, sitting up like a rocket, eyes ablaze with inspiration, "Hey...I know."

She hustled over to a coat closet near the front door. Pulled out an acoustic guitar, holding it up like a trophy. "Looka this. My ex left it."

"You're ex?" he said, sitting up a bit, wolf eyes flitting about nervously.

Waving it off with casual disregard. "Couple years back. A real piece of work, that one. 'Don't let the door hit your ass on the way out' I said. Didn't even take his toothbrush. And left this too."

She handed him the guitar. Ray took it, awkwardly feigning interest.

"Whoa, hey there. Isn't that something. Uh-huh... yeah." He spotted the name on the end of the neck. "A Harmony."

"You know your instruments."

"Says it right there."

Maggie turned it into a joke, masking her sly pleasure. "So you can read too, eh?"

They both laughed, their amusement laced with an undercurrent of tension. He had a creeping awareness that much more was transpiring in this moment than seemed readily apparent.

"Go on," she said. "Play something."

"Aw, no. We were talking. Having a nice conversation. Let's not ruin..." He let his words trail off, starting to lay the guitar down. But she didn't let him.

"Talk later." Pushed it back into his lap. "Come on." Putting on a little girl's pout. "One of your songs. Play, play."

Ray squinted hard into her glinting china blue eyes; tried drilling steel rods into her brain to turn her back. But his stern glare was easily deflected. He sensed she was inexorable

He tentatively plunked a couple strings, pretending to listen with serious concentration.

"Probably not in tune," he said.

"No. It is."

He tried a couple more strings, shaking his head slowly, summoning a pained scowl. "I don't know."

"My cousin was here at Christmas. Tuned it for me," she said. "It's right on the money."

Cornered, no easy avenue of escape, he continued to stall. Turned the instrument this way and that, checking it out from all angles. She observed him with a calm eye, sizing up every nuance of his behavior. Journalism school taught her *what* to look for, but it was those two psychology classes taught her *how* to look.

"You know," Ray said, "this might be one of those special, custom-made guitars." He studied it closely, eyes following the wood grain along the neck; a fastidious jeweler examining a rare diamond. "Yeah. See there. Where the wood joins the long part here. That's a particular special glue, I bet. And the strings, the way they lay down on the, uh..."

"Frets," Maggie offered.

"The frets, right. They're the same color as the, uh, turny things..."

"The tuning pegs," she said.

"Right." He looked right at her, deciding to play a *Joe* card. "We call 'em pips."

"Pips. Huh?"

"Or turks. Pips or turks. It's music biz thing," Ray said. Oh hell, he thought, why not just go whole hog? Jump in the deep end, see if he could tread water. "We got a whole different language. You'd be amazed by the history of the guitar."

She let her eyes go big, dazzled. "Yeah. I bet your version is really something."

"It's got plenty stuff you never heard before."

"I'll bet." She punched his arm good-naturedly. "But I wanna hear you play."

Dead end alley. No dodging this bullet. He clutched the neck of the guitar, trying to decide where to convincingly place his fingers. "Uh-huh, well, okay." He tried to recall his buddy, Thad, from Brooks Institute, fingering the strings of a Gibson and warbling *Kum-By-Yah* and all those other folky gems.

"Let's see, what can I play for you? Uhhh..."

"Do one from your show," she said, her voice steady, calm, smooth as ice.

He eyed the beer bottles on the table, glistening victims worthy of sacrifice.

"Okay. Yeah. Here's one..." he said, swinging the guitar into position on his knee. The neck slammed into the bottles, sending them flying. Beer gushed and the Pabst Blue Ribbon bottle shattered like tinsel. Ray scrambled to retrieve the broken glass.

"Damn! Geez, I'm sorry," he said. "Here..." Handed the guitar off to her like a hot potato. "Better take this damn thing away from me before I wreck your house. Get us both killed."

She held the guitar neck delicately between her fingers, watching him crawl around the carpet collecting bottle shards, his hands wet with foam. Didn't look like a rock star now, down there on his knees, she thought. Not at all.

42

Janey buried herself in the folds of a lumpy down comforter, the patchwork quilt that her grandma made, pulled up tight around the back of her neck to keep the chill out. She could still smell the familiar scent of her grandmother in the warm threads and crevices, inhaling the delicious warmth, soothed by its airy sweetness. Wrapping the downy edge of the quilt around her fingers, she scrunched it into a tight ball, pressing it against her face, eyes closed, consoled by the memories it conjured.

Ziggy had brought her home less than an hour before, parking at the end of the unplowed driveway. Neither of them had wanted the evening to end, so they huddled in the VW bus, slouched down in the cold seats, hands tucked into armpits, billows of damp breath fogging the windows.

"When your dad left, did you know he was going to?" Ziggy said, finally summoning the courage to ask one of the many questions on his mind all evening.

"No." she said, simple as that.

"Never said anything?"

"Not that I heard."

"Musta been tough. Coming right out of the blue like that."

She nodded. "I don't like surprises."

He waited for her to continue, but she didn't. He wondered if maybe he'd gone too far, become too personal. But he shoved the feeling aside, not wanting to cloud his new found confidence with doubt.

"You know where he went?"

She shook her head. "Far away, be my guess. Never came back, I know that. Never called. Never wrote."

"That must hurt."

"Not if you don't think about it."

Ziggy saw the curtains in the front window part slightly, a sliver of lamp light escaping, then they fluttered shut.

"Your mom..."

"She's okay," Janey said, not bothering to look. "She knows me."

"Hope you don't mind me asking about this stuff."

"I don't mind you asking."

"Okay."

"He was a miner. Mine supervisor they called it. But he sweated just as much as everybody else. Not much supervising involved."

"He told you about it?"

"I heard from others. Most the kids at school had somebody in their family worked the mines."

"Hard work, mining."

"All the work up here is hard."

Ziggy felt out of his element. His father had been a high school teacher, then an actuary for a small company in Chicago. What he did for a living didn't come close to the pure drudgery and hardship that Janey's father encountered.

"My dad had to double-out a lot," she said.

"Double-out?"

"Work two shifts in a row. Didn't see him much."

Ziggy wanted to commiserate — say something that would indicate he sincerely cared about her dismal plight. But the words in his head seemed thin and feeble, riddled with stale banality.

"He was at Consolidated Mineral for..." She hesitated, letting out a long sigh, having to think about it. Then shook her head. "I don't know how many years. Way before I was born. Then they shut it down. All he ever did was work that mine, his whole life. Didn't matter, they cut him anyway. One of the first."

"It's tough, losing a job," he said. Then wanted to bite his tongue. What did he know about it? Only job he'd ever lost was at the McDonalds in Skokie when he spilled Coke in the deep fryer, screwing up ten pounds of potatoes and backing up a long line of irritable customers out the door. He deserved to be canned.

"They argued sometime, yelled at each other, my parents. At night mostly. But I had my radio. Turned it up. Got a good signal out of St. Paul. Duluth too. On foggy nights even WLS in Chicago. Go down under the covers with a flashlight and my radio. So I didn't have to hear all that."

Ziggy fought a strong urge to put his arm around her and pull her close, let her know how sorry he felt. But he worried she might take it wrong. Think he was putting the moves on her, using her sad situation as an excuse to take advantage. But then she suddenly leaned into him, resting her head against his shoulder. It startled him for a moment, his whole body tensing.

"And then one morning, he was just gone," she said. "That's when my mom pretty much stopped talking."

After an empty space, Ziggy asked, "You think she's waiting for him to come back?"

"No," she said. "I think she's holding her breath, hoping he doesn't."

Later, in her own bed, drifting close to sleep, Janey heard a faint sound in the small room. She opened her eyes to see the glow of a lit cigarette in the darkness. Rising up on one elbow, she clicked on the lamp next to her bed.

Her mother sat in a nearby chair, a curl of smoke rising from the cigarette clamped between two plump fingers. Her face was a mushy blank.

"Mom?"

Her mother tapped the growing ash into an open palm, not even flinching.

"Your Granny," she said, voice smooth as silk, "she knew. You got a gift. When opportunity comes round, little girl, you best jump on it quick as ugly on a moose."

She pulled herself up out of the chair. "That's all I got to say." And turned off the lamp.

43

It was close to 3 a.m. when Gallagher set out on foot back to the motel. From Sally's place it was only a couple miles; down 4th Street, cut over at Birch Lane to Crest Avenue, six blocks or so on Howard, then 119 to the Ramada. He knew the route by heart now and walking gave him time to think about her, the crisp air stinging his lungs, the sharp bite of it clearing his brain of garbage.

She'd offered to give him a lift, but he'd said no, and she had rolled back over groggily muttering something he couldn't understand, falling right back into a deep slumber. He pulled the covers up over her naked back, admiring the graceful landscape of her youthful skin, pure as the winter drifts outside, nary a mole or flaw in sight.

While trudging over crunchy piles of plowed snow along Crest Avenue, he pondered the idea of insisting that his friends refer to him by his given name from now on. He imagined Sally calling him Anthony and he liked it. *Gallagher* seemed like such a flippant, generic dismissal of who he really was. There were plenty of Gallaghers in his family, but only one Anthony. It carried with it a distinct impression of authority and eminence, like Anthony Quinn, the Hollywood actor who kicked ass as Zorba the Greek. Or Marc Antony, Julius Caesar's good buddy in one of those Shakespeare plays. He let it echo over and over in his head, hearing different voices, each one lending the name a stronger sense of integrity.

HIDING IN HIBBING

He was so lost in his reverie he didn't even hear George's pickup truck roar up from behind, then abruptly swerve around him and skid hard on the slick ice, stopping diagonally in his path ahead, engine chugging like a heaving, breathless beast.

George and his buddies emerged from the truck, ominous silhouettes in the road, fists clenched, feet spread defiantly. Gallagher dropped his gaze to the fresh unbroken snow ahead, ignoring them, plodding relentlessly forward. This was Anthony walking now, unafraid and courageous, ignoring the obvious potential for disaster.

He strode right past them, never meeting their eyes, catching only a dark, hazy peripheral glimpse of George's boots on the road. Ten steps later, a rush of relief coursed through him. Five more steps and he found himself abruptly infused with a sense of rash confidence. Anthony Quinn as Zorba lit the fuse, but it was Anthony in *Guns of Navarone* that made him explode. He whirled around to face them.

"Hey!" he shouted, the sound of his voice raging louder than he intended in the still night.

George and his cronies didn't move.

"You're after the wrong guy," he said.

"Is that right?" George's silhouette said.

"Ziggy's not the one you want."

George took a few measured steps toward Gallagher, sliding into the dull glow of a distant streetlight.

"Ya don't say. Who'd that be then?"

"That would be me." He didn't intend his tone to be confrontational, but it came out that way.

Gallagher could see George's face harden as he turned to look back at his companions. They stirred restlessly, fists clenched tighter.

"But I swear," Gallagher said, "I don't know anything about your Pumpkin."

"Oh yeah?"

"I got enough to handle," Gallagher said, throwing in a little chuckle, hoping to ease the tension. "I got no interest coming anywhere near your Pumpkin."

"Well, that's real good, because nobody touches my Pumpkin, 'less I say so."

"Gotcha. We are totally on the same page. Understand completely."

George looked him up and down with a critical eye. "You're too damn scrawny and ugly anyway," he said.

"I agree. Hundred and ten percent," Gallagher said. "So... we're copacetic then?"

George tensed, shifting his body, tromping one boot down hard on the snow, as when a nervous horse irritably thumps the dirt with a hoof, challenging. "Copa what?"

"Copacetic."

George grimaced, perplexed anger bubbling up. He stepped toward Gallagher, coming toe to toe, towering over him.

"You being a smart ass?"

Gallagher caught a glimpse of George's buddies coming up behind him, their ominous dark shapes lurching forward.

"No, no. I'm sayin' we're copacetic, man. I got no interest whatsoever in your little Pumpkin."

The world abruptly stopped spinning. What began as a profound silence fell into an even deeper abyss.

"*Little?*" George said, teeth gritting, jaw set. "*Little?*"

Gallagher was bewildered. Rocked off balance.

"Yeah..."

George's fist shot out, a bolt of lightning slamming Gallagher's face.

The dull shadows behind George converged quickly. A torrent of punches and kicks rained down upon Gallagher in the darkness.

44

Ray knocked at Gallagher's door.
"C'mon Romeo. Let's go."
The door swung open. Gallagher's face looked like somebody had used it as a trampoline while wearing football cleats.
"Awww, Jesus!" Ray said. "I told you, man. I knew this would happen."
"Ziggy's in the clear now." Gallagher's proud grin was intersected and bent all cockeyed by a badly swollen cheek.
Ray pushed past Gallagher into the room, shut the door. "Those assholes did this to you, didn't they?"
"They won't bother him now."
"Christ. What'd you go and do, you dumb Mick?"
"I'm only half-Irish, Ray. My mother was Italian."
"So... you dumb Irish wop, look at you."
"I've seen worse growin' up in Philly."
"You're from Philadelphia?"
"Yeah, south Philly. Didn't you know?"
"You never said. I shipped out of Philly in the navy."
"No kiddin'. So, the streets then...you know."
Ray studied his pulverized face. "Aw, man. Christ. What happened?"
Gallagher shrugged. "Nothing, ya know. I ran into 'em last night. We just talked. Blah blah blah. Then this guy and his goons..."
"What guy?"

"The jerk who hassled Ziggy. Who'd you think I was talking about?"

"Yeah, him. Mean S.O.B. Thinks he's tough."

"Right. Big guy. He says, 'nobody touches my Pumpkin unless I say so.' And I told him, 'That's cool, man. I couldn't care less about your frickin' little Pumpkin'."

That's when it hit Ray like a frying pan to the noggin. Wham. Clarity. He blurted out a pained groan and laugh.

"Wait. You said *little* Pumpkin?"

"Yeah."

"And then he punched you?"

"Out of the blue. Bam. And his buddies too."

"Oh shit." Ray paced, shook his head in disbelief. "You dummy."

"What?"

"You don't get it?"

"Get what?"

"They're fruits."

"What?" Gallagher said, eyes blinking furiously, like he didn't hear right.

"Fairies, man. A bunch of pansies."

Gallagher's response was a dumb look.

"His pumpkin?" Ray said, as if it was blatantly obvious. "You know... his *pumpkin*." Unable to say it any clearer — he made goofy eyes down at Gallagher's crotch.

Gallagher stared, finding it hard to process this line of crap. Then, with a creeping awareness, "You mean his...?"

"Yes. His *little* pumpkin. You offended him, man."

"Nahhhh."

"You called his pecker a little pumpkin."

"Who calls their pecker a pumpkin?"

"Apparently fairies do."

"That makes no sense. A pumpkin is round. It's not shaped anything like a penis."

"Who knows why people come up with nicknames. My dad called his Aunt Thelma '*bulldozer*' and she was this skinny little thing, weighed no more than eighty-five pounds soaking wet."

"Maybe she drove construction equipment," Gallagher reasoned. "But a pecker does not, in any conceivable way, look like a pumpkin."

"I don't know. Could be it's orange or something."

Gallagher collapsed onto the corner of the bed, dazed. Was it really possible he'd been beaten to a pulp by a gang of backwoods fairies?

"Think about it," Ray said. "You insulted him very deeply."

Gallagher looked up. He still seemed unconvinced.

"They're human," Ray said. "Don't you think queers get their feelings hurt too?"

In the room next to his, Ziggy could hear a deep thrumming — the muddy rise and fall of unintelligible voices as Ray and Gallagher continued their heated debate. He pressed his ear against the wall, straining to interpret individual words in the muffled mush.

A fluttering of light and shadow on the curtains caught his eye. The steadfast groupies had reappeared once more, clustering outside the window of Ziggy's motel room. A temporary respite in the weather had now made their obsessive vigil—still driven by blind idolatry—a much more comfortable enterprise.

Ziggy peered out through a crack in the curtains, unsettled by the milling bodies seemingly driven by a secret hunger—waiting, waiting, waiting for some unspecified gratification.

Abruptly pushing the door open, Ray said, "Get away from the window, Zig. It just encourages them."

Ziggy turned to him, feeling queasy. "They're swarming again. We're like those poor suckers trapped inside that farmhouse in *Night of the Living Dead*."

"Yeah. Well check this out," as he moved out of the doorway, revealing Gallagher behind him.

Ziggy's stomach churned when he saw Gallagher's mauled face, marred by purple bruises and dull red splotches.

Two words blew out of him. "What happened?"

"Those bastards won't hassle you now, Zig," Gallagher said.

"You took all of 'em on?"

Gallagher shrugged. "One thing led to another..."

"Aw man. Why'd you do that? Jeez."

"Golden Rule. I believe 'Do unto others before they do it unto you'." Another shrug. "Or to someone else, ya know, who probably doesn't deserve it."

"You didn't even come close to saying that right," Ray groused. "And when did you become so freakin' religious?"

"I went to church. All the Gallaghers are Catholic. Not to mention the Marzettas."

"Your mom's side?" Ray said.

"Exactly. Irish and Italians, Catholic to the bone."

"This walking bruise, he grew up in Philly," Ray said to Ziggy. "You know that?"

"What? No." Then, to Gallagher, "I thought you were from Chicago."

"Come on. I told you guys a hundred-and-fifty times I'm from Philly. Don't you hear me?"

"We hear you," Ray said. "But we don't listen."

"How's that even possible?"

"Because we tune you out. Especially when you start talking all that Irish Italian Philly-wop shit."

"And on that subject..." Gallagher said.

"What subject?"

"My name."

"Your name? Who brought that up?"

"I'm bringing it up now."

"What about it?" Ray shouted, his voice climbing an octave.

HIDING IN HIBBING

"From now on I want to be called Anthony. Not Gallagher. Anthony."

Ziggy furrowed his brow. "Who's Anthony?"

"That's my name."

"I thought your name was Gallagher?"

"That's my family name. My given name is Anthony."

"Whatever," Ray said, throwing his hands up. "That's what you want, Tony, you got it."

"Not Tony. *Anthony.* Like Anthony Quinn."

"Who? Zorba the Greek?"

"He's not Greek. That's a movie. He's Italian."

"I thought he was Irish," Ziggy said.

"IRISH?" both Ray and Gallagher said, voices booming in unison.

"Quinn," Ziggy said. "Isn't Quinn Irish?"

Joe stepped through the open door, scowling. "What the hell is all the racket down here?" Then he saw Gallagher. "What the fuck happened to you?"

"Tony got a beatin'," Ray said.

"Who's Tony?" Joe said.

"I told you... it's Anthony."

"Who the hell is Anthony?"

Ziggy and Ray both pointed to Gallagher. "Him," they said together, like a Greek chorus.

"I thought your name was Gallagher," Joe said.

"It is. Anthony Maxwell Gallagher."

"Maxwell," Ray said, practically blowing snot out his nose, doubling over in convulsive laughter.

"From my uncle Max." Gallagher articulated each word with angry emphasis, not about to be chastised any further. "He got his leg practically shot off at Anzio in World War Two. And he was a fireman in Boston. Saved lives and... and..." A warm trickle of blood dribbled down the side of his neck from the cut on his cheek.

227

Joe eyed Gallagher's battered face with concern, carefully placing a hand on his shoulder. "Well, whoever they were, I hope you did 'em some damage."

"Not really," Gallagher said. "But I think they got it out of their system."

Joe turned a hard eye to Ray. "If he wants to be called Tony, call him Tony."

"Not Tony. Anthony," Gallagher said, tired of making the point.

"Like Anthony Quinn," Ziggy said. "The Irish movie star guy."

"He's Italian!" Gallagher said, fired up again.

Ray shrugged at Joe. "Apparently he's not Greek."

"The movie actor?" Joe said. "He's Mexican."

"What? No way. No!" Gallagher said.

"Yeah. We shot a Ford commercial with him. He was born in Chihuahua."

"Like the dog?" Ray said.

"Like the city," Joe said. "In Mexico."

Ray heaved a raw sigh. "We gotta blow Dodge. This whole freakin' mess was a bad idea right from the get-go."

"It's that kind of negative thinking got us into Viet Nam," Joe said, glaring.

Ray resisted an explosion, tucking it all back inside. But the flinty expression on his face said everything, despite the calm measure of his words.

"Yeah. Viet Nam was all my fault, Joe. I'll try real hard not to let that happen next time around."

"We got a break in the weather," Ziggy said, hoping to steer them back on track. "We could do it now."

"Yeah," said Ray, directing it at Joe. "Let's just go shoot this stupid beer commercial that you hold so near and dear so we can get our butts back home."

"We can't," Joe said.

"Sure we can."

HIDING IN HIBBING

"No, we can't. I met with the guy from Bemidji. A schmuck, this guy. The job's off. They had everything set up for Tuesday. Cheerleaders in bottle outfits..."

Gallagher brightened. "Cheerleaders?"

"Cool it, Gallagher," Joe said.

"Yeah," Ray jumped in. "Keep it in your pants for once, Tony."

Gallagher wanted to snap back at him, but was so happy he got a *Tony* out of Ray that he let it go. It wasn't exactly Anthony, but the day was young.

"Why not just simplify it?" Ziggy said, injecting a voice of reason. "We shoot some winter scenery. Snowcapped mountains. The forest. We stick a beer bottle in a babbling brook, icy water flowing over it. Then we superimpose one word...*Refreshing*. Then the name of the beer."

Stillness descended. They could all picture it in their heads.

"Don't go trying to solve this with solutions," Joe said. "Not your bailiwick."

"It's not bad, Joe," Ray said. "It does the trick, I think."

"No thinking," Joe said, as adamant as possible without yelling. "Doesn't matter. They don't care. Bottom line is, the job is off. No job, no money. We're screwed."

"So we came all the way up here for nothing?"

"Don't remind me."

"Hiding out here, floating a big lie."

"On my nickel, I might add."

"It hasn't been that terrible," Gallagher offered.

"There's a ringing endorsement for ya," Ray said. "Tony liked it."

"Out of my pocket. Every penny," Joe said.

"Except for all the great freebies we got," Gallagher noted, then wished he hadn't. Joe's caustic glare made it clear he would no longer throw any sympathy in Gallagher's direction.

"Pack up the bus, Ziggy. We're getting out of here this afternoon."

Ziggy nodded glumly at Joe, scanning the clutter of equipment cases.

Gallagher flung himself into a diving roll across the bed. "I gotta get some phone numbers." And raced out the door.

Ray rested his hand on Ziggy's shoulder. "Stardom is a fleeting thing, man. Top of the world one day, bottom of the heap the next."

45

Ziggy was about to knock on the door, when it flew open with a rush of air and a rusty squeak. Janey glowed with excitement

"Come in, come in," she said, waving him toward her with a flapping hand. "I'm on the phone with Carl. I'll be right out."

She scurried away down the hall to her room, leaving him alone in the cramped vestibule. He didn't dare move a muscle, for fear Janey's formidable mother might hear the squeak of a floorboard or sense a tiny disturbance of dust and come charging in to confront him with an axe, or worse.

But the air hung in layers of stagnant silence, a distant ticking clock and the normally undetectable settling of the ancient wood-framed house the only signs of life. Ziggy held his breath and leaned forward slightly, peering into the gloomy living room. It was empty. Curtains drawn tight, shutting out the world.

He stepped in with tenuous caution, gently rocking forward on each foot, from heel to toe, so as not to slap a footstep down on the hard surface or squeeze a creaking ache from the interlaced oak slats.

Small framed photographs and a few odd knick-knacks captured his eye. One ornate brass frame contained a creased photo of a man and woman. She was lithe and agile looking, with a kind smile and twinkling, spirited eyes. Her hairstyle seemed audaciously flippant for the apparent period of the photo, perhaps the early 1950s. The man beside her looked dour and irritable, as if awakened unexpectedly from an afternoon nap and forced into some horribly disagreeable activity. His foot rested on the front bumper of a Buick, a pose that would normally seem jaunty and casually cavalier, but here looked strangely aggressive.

Ziggy wondered... Could this be Janey's mother and father? He sucked in a sudden bite of air, pressing his lips together tightly. Did he just think that or had he actually whispered it aloud? He wasn't sure.

On a lopsided pine credenza he spied another picture, this one of Janey and a trim, wrinkled little woman with a captivating smile and bright eyes. They were arm-in-arm, their tangle of limbs clutching each other tightly. It had to be her grandmother.

Down the hall, he could hear the very faint sound of Janey's voice, muffled and distant. Another sound arose, a barely audible melody. Maybe a radio; he couldn't tell. The hushed music wafted from an open doorway off the small living room, undulating softly on the glow of warm light.

Driven by curiosity, he moved cautiously toward the doorway, feeling like an intruder even though he had been graciously—no, *enthusiastically*—invited in.

He peered around the doorframe edge, Janey's corpulent mother sliding ominously into view. He stopped abruptly, pulling back slightly holding his breath, undetected.

She stood at the kitchen counter, gazing out the small frost-covered window, her massive body pressed against the porcelain sink, splashes of water dampening her faded tent-like housedress.

At first he thought she was talking to herself, muttering in a random lilting manner. But then it came clear. She was singing. Softly. That pop ballad from the fifties about the pyramids along the Nile. Her voice was pure and sweet, flowing like a gentle river from her fleshy mass. Ziggy listened, transfixed.

You Belong To Me. That was it. He recalled his parents listening to it on the car radio, singing along, gazing at each other with goofy smiles and a secret look of euphoria that he couldn't decipher at his naive young age. Adult behavior is particularly elusive and inexplicable when you are only eight.

But now, standing in the shadows, he couldn't manage to connect Janey's imposing mother to the angelic voice he heard floating above the splashing in the sink. Its incongruity disturbed him, setting him off balance. He imagined Janis Joplin opening her mouth and the voice of Frank Sinatra emerging, distorting reality beyond all logic. But at the same time, it was beguiling; and in its direct soulful simplicity, truly enthralling. After a moment, he prudently backed away, discretely retreating to the foyer, relinquishing her to the privacy she deserved.

"Carl gave me the whole day off," Janey said, jumping into the VW bus like an ecstatic kid sprung from school.

"I've only got a couple hours."

Disappointed, Janey said, "Oh..." then bounced back. "Like my granny would say, 'two hours is better than no hours'."

"Sorry."

"It's okay," she said with sincerity so heartfelt that it made him choke up. "Where we going?"

"Thought you might show me around."

"Hibbing?"

"Yeah, and, you know, all around."

"Not much to see. Bunch of old mine tailings. World's biggest open pit iron mine."

"That sounds cool."

And standing on the edge of a monstrously vast scar scraped in the earth, snow whipped by harsh winds into rolling drifts resembling infinite white dunes of a sub-zero Sahara, it was more than cool; it was freaking freezing. Ziggy shivered in the blast of arctic air, spine gnarled up into tight aching knots that shot like icy lightning bolts up through his vertebrae into the base of his neck.

"See, not much to look at," Janey said. "Hull-Rust-Mahoning Mine. We just call it the Hull-Rust. Mostly we call it 'the pit'. This is what tourists would come to see if tourists ever came here. But they don't."

Ziggy shuddered, hands pocketed, nodding to disguise his shivers.

Janey eyed him with a canted grin. She was so used to the deathly cold and vile slashing wind that it never even entered her mind anymore.

He was first back into the bus, cranking it up while Janey climbed in. She found something terribly attractive about Ziggy's willingness to suffer the cruel indignities of a Minnesota winter for her, especially when he failed so miserably to hide his extreme discomfort. The engine turned over on the third try and the small heater spit out some pathetic coughs of warmth that did little to diminish his shivering.

They left the high ridge of the pit behind, dropping into the broad valley that ran past several long-abandoned mining operations. Rusted ore crushers and hydraulic grinders stood as mute testament to the once vibrant industry that had dominated the Misabi Range since the early 1800s. Rising ahead of them he saw a massive sprawling crust pulverizer, its broad splay of conveyor belts supported on graceless twisted appendages; a steel spider flipped on its back, corroded insect legs outstretched to the sky. Gelid snow powder clung to its rusted surfaces; the bleak dust of time.

Ziggy swerved off the road into a broad parking area adjoining a cluster of ghostly mine buildings, iron sheds and squatty Quonset huts.

"Wow. It's like some alien city of the future, only from the past," he said, jumping out with renewed enthusiasm.

Janey climbed out of the VW to join him, wrinkling her nose at his odd observation. She gave the decayed structures a second look to see if she might be missing something.

"Sometimes you're a little, I don't know, I guess, kind of... different?" Gently twisting it into a question instead of a judgment.

Still taking it in, he said, "Just 'cause it's ugly, doesn't mean it isn't pretty darn cool to look at."

She gave it a third try, but still couldn't see it. But then again, she thought, maybe he had the eye of an artist and she was just seeing it as it was, instead of as it could be.

Out of the biting wind now, the air felt more comfortable to Ziggy; it was almost bearable by Chicago standards. He locked on Janey's eyes with a steady gaze, long enough to make her wonder what was up. She raised her eyebrows, tilting her head quizzically, opening the door for him to let it all out. But he balked, pivoted away, pacing off a couple quick circles in the snow, his twitchy wandering an oddball prelude. Finally, sucking in a long fortifying breath, he ratcheted up enough courage to risk making a fool of himself.

"I've got this idea..."

"Oh boy, here we go again," she said, teasing him.

"I know, I know, but listen. You're going to think I'm nuts..."

"I accept that as a given," she said, enjoying this familiar bantering, beginning to feel that she could hold her own with him.

"I have this idea..."

"You said that already."

He paused, rocking back and forth from the waist. Raised a finger up, as if about to speak, then rotated his hand, wiggling the digit, summoning her to the back of the VW bus. Popped the rear door open, raising it to reveal a cluster of metal cases.

She waited with expectation, certain there must be something more to this. He flipped the latches on one of the cases, opening the lid, revealing an Eclair 16MM motion picture camera nestled in protective molded Styrofoam.

Janey reacted with a blink. "I thought you had guitars and music stuff in these."

It caught Ziggy off guard. "Oh, yeah. Well, we do. But, uh, we've got a camera too."

"For when you film your concerts," she said.

He hadn't even thought of that. "When we...? Right. Yeah. Exactly." He dropped a quick, inspired smile.

"Looks expensive."

"It is, yeah. I'm sure."

"You know how it works?"

"I could probably figure it out," he said.

The lies just kept piling up. Not lies, really. More like selective distortions of reality. Ziggy had been messing with movie cameras since he was seventeen when Wayne Long asked him to help shoot sideline footage at a Bears game with his dad's 16mm Bolex. Soon as he had that camera in his hands, he was hooked. The whirring sound of gears spinning madly inside, pulling celluloid strips past a chattering shutter; a mechanical symphony that changed his world. Wayne's father was head of the team's promo department, so it wasn't long before Ziggy was recruited as an assistant on the camera crew, loading film mags and pulling focus.

Janey touched the softly curved edge of the Éclair with a delicate finger, sliding it along so slowly it verged on sensuous.

"I want to film you," Ziggy said.

Janey snapped her hand away as if burned. "Me? Oh no. Uh-uh. I'd break the lens."

Ziggy laughed. "I don't think so."

She was clearly flattered, but did her best to hide it. Taking on a serious manner, cocked head, eyeing him askance, she said, "Why would you want to do that?"

He had her attention. "Okay, see, I film you singing..."

"Oh no," shaking her head, hands raised to ward off that image.

"Wait, wait, wait..." He flipped a smaller case over, unsnapping the latches and opening it; a Nagra tape recorder inside. "I play your tape, the song you did last night. You sing along with it while I film you. Then I edit the film together, add your song back in. It'd be like a movie of your song."

"You can do that?"

"Why not?"

"I don't know," she said, staggered by the unfamiliarity of what he proposed. "I don't know why not. I've just never heard of that before."

"You will."

"I will?" she said, taken aback.

"It's gonna be the next big thing. You'll be able to turn on the television and there'll be a channel with nothing but music films—these short music films—a whole song, top to bottom, around the clock, twenty-four hours a day."

"And you know this, how?" she said, smiling cutely, keeping it playful.

"I don't *know* it. I can just...feel it. Music TV. It's gonna happen."

"That sounds crazy."

"Sure it does. Isn't crazy what makes the world go round?"

46

Ziggy knew he couldn't throw this at Janey all at once. He needed to gain her confidence, nurture her trust.

That was a lesson he'd quickly learned when working on TV commercials with Joe and his crew back in Chicago. If you made the talent uneasy or spooked them, say, by screaming like a maniac—*get the goddamn scrim on that fucking fresnel!*—before they'd even had a chance to shovel in their doughnuts and coffee, the whole day could be ruined.

So rule number one was: *Always make the performers feel comfortable.* Safe. Secure. And never rehearse them too much because it kills their spontaneity and dampens their enthusiasm. This became abundantly clear to Ziggy when he worked on a regional commercial shoot for Krogers in Buffalo Grove. It featured three kids singing the praises of canned Spaghetti-O's.

The director was a Hollywood reject, a clueless goofball slumming after being booted from the hit comedy series *Get Smart* for insistently telling Don Adams how to read his signature line, "Missed it by *this* much."

Desperate to reestablish his wounded authority, the director forced the three hapless eight-year-olds to run their lines over and over as they devoured bowls of the pallid little pasta ovals drenched in bland marinara. By the time he felt he'd recaptured control of his life, the kids were burned out, listless and gorged on carbs. All it took was his impatient muttering of an expletive to stir their anxiety and cue an esophageal volcano.

HIDING IN HIBBING

One kid upchucked on the table, instigating the two remaining kids to spew on the director. Other than the unfortunate assistants forced to clean up the disgusting mess, the crew was delighted. The agency producer, however, was livid. As for the doofus director, he was last observed selling used cars in Livonia, Michigan.

Keenly aware that singing again so soon might spook Janey, Ziggy had already decided to gently ease her into it by first shooting some B-roll footage.

"I have an idea," he announced, as if struck by a sudden flash of inspiration.

"Another one? Oh, good, good," she said with a sense of great relief. "How about lunch? We could get lunch. I know this burger place on Donnel Street."

"I was thinking I could shoot some footage of the, uh, the landscape ya know. All this stuff..." He swooped his arm at the dilapidated buildings and monster machinery.

"Really?" Her mouth turned down, nose scrunched up, eyes scanning the stark scene, not seeing the potential.

"Yeah. And, uh, you, sort of...frolicking around in the snow."

"Me? Frolicking? I don't think I've ever frolicked."

"Okay, bad word choice," he said, chagrined. "Playing in the snow. You know, just having fun."

She tightly scrunched the fingers of one hand in the grasp of the other, swaying reluctantly from side to side, a small girl dreading her first day of kindergarten.

He didn't push. Just looked at her with calm stillness, his undemanding gaze gently enticing her into his circle of influence. "Come on," he said, "it'll be easy. You can do it."

She turned away, looking off, so he couldn't captivate her further.

"What would I have to do?" her small voice asked.

His smile suggested an impish complicity. He pulled a circular film magazine from the black case, opening the

239

camera body to expertly slide the teardrop loop of celluloid into the mechanism and slip the sprocket holes into place on the rollers.

She watched this with admiration; fascinated by the easy flow of skilled movements his fingers made, deft and precise, yet vigorous and sure. She flinched in reaction to the camera door snapping shut, its sharp finality announcing that her participation was imminent.

Without preamble, he rolled the camera, calmly talking her through a steady series of random actions: clambering over conveyors, twirling on snow-dusted hillocks of taconite tailings, teetering with precocious imbalance on loader arms. All the while letting the camera find its own way—tilting askew, spinning dizzyingly, then upside down, close and far, the glint of sun flares wiping the lens with rainbow smears— unburdened by rules or limitations. He filmed Janey with the freedom of someone unaware that "you can't do it that way"... driven by a flow of his own intuition, devoid of fear or hesitancy.

Ziggy swiftly changed film magazines with the slick ease of an experienced soldier reassembling his M-1 rifle, his gentle patter continuing unabated, keeping her in his easy embrace of confidence. She spun and danced and pouted for the lens, her brittle cloak of reticence melting away.

Janey jumped off the long conveyor arm protruding from the ore crusher, slipping on a slick mound of snow, landing on her butt. Ziggy plopped down next to her, laughing, breathing hard, clutching the camera firmly as if it was a precious infant.

Janey sucked in a long breath of crisp air, exhaling a damp vapor cloud that swirled lazily before her eyes. She peered into it, through it, an adorable smile on her lips.

"It'd be fun to be a beatnik," she said out of the blue.

"Beatnik? Why?"

She shrugged shyly. "Be different than what I am."

"I like what you are."

"Or a hippy," she said quickly, attempting to deflect the weight of his compliment.

"A hippy? Really?"

"Yeah. Sure. They're cool." She gazed off, delicately biting her bottom lip. "I always wanted to go off to San Francisco." She squinted one eye shut, looking at him with the other, a glimmer there. "I'd be sure to wear some flowers in my hair."

They both laughed at the familiar song reference, eyes fixed on each other, pausing to let the sappy, but undeniably silky smooth, vocal of Scott McKenzie float through their heads. After a weighty moment, Ziggy said, "Probably not all it's cracked up to be, being a hippy."

He instantly sensed her disappointment as the rush of exhilaration she felt suddenly drained away. He quickly added, "But I bet it would sure be fun for a while." He cast a forced twinkle her way, hoping to repair the breach.

Her dimples reappeared, cutting lively valleys into both cheeks. Those dimples. My God. They worked on him magically, sending an acute charge of elation coursing through his chest. He swiftly raised the camera, aiming the lens at her. Found her image in the viewfinder. Then, trolling for a clever composition, he caught sight of the bullet-dented, oxidized sign attached by twisted wire to the chain link fence behind her.

Mesabi Range Mineral — No Trespassing — Property Closed — Keep Out.

The mining company Janey's father had worked for, been fired from, been screwed over by.

Ziggy dropped the camera into his lap. "You know, we probably got all we can get here. Let's move on, see what we can find someplace else." He managed to keep his words logical, steady and unhurried. But no matter how hard he tried, he couldn't prevent his eyes from nervously darting to the sign over her shoulder.

Janey turned to glance behind her. "I know," she said. "It's okay, I don't mind. That stuff's all in the past."

Ziggy nodded, rolling his eyes back with relief.

She seemed able to effortlessly read his mind, plumb the private depths of his soul. It left him feeling naked, but unashamed; somehow vulnerable, yet undaunted. It was, oddly enough, a pleasant sensation.

"Are there any lakes around here?"

"It's Minnesota," she said, raising her eyebrows, tickled by the obvious nature of his question.

"Oh yeah. Right."

"Swan Lake isn't far."

"Seriously? *Swan* Lake?"

"Hey... I didn't name it."

47

The curvy road etched its way down thickly forested hills to Swan Lake, a vast expanse of ice blanketed by a layer of crystal snow. It was lightly crusted over from the trivial surface melt created on those rare days the elusive sun poked through, then frozen hard again at night. In the far distance, tiny specks dotted the lake; the shacks of ice fishermen, hardy souls—some would say foolhardy—who found solace and delight in squatting for long hours in makeshift sheds, staring down into small blue holes between their feet, clad in bulky layers of thick weather-resistant woolens and clunky boots, patiently waiting for hungry pike to chase hooks disguised with meager bits of bait. To outsiders, particularly those from the Deep South and sunny California, it appeared insanely grueling behavior. But to denizens of the far North Country it remained an inexplicably cherished tradition.

Just off the road, the shoreline leveled out, making access to the lake by vehicle an easy trick. Spotting a good entry point, Ziggy twisted the steering wheel to the left, launching the VW diagonally across the oncoming lane and out onto the ice, exploding a spray of dry snow drifted at the lake edge. The bus went into a slide when it hit the ice, skidding sideways, then twirling in a long lazy circle as Ziggy let off the gas.

Janey's arm was braced hard against the door, legs straight out and rigid on the floor panel, as the vehicle glided to a stop facing the road, now sixty feet away. Her face was a ghastly pale, eyes *Moon Pie* wide, as she turned to see Ziggy's enormous grin of delight. Air rushed from her lungs with a loud whoosh as she released the petrified breath she'd been holding, followed by a laugh-gasp-shriek of liberation on the intake of more air. Her heart tried to beat its way out of her chest with a crazed pounding rhythm.

"That'll get your pulse racing," Ziggy said.

She rolled her eyes broadly, a silly character in her own comic strip. Pulled herself upright in the seat, out of the low-slouched, tense-limbed crash position she had instinctively assumed.

"We used to do that all the time," Ziggy said, still giddy and grinning.

"What? Scare girls to death?"

"No," he said. Then shrugged, straight-faced. "Not intentionally, anyway."

The spiky rise-and-fall of adrenaline racing through her veins pumped another staccato laugh out of her.

"We'd stay at my uncle's cabin on Gun Lake in Michigan every winter." Ziggy twirled his finger. "Go lake spinning."

"Lake spinning?"

"You know. Wheelies on the water."

Janey looked into her lap with a whimsical nod and wisp of a smile. "We call it ice cruising."

"So you've done it then."

Shook her head. "Uh-uh. My first time."

"What? That's unacceptable." He revved the engine, popped the clutch and they shot away, spinning a dozen broad circles on the ice, tires spraying bursts of snow in their wake.

They rocked to a stop in the middle of the lake, laughing deliriously.

"There ya go," Ziggy said. "Second time's even better. You're no longer a virgin."

That plunged them into a weighty silence. The word had just slipped out; no suggestive implication was intended.

But the mere introduction of it had carried them into an unexplored realm.

Both of them stared out at the white panorama, as stark and empty as the stillness in their ears. Ziggy feared he had thrown down a troubling gauntlet, somehow signaling a questionable intent that would drive her away. Their relationship was already on a fragile course as he pushed and prodded her to move in directions she previously resisted. Push too hard and he could frighten her back into a dark cave of false security, hidden beneath the blankets of her bed, comforted by a flashlight and a radio.

But his gloomy fear was pleasantly capsized when she abruptly leaned toward him, kissing him on the cheek, then quickly leaped out the door. She raced out onto the lake, arms spread, twirling with uninhibited bliss, dropping on her back in a feathery berm of white crystals to make a snow angel.

Later they sat on a small hillock of snow they'd scraped together, a rumpled throne from which they could survey their vast glacial kingdom. It was uncomfortable, but they didn't care.

"I used to ice skate here," Janey said. "We'd shovel off a big patch where the ice wasn't rippled and just skate all day."

"Wish I could have seen that."

"When I was younger," she said. "Not for a long time."

Janey surveyed the snowfield, letting her mind drift forward and back; a random slide show of memories.

"I know there's probably some single moment when childhood ends and being an adult begins," she said, unprompted by anything but her own sifted memories. "It's already come and gone for me. But I'm not really sure when it happened. Like it was invisible. As if somebody sneaked in during the night and changed the channel on my life, then everything was different. I never felt it coming, being a grown-up, you know. And I never got a chance to say goodbye to being a kid." She rested her chin in the palm of her hand, elbow on her knee, unfocused eyes turned inward. "It would have been nice—having a little more time to let go."

Ziggy stared out at the frozen lake. He could relate to what she was saying and it gave him a chill. It hadn't come and gone for him, he thought. Not yet. Now he'd have to watch out for it, so it didn't somehow slip by without notice. Digesting her words, Ziggy concluded Janey was a whole lot smarter than he was, or at the very least, much wiser. He turned to gaze at the alluring dimple in her cheek. From the side it was even more beautiful.

"We better do this before the battery dies," Ziggy finally said.

He pulled Janey to her feet, then jogged back to the metal boxes stacked in the snow. Removed the Nagra recorder from its metal case and cued up the tape, plugging in a small portable speaker. She watched closely, heart beating faster, unable to tell if the pounding in her chest was prompted by a dread of singing again or the more complex fear of embarrassing herself in front of Ziggy.

He shouldered the Arriflex, casually grasping it with one hand like the pro she didn't know he was. Turning to her, a look of wonder illuminated his face.

"This is perfect. Those hills behind you. The woods. Sky. Perfect. Gonna look great."

She peered over her shoulder at the winter panorama, seeing it with new eyes. She had to admit, it was impressive, although until this moment she would never have thought of it that way. Winter was always cold and dreary and long and dark, but never perfect. Yet now, at this instant, it felt strangely flawless and even unexpectedly warm. She unzipped her parka, letting it hang open as she braced herself, feet set wide.

"Ready?" he said, raising the camera up into position.

"No."

"You sure?" he said with a laugh.

"Never."

"Great. I'll roll the tape and when you start singing... you start singing."

"Okay," she said, then muttered low, "I guess."

"You know what I mean."

"Yep."

"Okay...happy...upbeat...happy happy..." he said.

"What?"

"Nothing nothing," Ziggy said. "I was just trying to direct you."

"Oh. Better not. I won't know what to..."

"Okay."

"Just play it... I'll go."

"Okay, here goes. Three...two...one."

He started the tape. A few seconds of dead air passed as Janey bounced lightly in place, nervously preparing to slide into the rhythm.

The camera chattered softly. "I'm rolling," he shouted, his voice jumping up an octave to a shrill girly voice.

The music started and she began to move and sway. Ziggy started to sway with her, not even realizing it until he saw the image rocking and bouncing in the viewfinder. He stopped abruptly, getting a grip on his eagerness, forcing himself to stay focused.

Janey nailed the sync on the introductory *"come ons,"* clenching her small fists, glaring into the lens with brazen intensity, rolling with ease into the opening verse that traced a woman's journey from trust to a painfully broken heart and back again.

Janey's mom had once told her *"eyes are windows to the soul"* and it stuck with her, challenging her to peer inside others and find the truth, whether pleasant or not. And, she reasoned, if you could actually read someone's soul through those portals of wisdom, you should conversely be able to share a vision of your own true self as well. That is, if you dared.

Ziggy moved to his left, sidestepping gingerly in the snow, striving to keep the shot smooth. Instinctively, Janey responded to his lateral movement, shifting subtly to maintain eye contact with the lens.

And then, as she hit the final run of wailed *"come ons"*... Janey abruptly stopped, her mouth agape, eyes expanding wide in horrified distress.

"No no no. Keep going," Ziggy said, his eye glued tight to the viewfinder.

But Janey's body went limp. She seemed to shrink within her parka. As the relentless music pounded on, Janey numbly raised her arm, a trembling finger pointing at something behind Ziggy, over his left shoulder.

He turned to see the VW bus slowly sinking through the cracking ice, the front end tilting skyward, as if taking a last helpless gasp.

On the audiotape, the intrusive clamor of the two drunk creeps cut through the music, howling wildly as they pounded their table. Janey's recorded voice abruptly wavered and splintered, then vanished in the wake of a mumbled sob.

In nearly sadistic comedic fashion, the tumultuous instrumental climax accompanied the sinking vehicle as it disappeared beneath the frozen surface of the lake.

Ziggy first, then Janey, collapsed onto the ice, sitting like lumps, deflated, staring numbly at the starkly empty snowfield, as the tape ran out.

48

"What the fucking hell, Zig!"

Ziggy sat on the edge of Joe's bed, head slumped, chin digging into his chest with remorse.

Joe paced around him, an angry bull. He was so lividly pissed he could barely find words profane enough to express himself.

"I just thought..." Ziggy said.

"Don't. I told you not to do that. No thinking. You're not qualified. Leave thinking to people got the capacity for it."

Joe's words were articulate and certainly coherent, but if he could have added a verbal exclamation point to every one of them, he would have. Little dabs of angry spittle had gathered at the corners of his mouth.

"I saved the camera..." Ziggy said.

"Jesus Christ."

"And the Nagra. I saved the Nagra."

"You lost the goddamn *BUS*," Joe said, exclamation point assumed. "And why? Because you were filming a *girl*."

Ray said, "I told you, man. She's a user." Ray was in the room too, slouched in a chair, comfortably secure in his early prediction that this was all going to go haywire.

"She's not a user," Ziggy said.

Joe's eyes jumped between Ray and Ziggy. "The waitress, right?"

"She got you to film her, didn't she?" Ray said.

"It was *my* idea," Ziggy came back.

Gallagher sat on the dresser, taking it all in. "Which one? The cute one? Dark hair with the big...?"

"The whacko one," Ray said. "Who pulled the cryin' jag to sucker this poor idiot."

"The cry-baby?"

Ziggy lunged at Gallagher, growling, knocking him off the dresser. Gallagher scrambled to his feet, flailing his arms defensively. Ziggy took a sloppy swing at him, missed by a good six inches. Lost his balance and fell against the dresser, bumping his head into the wall.

Joe and Ray grabbed Ziggy's arms, trying to get the unexpected tornado under control.

There was a knock at the door. A gentle rapping.

"Okay okay, hold on. Cool it," Joe said.

They all froze, listening. The loudest sound was Ziggy's heaving breath, sucking in and out of his lungs like a wheezing fireplace bellows.

Another knock, this one more pronounced. Nobody moved. No one seemed to know what to do. If they waited long enough and didn't make a peep, maybe whoever it was would go away.

Finally, Ray got fed up with their chicken-shit vacillation. He pulled the door open.

Mayor Happ Grunwald hustled into the room, all smiles and fidgets.

"So you're all here then? Good good." He puffed out his chest a bit, pulling in a solid breath to sustain the official nature of his announcement. "On behalf of Hibbing, I want to invite you... official, from the city, ya see... invite you to a dinner in your honor at the Elks Club tonight."

Joe turned to Ray, then looked at Ziggy and Gallagher, both their faces still ruddy from the scuffle, eyes flitting around with dazed apprehension. That's when Happ caught sight of Gallagher's mangled mug and froze; his own face became a troubled visage, furrowed by concern.

"What the holy heck, eh..." was all Happ could manage. "You get smacked by a truck?"

"Yep," Gallagher said, at the same moment that Joe said, "Ice." A flurry of awkward looks and ricocheting glances followed.

"Slipped on the ice," Ray chimed in, running with it.

"Then ran into a door," Gallagher said, figuring a little embellishment couldn't hurt. After all, he was pretty beat up.

Happ seemed confused. "What about the truck?'

"There was no truck," Joe said.

But Gallagher's words were already spilling out. "Truck door...Bam! Right into it." He flashed an apologetic look at Joe but the subtle inference was lost in his landscape of bruises. "Kinda slid off, then, ya know. Plowed right into the side mirror, and, yeah..." his voice trailing away.

The others just nodded helplessly, not wanting to add any more fuel to Gallagher's imaginative fire by offering further explanation.

Happ stared numbly, then said, "Winter's a real bitch up these parts. Jest keepin' your footing can be a tribulation, don't cha know."

More nods of agreement all around, gazes aimed downward to avoid revealing their lying eyes.

"You fellahs been put through the ringer, that's for sure. That's why the whole town's coming out—kind of a 'thank you' for all ya done by way of picking up our spirits and stuff. Making you honorary citizens of our town...of Hibbing, ya know." Cleared his throat, uneasy, then added, "Elks Lodge tonight. Seven sharp, it is." Announcing the time and place seemed to make it official. And, hopefully, conclusive.

Their awkward discomfort was obvious, flickering like a neon sign. But the lack of a verbal response left a chill of dread in the room.

"So...you'll be there, eh?" Happ said, working hard to keep it positive.

"We can't," Joe said finally, trying to summon enough regret and sincerity that the Mayor might let it go at that.

"Oh, gosh," Happ said, reeking with disappointment. "Town's been real good about keepin' your secret. Just like ya asked."

The lingering intervals of silence were getting more uncomfortable. Happ looked at Joe with a squint. "Could we, uh...?" Nodded toward the bathroom.

Joe gave him a cockeyed look, unsure. Then he got it; time for a man-to-man, one-on-one chat in the privy.

Joe shut the bathroom door as Happ flipped the toilet lid down and sat on it. Feeling out of place towering over the troubled mayor, Joe searched around for a lower berth. Ended up squatting down on the edge of the tub.

Happ hunched over, studied his hands, opening and closing them, his forearms braced on his knees. This was clearly not easy for him; a knotty seed of humiliation grew within, urgently craving a course of escape.

"Didn't want to say this in front of Ziggy and the boys," he said finally. "I'm kinda against the wall on this thing, Joe. See, it was me, uh..." His eyes came up. "It was me chased Bobby Dylan off."

"How you figure that?"

"I was the one pulled the plug on him. Back at Hibbing High. Was principal then, see, before mayor. Bob and his Golden Chords were playing *Rock and Roll Is Here to Stay* at the annual Jacket Jamboree; was what we called it, Jacket Jamboree. No jackets involved, per se, but...anyhow, he was acting crazy, Bob was. Singing real loud. Thought he was Jerry Lee Lewis, beatin' on the keys like a madman. Broke the darn piano. The foot pedal, ya know. Got way out of hand. So I cut off his mike. But he just kept on hollering, strutin' around—*singing*, he'd call it—kids out there all jumping, screaming and going crazy. So I shut the curtain on him. Wouldn't let him play any further on account of the ruckus."

He let out a long sigh; a weight lifted, but not gone. "Bad call on my part. Once he was out of school, he took right off for New York. Left Hibbing in the mud. Everybody blamed me. Said I screwed the town. Run off our one and only true celebrity."

"And you actually think that's why he left?" Joe said. "Because you pulled the plug?"

"Why the heck else? Hibbing's a great place to live."

"Could be he had other plans."

"Aw, no matter. My fault. Whatever the reason, that's what everybody thinks anyhow."

Joe gave it a decent pause, so Happ wouldn't think he was just impulsively pulling words out of the air.

"Well... I have a real strong feeling he would have left Hibbing anyway."

"Might be how you see it. Not me. Not them."

Joe couldn't argue with that.

Happ withered, sapped of spirit. "I let 'em down once, Joseph. I can't let 'em down again. I just can't."

"We're going to dinner, fellahs," Joe announced as he and Happ emerged from their bathroom summit.

There wasn't a move or peep from any of the three. To a man, all they could muster was a blank look and a fervent hope that Joe had some miraculous strategy up his sleeve.

Happ, on the other hand, was beaming like a child on Christmas morning, his entire being electrified with joyous anticipation. "We'll send Bert Humphrey's taxi to pick you all up. It's an old hearse, is what it is, but never mind that," he said, a gush of relief opening the floodgates of honesty. "Bert fixed it up real slick. We use it for all our official city events, like a fancy limousine. It'll carry the whole bunch of ya in one trip."

Joe felt the glaring eyes of Ray, the stunned gaze of Ziggy, the glimmer of anticipation from Gallagher. He tilted his head with a helpless shrug; *this is how it's gonna go, guys, so live with it.*

"Thanks, Joe," Happ said, gushing with gratitude. Then, all keyed up on optimism, he took a wild flyer. "And since you're gonna be leaving us soon, maybe you'll play us a tune tonight."

The reaction from the four bogus musicians was a matched display of staggered panic.

"Uhhhh, phew," was about all Joe could come up with, inspiring little confidence from his cohorts.

"Just a short one?" Happ said, ever hopeful.

"Can't," Joe said, abruptly grabbing at his only option, envisioning a way out. "Our vehicle went through the ice today."

Happ's face scrunched up, morphing into a grotesque portrait of gnarly clefts and deep fissures shadowed with gloomy concern. "Oh yah?"

"Yep, out on lake, uhhhh..." Joe's eyes flashed to Ziggy.

"Swan Lake," Ziggy said.

"Yeah, Swan Lake. All our instruments, gear, the works... all at the bottom of the lake."

Happ gave it a beat, mouth agape, soaking this in. "Ice fishin', we're ya?"

49

It took less than an hour for a good-sized crowd of curious townsfolk to assemble on the ice of Swan Lake. Word had spread quickly through hastily dialed phone calls and fervent whispers on the street. A cluster of bundled, scarved and mittened observers cautiously edged their way across the slick frozen surface toward the gaping fissure. The reputed perpetrators of the ignominious calamity—Joe, Ziggy, Ray and Gallagher—trailed behind as diffident spectators.

The only vital player who'd missed out on the unfolding foofaraw was Maggie Thorson, the one person who could have potentially benefited most from such a newsworthy event. She had already gotten wind of the big affair being planned that night in honor of Ziggy and the Jetstream at the Elks Lodge and was shopping at Barclay's for a new pair of shoes to wear. If she was going to break the biggest story of her career then, by golly, she'd do it dressed in style. Floating on this rationalized piece of logic, she eagerly eyed a dazzling pair of red high-heels.

Ironically, indulging her ego in a stack of shoeboxes had left her out of the loop on the latest wrinkle. The real newsflash was out on Swan Lake.

Daryl Mitchell shuffled close to the jagged rupture in the ice, peering down into the dark blue/black water. A chuckle caught in his throat, causing his arthritic shoulders to bounce.

"Musta give the pike a start," he said. "Won't bite for a month now."

A flutter of appreciative laughter rippled through the crowd.

"That's a sure bet," Pete said. "Scared the dickens out of 'em I'd say."

Happ glowered at the wretched hole, no sign of the VW down in the deep chilly gloom. "How we do this then?"

"Could borrow Delmer Putnam's tow truck," Carl said. "Use the winch."

Pete shook his head. "Have to hook 'er first. Who's gonna dive down there?"

"Get Harvey Two Trees over to Squaw Lake," Pete said. "He's got one of them scuba dive rigs."

"He ain't cheap."

"I'll kick in," Bob said.

"Me too," Daryl said, even though everyone knew he didn't have a nickel.

"I can set a can out on the registration desk, slit in the top," Pete offered. "Take donations from the guests."

"Heck yeah," said Wayne Everson. "And we can put it out on the radio, get contributions from our loyal listeners."

Joe couldn't take any more of this rampant generosity. "Oh, hey, that's not necessary," he said. But his protest went unheard and unheeded.

Happ stepped forward, raised his hands. "No need for any of that. City'll pick up the tab."

"Well, shoot," Pete said, "we can all pitch in, don'tcha think. I got a few dollars tucked away."

"Sure thing," Carl said.

Bob inched closer to the abyss, but didn't lean in. Stayed straight and rigid as one of his bowling pins, afraid the dark void might reach out and grab him. "Heckuva deal."

A grinding moan shuddered beneath their feet. The ice field gritted its teeth, generating a dull wave attended by sharp cracking.

Everyone scattered back from the yawning chasm, retreating in all directions. They shuffled to a stop about thirty feet out, gazing back over their shoulders with wide-eyed trepidation as the prickly lightning crackles in the ice subsided.

Instinctively they spread out in a loose circle around the hole, distributing their weight more evenly across the tenuous surface.

Puffs of heaving breath clouded the air; human factory stacks releasing their pent up steam.

Joe caught Gallagher grinning like a fool and shot him a penetrating glare, complete with a hard furrowed brow and clenched jaw. Ziggy and Ray just gawked in numb silence, all expectations quashed.

"That tears it," Pete said.

"Yah," said Carl. "I think she's parked til spring."

50

Maggie pranced down the carelessly shoveled sidewalk, an ornate bag from Barclay's Shoes hooked on her arm. She had finally rejected the red open-toed slingback patent leather heels with sparkles as too flashy and settled for a pair of plain black pumps. After all, the gala evening ahead was destined to mark a significant professional achievement in her life; it was not some glamorous celebration saturated with champagne and limos. She would save the shiny crimson sparklers for her eventual acceptance of the Pulitzer Prize for broadcast journalism.

She paused on the street, wondering if they even give a Pulitzer for broadcast journalism. She'd have to check that out. Oh well, she thought, there's always an Emmy. They invariably hold a big gaudy shindig every year.

That's when she saw Stromberg and Rafferty enter the Donut Palace across the street, a pair of walking red flags wearing overcoats and fedoras just like the reporters in those fast-talking Cary Grant movies from the 1940s that she often loved to watch on the late movie.

Maggie paced in a couple quick circles, trying to make up her mind. She had intended to track them down later and lay out the whole plan. But maybe now was better. Get it all set. Put the gears into motion.

She tromped back and forth on the sidewalk, restlessly working out the best approach, creating a chunky puddle of dirty slush under her feet.

HIDING IN HIBBING

Stromberg shoveled sugar into his steaming coffee, disgruntled. "Should have known it was a crock of baloney," he said, throwing in a couple more big spoonfuls to sweeten his mood. "Goddamn wild goose chase."

"Sure sounded like the real thing, though," Rafferty said, staring glumly at the chocolate donut on his plate. "Think it was some kind of practical joke?"

"For what purpose? I mean, you know, what *practical* purpose?"

Rafferty simultaneously cocked his head, shrugged his shoulders and popped his eyebrows up in bewilderment. "Well... what's the purpose of calling a stranger, asking him if his toilet is running and if he says 'yes' you tell him he'd better chase it?"

"You actually did that?" Stromberg said.

"Not me. Some kids I knew."

"That's just stupid. What're the chances some guy's toilet will be running at the exact moment you call?"

Rafferty thought about that. "Okay, how about dialing up a tobacco shop and asking if they got Prince Albert in a can, and if the guy says yes, you tell him 'well, you better let him out or he'll suffocate'?"

"Well that's funny."

"So you think *that's* funny?"

"Yeah. My dad, he used to smoke Prince Albert in his pipe."

"Mine too."

"You pull that one?"

"If you think it's funny...yeah."

Stromberg sipped his coffee, wrinkled his nose at the sweetness. "We're gonna catch hell if Ed ever gets wind of this. Could mean we're done, you know."

Rafferty pulled the envelope from his coat pocket, checked the plane tickets. "We could change 'em. Leave on the red-eye at twelve-thirty."

259

Stromberg gave a little nod, pursing his lips in serious consideration. "Back to work in the morning. Come up with some bullshit story to excuse the expense report. Might save our butts."

Maggie opened the door, did a quick glance around. Found them in a snap. Walked directly to their table, pulled up a chair and sat down, sliding the shoe store bag onto the floor beside her. Stuck out her smooth hand.

"Maggie Thorson. KHIB-AM."

They stared at her in mute surprise.

Maggie leaned toward them, striking an air of confidentiality.

They both rocked back a bit, wary. Threw curious glances at each other. Rafferty recognized her name and voice from the first phone call.

"So," Maggie said, a sly smile on her lips. "From the Times, eh?"

They continued to stare in stony silence, wondering where this was going.

"New York Times," she said. "All the news fit to print, etcetera."

"Actually, we're from the..." Rafferty started.

But Stromberg jumped in to cut him off. "And if we were?"

Maggie locked eyes with each of them in turn, a knowing smile emerging.

"Oh yah, suuuuure," she said with a confident, slow nodding of her head. "That's how the pros do it. Incognito kinda deal. Reverse psychology. Tell 'em you are what they already think you are...then they'll figure you're actually not."

She winked slyly. "I gotcha. I'm in the club, ya know." Then winked again in case they missed the first one.

"The club?" Stromberg said.

"Professional journalist."

She scooted closer to the table, speaking covertly. "So, tell ya what I'll do here. I can getcha into the Elks Hall thing tonight, okay, but the deal is you gotta give me a shared by-line when ya break the story in the Times."

They froze their impassive expressions, not daring to upset the delicate mystery of these puzzling negotiations. Choosing his words carefully Stromberg said, "What story would that be?"

Maggie rocked her head side-to-side; with a sly smile, she raised her eyebrows temptingly. "Oh, you'll see."

Stromberg and Rafferty exchanged looks, while Rafferty nervously tapped the chocolate donut with his finger, as if trying to send an excited message to his cohort with Morse code.

Maggie abruptly extended her hand again with a broad smile. "So... we got us a deal then?"

Being no fool and not wanting an opportunity to slip away, no matter how strangely obtuse it might be, Stromberg grasped her slim hand and shook it firmly.

"Sure thing. Deal"

When Maggie strutted back into the radio station shortly after three o'clock, shoe bag in hand, Donnie met her at the door with a big lopsided grin.

"Shoulda seen it, Mags?"

"Margaret to you," she corrected. "Seen what?"

"Out the lake. Their VW...the bus, ya know...right through the ice. Big ol' gaping hole."

"Who did?"

"Who else? The band. Ziggy Jett and those other guys."

"Went *through* the ice, ya say?"

"And all their stuff in it. Straight to the bottom."

"Well, I'll be gosh-darned," Maggie said, staring off, envisioning pieces falling into place that Donnie couldn't see. "Whole thing went down, huh?"

"Like a stone. I was there to see the actual hole myself. And that hunk of German rust isn't comin' back up. Not til June maybe when they winch it out."

"Huh. What a co-ink-a-dink."

"How's that?"

"They gotta play tonight and suddenly no instruments. Fishy, I'd say."

"A shame, is what it is. I feel for 'em."

"Yah, well don't waste your sobs. They're not slipping out of the noose that simple."

"What noose?"

"No noose, Donnie." Then, just because she thought it was funny, added, "No noose is good noose."

He scrunched his face up in a knot, perplexed by her disconnected rambling, unaware that just a few minutes earlier she had traipsed into the Donut Palace to cut a deal with those New York sharpshooters.

But this new twist—this tragedy out on the lake—warmed her heart. She began to concoct a new angle that would absolutely cinch her journalistic future.

"Hey, you got Tegner's number in that rolodex thing of yours?" she said.

51

"**Hey Zig. Let's go,**" Ray said, impatiently rapping on the bathroom door with a sharp knuckle.

"I'm in the shower," Ziggy yelled back, a harsh tinge of irritation in his voice.

"Come on. Last chance to be a big shot."

The drive back from Swan Lake had been a long miserable journey, all four of them jammed into Happ's Ford Country Squire station wagon, the Mayor behind the wheel, chattering with incessant cheerfulness about how whenever the barn door to success slams shut, a window to wonderful opportunity always gets flung open.

But his cockeyed message of blind optimism didn't stir their souls. They knew they'd screwed up royally, pretty much turning ice cream into bullshit. And now they had to spend an agonizing evening politely accepting the praises and gratitude of all the generous people they had so callously bamboozled. They were steeped in shame, none more so than Ziggy who had been elevated to the unwanted position of *star*. The spotlight would be on him and he would have to graciously accept the adulation and accolades he knew he didn't deserve. Not only had he perpetuated the ruse, but he'd also committed reckless acts that could bring the rickety tower of deception they'd created crashing down on them.

"Where the hell is Ziggy?" Joe said, sticking his head in the motel room doorway.

Throwing a thumb toward the bathroom door, Ray said, "Shower. Trying to wash his guilt down the drain."

"Or drown himself standing up."

"He did save the camera and recorder." Ray cocked his head at the Eclaire and Nagra on dresser. "That's something."

"Yeah, if something is nothing."

"Of course, then there's the bus."

"V-dub was owned by the agency. It's insured. They only used it for run outs on local crap. Shuttles to O'Hare." Joe shrugged, indifferent. "Rest of the gear was all insured too. Frankly, I couldn't care less if the agency gets stiffed."

"Not gonna nail a promotion with that attitude."

"Fuck 'em."

"What're you trying to do, make me respect you?"

"I don't seek the impossible." Joe shuffled uneasily in the doorway, troubled by the shattered mirror, broken lamps and damaged bedside tables.

Ray shrugged. "It's rock-and-roll, man."

"They're gonna pick us up soon," Joe said. "Where's Gallagher?"

Ray gave a shrug, shook his head. "Hell if I know. And I'm trying really hard to find a reason if I even care."

Joe just raised a knowing eyebrow and nodded.

After Joe left, Ray shut the door. The shower was still running. He knuckled the bathroom door again. "Snap it up, Elvis."

Pacing the room, he paused to touch the camera. Picked it up, checking the lens to make sure it hadn't been damaged. Caught a glimpse of the Nagra recorder plugged into the battery pack, a tape reel cued up. Glanced toward the bathroom. The rush of water continued unabated.

He turned the Nagra switch. The reels rotated. Music began; the Brewskis, playing the jazzy riff that slides into the first verse of *Piece of My Heart*. Ray reached for the switch to turn it off, when Janey's voice abruptly emerged, softly insistent, imbued with enticing purity.

After a few moments, he turned it off. A piece of white tape was stuck to the reel, something scrawled on it with a blue marker. It was upside down. He rotated the reel with his finger until he could read it. It said simply: Janey.

Ray started the tape again, captivated by her deep, soulful sound, breathy yet strong, sultry and warm, drawing him in. He smiled, impressed. Turned to look toward the bathroom door.

"Ziggy, you dog," he said.

52

"**Right here,**" Gallagher said. "I'll never wash it off."

He showed Sally the phone number scribbled in ink on his forearm. She twisted his arm around to be sure, checking the number closely. Giggled, then squeezed it tightly in her hands.

"You better not."

She grabbed his other arm, tugging the sleeve up. "And you better not have any other phone numbers tattooed on you either."

He pulled her to him and nuzzled her neck playfully. She shrieked and laughed, halting little gasps interrupted by more kisses. Then she stopped short, earnestly examining his battered face.

"That was so mean of them," she said, fingers gently tracing the swollen edge of a darkened bruise.

"Naw, it's the game. No big deal."

"It is to me," she said. "I don't want anybody to mess up your beautiful face."

"Hockey's a tough sport. You play, ya gotta play hard."

"I know, but..."

"Pucks and sticks and fists flying everywhere. It's a regular melee." He squinted at her. "You know that word? Melee."

"No."

"It's like a brawl." He kissed her forehead with his cut and swollen lip.

"Oh,' she said, kissing him back tenderly.

They were fooling around in the rear corridor of the motel that connected the two longer parallel hallways. It would have been an easy find for Joe had he simply walked the halls of the motel until he happened upon them. But instead he went to the lobby first where, in a last minute bid for a stash of celebrity memorabilia, Pete pressured Joe into autographing a stack of motel brochures.

"And if you could just forge Ziggy's signature on a few of those there, I'll never tell," he said.

Joe obliged, in so deep now it didn't seem to matter.

Meanwhile, Sally sympathetically stroked Gallagher's cuts and bruises with her fingertips, soft as a butterfly. He savored the attention, but the delicate touch was beginning to tickle. He pulled her hand away with as much diplomacy as he could muster.

"Gonna have to go," Gallagher said. "Gotta get ready for tonight,"

She twisted her mouth in a childish pout and then let it slide into a wistful smile. Hugged him again quickly, planting another kiss on his bruised cheek, then scampered off down the hall, pausing briefly to toss him a carefree wave before disappearing around the corner.

Gallagher turned up the long corridor, ambling toward his room. The lobby door at the far end of the corridor swung open. An imposing figure appeared. Gallagher slowed, then stopped. He couldn't make out who it was right off, then it came clear. George was headed directly toward him, the speed of his resolute stride escalating when he saw Gallagher. Directly behind George, a seemingly larger, more imposing form could be seen advancing as well.

Gallagher backpedaled a few quick steps, then spun around and dashed around the corner into the rear corridor. He didn't have time to reach the exit door, so he quickly twisted several doorknobs on the run, hoping one would open. Of course they wouldn't; not without a key.

But then one did. Not a guest room. The supply closet, filled with towels, soap, shampoos, sheets, plus a mop and bucket. He hustled inside, pulling the door shut behind him. Stood motionless in the pitch darkness. Then slid down to the floor, huddling against the back wall.

Gallagher was normally not one to run from a fight, as he had previously demonstrated. But getting yet another beating on top of the cuts and bruises he already endured was not something he relished. And who knew what else that big bruiser and his buddies might have in mind?

He heard the mushy plod of heavy footsteps on the hallway carpet. They stopped. He held his breath, and then could hear the raspy inhale/exhale right outside.

The door flew open, illuminating Gallagher huddled in the corner, cringing with arms wrapped around his drawn-up knees, trying hard to be invisible and failing miserably.

George towered over him in the doorway. Gallagher awkwardly attempted to stand up, but George placed a huge hand on his shoulder and shoved him back down.

"I don't...I'm not...I'm just..." Gallagher said, struggling to stitch together a coherent thought.

George ignored him. Turned to the side, motioning someone in the hallway toward him with his meaty hand. A dark form moved into the doorway, consuming much of the incoming light. A startlingly burly girl, maybe six foot two, with the body of a Green Bay linebacker and a puffy sweet face. A bulky down jacket, unzipped and draped open, exaggerated her brawny girth even more.

"This him, Pumpkin?" George said. "The one's been chasin' after ya?"

She shook her head very slowly side-to-side. Heaved an irritated sigh. "I tolt ya, it's Delmer Putnam over ta Duck River. Runs the bait shop in summer. With the grabby hands and the funny eyeball."

"So...not him?" pointing at Gallagher. "Or them other hippies?"

"I tolt ya. No." Then, mumbling to the side, "You never listen to me."

She looked at Gallagher and crunched up her face in a sour expression of repugnance, as if he was that dead frog you pin to a table for dissection in high school science. Then she turned and shambled off.

George looked down at his feet, shuffled a bit, contrite. Sneaked a fleeting sidelong glance at Gallagher.

"So that was Pumpkin, huh?" Gallagher said to break the silence.

"Yeah. Real nice girl. Not the best judge of character."

And definitely not *little*, Gallagher thought.

"Seemed nice."

"Yep, sure is." Then, direct to Gallagher, George said, "Guess we mighta jumped the gun on that ass whuppin' we give you."

"Sort of, yeah."

"Sprung the trap on the wrong skunk, I'd say." Which was the full extent of any apology George could pull together.

"It'll heal," Gallagher said.

"Well, okay then. So, uh, we're, uh...whatever you said before."

"Copacetic?"

"Yeah. That."

Gallagher nodded.

George shut the supply closet door. Gallagher was consumed by utter darkness. And silence. He could smell the sweet fragrance of hand soap and shampoo, the fresh breath of washed sheets and towels. It called to mind the linen closet in their small brick home in South Philly; his mother carefully stacking meticulously folded sheets and pillowcases, the clean scent of April wafting out, even in the dead of winter. It was a simpler time back then, when a tiny moment, disconnected from anything else, could be fondly appreciated and cherished, then tucked away and cataloged, brought out again whenever needed.

Ray was wrong, he thought. George and his buddies weren't some breed of strange sissified sadists. They were just a bunch of regular guys looking out for their friend. Gallagher could let it all go now. He'd had his face stomped plenty growing up in Philly and lived to tell about it. And had his heart stomped by lots of girls with nicknames a whole lot weirder than Pumpkin. So he could understand.

Sitting there in the dark, he felt wrapped in a warm blanket of security, safe from the jarring light of day that cruelly exposed all his fears each morning, illuminating a creeping dread of what his future would bring.

This black void, perfect in its nothingness, offered unlimited possibilities. It gave him hope, a growing belief that he might even have a future all his own. Not the dismal existence of his father, fraught with alcohol and disillusion; or his mother's troubled days, dreams shattered by sorrow and deceit. Or even the dismally stunted lives of his few friends, pummeled by plans gone awry, casually kicked aside by fate.

He could sit right here for eternity, he mused. This snug hollowness was pure heaven.

That's when the door burst open. A startling blast of bright incandescence splashed his face.

"You're not getting outta tonight that easy, Gallagher," Joe's voice rumbled like some fairy tale troll. "Let's go."

53

The Elks Hall was considerably more impressive and ornate than one would ever have anticipated. But perhaps this wasn't so surprising. Hibbing had become, after all, the unlikely home of a world-class high school, widely hailed as a veritable Versailles of education. Majestic murals greeted students as they entered the hallowed halls. And its massive auditorium, where a wild young Bob Zimmerman had once bought down the house, featured elaborately gilded paintings and intricate stained glass windows, not to mention four grandiose chandeliers imported from Czechoslovakia.

Not to be outdone, the B.P.O.E—the Benevolent and Protective Order of the Elks—had followed suit, designing a spaciously sumptuous gathering place where they could consume their venison stew and hot pasties while immersed in delusions of opulent dignity. Following the collapse of its vigorous mining boom, the once affluent town had been gripped by the sad curse of invasive poverty and rampant unemployment, yet the hardy citizens continued to proudly maintain a mantle of stubborn confidence, surrounded by the veneer of their rich historical legacy.

The plush atmosphere was an odd contradiction to the utilitarian folding tables, paper plates and plastic utensils, neatly arranged on brown butcher-paper tablecloths.

A string of buffet tables stretched along one side of the cavernous room, littered with an abundance of delectable dishes—cheesy casseroles, thick stews, Jello salads, savory roasts—not unlike the cornucopia of scattered offerings Ziggy and the guys had found outside their motel room doors, left by blindly adoring fans and groupies.

A modest stage with a faded brown curtain extended into the room at the far end, a sturdy oak podium located off to one side. A hand-carved proscenium arch over the stage added a touch of delicate flamboyance to the otherwise austere rostrum. A folding table of honor, with an actual linen covering, was situated just below the stage. This is where the four members of the faux band would be seated, spotlighted in all their counterfeit glory.

Mayor Grunwald flitted around, anxiously overseeing the placement of every detail, determined that nothing would go wrong. This was to be his redemption; his long sought emancipation from shame.

Notable local citizens began to arrive, along with assorted family members, including a growing number of budding teenaged girls who trembled with barely restrained excitement. Most of these feverish young females had been forced to plead their case to stubbornly reluctant parents, arguing with insistent logic that attending the event on a school night was crucial to their educational advancement, especially in the cultural arena of musical appreciation. Though parents were seriously out of touch with current teen whims and devilish obsessions, they were not entirely stupid. However, the majority of fathers were also precariously vulnerable to the sinuous charms and desperate pleas of daughters quivering on the verge of tears. And so, though adult resistance was well mounted and valiantly fought, the battle was widely lost.

Bert Humphrey drove the boys over in his renovated hearse, excited to be shuttling real celebrities instead of the usual inebriated traveling salesman trying to find his way back to the Androy Hotel after a bender. Even wore a funny little sea captain's hat, the anchor patch ripped off, looking much like the jaunty caps he'd seen on limousine drivers in Hollywood movies. He chatted them up on the way over, speculating with uninformed wisdom about the trajectory their musical career might take.

When Bert got a glimpse of Gallagher's face in the rear view, he said, "Get yourself mangled by a grizzly, did ya?"

"Couple of 'em," Gallagher replied without hesitation. "Came up on me sudden like out back of the motel." He cast a lopsided grin, thoroughly enjoying his flourishing legend. "But I chased 'em both off by pounding my chest and yellin' like a mad man."

Bert chuckled to himself. Spinning tall tales steeped in provocative exaggeration was a cherished Hibbing tradition. Truth was beside the point.

He dropped them off at the rear alley door—called it the *backstage entrance*—where they were greeted by Pete Peterson, Bob Koenen and State Trooper Ron Von Ahlen, who quickly flanked them like bodyguards, hustling them in past the trash dumpsters, through the boiler room and kitchen, and out into the main room, with barely a ripple of recognition from anyone. Most who had gathered early were deeply engaged in eager conversation around the buffet tables or busy staking out the best seats, so they paid little attention to the stealthy escorted entourage that slipped in surreptitiously to sit at the folding table of honor.

Given the weight of pretense they shouldered, the four charlatans embraced whatever anonymity they could get, huddling in the shadows of their earnest bodyguards as they entered, slouching low into their chairs, heads averted, faces furtively concealed behind arms and hands. Gallagher was the only one who sat up straight, energized by the crush of people, eyes darting around the crowded room searching for Sally.

Across the room, out of their eyesight, Maggie escorted Rafferty and Stromberg to a table with a neatly printed sign on it—RESERVED FOR WHIB-AM.

"Gentlemen," she said, her manner unusually decorous, "have a seat here at our reserved table. Enjoy some delicious food at the buffet if you'd like. I'll return shortly." Then scuttled away in her plain black pumps that went perfectly with the conservatively drab, slate gray dress she had happily worn to her Aunt Rosemary's funeral last year, where she had smiled broadly as damp dirt was shoveled onto the casket.

Rafferty raised his dark eyebrows at Stromberg, then turned to assess the many contradictory aspects of the vast room, particularly struck by the big mounted moose head surrounded by delicate gilt-laced brocade.

Happ intercepted Maggie as she set course for the stage, his face a troubled sea.

"Geez, Maggie, what you doing bringing them two New York fellahs in?"

"Cool your shorts, Happ," she said, waving him off. "Guests of the station is all."

"But they're the two's been pokin' around. They're gonna throw a wrench..."

"Under control."

"They could blow the lid off..."

Maggie stopped short, turned to him. "Look in my eyes, Happ." She fixed him with an unblinking stare, trying real hard to shoot those little cartoon arrows right into his head. "I got this handled. It's under control."

Spun on her heels and marched off. Happ squinted over at the two east coast interlopers, not at all reassured.

A squad of Carl's perky waitresses descended on Ziggy and his bogus band shlepping armloads of lime green and turquoise Melmac plates heaped with food. This grotesque outpouring of generosity and idol worship weighed heavily on them; it made them feel like captured jungle explorers masquerading as false gods, seized by adoring natives, then wined and dined and fattened up, and once unmasked, unceremoniously tossed into a raging volcano. The feast being laid before them took on the ominous pall of a ritualistic *last meal*.

HIDING IN HIBBING

Ziggy felt a brief respite from the dread when Janey finally appeared in the crowded B.P.O.E Hall. She stood out with such clarity, as in the movies, a glamorous starlet in perfect focus against the hazy milling bodies behind her. Even at a distance he could see the flawless radiance of her young skin through delicately applied makeup. She appeared unexpectedly confident in her demeanor, revealing little of the tension that roiled within.

Earlier, they had trudged off the lake carrying the camera and recorder, their hearts heavy with gloom, not speaking at all. At the road, they eventually caught a ride with a sympathetic trucker who gave them a lift back into town. The driver sensed a murky tension and refrained from asking questions, commenting only a couple times on the weather, which was predicted to change again soon, from bad to worse. But inclement weather was the least of Ziggy's troubles, and Janey now existed within the dark circle of his misery as well.

They walked several blocks to Janey's house, where they stood outside in the snow for a long time. A somber silence was their salvation. The portent of harsh punishment hung over them with such enormity that spoken words would only have magnified the potential consequences, making them unbearable to imagine.

"So, guess I'll see you there tonight," Janey finally said.

Ziggy looked at her with surprise. Her hopeful words, boldly expressing an assumption that he would still be alive and not in jail or perhaps even hell itself, instilled him with encouragement. He took the Nagra recorder from her arms.

"Yeah," he said. Nudged her shoulder playfully with his arm, then walked back to the Ramada, steeling himself to face the terror of Joe's wrath.

Upon entering the Elks Hall, Janey caught a glimpse of Ziggy at the same moment he saw her.

She offered an endearingly shy smile and a tiny wave, her delicate hand held close to her chest. A voice called out to her. It was Danny, sitting at a table behind Janey with the other Brewskis, Mike and Hal. True to their band moniker, they were already enthusiastically chugging suds, gleefully raising their foamy plastic cups.

She stepped over to greet them. Danny gallantly pulled out a chair for her. Janey hesitated, throwing a quick helpless glance at Ziggy. Then sat down, perching on the edge of the chair to signal her visit might only be temporary.

At the lip of the stage, Maggie snagged Donnie by the sleeve as he emerged from behind the curtain.

"Ya get it all set up then?"

"Yeah, sure. I'm on top of it, Mags."

"Margaret to you, kid."

He let the curt admonition slide. He'd heard it too many times before. "Tegner gave us everything you asked for. I went down to the store, used his pickup to haul it over."

"His? How come his truck?"

"Well, cuz," Donnie said, taking it as obvious, "I don't have one."

Maggie nodded blankly. Her nervousness was making her lose focus. She glanced at the KHIB reserved table, just to be sure Stromberg and Rafferty hadn't fled. The table was empty. Her eyes shifted back and forth frenetically, wildly ricocheting gumballs. After a moment of panic, she caught sight of them snaking their way back from the buffet, paper plates piled high. She shut her eyes, relieved, taking a breath and a moment to compose herself, straining to summon calm from the darkness.

Maggie had seen right through the fake band's clever ruse the moment Ray fumbled an incompetent escape from strumming the guitar in her living room. Breaking the big revelation of a con job by a bogus band would have been triumph enough for Maggie, but actually orchestrating a meltdown of their grandiose fraud in front of a huge crowd of Hibbing citizens would be truly spectacular.

"Oh boy," she muttered aloud, gazing at the crowd filling the Elk's Hall. "When the scam hits the fan..."

"What scam is that, Maggie?"

She snapped out of her reverie, shooting an icy glare at Donnie. "Just mind your p's and q's there, Donnie. Wasn't speaking to you."

"That the scam that's gonna get you outta here...?"

"You want me to talk to Beth?" she said, threatening.

"I, uh..."

"Tell her about your grabby hands and improper behavior?"

"But I didn't do..."

"Cuz I will."

Carl inched his way next to Happ, muttering covertly out one side of his mouth, lips curled tight.

"What's with them bein' here?"

They both stared at Stromberg and Rafferty devouring hot pasties.

"Maggie's got it all under control," Happ said, voice wavering a bit.

"Under control?"

"What she says." Then bent toward Carl, whispered, "I think she mighta paid 'em off. Under the table so to speak. Keep their mouths shut."

"Oh you think, huh?"

"Be my guess. Said she had it handled."

"You believe her?"

"Somebody got compensated."

"Think it'll stick?"

Happ cocked his head, unsure. Threw in a little shrug to sell it. "You know Maggie. A real corker. Gets a bug up her butt, she's a steamroller."

"Let's hope," Carl said.

277

54

At their special table, Rafferty poked the mound of lime Jello with his fork, watching it jiggle.

"How the heck do they get those little marshmallows inside?" Peering at the tiny white puffs floating in a rubbery green pond.

Stromberg looked over at him, his face scrunched up, perplexed. "What?"

"How do they get 'em in there? The marshmallows and tangerines and cherries?"

Stromberg looked down at his block of red Jello with pineapple triangles inside.

"Not much of a cook, are you?" he said.

"Me? No. That'd be the wife."

"The wife."

"Yeah. She does all the cooking."

"The *wife* does."

"Yeah."

"You mean Gloria?"

"Yeah."

"She's got a name."

"Right. Gloria. You know her, for crying out loud."

"She's not just a *thing*."

Rafferty stared at Stromberg, eyebrows knitted tight, not getting it. "You've been over for dinner. More than once. She did the cooking."

"And so you think she'd know how to get stuff inside the Jello?"

"The wife? Sure."

"*The wife*. Do you even hear yourself?"

"Geez, I just was just asking about the Jello, for criminy sake."

They were already starting to fit in. Conversation was a tricky art up in the North Country.

The table of honor, meanwhile, was immersed in a veil of silence; a physical stillness so profound Mount Rushmore would have appeared animated.

"Okay guys," Joe finally said, exercising that smooth, unruffled tone he always managed to pull off in the face of crisis. "Let's just stay cool tonight, be friendly, shake hands with everybody, avoid answering any questions, 'specially if it's got to do with the music business. In the morning I'll rent us a car and we're outta here. By tomorrow night we'll all be sleeping in our own beds."

That sounded pretty good, but the evening was still young. And as Robert Frost put it, there were miles to go before they'd sleep.

Ziggy looked intently across the room at Janey, wondering what she was talking to Danny about, an ache of insecurity creeping through his bones. He strained to read their lips, but quickly realized only spies and deaf people were adept enough to pull that trick off.

Gallagher watched Ziggy watching Janey, his eyeballs flashing back and forth between the two of them, amused by the obvious adoration churning in Ziggy's gaze, and acutely aware of the squeeze of jealousy that must accompany it.

Danny leaned on one elbow, moved closer to Janey. "Me and the guys were talking. Wondered if you might, ya know, think about comin' back to the band."

She opened her mouth, but nothing came out. Instead, she took a healthy bite of air, pulling it into her lungs. Managed a faint, "You serious?"

"Not a joke. Dead serious."

"I, uh, I..." Looking down shyly. "Why would you want that?"

"Well shoot, when you sang with us over to Chisholm the other night, you were great."

Her eyes came up and rolled left, checking to see if Hal and Mike might be laughing now, mocking her. But they just nodded their heads with solemnly sincere encouragement, wearing looks she'd rarely seen from them before.

That was when Gallagher stepped up behind Janey. "Hey there. How's it goin'?" he said to everybody, cordial as a kitten rubbing up against your leg.

Ziggy saw this. Snapped a quick look at Gallagher's empty chair beside him. Hadn't even seen him get up. Never even heard or felt him slip away. His gaze whipped back to Janey.

"Didn't mean to interrupt or anything," Gallagher told them, reeking with deferential politeness. He turned to Janey. "I kinda wanted to talk to the guys here for a minute. You mind swapping seats with me?" He motioned across the room, toward the empty chair next to Ziggy. "You can grab my seat right over there. Just for a few...I'll be real quick. Promise."

Janey became more flustered, trying to process the unexpected offer to swap seats, oblivious to Gallagher's battered face. "Uh, well, I, um...okay." She looked toward Ziggy, feeling the sudden strong pull of his security. "Sure. I guess. Sure."

She stood up in a daze. Walked zombie-like toward Ziggy, her head in a bubble of muted echoes, like the bad cold that plugged her ears last winter and left her floating helplessly in the disorienting soundless void of outer space for a week.

As Janey approached, Ziggy jumped up and pulled Gallagher's empty chair out for her, wondering what the hell had just transpired.

Gallagher had already planted himself across from the Brewskies, pulling himself up close to the table, hunching toward them with an enthusiastic gleam. They stared uneasily at his mauled mug.

Gallagher caught their anxiety, shrugged it off. "Music biz is a rough gig. Beat on the drums long enough, they beat ya right back."

Mike shifted tensely in his chair. Gallagher said, "But I don't have to tell you guys that, since you're a real band and all."

Danny hesitated, then said, "Well, we're not big time, like you. But, yeah, we play around some."

"Cool," Gallagher said, head bobbing, sneaking a glance at Janey now sitting with Ziggy. "Very, very cool."

Ray caught a glimpse of Maggie conferring with Happ at the far side of the stage. Happ abruptly leaned back, giving Maggie a sharp look of surprise. Whether it was delight or dismay, Ray couldn't tell. But either way, the covert nature of the exchange made Ray deeply uncomfortable.

Janey gazed at Ziggy, relieved to be in the comfort of his presence again. Her eyes swept nervously across Joe and Ray, who both watched her in silent fascination, their blank stares providing no clue to the rush of crazy thoughts scampering through their heads. What she also didn't detect, tucked deeply inside Ray's mind, was his newly acquired appreciation of her true talent.

A *ticka-ticka-ticka-ticka* sound drew their attention to the stage. Happ was at the podium, holding a plastic glass near the microphone, tapping it insistently with a plastic spoon. Maggie stood off to his side, working hard to conceal a self-satisfied grin.

"So... heckuva week, eh?" Happ said, leaning into the mike. "I 'spect you all heard that Ziggy and the boys had a little episode of bad luck today. Tried to pull a hit-and-run on some muskies with their vehicle. Now she's parked down bottom of Swan Lake."

Those who had already heard about it laughed uneasily at the reference. Those few who hadn't been privy to the news gasped and groaned, exhibiting an array of shocked reactions.

Stromberg and Rafferty just exchanged curious looks, wondering if they were about to discover the secret behind Maggie's *big story*.

"Not to worry," Happ said, flapping his hands to calm the rumble of concern. "Garth Poleson and some other merchants got together...donated a used Chevy van to the boys right offa his car lot."

This was greeted with a flash of relieved applause and scattered whistles.

"Oh she's got a few dings and dents, don'tcha know, but she runs like a top for a junker," Happ said. "It'll get the boys where they're going."

Stromberg and Rafferty craned their necks hoping to get a look at *the boys* Happ kept referencing. But their eyes swept right over Ziggy, Ray and Joe, now slouched even lower in their chairs, undetectable to the common eye, wearing their mortified immobility like camouflage. And even though Gallagher sat up tall at the Brewskies' nearby table, sporting a joyful smirk, thrilled by Happ's surprising car announcement, he went unnoticed as well.

"What the hell..." Joe grumbled low into his arms folded up tight across his chest. This incredible act of communal generosity drove him into an even deeper remorse. He rued the day he had launched the ill-conceived charade. But you pull enough cockeyed schemes, eventually that dumb bird comes home to roost. It's in the numbers. Like it or not, the odds are against you.

Janey squeezed Ziggy's arm, happy to learn their unfortunate mishap on the lake had spun into a positive

HIDING IN HIBBING

outcome. But her effort at encouragement only made Ziggy feel worse. He turned ashen, plagued by a rocky queasiness.

"And that's not all," Happ continued.

Ray's head slumped low, eyes shut; he sensed the walls closing in.

"The boys lost everything they had when their VW bus turned into a U-boat," Happ said.

The entire crowd groaned in a harmonized chorus of sympathy; one of those elongated *Awwwwwwwwws* that usually emanates from a sitcom audience in response to the disclosure of unexpected tragedy, as on *Family Affair* when Buffy learned that her doll, Mrs. Beasley, had fallen six stories out of an apartment window into a trash bin.

"But hold on now. Hold on. Maggie Thorson, from over the radio station—you all know Maggie—she just told me, well, here, why don't I..." He stepped aside, turning to Maggie, motioning for her to come over. "Maggie, why don't you tell everybody..."

Ray looked up when he heard her name. Felt a sharp stab to the back, rocking his world even further off its axis.

"Thanks, Happ," Maggie said, adjusting the mike. "So, yah. Station WHIB-AM and Adam Tegner, down at Tegner's Music Store, have generously provided all new instruments —guitars, drums, amplifiers, speakers—so Ziggy Jett and his band can perform for us right here on our stage tonight."

The crowd broke into a rumble of applause as Donnie pulled the curtain open. A full drum kit and three electric guitars perched on instrument stands were neatly arranged center stage, an amp and several speakers stacked up behind.

This threw both Rafferty and Stromberg into full rubbernecking mode, rising up a couple inches out of their chairs, knees bent and flexing, trying to locate Ziggy and his group.

They should have been easy to spot now. Joe looked as if he'd been cold-cocked by a 12-inch fry pan, eyes practically crossed, stars spinning around his head like in a Bugs Bunny

283

cartoon. Ziggy so pale now that freshly fallen snow would have looked like a bed of charcoal beside him. Ray imploding slowly, the cold validity of his pessimism realized, any light of hope he had secretly envisioned now flickering out. But the visual pandemonium that spun chaotically around them concealed their stunned reactions from detection.

Only Gallagher blazed with delirious excitement. He hadn't yet grasped the reality that he was *not* a musician. He didn't know how to play, how to sing, or how to be the celebrity that most of the girls in Hibbing already thought he was. But it didn't stop him from momentarily dog-paddling in his pool of delusion.

Rafferty and Stromberg were lost at sea in this curiously odd collision of unfamiliar elements, flummoxed by the discordant patchwork tapestry of flannel shirts and business suits, hand-knit winter scarves and neckties, checkered hunting caps and party dresses. These two big city showbiz mavens from Manhattan never felt more alien and out of touch with reality.

Ziggy turned to Janey. She was beaming with pride, a hot glow in her pink cheeks.

"Janey, I need to tell you something," he whispered.

She peered into his eyes, lightly biting her bottom lip with expectation.

"How's about that, eh?" Happ said.

His booming voice pounded their ears as he practically gobbled up the microphone with excitement. "Tonight we're gonna get a preview of what these young fellahs are all about."

Another loud surge of applause pounded Ziggy's ears, pushing the dizziness down into his stomach, where it swelled the nausea already churning there.

"And to escort our guests of honor to the stage, we got some of our own local, uh, lemme just..." Happ dug into the pockets of his ill-fitting suit coat, fumbled around, finally coming up with a folded piece of paper, squinting to read. "Hang on here, uh... first up, we got Sally Johansson, our own 1970 Miss Boat Landing."

The pony-tailed waitress bounced up onto the stage, exhilarated by the applause. Gallagher grinned, relieved to see her.

Happ continued, "Tonight Sally will be escorting, uh..." He checked the paper in his hand. "Says here...Anthony Quinn."

To the burst of raucous laughter, he added, "Probably not that one though, be my guess."

Sally's face fell when she looked toward the table of honor and didn't see Gallagher there. But then he abruptly leaped up at the Brewski's table, waving his arms at her, teeth flashing, mile-wide grin creasing his face. Seeing him, she bounced up and down eagerly, scampering from the stage to fetch him, hooking his arm with hers.

"You didn't tell me you were Miss Boat something," he said to her as they walked toward the stage.

"Landing. Miss Boat Landing," she said, squeezing his arm tighter. "And you didn't tell me that your name was Anthony."

"It's Tony. Just Tony."

Watching all this numbly, Ray muttered, "We are so fucking screwed."

Joe surrendered to their fate, squeezing out a wry smile at the only thing he still found ironically amusing. When Happ had asked him for a list of the band member's names, he had given it to him. Not that it was accurate in any way. But then, the mayor hadn't specified wanting an *accurate* list.

Ziggy huddled close to Janey, holding her hand between the two of his, staring down at the fleshy knot of fingers, not wanting to look into her eyes yet.

"Janey..." he said, really struggling now. "We, uh..."

"What is it?" Trying to encourage him without pushing too hard.

"We are...not a band."

Ba-dum-bump! Gallagher hit a sloppy rim-shot and cymbal crash, grinning with delight behind the drum kit. The crowd whistled and hooted and applauded.

Ziggy's baffling declaration was left hanging in the air. Both he and Janey looked at Gallagher, trying to bring what they were seeing into line with the words Ziggy had just spoken.

Happ laughed jovially at Gallagher's rowdy enthusiasm. He had no intention of pulling any plugs on anybody this time, no matter how wild they got.

"Next up," he said, "Connie Myers, Miss Junior Jaycees Sweetheart."

Connie sprang up, blond and supple, brazenly working the Juicy Fruit in her mouth as she hip-swung her way toward the table of honor with a sassy smirk.

"Connie will be escorting Ray Gunn," Happ announced with a big eye-roll to the crowd. "I didn't make that up, folks. What it says right here," flapping the paper, prompting another wave of laughs.

From the crowd, somebody shouted, "Go get 'em, Gunn!"

Ray scowled at Joe, who gave an ironic shrug, keeping his inner smirk under control. Before Ray could say a word, Connie was standing in front of him, her hand extended with lissome grace, the other resting on her jutting hip, striking an enticingly insouciant pose. The fuse had been lit. There was no going back now. Ray took her hand and stood up, letting her guide him by the arm.

Climbing up the three steps to the stage, he caught Maggie's eye and glared with stony enmity, hard and cold as he could manage. But she gave as good as she got, firing back a vacant regard of smug confidence that shamelessly declared *gotcha sucker*.

HIDING IN HIBBING

Ray hooked thumbs in his jeans pockets, took up a slack-legged position next to one of the guitars; it didn't matter which one, since he couldn't play any of them. He shot a wide-eyed look of teeth-gritted disdain at Gallagher, who couldn't have cared less, wallowing happily in his incandescent glory as the world's greatest fake drummer.

Joe knew that he was probably next to walk the plank; Ziggy had been ordained the star and would obviously be saved until last. He imagined slipping out before they called his name, magically disappearing into the night, dashing to the far ends of the earth and starting a new life as a monk or forest ranger or a pirate. But he could never abandon his trusted accomplices. Not after being the instigator of this outrageous hoax, heedlessly setting the wheels into motion without regard for the consequences. All this raced through his mind in less than a second, leaving him slouched in his chair awaiting the inevitable.

Across the table, Janey gaped at Ziggy with puzzled eyes.

"I don't understand. You said..."

"I lied." He turned to meet her troubled gaze. "I didn't mean to. It just got out of control."

"What did?"

"We we're just trying to get rooms and there weren't any, because of the storm and roads being closed..."

She tried to sort his words, scattered puzzle pieces dumped on the floor. "So, then you don't...?"

"Have a band? No. We don't have one. I'm not in one. There is no band."

Janey went limp, her confusion turning to hurt. The atoms spinning in her body slowed, thick molasses in her veins.

"I'm not a rock star... or a musician," he said. His tone flattened out with the shame of confession. "I'm an assistant cameraman. We're a film crew from Chicago. We came up here to shoot a commercial for this brewery over in Bemidji."

Her smile was long gone now. Replaced by tight lips and misty eyes, her heart in a vice.

"I wanted to tell you. Every day, I wanted to tell you," he said.

After a moment, Janey said, "You should have. It wouldn't have mattered to me."

Up on the stage, Happ manhandled the microphone again, creating a jaggedly amplified rumble. "Here she is, Sandy Wingert...Miss Main Street Hardware in last year's Founder's Day Parade."

Scattered whistles and catcalls greeted the appearance of a tall, Nordic blond, her lustrous hair cascading over her shoulders. She waved at her fans, walking arrow-straight, back perfectly arched, a natural at this runway walking stuff.

"Sandy will be escorting Joe Smith," Happ announced, then broadly swung his arm in a sweeping arc to flag her attention from the show she was putting on, pointing her toward Joe at the table of honor.

"I'm Gunn and he's *Smith*?" Ray muttered in disbelief.

Gallagher executed another goofy drum roll and rim shot, getting better.

Ray rolled his head around to find Maggie off to the side in the wings. She shrugged at him dismissively. *Sorry, but hey, it's a tough world out there. You screw me, I screw you. Don't ever try to fool me, pal. I'm nobody's patsy.* If it's possible to express all of that with one effortless look, Maggie certainly pulled it off.

Sandy sashayed over and grabbed Joe by the arm. He went with her, surrendering without a struggle. There are times when your fate is sealed, your destiny locked in stone. No matter how much you may resist, it's going to play out anyway. Only thing you can do is demonstrate enormous grace under pressure.

Ziggy searched Janey's glistening eyes, hoping to find some pale glimmer of forgiveness. "It was just a stupid joke. And really, really stupid. We never thought it would..." His

HIDING IN HIBBING

words trailed off helplessly. Where was that classroom full of loyal junior high kids, inspired by Spartacus, standing up beside him and declaring they were *all* Ziggy Jett? Freeing him from the chains of his unintended deceit.

"Okay then, now I know ya all been waiting for this," Happ said. "The guest of honor hisself, Ziggy Jett."

The crowd exploded in a wild frenzy of applause and whoops. Several teen girls leaped up, shrieking with tearful abandon, dragged back down into their seats by mortified parents.

A hot spotlight beam swept across the room like a meteor; it illuminated Ziggy with a blast of blinding light. He reacted, hunching down in the entrenched manner of a protestor dodging fire hoses in Selma.

"That really him?" Rafferty said. "Sure doesn't look like much."

"Gotta get famous first," Stromberg said. "Grow into it."

"Not exactly a pop idol."

"Remember Rick Nelson...when he was still Ricky? Just a kid? Geeky little nerd with a stupid pompadour, slicked back on the sides into a D.A.?"

"But he could sing."

"Yeah, point is he was a dork first. Then he got cute."

Rafferty considered this. "How you explain Mick Jagger then? Good looking young kid, just keeps getting uglier."

"You're not a girl."

"What? No. What's that got to...?"

"That's the ironic contradiction of the whole thing, see. More famous you get, the less good looking you need to be."

"That your expert opinion?"

"Been in the talent game a long time, my friend."

"And to escort Ziggy...here she is...you all know her..." Happ paused, expertly whipping up the crowd's expectation. "Sarah Rehborg, 1970 Prom Queen over at Hibbing High."

Sarah popped up, grinning through her braces, about to burst with unbridled excitement. She shuffled toward Ziggy, her legs constrained by the strange crazy-quilt dress she was wearing.

Happ lifted his glasses, squinted to read the crumpled paper. "Says here, Sarah's got on a dress she made herself outta some old football jerseys from the 1967 championship Hibbing Warriors."

The crowd howled wildly. That 1967 team was held in extremely high regard, exalted to the level of gridiron gods, having beaten every team on that season's schedule by more than fourteen points.

"Let's hope she washed them jerseys," Happ said, before realizing it was a pretty tasteless joke, given that people were eating. But nobody gave a hoot. When you can tie Ziggy Jett, Superstar, together with the championship Hibbing Warriors, that's a combo that can't be diminished by bad taste or lame humor.

Ziggy could see Sarah coming for him out the corner of his eye. He gasped for air, lightheaded.

"I don't know what to do," he whispered to Janey.

Calm and clear as morning air she said, "Maybe what you should have done in the first place."

55

Sarah's hand touched Ziggy's shoulder.

He shuddered, an electric shock shooting through him. Flashed a sidelong glance at Janey, searching her eyes. She was steadfast, unwavering, neither angry nor sympathetic, leaving it all to him now.

Sarah reached down and gently tugged Ziggy's arm, guiding him up out of the chair, braces flashing. She hooked his arm with hers, steering him toward the stage. In Ziggy's head everything moved like thick tree sap.

Sarah led him toward the short stairway at the far end of the stage, forcing him to traverse the entire breadth of the proscenium, the harsh spotlight tracking his every step, stirring a caustic anguish in his stomach. Joe and Ray watched Ziggy pass by below them with blank expressions, eyewitnesses to an execution. The phrase *"good day for a hanging"* stumbled through Ray's brain. Only it wasn't just Ziggy on his way to the gallows. They were all going to swing.

Climbing the three stairs to the stage, Ziggy barely registered Gallagher, dimly visible behind Ray and Joe. But he did clearly perceive an aura of exultant anticipation radiating from Gallagher's hazy face.

Sarah led Ziggy to the microphone in front of the band, giving him a quick peck on the cheek. He flinched at the cold sting of her metal braces on his skin. The sweet gesture elicited a cheerful response from the crowd, punctuated by an array of other appreciative noises as Sarah departed with a breezy wave.

Ziggy stared out at the crowd, grateful now for the harshly bright spotlight that mercifully blinded him to the large gathering of his witnesses, judges, and soon-to-be executioners. A few seconds passed as the room quieted; it felt like an eternity to him.

"I, uh..." Ziggy said. The sound of his voice boomed through the room, causing him to jerk back from the microphone as if it had bit him on the chin.

Squeals of feedback followed as his hands wrestled the mike into place, finally relinquishing the futile struggle and backing off a bit.

"I, uh...I'm sorry. We, uh...We can't play."

A mumble of disappointed confusion rippled through the crowd. At the side of the stage, Happ furrowed his fuzzy brows. Beside him, Maggie smirked, shifting from one foot to the other, ready for the next peeling back of the onion.

Stromberg looked toward Maggie. She found his gaze, her eyes locking on his with radar precision. She winked. Not a flirtatious wink or a coy wink. It was a Machiavellian glint that clearly announced: *Get ready, boys...here it comes.*

The big reveal. Maggie's big news flash.

A voice from the crowd shouted out, "Sure ya can!"

Another followed, "Go for it, Ziggy."

The Brewskis started bellowing, "ZIG-GY! ZIG-GY! ZIG-GY!" The pumped their fists in the air with beer-fueled abandon.

A chorus of voices from the audience joined in, shouting out its ardent encouragement. The random shouts soon turned to a singular chant, escalating in fervor and volume. "Ziggy! Zig-gy! ZIG-GY! ZIG-GEEE!"

"No, no, listen," Ziggy said. "Wait, wait..." Raised his hands to quiet them, anxious to throw himself on the pyre and get it over with.

Hearing his pleas, the chanting gradually subsided, with scattered shrieks, shouts and snatches of rowdy applause erupting from zealous pockets of the crowd.

"What I'm trying to tell you is..." He paused for a strong intake of breath. "I *can't* sing."

A tense hush descended. A confused murmur washed through the crowd, rising and falling on a wave of discontent.

Ziggy felt like barfing, fainting, curling up and dying right there on stage, a melodramatic reaction so freaking Shakespearean that he flushed with shame.

Joe and Ray stared wide-eyed. Neither of them had blinked since Ziggy stepped up to the microphone.

Gallagher raised his drumstick over the snare, poised to hit a rim shot to shatter the tension and then, wisely, thought better of it.

"Ya can't? Or you *won't*?" shouted ornery curmudgeon Gunnar Stout, fingers massaging the ten spot in his pocket Maggie had slipped him earlier.

An expectant hush fell. Ziggy had no choice now but to confess all and let the mob start pounding him.

Joe abruptly appeared at Ziggy's side, slipping an arm around his shoulder, bobbing a confident nod. Leaned into the microphone with sober sincerity.

"What he's trying to say is..." He paused for dramatic emphasis. "Ziggy's developed a critical throat condition."

That got things real quiet. Ray gave Gallagher a knowing glance. They both recognized that tone in Joe's voice. The magic man was back at work, weaving a brand new fantasy.

"Doctors tell us he's got a terrible bad case of damaged bifibulatic vocal cord demystification," Joe said, rolling the words out quickly before anyone could parse their meaning.

Ray swung his head to the side so no one but Gallagher could see him roll his eyes; Joe's line of bullshit was truly testing the waters.

"And, sorry to say," Joe continued, "looks like this awful affliction could be permanent."

A disappointed groan arose in the majestic Elk's Hall.

Maggie's fleeting eyes surveyed the hubbub erupting around her. That was a twist she hadn't seen coming.

Deep in the crowd, State Trooper Ron Von Ahlen folded his arms across his chest; shook his head with a woeful frown. "That poor fellah's cursed. First that darn hernia, now this here throat deal."

Next to him, Gunnar irritably grumbled, "They're all hooked on drugs, them goddamn hippies." Raising his voice at the end, figuring his crusty ad-lib should be worth at least another five bucks. He'd have to talk with Maggie.

The surge of grim disappointment and confusion that slithered through the crowd began to grow into a loud rumble of dissent.

Stromberg and Rafferty sat upright, casting worried glances at the rising commotion.

Ziggy grabbed the microphone. "Wait, wait, wait. Just because I can't..." His eyes flitted to Janey. "There's someone else I want you to hear. One of your very own." He pulled in a breath. "Janey Olsen."

She was startled to hear her name, the shock of it reverberating through her whole body. A startling sense of inevitability gripped her throat, both fearsome and acutely exhilarating. She wanted to run, but wasn't sure which way, toward the stage or away from it.

The chorus of abrasive comments and grousing rising around her became a troubling dirge of discontent; flapping dark wings of crows beating hard against her ears.

Ray pushed his way to the microphone, nudging both Ziggy and Joe aside.

"He's right," Ray said. His voice boomed off the walls, rattling the restless natives to attention. Faces turned to him, frozen eyes expectant. "She's the real talent been hiding here in Hibbing. Right under your noses."

Ziggy did the closest thing to a perfect double-take since Martin and Lewis, mouth agape, eyes bulged like grapes; he couldn't believe he'd heard those words from Ray's lips. Equally farcical, Ray shot Ziggy a big smart-ass grin and made a feisty little click sound between his teeth and cheek.

"Janey, get up here," Ray said, looking right at her, brashly insistent. He quickly swooped to the edge of the stage, dropping to one knee, extending his hand toward her with a gallant gesture.

She audibly gulped, surprising herself. A look of terror was the mask she wore, but her leg muscles were already flexing, ready to stand, walk, leap forward.

Seeing her hesitation, but knowing her heart, Ziggy joined Ray, kneeling beside him, reaching out toward Janey.

The vast pause of anticipation, drenched in a silence that accentuated every tiny creak of floorboards and metallic squeak of folding chairs, let Janey know this ponderous moment would not end until she made a move.

Ziggy motioned her toward them. She abruptly sprang from her chair, as if leaping from a perilous perch across a chasm to the safety of rescuing arms. Ziggy and Ray, each taking a hand, pulled her up onto the stage, her body so light and their effort so exuberant that she rose like a feather in their grasp.

Moving close to her ear, Ziggy coaxed her with a gentle whisper. "From up here you can't even see their faces. Just look way out, right over their heads."

She swallowed the lump of fear in her throat and took his hand, walking slowly with him toward the microphone. Ray trailed behind, looking off to Maggie in the wings with a swaggering grin.

In the front row of tables, Carl said, "That poor girl's been through enough crap. Why can't they just let her be?" Muttered to himself, but those close around him heard it.

"Let's get the Brewskis up here too," Ziggy said. He waved them toward the stage with a big swoop of his arms.

Ray and Joe both joined him in his grand gesture, desperate for replacements to get them off the hook.

Taken by surprise, Danny touched his chest, miming a broadly incredulous *who us?* gesture, flipping wide-eyed looks of disbelief at both Hal and Mike. But it was just an instinctive show of fake humility. All three scurried out of their chairs, vaulting up onto the stage like klutzy Olympic tumblers, clambering to their feet.

Danny and Mike went straight for two of the guitars, strapping them on. Behind them, Hal was forced to wrestle the drumsticks away from Gallagher who stubbornly resisted being dethroned.

"Oh-fer-geez... going from bad to worse," Carl said, turning away. "I can't watch."

Pete grabbed at the coat hooked on the back of his chair, trying to unravel it. "Heckuva thing. I already seen this damn fiasco down at the high school. Not a pretty sight then, and not one now neither."

Three tables away, Stromberg and Rafferty sat there dumbstruck and deflated.

"Amateur night," Stromberg grumbled. Shook his head mournfully.

"Made us out to be a couple of shmendriks," Rafferty said.

"Worse. Schmucks."

Rafferty checked his watch. "Still make that red-eye outta Duluth."

"Think so?"

"Drive like hell, maybe."

"Gonna save our jobs, we better."

Rafferty mulled it over, serious now. "Think maybe we wanted it too bad?"

"We hear what we hear, I guess."

"Sounded good at the time."

"Promising...crazy as it was."

"Ya take your chances."

Stromberg grimaced in frustration. "Shit." Stabbed the red Jello with his spoon.

Feeling alone and vulnerable, Janey looked back over her shoulder at the Brewskis. Gallagher floated behind them, wandering like a petulant puppy that had his chew toy stolen, plotting to get it back.

Danny smirked at Janey, giving her a confident nod of assurance, impulsively flashing a *thumbs-up*. He knew what to play.

As Janey's head came back around, the spotlight slammed on with a metallic thud, hitting her with a blinding blast of light, forcing a tight squint.

"Told you," Ziggy said as he brushed by her ear and moved away.

The Brewskis dropped seamlessly into the lilting blues preamble of *Piece of My Heart*. Janey swayed with it, both hands reaching up to softly embrace the microphone atop the stand.

The crowd stirred, but not in a good way, restless and disheartened that the big night had now taken a turn toward the tragically familiar.

Stromberg and Rafferty were up out of their chairs now, moving toward the main doors leading to the street. Most others were gathering their hats and coats—the murmur of disappointment colliding with the raw scrape of chair legs and shuffling feet on the creaking hardwood—desperate to escape before the pathetic embarrassment began.

Janey rocked gently from foot to foot as the music built, eyes nearly closed in the searing heat of the spotlight. She was about to throw herself on the same altar of sacrifice, in front of many of the same people who had once laughed at her, pitied her, mocked her with cruel reenactments of her shame.

And then it came. The powerful crush of her voice, coursing through the room like pure thunder. "*Come on!... come on!... come on!... come on!*"

Like a tide turned by the tilting of the ocean floor, people slowed, legs churning to a halt in thick sludge. Passengers on the Titanic, hearing the clarion call; *the lifeboats are the other way!* Some looked down, pausing to listen. Others rotated their heads, ears pricked up, peering back toward the stage.

Janey's mesmerizing voice, unexpected in its clarity, oozed out the bluesy lyrics of the first verse; words often lost in a drug/whiskey haze when sung by Janis, now soulful and aching, making the familiar new.

Stromberg stopped dead in his tracks, closing his eyes for an instant, letting the sound permeate his senses, then spun around on his heels to stare at Janey.

Rafferty, oblivious at first—focused more on elbowing his way toward the door so they could make their escape to Duluth—suddenly distinguished what he was hearing as something exceptional and froze, chin dropping slowly, his mouth agape. He turned slowly, along with those around him.

Backstage, Donny ambled over to Maggie who was transitioning to a whiter shade of pale.

"This it, Maggie?" Donnie said. "The big scam?"

"Shut up, Donnie."

Blinded by the glare of the spotlight, Janey couldn't see the mass retreat or subsequent resurgence of the crowd, but she could feel the energy mounting as looming shadows crushed toward the stage, a tsunami of breathing souls rising from the darkness to embrace her with their fascination. It cleansed her of fear, driving the mauling spirits of self-doubt into submission. Her voice soared, funneling all the crazed passion of youth into a glorious aria of hurt.

Standing just a few feet away, Ziggy was elated by the sheer power of her performance, his mind spinning. He imagined Janey reaching out to him, beckoning him to her side, encouraging him to join her in the dynamic refrain. Both of them at the microphone, in perfect harmony, his voice soaring just like hers as they traded raucous shouts of *come on... come on... come on.*

But then a sharp vision of high school chorus practice materialized in his head; a phalanx of teen girls yawning, droopy-eyed and bored stiff, giving him the evil eye for luring them into an overpowering yawn fest. He was the joker revealed. The fraud exposed. And that killed it. His fantasy dissolved in a dreary mist.

This was Janey's moment, not his.

A thundering applause snapped him back to reality. The song had exploded in a rousing crescendo, segueing into a cacophonous audience response.

At that moment, everything accelerated. The crowd surged toward Janey, young people effortlessly flinging themselves up onto the stage, crushing around Janey, bees converging on their queen, dancing the boogie-woogie of adoration.

Words of praise flowed with the ease and refreshing tang of cold lemonade on a hot summer day.

Stromberg and Rafferty pushed through the throng, using elbows and knees as battering rams. Flinging his arm out, Stromberg thrust his business card past heads, over shoulders, toward Janey.

"Miss Olsen, Miss Olsen," he said over the din of adoring voices, "I'm John Stromberg. Talent coordinator for The Ed Sullivan Show."

A hush descended on the horde of admirers as his words registered with them.

Janey stared numbly at him, not sure she heard right. All eyes around them focused on Stromberg. Rafferty squeezed in beside him, struggling with flailing fingers to fish a business card out of his own wallet, arm trapped by the press of people.

"How would you like to audition for Mr. Sullivan?"

Janey couldn't focus, now loopy with surprise.

Rafferty tried to chime in. "Yeah... uh, Mr. Sullivan... we, uh, could...I'm...just lemme get my..." Descending into an incoherent jumble of half-words until he finally came up with his card. It was immediately snatched from his fingers by Carl, who gave it a skeptical once over.

"Next week, if possible," Stromberg said. "We can fly you to New York."

"Yeah, fly you in, set you up in a hotel," Rafferty said.

"Well, I...I, uh...gee, I guess," Janey said, breathless, trying to stave off the dizziness pressing at the back of her skull.

"All expenses paid," Stromberg quickly added, trotting out the standard spiel for roping in cooperation from a potential talent.

Ziggy shouldered his way closer, squeezing next to Rafferty, who looked at him with total disregard now.

"And-and-and listen," Ziggy said, "I shot some film of her singing."

Janey jumped in excitedly. "It's true. He did." Trying to shift the attention to Ziggy and away from herself, hoping to ease the raw flush of fame seared into her skin by the spotlight.

"I can cut it together. Music...the song...whole thing. You could run it on the show too."

"Yeah yeah, thanks, pal," Rafferty said. "But no film. Ed Sullivan is a *live* program."

"We don't run film segments," Stromberg added, terse and tight lipped, completely ignoring the obvious truth; the show had often previously broadcast music film segments by performers, including the Beatles.

"But you don't understand," Ziggy said. "I don't want any money. You can have it. It's all yours. Free."

Stromberg grew defensive. "If she *was* on," he said, "we'd only want her on *live*, see."

"You get that, no?" Rafferty said, giving him the stern look that says *end of discussion*.

Ziggy continued to press. "But this is gonna be the next big thing. Music performance films. On television."

"Yeah," Stromberg said, "you're the prognosticator, kid. You and Marshal McLuhan."

The crowd squeezed tighter, pushing the mass of people one way, then the other, as everyone strived to get close enough to hear what was going on.

With each surge and heave, Ziggy was pushed further away from Janey.

He raised his arm straight up, an elevated submarine periscope with wiggling digits, disappearing in the tossing swell of humanity. "Just wait. You'll see. It's coming," he shouted. "Music television."

But his voice was lost to them as he was shuffled to the fringe of the crowd where his three cohorts waited—ignored by everyone now—relief in their eyes. Except Gallagher, who continued to burn with feverish excitement.

"We coulda played as good as those guys," he said, somehow still believing it. The others let it ride. Why pop the bubble of a true optimist and gallant fool?

Later, while driving back to Chicago in the dinged-up donated Chevy, Joe slapped a firm hand down on Ziggy's shoulder. "I take it back," he said. "This thinking stuff just might be your bailiwick after all."

Ziggy smiled, let that soak in, enjoying the vote of confidence and the warm feeling it gave him. After a half-mile or so, he turned to ask Joe, "What exactly is a bailiwick?"

Joe gave it a pause. Stared straight ahead at the road, tires humming steadily on the highway. Finally said, "Hell if I know. Heard Paul Harvey say it on the news once."

"It's a West Germanic word borrowed from vicus, the Latin for village," Gallagher said, as if it was perfectly normal for him to know this stuff. "It means *special domain*."

After that it grew very quiet. There were many miles to go before they'd sleep and many promises to keep.

PART TWO
AFTER HIBBING

*"In plucking the fruit of memory
one runs the risk of spoiling the bloom"*
Joseph Conrad

DAVID O'MALLEY

HIDING IN HIBBING

JANEY

Janey never got her chance to audition for Ed Sullivan.

Stromberg and Rafferty had returned to the familiarity of Manhattan immediately following Janey's performance at the Elks Hall, racing on icy roads to Duluth, barely making the red-eye as the main cabin door was being pulled shut.

While attempting their hasty escape from Hibbing, Maggie had relentlessly dogged their heels all the way to the rental car, babbling about her big story and how she had been the one who actually discovered Janey; *that*, she claimed, was the urgent breaking news flash she had promised to let them in on.

We're not reporters, they insisted, hustling away. *We're not from the NY Times!*

But she didn't get it, lost in the confusing jumble of her own reality, still playing the role of a hot shot news hound with a Pulitzer in her future.

When they rushed into the Ed Sullivan Theater at daybreak, unshaven and disheveled from the flight, they were met by an aura of despair brought on by the looming shadow of a very large network axe about to fall.

They defended their actions, strategically evading any discussion of the dubious motivations that had prompted their unannounced trip. Rafferty heaped praise upon the astounding treasure they'd unearthed in the heartland of America, extolling Janey as the vanguard of a new age of performers.

"She's more than a breath of fresh air," Rafferty said, popping out the first in a series of showbiz clichés. "She's a furious hurricane of pure oxygen."

Keeping a cool lid on his own hyperbole, Stromberg assiduously explained that Janey represented a blend of the evolving rock genre and classic pop music.

Rafferty frosted this rational line of reasoning with gooey embellishment, declaring that she would blast open a door to the burgeoning youth market while also capturing the aging fuddy-duddies and geriatric killjoys.

"She's like a pristine mountain stream, pure and fresh," Rafferty said, already figuring how to sell her to the entertainment press. "But with a raw edge of danger that makes Janis Joplin look like an angel."

Stromberg rolled his eyes, but kept his mouth shut. Bringing up the fact that Janis *was* dead—and therefore already an angel of sorts herself—would only prove to be an unnecessary distraction.

Rafferty's spiel was all a crock of bullshit, of course. But that obvious flaw was lost in the foggy buzz of panic that was growing as CBS continued to put the squeeze on the show to defend its relevance.

Ed was pissed at Stromberg and Rafferty for running off on a wild goose chase without his approval, but also intrigued by their glowing reports of an incredible young performer discovered in Hibbing, hometown of Bob Dylan.

John Stromberg had been right on the money; Ed saw this as a golden opportunity to redeem himself in the eyes of the television audience, digging into the American heartland to discover the stars of tomorrow. He would re-imagine his *Ed Sullivan Show* as a crystal ball for talent that reached into the future, not the past. And he could use this unknown girl from Bob Dylan's hometown as the signature prototype of a new generation.

Following several weeks of protracted back-and-forth discussions to hash out travel details and other nuances, Janey had finally been flown to New York City and ensconced in the Statler Hotel, just down the street from the Ed Sullivan Theater, to await her audition.

HIDING IN HIBBING

She spent the entire first week in her hotel room, biting her nails while watching television or gazing with lonely eyes at the tiny scuttling ants of dithering civilization below her window, unaware that the machinations of a television classic were already winding relentlessly toward self-destruction.

She phoned Ziggy every night, dazzling him with imaginary tales of all the new adventures she'd experienced, infusing her voice with false enthusiasm as she related summarized highlights from the tourist guide discovered in the desk drawer, claiming them to be her own thrilling escapades. She left no doubt in Ziggy's mind that she was clearly smitten with the Big Apple.

After six days, bored to sobs, Janey forced herself to finally venture out. She took a cab to Greenwich Village; a rollicking, bouncing, honking, swerving, frightening ride that shook the fear right out of her bones. Recognizing her naïve vulnerability, the Jamaican taxi driver—with wild dreadlocks flaring like the snakes of Medusa and a broad grin hanging from two ears—graciously let it slide when she neglected to tip him.

She wandered into the Bitter End, a club she'd read about in a copy of the Village Voice found discarded in the hotel lobby. Slipping into an empty chair at a small table in a darkened corner she ordered an Irish coffee; it sounded romantic, even daring. That was the moment her fascination with Manhattan—so convincingly faked to Ziggy on the phone—began to evolve into something truly tangible.

She felt a resurgence of belief that this dream might be real, not just some midnight flight of fancy experienced beneath the safety of her grandmother's quilt. An audition for the Ed Sullivan Show was no minor achievement. The possibility of her actually singing on national television— witnessed by millions of viewers—was itself a wondrous phenomenon.

A warm glow of confidence swept through her. *This could really happen*, she mused over and over, graced with a smile of contentment. *This is happening. I'm here now. Right now. I could become a singing star on the Ed Sullivan Show.*

But as the quaintly bucolic saying goes, *that horse had already left the barn.*

By the beginning of March the *Ed Sullivan Show* had plummeted to 43rd in the ratings. On the 17th of March, following a painfully prolonged and contentious controversy over the long-running program's viability in the crazed pantheon of contemporary media, the dreaded phone call came.

The last *Ed Sullivan Show* was broadcast on March 28, 1971; a final bloody sacrifice to the indifferent gods of commerce.

The series was way past its prime, the CBS network executives successfully argued. It had run out of steam in a world operating on petroleum, electricity, solar power and, soon, microchips. The viewing audience no longer craved a smorgasbord of drastically incongruent acts that spanned cheap vaudeville and esoteric ballet, Italian opera and cute animal tricks, Broadway tunes and the messy guts of rock-and-roll, not to mention the gritty bump-and-grind of black R&B. The times, obviously, had been changing all along.

When word finally came to Janey that the show had been cancelled and her audition was off, she was crushed. She never even had the opportunity to meet the legendary Ed Sullivan. Nor did the great *stone face* ever get a chance to see or hear the lovely gem that his two ambitious talent coordinators had plucked from obscurity. In a flash, all that evaporated.

But an emerging New York resilience had already begun to coalesce with Janey's stubborn Minnesota tenacity; infused by a newly forged unwavering spirit, she decided to stay in Manhattan rather than return to Hibbing and face humiliation again.

Upon learning that Janey's shot at stardom had been callously dashed, Ziggy told her he would jump on the first flight to New York. But she quickly assured him she was okay, pleading with him not to waste the money. "I'll be fine. I will," she told him. He listened. She waited.

"I came to the mountain," she finally said, hoping the familiarity of the phrase would ease his concern. "Now I have to see what's on the other side."

His palpable silence prompted Janey to gnaw on her bottom lip, worried she might have somehow crushed something precious in him. It wasn't that she didn't want to see Ziggy. She craved his comforting presence and the easy way he nudged her confidence to the surface—the magic that had entranced her in Hibbing. But something told her that what lay ahead she must now face on her own. Ziggy had already emancipated her from so many doubts; lovingly pushing and prodding her to overcome the fear and shame that had immobilized her far too long. But now she needed to know she could do it by herself. All of this raced through her mind during his unbearable silence on the other end of the line, while she struggled to find the right words to describe her clashing emotions.

Then, just as she began to wonder if the call had been disconnected, she heard Ziggy's voice cut through the ocean roar of hissing static.

"I understand," he said. Simple as that.

Janey exhaled a gush of relief, not questioning how he knew what she was thinking, feeling. Hoping that was why he'd said it.

Later, after they had hung up—following numerous sincere promises to call each other as often as possible—she experienced a plummeting sadness. As if she had cruelly betrayed him by not accepting his gallant offer to fly immediately to her side. But as soon as she stepped onto the street, breathing in the raw dirty energy of the city, and later gobbled down a pastrami-on-rye at the Broadway Deli, the murky feeling of guilt passed.

Janey had made new friends during her forays into the Village and, upon hearing her disappointing news, they generously offered her a place to crash as long as she wanted. It was, she mused to herself, as if this was all meant to be; the pieces were tumbling into place with the guidance of benevolent fate.

Manhattan was like Oz to her, filled with glorious sounds, lights and colors. Aromas in the streets, at first pungent, sometimes repellant, soon became delicious as they took on personal meaning, affixed to the mounting pleasant memories of recent days. It wasn't a step up for her; it was a magnificent leap ahead.

On the flurry of nights that followed, Janey and her friends made the rounds of all the coolest clubs in the Village —the Bitter End, Café Au Go Go, Café Wha?—becoming regulars at the Village Gate where a couple of new guys on the block, John Belushi and Chevy Chase, tore things up every night in *National Lampoon's Lemmings*. This led to hanging at a dinky hole-in-the-wall at Bowery and Bleecker that eventually became the famous punk haven, CBGB. But before being swallowed up by the crass New Wave beast, she migrated to the siren call of jazz at the Village Vanguard, and then the Blue Note, where the hip bohemian atmosphere was decidedly seductive, and the sounds even cooler.

For a while Janey had a semi-serious boyfriend, an aspiring folk musician named Stephen who played banjo and told rambling philosophical jokes—*"So Aristophanes and Aristotle walk into a library..."*—that were way too esoteric to generate honest laughs. Eventually their tenuous relationship dissolved in a strident rush of contentious blather.

Alone and miserable, Janey finally called her mother to tearfully unload her mantle of misery with a cascade of tears, hinting that she might return to Hibbing. Her mom told her, "Don't you come back here girl. Do that, you'll miss out on life."

HIDING IN HIBBING

Knowing her mother was right, Janey once again vowed to stay.

Like many caught up in the swirl of Manhattan madness, she soon found herself drawn into the enticing world of theater, secretly hoping to sing on the Broadway stage. Dedicated to this new course of action, Janey waited tables at the Stage Deli, occasionally trying on a horribly rendered Brooklyn accent, prompting puzzled looks from the Jewish regulars and a muttered rumble of *"oy veys"* and *"the shiksa is mishuga."*

She threw herself into the heartbreaking, soul-numbing grind of auditions for endless months that ultimately segued into years, until she finally lost all hope, being told too many times that she was "really really very very good, but maybe, much too nice." It was the New York City version of Hollywood's *we'd love to be in business with you* or, as Stephen called it, the *long friendly "hell no."* Stephen had also told her, "In L.A. they stab you in the back, but in New York they stab you in the chest, right in the heart, so at least you know it's coming." Either way she was tired of being stabbed, weary of the incessant warnings. She knew it was time to ditch her wayward dream of a career in the theater.

The very next day, on June 12, 1975—wracked by an especially unruly monthly cycle—she shuffled to the Belasco Theater for her final scheduled audition.

Following a particularly listless tryout for the latest recasting of *Grease*—capped off by a curtly dismissive shrug and indignant groan from the bored director—she finally uncorked her bottled-up rage, angrily telling him off with an unexpected repertoire of raw expletives she had only recently seen in Jerry Rubin's *Steal This Book*, plus a few from that dog-eared copy of *On The Road* she'd found lying around Stephen's loft; words she'd never spoken before, some she'd never even heard. Janey had burned her fuse to the very nub, and then exploded, collapsing on the stage after her crazed tirade, red-faced, convulsing, tears smearing her cheeks.

DAVID O'MALLEY

And she got the role; Marty, one of the Pink Ladies, plus understudy for both Rizzo and Sandy. *Grease* ran at the Royale Theater until November 21, 1979. Her Broadway career was off and running.

Go figure.

ZIGGY

Ziggy and the guys had made a hasty retreat from the B.P.O.E. Hall that memorable night, quietly slipping out before anyone could corner them with any probing questions, or worse, threatening accusations. They didn't expect to be greeted by Happ standing in the parking lot beneath the dim halo of a streetlight, bundled in his puffy down jacket with an Elks patch sewed on, a hearty grin pushing his red apple cheeks all the way back under his earflaps.

"Nope. No limousine, fellahs," he said. Stepped toward them, reaching for something in his pocket.

They stopped in their tracks, braced for the worse, anticipating that a much-deserved retribution might be at hand.

Happ held out a plastic fob with a single key dangling from it.

"Got your Chevy van right here though," he said, handing the key off to Joe. "She rattles a bunch, but pay it no mind. She'll likely hang together alright."

"Thanks," Joe said, his voice squeezed and raspy, the huge relief he felt drawing the air through his dry throat.

Not wanting to risk the prospect of further discussion, Joe motioned the guys toward the rusted heap. They wasted no time, tromping off with a steady gait, all the while resisting a desperate urge to dash away like fleeing convicts.

"Joe," Happ said, nodding him aside. "Could we, uh...?"

Joe froze. He made an odd shuddery movement of conciliation and then tossed the key to Ray, who hesitated for only a brief instant before leading Ziggy and Gallagher to their getaway car. Joe turned to Happ with quizzically raised eyebrows and a wrinkled smile, striving to paint a portrait of innocence on his face.

"My old friend, Dr. Michelson, works up the miner's hospital, he was here tonight. All excited to hear you fellah's play." Happ stepped closer to Joe, keeping his voice low and confidential. "Told me he never heard of that particular affliction...that bifibulasta-whatever-whatever you said."

Joe felt a chill run down his spine. Looked at his feet with a little nod, trying to keep the guilt on his face in deep shadow.

"But he did recommend some hot black tea with a little lemon and honey oughta do wonders. Clean it right out of poor Ziggy. Get him good as new," Happ said, before noticing the blank look on Joe's ashen face. "Oh, I know, it's not your fancy modern medicine and what not, but sometimes the old way is best."

Joe looked up at Happ. Saw the twinkle hiding back there behind his eyes.

Awash with remorseful gratitude, Joe said, "We, uh..." It ended there, the rest unspoken and unnecessary.

"No need," Happ said with a flap of his hand. "What you did for us... giving one of our own a shot at something better, that there's a gift."

Sitting in the van waiting for Joe, Ziggy anxiously watched the back door of the Elks Hall, hoping that Janey would somehow magically materialize, her lovely face aglow with tearful gratitude. He imagined she would rush to the van, embracing him with trembling passion, casting aside all feelings of cruel betrayal, swooning in the caress of a personal dream now realized. And then, uttering her undying love for him with those softly sensuous lips—her sweet compassion a welcome balm to soothe his curse of culpability—she would beg him to take her with him.

But she didn't appear. When the van door opened, illuminating the roof light with a startling blast of brightness, it was only Joe climbing in, exhaling a long slow breath of relief.

HIDING IN HIBBING

Riding in silence on the way to the motel to get their bags and personal items, Ziggy asked Joe if he could keep the film footage he'd shot and the tape he'd recorded.

"Well, ya messed it all up by shooting stuff I can't use, so might as well," Joe said. "No good to me now." His tone was cranky and displeased, but Ziggy could hear through it, sensing the generous granting of a wish.

When they hit Chicago the next afternoon, hastily dropped off in The Loop by Joe to go their separate ways, the parting was desultory. Joe's terse farewell to Ray, Gallagher and Ziggy was clouded by an unexpected finality.

The local train to Wheaton seemed to crawl, leaving Ziggy in a tense funk. Thoughts of Janey filled him with anxiety. It was nearly dark by the time he raced up the stairs and fumbled to unlock the door of his cramped studio apartment. He had to dial the phone three times before his fumbling fingers finally got Janey's number right.

Hearing her voice caused his stomach to flutter wildly, spinning with the sweet nausea he used to get when plunging off the high dive at the community pool, floating untethered and helpless.

His rapid jumble of words mashed together as he struggled to make amends for his abrupt departure the night before, begging her forgiveness once again for misleading her. But she assured him that he didn't need to explain or apologize for anything.

"I don't care who everyone thought you were," she said. "I only care who you are to me."

He hit the water, the harrowing plunge complete. The welcome comfort of gravity returned in soft waves, warm silence engulfing him with calm.

Her excitement poured through the phone in a torrent. Yes, they are going to fly her to New York. Yes, she is going to audition for Ed Sullivan...*the* Ed Sullivan. When? Soon, maybe, she's not sure exactly. There are still so many arrangements to be made and paperwork to sign. And interviews. The TV station in Minneapolis wants to interview her. They're sending someone next week.

After nearly a half-hour of garrulous and unbridled elation, Janey paused, then softly told Ziggy how grateful she was that he had believed in her. A long pause followed... a space that was full, not empty.

They promised each other they would talk every day and write often. And for a while they did.

When Janey called him upon her arrival in New York at the beginning of March, her excited description of the flight —her very first time ever on an airplane—was laced with the delirious exhilaration of a sugar-charged child. "My plane was pink! Or lavender! Can you believe it? It was Braniff. All their planes are different colors. Green, yellow, even one with polka dots."

He was thrilled by her delighted exuberance, pleased she had focused on a goal that might ultimately define her life; the kind of reliable certainty that continued to stubbornly elude him. He often found himself floating on the cockeyed dreams of others, wandering without a compass, peering toward horizons that never came clearly into view.

He laughed encouragingly at her dizzy first impressions of the Big Apple, unaware they had all been conjured by nickel-a-word travel writers who had likely cribbed them from other brochures and tattered guidebooks that came before. They seemed to pour from Janey with such pure conviction, prompting him to smile with an unbridled pleasure. It was exactly what he'd hoped for her—an innocent explosion of enchanted joy at discovering a world that seemed to lie far beyond her comprehension. And he had been the one to open that door for her.

Ten days later, when Janey called with news that the show had been cancelled and her audition was off, Ziggy felt strangely unmoved. He was, of course, very sympathetic, and expressed sincere disappointment. But a veil of acceptance surprisingly enveloped him in a dull cocoon.

"I'll come there today," he said, impulsiveness trumping reflection. "I can get the next flight out." Upon hearing his own words, he felt startled, as if someone else in the room had spoken on his behalf.

In a single prescient moment, his life flashed before him, as in the movies when all the past highlights of a dying man's existence race by in an artful montage. Only this was a herky-jerky flash-forward—a sloppy muddle of tumbling images and swirling emotions—revealing what lay ahead. He saw an endlessly spiraling quest to convince the powers-that-be of Janey's incredible talent, with him trudging by her side every step of the way; the fake Ziggy, the sham from Hibbing—touting, cajoling, promoting, reassuring, prodding—ultimately becoming an unwelcome anchor that would drag her down. He'd be a pathetic proxy; the blind leading the blond.

Ziggy opened his mouth to speak, unsure what words would follow, yet willing to let his subconscious take the reins. But before he could utter a sound, Janey let him off the hook. "I'm okay. Really. Don't waste your money on a flight," he heard her say. "I'll be fine. I will."

He waited for his own words to come, but they remained trapped and elusive.

Then he heard her say something about the mountain and seeing what was on the other side. Echoing their hushed moonlight talks in Hibbing, the soft steady calmness of her voice filled him with an inexplicable and unearned assurance.

A pause longer than baseball season held them glued to their respective phones, the long-distance abyss a symphony of celestial clicks, pops and sizzles.

Finally, Ziggy said, "I understand." And, somehow, he did.

As weeks passed, Ziggy felt the tenuous bond between them gradually begin to dissolve, soon convinced that the once strong link in their chain of shared experience had been irrevocably broken.

In the course of their nightly phone calls, Ziggy couldn't tell for sure if she might now have a boyfriend. Janey never clearly identified the friends she had made—whether male or female, tall or short, crazy or sane—and never uttered their names. He was reluctant to ask her directly if she was seeing someone, dreading the long vacant pause that would surely follow as she considered whether to lie or confess.

Over time, the skirting of this sensitive issue led Ziggy to believe she was sheltering some dark secret, trying to avoid hurting him at all costs. Eventually their letters grew shorter, arriving days, and then even weeks apart. The phone calls were marked by longer pauses, filled with an ominous soft hollowness that bore a dreaded implication words would only have further misconstrued or improperly minimized.

The effort to communicate with Janey was now shrouded in too many painful contradictions. A fog of sadness and regret loomed over a dream crushed, a naive innocence shattered. Picking up the phone became an ominous weight he no longer wanted to bear.

Following a period of self-imposed misery, he finally awoke one morning to the vibrant cacophony of loud car honks, wailing sirens and blaring roar of the city, coming to an incisive realization. The world was alive and he'd been playing dead; a pathetic possum grotesquely wallowing in self-pity. He kicked himself out of his own bed, cursing the useless loser he'd become.

Desperately short on cash, he begged a job chopping cabbage and slicing liverwurst at the deli around the corner and three blocks down from his apartment building. He walked to work each morning right down the middle of Pulaski Street, imagining himself on the legendary album

HIDING IN HIBBING

cover of *The Freewheelin' Bob Dylan*, hands jammed recklessly in his pockets, only without the cute girl on his arm.

With the help of Dennis Hugee, a high school friend who worked on educational films at Scholastic Productions, he was able to get his 16MM footage covertly slipped into the night lab run for processing and printing. Then, sometime after midnight, Dennis would sneak him into the editing room and they would work until dawn on a KEM flatbed cutting together the footage of Janey lip-synching her song at the Misabi Range Mineral operation and out on the vast starkness of Swan Lake.

"She's a babe, man," Dennis said. "You get in her pants?"

"Shut up," Zig said, cutting him off with a withering look.

They got a sound guy who was bored stiff doing graveyard-shift sound transfers to unlock the mixing booth so they could clean up and edit the audio of Janey's performance with The Brewski's at the Holiday Inn.

"Not bad," Biff, the sound guy, said. "Sexy thang. She got nice tits?"

"Shut up," Ziggy said.

Dennis and Biff flashed knowing looks at each other. They easily recognized Ziggy's helpless emotional condition —unrepentant infatuation.

When it was all edited, synched and mixed, they transferred it to video, laying off a copy to Betamax, the hot new format that had captured the public's fascination. Screening the final music video, Dennis leaned back with a huge grin.

"I dig the VW goin' through the ice," he said. "That's some radical shit, man."

Ziggy took the final videocassette to all the network-affiliated TV stations in Chicago, insisting that he personally screen it for whoever was highest on the executive chain.

Impressed by his enthusiastic chutzpah, the station manager at WGN—a programming leader in the Midwest market—agreed to sit down with Zig to give it a look.

When the final shot swept from Janey's traumatized expression, swish-panning with shaky conviction to the VW bus sinking slowly into the frozen lake, the station manager barked a startled laugh.

"Great! Great! I love the bus taking a nose dive," he said. "How'd you do that? Some kind of special effect?"

All that effort, plus Janey's unquestionable talent, and the guy loves the one genuine tragedy that had befallen them.

Ziggy kept his cool. Tried to shift the focus back on Janey. Described his idea for a new television channel featuring nothing but music videos.

"Not gonna happen, "the WGN guru said with brash certainty. "Aren't enough of 'em around. And who cares anyway? Music is auditory. People listen to it, they don't watch it. You want pictures, go to the movies."

Frustrated by such blind pigheadedness—but clearly undeterred—Ziggy continued to pitch his concept all over town, bending the ear of anyone who would listen, showing his video to whoever he could lure into a chair with his earnestly appealing patter.

Everybody loved the VW bus crashing through the ice, sinking like a German Titanic. But the moment was a freaky quirk; the song preceding it now seen as merely a shaggy-dog preamble to the unexpected silly twist at the end.

Refusing to be vanquished by the pedestrian lack of foresight that greeted him, Ziggy took a different approach. If he simply denied people the ability to *see* the submerging automotive U-boat, they couldn't become fixated on it.

He set up a meeting with Chuck Walters, program director at radio station WLS-AM, the 50,000 watt dynamo that fed the hottest hits to America, convincing him he possessed a recording that would change musical history. Once again, it was not what he said but how he said it that nailed the meeting for Ziggy. His lively enthusiasm and cockeyed imagination were proving irresistible.

Walters politely listened to the entire recording of Janey's song, all the way through the tremulous ending as her voice dramatically stumbled, broke, then crumbled, overrun by the Brewski's cacophonous instrumental climax.

An expectant silence followed as Walters gazed out the window at the Chicago skyline, finally turning to Ziggy.

"It seems to lack a satisfying conclusion, doesn't it?" he said.

Ziggy's brain took a wild spin in his head. A lightning bolt of pessimism struck, rattling his core. Doesn't anybody get it? Can't they hear it? Can't they hear *her*?

He snapped. Bypassing the community swimming pool and the dinky high dive, he leaped right off a towering cliff, plunging toward the pounding waves in a stormy sea below. He didn't even hear his own words as he recklessly hurled himself into a rabidly eloquent dissection of music and technology and the changes that were soon to shake the world. It was a circuitously rambling, yet strangely coherent, defense of pure talent and the sturdy thread of humanity that courses wildly through popular music; revealing our fears, concealing our love, always searching for solutions to the conflicts that drive our personal quest to be better, stronger, truer to our destinies.

Thoughts he didn't even know he had. Ideas lurking so deeply within his soul they were invisible by day, wearing masks to avoid detection, emerging at night in his dreams, colorful phantoms of inspiration that often tripped into his waking days without notice, lurking on the very edge of awareness.

Walters didn't interrupt him, perhaps knowing that, as when awakening a deep sleepwalker, the outcome could be dangerous. But as Ziggy came drifting back to awareness, his jagged breathing settled into a steady rhythm. His eyes became focused and clear. Walters smiled at him kindly.

He had no interest in the song or the singer. Instead Walters offered Ziggy a daily fifteen-minute show on WLS to talk, rant, speculate...providing an entertaining analysis of the numerous current technological and social developments he envisioned on the horizon—peppering it with his own personal predictions of future breakthroughs. He urged him to be as radical, crazy and extreme as he wanted to be.

Chuck Walters clearly understood the true value of controversy in capturing the ears of more listeners—securing a greater share of the highly competitive broadcast market, thus allowing the station to raise ad rates. And so, *Ziggy Zigmond's Over the Edge* was born.

Ziggy settled into a decade-long run on the station, garnering a relatively small but dedicated audience of oddball listeners who could somehow appreciate his weirdly speculative musings.

After recording his daily show for later broadcast, Ziggy often hung around the station, regaling various disc jockeys coming off shift with his latest inspirations. His persistent reiteration of the "music television" notion—something he had unconsciously restrained himself from ever mentioning on air—had pushed his co-workers to mock him with straight-faced sarcasm, baldly ridiculing him for harboring an obsessively unrealistic desire to somehow get his one-and-only music video on television.

"Give it up," Dan Feretti, the morning drive-time DJ told him. "Stick that babe in your '*it was nice while it lasted, but it's time to move your ass on*' file. Life goes on, bud. Don't get stuck in the shitty rat hole of the past." Feretti had a way with words.

Eventually, Ziggy followed his advice. Tucked the Beta video and audio cassette in the bottom of his sock drawer, pulling them out only on those rare occasions when he had too much to drink and became seriously sappy, watching the video over and over until he passed out on the couch.

HIDING IN HIBBING

Ziggy dated numerous women over the years. Many of them were extremely attractive, often possessing distinctly elusive charms. Some were even quite easy to listen to as they colorfully recounted their many disappointments and triumphs in life. While others seemed to forget they were actually out on a *date*, endlessly complaining in painful detail about previously unfaithful boyfriends, as if Ziggy was some kind of supportive gal-pal who would happily lend an ever-present sympathetic shoulder to cry on, while freely offering intimately compassionate advice.

When he zoned out during those depressing evenings, he would think about Janey, grow despondent, drink too much, then go home and watch the video again. He was stuck in the eternal looping re-run of an agonizingly cruel sitcom.

Then, just after midnight on August 1, 1981, Dan Feretti called, woke him up, excitedly demanding he turn on his TV. "Channel thirteen, dude. Do it now." Ziggy rubbed his groggy eyes, turning the set on, switching the channel. And there it was, in all its crazy glory...a rock group called the Buggles singing *Video Killed the Radio Star*. A music video. On the premiere of MTV. Music Television.

He sat with mouth agape, listening to Feretti laughing over the phone, giggling like a goofy kid. "You nailed it, you son-of-a-bitch, you nailed it," he heard the filtered voice say, drifting up faintly from the receiver now resting on the coffee table.

When The Buggles video ended, a shot of the moon landing appeared with an astronaut planting a flag on the lunar surface. But instead of the American flag, it was a flag with the MTV logo on it, clearly staking its claim on immortality.

Then *Video Killed the Radio Star* played once again, followed by the MTV astronaut, then the video, then the astronaut, then the video... over and over.

323

They only had a limited number of other music videos, cycled and recycled throughout the night. But who cared? The future had arrived.

The following week Ziggy finally told Chuck Walters about his prescient prediction regarding the advent of MTV. But Walters just laughed it off.

Ziggy squirmed, uncomfortably perplexed. "I thought you respected my ideas?"

"I did," Walters said. "I do. I *do*."

"But not this one."

"How come you never told me about it before?"

"I thought you'd laugh."

"What? Like I just did?" Walters scratched his head, tugged at his shirt cuffs, stalling, on shaky ground. "Come on, Zigmond, any bum out there can predict something *after* it fuckin' happens," he said. "When my wife left me, I told everybody that I saw it coming way before. Knew she was gonna dump me. I predicted it...years...*three* years...before we split."

Ziggy chewed this over with a grimace. "I don't see how that's relevant."

"Yeah, maybe not," Walters said, giving it a second thought, slumping back. "Guess they just bought into it because I was such a dick to her for so long."

"Yeah, that's sorta different than what I..."

Waved it off dismissively. "No matter. Point is, kids are gonna get burned out on all this jumping around, shaking their butts to rock songs. It'll never last."

"Oh, it'll last," Ziggy said. "It'll just change. Everything changes."

The next summer—June of '82—Ziggy got a phone call out of the blue from Janey. It took him completely by surprise, causing him to drop into a chair when his legs turned all rubbery.

"How'd you even find me?" he said, throat tightening.

"In the phone book, silly."

"Oh, yeah, sure," he said. He didn't even know he was listed, having never had a reason to look himself up.

She was in Chicago to help with auditions for the new road company of *Grease*, which was set to launch nationwide in the fall. She asked if he had time to meet her for lunch so they could catch up. Her request was brisk and off-handed, as if their encounter in Hibbing had happened only yesterday.

He stuttered a bit, trying to wrap his head around Janey's casually flip request, her ethereal face floating through his consciousness, foggy at first as he tried to fit the disparate pieces— eyes, nose, lips, hair— into a complete picture. Queasily disturbed by his inability to bring her sharply into focus, he reverted to his memory of the filmed images he had viewed over and over until they'd ultimately become the reality that replaced actual reality.

"Where are you?" he asked. It felt like such a stupid question, as if asking the location of a disembodied spirit floating somewhere in another dimension.

"Downtown," she said. "I'm not that familiar with Chicago. I think someone said we're near something called the Loop."

They settled on the Green Door Tavern on North Orleans Street, a burger and beer joint cherished for decades by locals. It was truly unpretentious but offered a warm familiarity that Ziggy hoped would serve to calm his frazzled nerves.

Catching his first glimpse of Janey, his blood surged. The manic flapping of wildly beating wings coursed through him. She still embodied the same sweet loveliness that had captured him a decade before.

They embraced and it did, indeed, feel like no time had passed at all. But there was something altered; a burnished strength that made her stand taller and move with assured grace, no longer alarmed by the small shocks of life.

"This is quite a place," she said, her eyes sweeping over the rough-hewn wooden beams, inhaling the sweetly sour aroma of ancient floorboards soaked by more than a century of spilled ale.

"It's one of the oldest buildings in the city," he said, glad to be talking about anything but feelings at this early stage of their reunion. "Built right after the Great Chicago Fire back in 1871."

She tilted her head, squinting with one eye at the far wall. "It feels like it's crooked."

"It is," he said. "It's been settling for a long time. One end actually tilts on a ten degree angle."

"Really?" Her eyes getting big. "Could it collapse?"

"Everbody's been waiting," he said, the corner of his mouth twisting wryly. "Could go any time now."

She joined easily in his droll speculation. "So the whole building could just crash down on us and we'd be trapped in here forever—together."

Their eyes met and held, the suggestion of eternity floating between them, the magical suspension finally shattered when a loud cheer for a Cubs triple arose from the patrons watching the TV above the bar.

Janey spoke with brightly animated excitement about her new life in Manhattan, eyes glinting neon, lashes fluttering, her slender expressive hands swimming in the air. Her words spilled out with the garrulous rapidity of an automatic weapon.

She told him of her great run in *Grease* on Broadway playing three—*three!*—different roles. And the incredible experience of studying with Stella Adler... "well, not Stella herself, but one of her *amazing* instructors." She raved about the restaurants, the bars, the clubs, the lights, the energy of a city that is truly a living creature. Not just bricks and steel and light, but a living, breathing animal that chases you all day and then curls up around you at night like a big furry Alaskan Husky keeping you warm and safe.

HIDING IN HIBBING

But she never mentioned a boyfriend or dating or anything that even hinted at a romantic entanglement, perhaps out of respect for Ziggy's feelings, or maybe just from the shame of having dodged the subject for so long.

For a while they even avoided reflecting on their time in Hibbing, fearing that if they danced too close to that fire they would both get burned. But Ziggy knew they couldn't continue to ignore it.

"Sorry the Ed Sullivan thing didn't work out," Ziggy said. He looked down at the table with sincere regret, as one would when eulogizing an old friend. It seemed like the right thing to do, although the obvious gesture felt somehow inappropriately melodramatic.

"Oh my God, no," Janey said. "I'm not. What if I had been on the show and *then* they got cancelled. I'd be blamed as the girl who killed *The Ed Sullivan Show*. No, later I heard it was coming on for a long time. The ratings were way down. It was inevitable."

He blinked. *Inevitable* was not a word he expected to hear from Janey. Nothing seemed inevitable to her now. She steered her life with such bold assurance.

"They're taking *Grease* on the road. It's a big hit. Really super popular. Have you seen it?" Not waiting for an answer, catching Ziggy as he started to shake his head, she moved on. "I'm gonna help with casting here and then in Denver. Then I'm back to New York. There's an audition for a revival of *Hair*. I can't miss that. I'd love to do *Hair*."

"Did your mom get to see you on Broadway in *Grease*?"

"No. She passed two years ago. Emphysema."

"Oh. I'm sorry."

Ziggy wondered, *why do people always say someone passed? What they did was die. You pass a history exam. You pass a note. You pass a bakery and don't go in. Lawyers even pass the bar. But when you die, you're dead. You're gone.*

He stared at the napkin in front of him, and the soggy cardboard coaster beside it. The mention of Janey's mother had put a gloomy damper on their reunion. Ziggy regretted bringing it up, sadly reminded of Janey's mom singing sweetly in her kitchen, thinking she was alone and unobserved.

Fortunately, the arrival of icy beer mugs and juicy burgers helped distract them from the intrusive pall.

With a bright smile, she mentioned seeing MTV, praising his brilliant intuition. "We all watch it. You knew it would happen. How did you know? It's just so amazing." Her words gushed forth rapidly, thoughts running together in sparkly bursts. "I think you knew because you have insight. Imagination. Stella, not really Stella, but her instructor, she says that imagination is reality preconceived. Or something like that. I can't remember. But you have it. Preconception. Or precognition. They're different, but it's subtle."

A dab of catsup on her lip looked like blood, reminding Ziggy of a rose, a red rose, and the sharp thorn that can so easily pierce the skin, the heart, of someone blissfully unaware. Her darting tongue licked it away, bringing his gaze back to her eyes; the bright long-ago eyes of Janey on that frozen Minnesota lake.

"Oh, I almost forgot," he said, reaching into his jacket pocket, retrieving a Beta videocassette.

Her eyes widened. "What is it?"

"It's you," he said proudly.

"Oh my God, you did it?"

"Yep. Edited, music all mixed and everything." He hesitated, nudged by a twinge of remorse. "I would have sent it to you, but..."

She cut him off. "Oh my God, I can still see that bus going through the ice, sinking into the lake. That was so freaking crazy!"

With a flat stillness he said, "Then you'll love it."

"Can you believe we did that?"

"It's Betamax, so..."

"No problem. All my friends have Beta players." She hugged the cassette like a doll, getting a smear of catsup on it. "Thank you so so much."

After lunch they walked back down North Orleans toward the Loop. The banter was light, skipping around the periphery of their varied experiences, touching on nothing with a pulse. At the corner of LaSalle and Randolph they hugged for a long moment, promising to call and write, ignoring the fact that they hadn't shared any new contact information.

He watched her walk to the corner, where she quickly turned and tossed a cheerful wave before disappearing from sight. He knew it would probably be the last time he'd ever see her.

On the train back to Elmhurst—where he'd moved the previous year into a new apartment—Ziggy marveled at how easily he had convinced himself he and Janey could have ever been a couple. Whatever volatile chemicals had collided in those chilled environs of Minnesota had somehow been neutralized by time and distance. He still adored her, but his enchantment was now steeped in a rusted coat of reason and rationalized perspective.

Then, almost home, he stopped on the sidewalk, leaning weakly against the wrought iron fence in front of a three-story brownstone, garbage cans propped obtrusively out front for pickup, tin monuments to the purring current of everyday life in the city.

Ziggy realized what had happened. That extraordinary moment when childhood ends and adulthood begins—when the boy becomes a man—had finally come and gone. He had promised himself to vigilantly watch for it, so that he might experience the elusive transition with full knowledge and awareness, taking the time to linger in its glory and brooding mystery. But in the charged muddle of life, it had cleverly eluded him; arriving in the middle of the dark night as he slumbered, creeping in undetected and robbing him of his cherished past, leaving him with an uncertain future.

Janey had undeniably changed. But it was his own transformation that now defined his world.

Contrary to Andy Warhol's glib prediction regarding the merciless brevity of fame, Ziggy's fifteen-minute radio show soon began to gain serious traction and expand, first to thirty minutes on Saturdays, then to a full hour during the Sunday morning news block. It proved to have a respectably successful run, capturing a loyal audience of forward-lookers, early adopters and open-minded dreamers.

But by 1987 WLS had abandoned its wildly successful leadership in music radio, phasing out the long-cherished Silver Dollar Survey and then drifting lugubriously into the burgeoning quagmire of talk radio.

Put off by the contentious mix of showboating blabbers and extremist political proselytizers, Ziggy jumped ship when offered the position as a daily columnist for the Chicago Tribune, finding a new home that suited him perfectly.

As the years crept by, Ziggy gradually shook the hold that Janey had on him. She rarely entered his freewheeling thoughts now unless prompted by some cogent phrase or potent aroma that would hold no place in his mind without her. And even then he gave the sudden reflection only a wisp of regard before consigning it to his cluttered warehouse of remembrance.

The boy he had once been fearlessly reveled in the fond recollection of the golden times; the man he had become recognized the potential for regret and loss lurking in the deceptive shadows of his memory, keenly aware that a bittersweet sting of melancholy could easily accompany the summoning of things past.

While walking five blocks each day from the Randolph Street Station to the Tribune Tower on Michigan Avenue, Ziggy began to take fleeting pleasure in scrutinizing the multitude of faces floating past him as he moved upstream. He analyzed the unending diversity of facial expressions, marveling at the crazy patchwork spectrum of attire, often ridiculously mismatched, ill-conceived and, more often than not, sweaty.

Over time he began to recognize faces that had appeared before, reading their emotional states with ease, mentally admiring or sharply critiquing their distinctive choice of shoe, sock, skirt or jacket on any given day.

As days passed, moving from the oppressive heat of summer into the briskly crisp coolness of autumn, one face in particular began to intrigue him; her porcelain cheeks and lively eyes framed by an explosive cascade of blond curls. His rapt attention was drawn to her lithe body as she navigated with vivacious ease through the morning crush on clicking heels.

He tried to scrutinize her as she passed by in a flash, there and gone, before he could manage to rivet his focus on her spirited dimples, adorable nose, delicately petite chin; his uncooperative eyes ricocheted like pinballs as they tried to take in the whole of her at once.

After a week of fleeting incursions, he took a different tack. Each morning, as he neared the bridge that crossed the Chicago River, he would crane his neck in hopes of spying her at a distance, giving him a longer period in which to observe her approach. When he would finally see flickers of her golden ringlets within the crush of people, he quickly maneuvered his trajectory so he could pass closer to her.

With each brief fly-by he would strive to study another tiny aspect of her attractive countenance: the gentle curve of her neck, soft luster of her skin, the eager concentration of her delicately sculpted brow, the glow of her rosy lips. Within a week or two, he had assembled a reasonable facsimile of her in his mind, able to recall it with relative ease while staring vacantly at the tank-like IBM Selectric on his desk.

Eventually, on a mid-October day warmed by a gentle Indian Summer breeze, their eyes met. Ziggy looked away quickly, pretending to admire the façade of a building, wincing painfully once she had passed, feeling like a clumsy criminal caught in the middle of a botched burglary.

The next morning, their eyes met once again, but this time he resisted the chicken-hearted urge to avert his eyes, tightening his neck, holding steady. Their gaze linked firmly, unblinking, for two...three...four...five seconds—which feels longer than one can possibly imagine—until they nearly brushed arms, wiping through each other's warm space and gauzy peripheral vision. Then...gone. Moving away; ships rocked by the tremulous wake of near collision. But they did not look back.

Ziggy was determined to end the anguish of this farce. He vowed the next time he saw her, he would not only look her in the eye, he would speak. There was a strange spark of familiarity that drew him to her and he felt daringly compelled to acknowledge it. And he would do it without preamble or agenda; he'd simply tell her what he felt at that very moment. If she slapped him or walked away or cursed him or just looked at him like he was a lunatic, so be it. What did he have to lose?

As luck would have it, his train was a few minutes late the next morning. He rushed up Michigan Avenue, making up for the delay with a skip-hop-step stride that altered between bursts of jogging and a goofy fast walk, breaking a slight sweat driven more by anxiety than exertion.

When he finally spotted her moving steadily toward him, he wondered for a moment if she might have arrived on her normal schedule, realized he wasn't there yet and had circled back to repeat her route so they could still meet. He dispensed with this ludicrous thought instantly, knowing it was the work of a foolish ego.

As she approached, her eyes found his without hesitation, locking on them like a vise. A warm charge gripped his thumping heart, his lungs squeezed bone dry as he struggled to slow his pace.

Look normal, casual, at ease, he thought, repeating the words like a self-help mantra, hoping it would calm him.

With just a few feet remaining between them, Ziggy opened his mouth to speak. He thought he saw expectation in her face, a glimmer of hopeful anticipation and the vague hint of a smile at the corner of her lips.

And he froze, mouth open, gripped by the certain knowledge that he could not possibly manage to speak. No sound would come forth because his mind had completely emptied.

There really *is* such a thing as a blank mind, he thought, terrified by the very prospect of providing a public display of pure idiocy. Instinctively—and remember, wisdom has no bearing whatsoever on instinct—he transitioned his *about to speak* open mouth into a terribly obvious imitation of a casual yawn: gaze drifting off, eyes squeezed in a squint of faux drowsiness, slack-fingered fist raised to his lips, politely shielding observers from the offensive indication of gross disinterest or boredom. The whole shebang.

And suddenly, she was gone.

He took a few more steps. Stunned. Mortified.

"Arthur?" a woman's voice said behind him.

He stopped, not sure if he'd imagined it.

"Arthur Zigmond?"

He turned around.

She had paused less than ten feet away, balanced lightly on one foot, the other extended out slightly in a graceful pose of tentative interest. Like a ballet dancer, he thought.

"I thought it was you," she said. Her smile was undeniably enchanting.

He cocked his head a bit, feeling that he knew her but unable to find the connection, wondering how long he could keep up this ruse of recognition.

"Susan Mitchell," she said, lightly touching fingertips to the center of her chest, just above her heart. "Taft High School."

Awareness flooded Ziggy, with a rush of images and emotions that caused his eyelashes to actually flutter like a flustered schoolgirl. "Suzy?"

"Well, Suzy back in school," she said, taking a step closer with a bashful shift of her shoulders. "And Sue to my parents..." a cute head wobble and a mortified roll of her eyes, "but you know parents. Then, I was Suzanne with a 'z' in college. Yeah, I know, kind of pretentious." Talking fast because she was nervous. "Now, I'm just plain old Susan."

"No, not plain. You look great. I just didn't..." he said, making a vigorous gesture that had no specific meaning.

"It's the hair," she said, anxiously twirling her finger in the gush of lovely curls. "In school I always had a pixie."

"Yeah. Short."

"Very," she said. "Very very."

"I remember. I liked it."

"You did?" She blushed faintly. "I didn't think you even noticed. "

"Are you kidding?" he said with fervor. Then, drawn again to the exquisite twisty convolutions resting against her cheek, he quickly added, "But I really like this too. A lot. It's so...wow." *Words fail me*, he thought. Then said it. "Words fail me."

She smiled at his frankness.

"I remember how you used to do that crazy fake yawn in choir and get us all started and in like less than a minute we were all yawning and giggling and we couldn't even sing a note."

"You remember that?"

"Well, yeah. How could I not?"

He looked down, shuffling his feet. "Really stupid stuff, I know."

"I loved it. I thought it was hysterical."

HIDING IN HIBBING

"Really?"

"Yeah, it was truly funny, the way you..." She hesitated, but only for a heartbeat. "I thought it was kind of sexy."

"You did?"

Was she pulling his leg? He couldn't be sure. But the flush in her cheeks and shy smile told him she was entirely sincere.

"So what are you doing now?" she quickly interjected, hoping to steer the conversation onto a less dizzying path.

Strangely comforted by her directness, he felt abruptly compelled to lay out his whole life, disclosing every incident, every doubt, every relationship, every tangled road he had followed to this point. But, reigning in the reckless urge, he simply said, "Oh, uh, I write a column for the Trib."

"You *do*?" she said, her dramatically arched eyebrows, steady smile and unblinking expression unable to totally obscure her decidedly muted enthusiasm.

"Yep. Five days a week. Sometimes for the Sunday edition too." He sensed something in her awkward silence. Finally asked her, "You read the Trib?"

Susan bit her bottom lip, embarrassed, her eyes darting demurely. Squinted her lids shut so she didn't have to see his face when she confessed, "I only read the Sun Times."

He looked right at her, unflinching, lovingly allowing her to wallow for a moment in her mortification, concealing the pleasant thrill growing in his heart.

"Not anymore," he said with surprising certainty.

JOE

It was already close to 2 p.m. when they finally hit the Loop, exhausted by the long drive back from Hibbing.

Joe dropped the guys off at Union Station so they could catch the El to scattered destinations, then headed straight for the Young & Rubicam office. He was anxious to report that the company utility van had been damaged way beyond recognition in the recent winter storm. Get it over and done with before he had second thoughts.

Matt Campbell, the comptroller said, "What? That VW piece of shit?" Making a face you usually see when someone has bad indigestion.

"Yeah. The bus."

"Fucking tin can death trap."

"Totaled," Joe said with a shrug.

"Good. May it rest in pieces. Now we can pick up one of those new Dodge vans with the floor heaters."

"No kidding? On the floor?"

Nodding yes. "In the back seat too. Sick of freezin' my feet off when they shuttle us to O'Hare."

"You need paperwork on it?"

"Anybody injured?"

"Couple of scrawny pines lost their needles." Joe gave it a beat, then added, "Slid right off the road into a lake."

"Seriously? A lake?"

"Through the ice. Right to the bottom. Everything in it. Lost it all."

Matt stared straight ahead, flummoxed. "Well, shit."

Joe gave him a few more moments to absorb this. "So... need anything?"

"Nah." It was exactly what Joe wanted to hear. "Our insurance guy, you know, Bob—sends us over a case of

Seagrams every Christmas?—he's cool. I'll just have him file the claim. Tell him we're getting a new vehicle. Maybe one of those Range Rovers with an eight-track."

Joe gave him a look, imagining the Y&R execs in ten-gallon cowboy hats and bolo ties, bouncing across the plains in a Range Rover listening to Willy Nelson. It was just a faint glimmer, because he really didn't care. But Matt caught it.

"Yeah yeah, I know, this is Chicago," Matt said, "not friggin' Montana. Screw it. We get a nice discount. Brian says he's got the account in the bag."

"Sounds good," Joe said. Made no difference, he wouldn't be around long enough to ride in it anyway.

That handled, Joe went looking for Saul Johnson. Found him in the main conference room bent over some lame storyboards for a Froot Loops pitch — clowns and brightly colored cars and circus animals — sweating a two-o'clock sacrificial dog-and-pony slaughter in front of a solemn panel of frozen-faced suits flown in from Kelloggs of Battle Creek.

Joe peered over his shoulder. "Seriously? Clowns?"

"What do you got, smart guy?"

"I don't. But for sure not clowns."

Saul slid a blank panel over the storyboard sketches, ending that debate. Rubbed his thinning comb-over, messing it up. "I got a call from Harvey Benson."

"Kind of a jerk."

"Not a happy jerk," shaking his head with a sigh, beads of sweat popping out between the squirmy threads of hair. "Said you blew him off."

"We couldn't get there. You mighta heard, the snow. Made Chicago look like Miami."

"Went out of his way to set it up for you."

"He had cheerleaders dressed like beer bottles."

"His company, his beer, his call, know what I'm sayin'?"

"When we got dug out, we offered to do whatever he wanted."

337

"He said you said talking fish."

"The guys and me, we were just brainstorming."

"With your crew? What the hell do they know?"

"Let's leave them out."

Saul rolled his head. It was all a pain in the neck. "You left me in a real bad spot, Joe. He's pissed."

Joe went around the table, standing across from Saul so he'd have to look him in the eye, know he's serious. "I'm done doing favors for guys who owe favors to other guys who are up to their asses in favors they owe."

"Oh really," Saul said, a little belligerent now.

"I'm out of the favor business."

Both locked in a stare-down, seeing who would blink first. Saul's left eye started to water from the strain. He looked down, wiped his eye with a finger, like he had something in it.

"So how we gonna resolve this here?" he said.

Joe crossed his arms, leaned back. "Fire me."

"I can't fire anybody. That's Stan's call. Or Bob. But this is personal, off the books, so they have no say."

"Okay. Then, how about I go the hara-kiri route?"

"Harry who?"

"I'll fall on my sword."

Saul squinted, only hearing the *sword* part. "I don't want to fight about this..."

"I quit," Joe said.

And that was it. Joe was done. Walked out leaving Saul to his Froot Loops and clowns.

It took him a few weeks, but he set up his own production company in an unfinished shell of a fourteenth floor office on Van Buren. Not much to look at, but a great view down Michigan Avenue, and if you pressed your cheek against the glass you could even catch a little slice of the lake.

He pulled in a couple of creative guys who'd recently been canned by smaller agencies for floating concepts that were way too radical for the room. Just the kind of guys Joe

HIDING IN HIBBING

liked. If you're going to start somewhere, better to start crazy and work your way back.

After he managed to scrounge up a couple of used desks, some chairs, couple lamps and stuff, he found a tiny production house that had gone belly up a week before and bought their entire equipment inventory for pennies on the dollar. He'd kept the Éclair camera and Nagra recorder that Ziggy had rescued, but they weren't worth much. Good for backups if something went haywire.

Each step he took gave him a greater sense of freedom, lightening his load, pointing him in the right direction. With everything ready to go, he dialed up Ray, asking him, "You want to shoot some film?" It was the first time they'd talked since returning from Hibbing. Ray hemmed and hawed, making clumsy attempts to change the subject, finally saying, "You know the last time didn't work out so great."

"That was a fluke. How many times is a Hibbing gonna happen?"

There was a pause. Then Ray said, "You want me to speculate on a number?"

"We came through okay, didn't we?"

"Had its moments," Ray said. He smiled a little, but Joe couldn't tell that over the phone.

"So what do you say?" More dead air, so he continued. "I quit the agency. Cut all the ties. Got a little production operation going. Not under anybody's thumb now."

"That's cool."

"Told you I'd bring you along. Keep you employed."

"I been thinking..."

"What?"

"Trying something else maybe."

"Like what?"

More silence. Too much it seemed. Then, "But thanks for thinking of me, Joe. I really mean it."

"Why the hell you wanna...?" Joe started, then heard the *click*, followed by nothing.

DAVID O'MALLEY

It was the last time he talked with Ray. Three months later, when things were really starting to pop and he needed someone to shoot A-camera on a Wendy's spot, he tried calling again. But Ray's number had been disconnected.

As Joe's reputation for wildly offbeat characters and a unique in-your-face style started catching on with agencies and clients, the number of production days doubled, then quadrupled. He created a series of innovative spots featuring fast-talking pitchmen, oddballs and eccentrics; they were everyday people but with unforgettable mugs. Companies clamored to get a Joe Studebaker commercial on the air so they could be the number one topic around the water cooler.

In the early '80s he created a national sensation by having a crotchety grandmother open the bun of a fast-food competitor's pathetically meager chicken sandwich and gripe in a gravelly voice into the camera, "Who stole the bird?" Sales for the Chicken Chucky chain went through the roof as America gobbled up millions of their Jumbo Chicken Chucky Tall Stack Sandwiches. From there it was straight up.

Over the years, Joe lost Gallagher's phone number. And as for Ziggy...Joe never called him about working again. But he did think about him often.

HIDING IN HIBBING

RAY

Before Ray caught the 3:30 train to Elmhurst, he pulled Ziggy aside and told him with grave seriousness, "Remember, Zig, it's not how many threads you have, it's how you weave 'em together." Gave him a rough guy-shove—actually more like a punch in the arm with a sharp knuckle bite to it—then pushed him out into the crush of dull-eyed commuters shuttling upstream like salmon.

A week later Ray got his hair cut short, pledging to get serious about his life. He forced himself to go see a movie at the Music Box Theater—a revival of the 1963 classic *Charade* with Audrey Hepburn and Cary Grant. First movie he'd seen in three years. The title sounded artsy-fartsy, so he figured it must have some real substance. Surprisingly, it was light and frothy, making him laugh a lot.

He even bought a book—his first one ever—which he promised himself he would read, but never did. The title, *The Organization Man*, appealed to him at first, then made him feel queasy. He buried it in a pile of magazines and old newspapers in the corner so, out of sight and out of mind, its presence wouldn't haunt him.

On a cold, rainy Wednesday afternoon he visited the Art Institute of Chicago, wandering the connected galleries staring vacantly at unfamiliar landscapes and meticulously shaded people frozen in hazy moments of indecision or listlessness.

His eyes were drawn to several attractive young women, each of them ambling around slowly, pausing to gaze with very serious expressions at framed tableaus, heads tilted slightly in contemplative reflection. One in particular, with soft brown hair and luscious delicate skin, turned to glance at him briefly and appeared to wink, winsome and coy. A few moments later he noticed she had moved away and was standing by a Monet, head bent forward as she daintily wiped a finger across her fluttering eyelash, trying to extricate some annoying speck. He realized the flirtatious wink had simply been a wishful fabrication of his own desperate imagination; that is, unless her gesture had been initially genuine, then reconsidered on second glance and masqueraded as an eye irritation to ward off further contact. Either option left him adrift, without consolation.

All of this cultural indulgence—the movies, the books, the museums—was in preparation for applying to college. If he was going to challenge himself by plunging into the frightening world of academia, he wanted to be as well prepared for the unfamiliar milieu as possible. Otherwise, he feared he would be easily recognized as an interloper, or at worst an outright fraud, and quickly excluded.

Northwestern was out of the question, but DePaul seemed like it could be within his grasp. If not, there was always the University of Chicago or Columbia School of Broadcasting. Or even Skokie Community College. Each new option he considered seemed to tumble lower on the scale of educational credibility. *Why not freakin' trade school?* Ray thought, prodding himself with his sharply honed bitterness. *You can run a belt sander or crank a friggin' monkey wrench.* Moments like that made him resent his hapless inclination for pessimism.

Occasionally he thought about Maggie, picturing her in his mind; her once captivating smile and sparkling eyes so effectively concealing a host of darker motivations. He wondered how he could have fallen so easily into her cold trap, ensnared by her seductive deception. He still didn't understand why she had used him in such a callous way, why she had betrayed him without a blink. His devoted cynicism should have allowed him to see through her charade.

Ah, yes. *Charade.* It became his byword; the lightning rod that allowed him to escape the dark torment of guilt and regret. Whenever he was robbed of sleep, plagued by self-doubt, second-guessing how he might have somehow seen Maggie with clearer eyes and escaped her treachery, he thought instead of Audrey Hepburn and Cary Grant playing *Pass the Orange*, that silly party game in the movie *Charade*; trying to transfer an orange between each other without using their hands. The image was vivid. A bright sphere of citrus embraced delicately beneath Audrey's celebrated chin, soft against her svelte neck, as she tried to pass the fragrant orb to Cary Grant, he having to grab it under his roguishly dimpled chin, their bodies pressed together, writhing with panting effort, his lips brushing her cheek softly.

Seduction in the guise of innocence. The inadvertent touch of their skin, electric. The tease. The dance. The whirling swoon of anticipation holding more erotic appeal than actual culmination. And riding on this wave of sweet cinematic fantasy, Ray would finally drift off to sleep.

The cost of attending college would not be inexpensive, he reasoned. Highway construction paid well, but a couple weeks of strained muscles and a damaging sunburn put an end to that misguided adventure. So he applied for a job downtown at Marshall Fields in the stockroom. But the sheer boredom of it soon drove him to request a sales clerk position in sporting goods, lying about his past experience with the casual ease that Joe had exercised when knitting one of his imaginative tales.

As days rolled into weeks and months, the comfort of avoiding the start of college became more attractive. The portion of his paycheck he put aside for tuition and books, stashed each Friday in an empty glass Heinz pickle jar, soon began to shrink and the cache so diligently saved withered to a few singles and some random coins.

That was when Larry showed up at his apartment, wired with adrenaline and who knows what else. Ray had met Larry Higginbotham in the Navy, when they were both stationed near Norfolk. A dedicated schemer, Larry always had an angle, anxious to play it.

"Okay okay," Larry said, pacing around with restless agitation, continually catching the toe of one shoe or the other on the curled flap of rug under the coffee table. "Here's the deal, see. You drive me to Mexico, okay..."

"Mexico?"

"Yeah. It's cool. Nice drive. Couple days, three tops."

"Why?"

"Business. I got business."

"What kind of business?"

"Just some business. Not important." Moving, moving, never stopping. Skittish, like a dog in a pen, back and forth.

"Why you need me?"

Larry stopped for the first time, as if he didn't expect that question. "I don't have a car."

"Where is it?"

"Long story. Not important." Pacing again. "But here's the thing, see. You drive me to Mexico, we cross the border at Nogales, I take care of the business and stuff, we come back up through Tijuana, go to L.A. and Frisco. And I pay you a thousand bucks."

"What for?"

"For driving me. That's it. Plus I'll pay gas, food, beer, whatever. You get a grand." Spread his arms, rocking back on his heels, pitchman supreme. "What a deal, right?"

It was Ray's turn to pace, only slower, looking down at his feet pensively.

"I don't know," Ray said. "There's something that just doesn't..." Letting it hang.

"What? It's not brain surgery. You drive me. I pay you."

The phone rang. Ray didn't react to the first ring, still thinking. Then he walked to the phone sitting on the stack of newspapers next to the bedroom door, picking up the receiver on the third ring. Listened, eyes rolling up to Larry, mumbled some random *non sequiturs* then turned into the bedroom, carrying the phone with him, stretching the cord around the doorjamb.

"You know the last time didn't work out so great." That's what Larry heard him say as Ray disappeared into the bedroom, the rest of it falling into a muted jumble of half-words, traffic noise from outside obscuring the rest.

Larry paced around the couch, circling it with the nervous movements of a jittery shark. Bit at a hangnail on his thumb, fidgety and impatient.

As Ray stepped back into the room, Larry heard him say, "...for thinking of me, Joe. I really mean it." Then Ray dropped the phone in the cradle, seeming to sever the call prematurely.

Larry looked at him, shifting from one foot to the other, staring him right in the eyes, wearing a mask of enthused expectation. "So? You in?"

Ray exhaled, letting a lot go in that single breath. "We drive there and back... and I get a thousand bucks?"

"There it is."

Ray took a few random steps, not going anywhere, just moving. "I've been struggling, man. With this...tendency. I'm so fuckin' cynical all the time. The glass half empty, ya know? Instead of half full."

"It's a curse, dude."

"Like to start seeing that glass half full."

"Fill it up, man."

"Put a lid on my constant skepticism."

"So, yeah." Larry said, still all twitchy, fingers pushed deep into his jeans pockets, rocking, shifting foot to foot. "Whatd'ya say?"

A pause. Long enough for the traffic sounds to intrude again. Ray looked off. At nothing.

"Sure."

They left on Thursday morning, following the roads that threaded through the hills of Missouri and rolling plains of Oklahoma, then knitted across the silky desert of New Mexico and Arizona. On Saturday they crossed the border at Nogales and gently weaved their way into the lonely wilds of Mexico.

There's probably more to it.

Who knows?

That desolate rocky realm below the border tells no tales.

HIDING IN HIBBING

GALLAGHER

After being dropped in the Loop, Gallagher simply told Ziggy and Ray to "hang loose"—no handshakes, no hugs, nothing final or sappy like that—then bounced away and caught the blue train out to Addison Park, where his sister had an apartment just a block off Pulaski. She was a teacher and had a soft spot for her younger brother, letting him crash on her couch whenever he needed to.

He had been counting on the meager pay from the Minnesota job to help cover the back rent he owed on his one-room walkup in the city, but that was a bust. So now he had to tap dance, make a course correction.

Got a job at McDonalds, which he swore he'd never do, and saved up every dime he could for eight months; the kind of dedication his sister, Annie, had never seen from him before. Put $50 down on a drum kit, paying it off in tiny increments every week. Snagged a cheap eight-track player and some used speakers at a garage sale. Talked his uncle Marty into letting him set up in the dingy cellar under his metal stamping shop on East LaSalle Street, then locked himself in and started banging on the drums, pounding along to hit records until he learned how to play.

Took a second job washing dishes at Sammy's Italian Café, basically dividing each day into thirds; eight hours at McD's, eight with his hands in hot greasy water at Sammy's, and the other eight banging the skins. Sleep? That was for pansies. What he didn't scrounge from Sammy's and McD's to eat, he'd get at Taco Bell, since everything on the menu still only cost a quarter.

By June of '73 he'd saved up enough and felt he was ready, so he bought a used Plymouth off his sister's girlfriend and headed west. It was rusted out with crappy shocks, but had a decent engine. As long as it kept moving who cared if air blew in through spaces where the trim had been ripped off and occasional potholes rammed the cheap coiled-spring seats right up into your tailbone?

Fifty miles out on I-90 he swerved north, heading for Route 53, rolling into Hibbing eight hours later, swinging by Sally's place to pick her up, like some medieval knight charging in on a white stallion to rescue the damsel.

"Portland awaits," he said, throwing the car door open with foolish gallantry.

"I don't get it," she said, demurely dragging the toe of her shoe across the ground, "Why do you want *me* to go with you?"

"Yeah, suppose you're right," Gallagher said, a coarse twinkle of sarcasm in his voice. "Guess we could just stay here, hang out, eat bad pizza, get old, sick, and wait to die."

His dismal parade of bleak one-syllable images cut to the bone. She broke out in a cold sweat, jumped right into the car. Didn't even pack a bag.

In Oregon they slipped into an easy groove, loving the moody rain that pelted them and the gloomy clouds that kept their youthful expectations of too much happiness at a safe distance.

When money ran low, they stooped to panhandling outside Powell's Bookstore, figuring that if people could afford the luxury of books they could easily toss a few coins their way. But theories predicated on hope rarely prove accurate. So with empty pockets they drifted up to Seattle, where Gallagher immediately got a gig playing drums in a half-assed band called Smelly Fried Fish. Relying only on simple four chord covers they played six-hour shifts in every crappy college bar within pub-crawling distance of U-dub, allowing Gallagher to tuck away enough bucks for rent, while Sally brought in some real money waiting tables at the popular seafood emporium, Ivar's Acres of Clams.

HIDING IN HIBBING

Seattle had always been a musical town. The jazz scene was anchored for years by the cool, conga-flavored sounds of percussionist Gerard Breashear and singer Wanda Brown. But it was radio deejay Pat O'Day and his ubiquitous dance parties that pushed the Emerald City into a music frenzy, giving birth to a burgeoning conflux of hastily formed cover bands in the early '70s. A roaring tidal wave of homegrown garage bands soon followed. By 1976 jazz, folk and rock were eclipsed by the musical devil seed of punk, which would eventually lead to the tumultuous birth of grunge.

Through all this, Gallagher managed to secure a continuous run of gigs filling in for drummers who had either quit, been fired or deemed by their band-mates as too wasted to play. Banging away without any more finesse than he had briefly demonstrated on stage at the Elks Hall in Hibbing, Gallagher managed to anchor the propulsive bands with a steady thundering beat that equaled the ear-splitting jangle of their artless social rebellion.

Quicker than they expected, Gallagher and Sally had pooled enough to cobble together a basement recording studio in Redmond. Given the number of new rock groups popping up, there was always a shortage of studio space and never a shortage of work. Looking back, they were always amazed at how fast and easy things happened when they were blissfully young.

Eventually Gallagher forgot all about wanting to make his mark as a working drummer and stuck with becoming a master of the mixing board. He even dumped wanting to be called Anthony. He liked Gallagher just fine and it stuck.

Bob Dylan launched his world tour in late 1978. When Gallagher heard on the radio that seats had gone on sale, he drove straight to U-dub and got two tickets for the November 10th concert at the Hec Edmundson Pavilion. It was an instinctive move on his part, devoid of the usual deep thought, serious consideration and lengthy discussion that normally preceded such an important decision. He didn't even stop to call Sally knowing that her recently developed caution in all things financial might kick into gear, exposing them to their usual frustrating cycle of hesitation, doubt, reconsideration and, ultimately, inaction.

Besides, certain things in life are meant to be a surprise.

The Pavilion was sold out that night. Dylan's world tour, his first major run of concerts in nearly ten years, had generated huge interest. After endless rumors of a puzzling premature retirement, as well as running controversies over his reviled electric phase and his suspicious detours into Christian gospel, the legendary Phoenix was rising again. He would either blaze like a guiding light or gloriously crash and burn. There was no shortage of willing witnesses.

Sally leaned forward in her seat, anxious eyes anticipating the appearance of the true superstar who hailed from her very own hometown, who had attended the very same high school she did. She never gave a passing thought to the irony of the fake star at her side and the failed deceit of his past pathetic charade. She had never cared if he really was a musician or a star or a celebrity; right from the start, she saw the man, not the façade.

It was halfway through the concert, somewhere between *It Ain't Me, Babe* and *Girl From the North Country* that Gallagher abruptly realized he had never actually fallen in love with Sally. Not the head-over-heels, love at first sight, crawl-on-your-naked-stomach-over-broken-glass-to-be-with-her kind of love. It was something else. Something bigger.

When she first flirted with him at Carl's Diner — what was that coy wink but an invitation to step into her life? — he had sensed a subtle shift in his world. When they first made love, convulsed by endless fits of helpless laughter, it felt more delirious and delicious than any orgasm. When they first talked about something of real substance, something that truly mattered, a tiny seed planted itself deep in the furrows of his heart, within his lungs, taking root and growing slowly. Undetected, its tendrils encompassed and infiltrated all his organs and veins and bones and muscles and blood. Until now, finally, at this time, in this place, both he and Sally had become stronger together than they ever were apart. Unaware, he had pursued her, embraced her, without agenda or purpose. It was because *it was*, needed to be; two lines converged in precisely the same direction, invisibly entwined.

There had been no falling. No first sight. No crawling or suffering or angst. They had simply been drawn into each other's vortex of irresistible influence, happily surrendering to it without ever consciously taking notice.

After several years living together in a crappy one-room flat, Gallagher and Sally moved to an equally unremarkable four-room walk-up near Pikes Market, producing three children, Dylan, Zig, and their youngest, Pumpkin. Her real name was Pamela, but he loved calling her Pumpkin, grinning in sly reflection, still feeling the harsh aching bruises of experience buried deep under his skin.

When Pumpkin was eleven-months old, she uttered her first word. "Dance." Her dad thought it was "dense" or "dunce" but Sally was certain it was "dance." When she was not yet three she said, "inflatable" with perfect clarity. A bit surprised, Gallagher asked if she knew what it meant. "No," she said, shrugging her tiny shoulders, "I just like the sound of it."

That evening, Gallagher finally asked Sally if she'd "entertain the proposition of establishing a commitment of connubial conjugation."

"Fuck that," she told him. "Let's get married."

He grinned. "Fabtaculous."

"I like all your big words," Sally said, cuddling down in his arms. "They make me feel safe."

"Oh yeah? How's that?"

"It's like a big high wall. Keeps the stupid out."

"Impenetrable."

"Yeah." She laughed. "See, you coulda just said *thick*."

EPILOGUE

In May of 1988 Ziggy and Susan were married. It was a modest ceremony attended by only a few close friends and Susan's parents, Bob and Jean, lovely people with hearty laughs who shared six dogs, a conventional outlook on life and little concern for sports or politics.

Ziggy's own parents had already passed away, which is how he now chose to describe their fated circumstance, finally accepting that he never really wanted to think of them as *dead* and *gone*, vanished from all existence and memory. Like most of us, he preferred to believe they had simply moved on, taking up residence in some distant inaccessible place like Antarctica or China, a remote region of the world that defied convenient visitation.

To celebrate their first six months of marriage, Ziggy decided to splurge and take Susan to see the 20th Anniversary production of *Hair* that had opened to rave reviews at Chicago's historic Vic Theater. The ticket prices were steep but they both felt any cost of celebrating their life together was well worth it. As icing on the cake, Ziggy also booked a room for them at the luxurious Palmer House Hotel.

As they stepped under the Vic Theater marquee, Ziggy caught sight of the play's poster, a psychedelic splash of brightly colored hippies leaping and dancing with carefree abandon. He was struck by a sudden twinge, recalling that freezing day at the iron pit near Hibbing when Janey had talked with such affectionate fascination about beatniks and hippies; how it would be so much fun to be one, even for a short while. He wondered if she still felt that way.

"Great seats," Susan said, hugging his arm tightly as they settled into the center orchestra section.

HIDING IN HIBBING

"You deserve only the best," he said. Ziggy had sweated indecisively over the seating chart for nearly a half hour when buying the tickets, so hearing her grateful words brought a welcome measure of relief.

As he thumbed casually through the vividly designed playbill Ziggy was startled to see Janey's name listed in the cast. He had to blink twice, unsure he had read it correctly. But there it was. Janey Olsen. In the role of Sheila. And it was right up there near the top of the list. Did that mean she was a major character? He closed his program book sharply, as if trying to trap a mouse in a box so it couldn't escape.

"What's wrong?"

"Nothing. I just...why sit here and read when I can talk with you."

"That's sweet. You always know the right thing to say."

"Not really," he mumbled aside.

A traditional Broadway overture was replaced by a parade of cast members in garishly colored rags and tatters, dashing up and down the aisles, where they whirled, flounced, coaxed and taunted audience members, striving to drag them from their straight-jacketed conformity into the frenzied, free-spirited world of the flower-power generation. The house lights lowered as the revelry concluded and the carnival of players blended seamlessly into darkness. Susan squeezed Ziggy's hand. The stage lights came up. And there she was. Ziggy felt his chest tighten.

For the next two-hours and twenty-six minutes he sat transfixed.

Afterwards, as they stepped out of the theater, standing with the milling crowd beneath the blazing radiance of the marquee, Ziggy recognized some of the cast members, now out of costume, drifting from the broad alleyway that led to the backstage entrance. He hesitated, inspired by a reckless thought, trying to push it away.

"What is it?"

"Nothing. I thought I saw someone I knew."

"Really? Who?"

"Oh, just someone..." He looked toward the alleyway. "But I'm not sure."

She nudged his elbow lightly with her own. "Go ahead. You know it'll drive you crazy if you don't."

"No, it's okay. I, uh..."

"Go on. I have to run back in and use the ladies room anyway. I'll meet you back here."

Ziggy turned into the alley as three members of the rag-tag chorus ambled past, blurting the laughter of unbridled youth, ready to party.

Nearing the stage door, he slowed his pace; he watched as it opened and closed, cast members traipsing out alone or in small clusters. He looked down, then away, not wanting to appear like some obsessed theater fan in the annoying pursuit of autographs.

After a long moment, he began to feel ridiculous, a sentimental madman on a fool's errand. He paced a quick agitated circle and then turned to retreat back to the street. He barely heard the door open behind him.

"I saw you."

He stopped. It was Janey. There was no doubt. Her voice was silvery and clear in the crisp November air. He turned slowly to see her, taking in the ethereal glow of her face.

"I saw you," she said again. "In the audience."

With a crooked grin, he said, "No you didn't."

"We never look out there. Most of the time we can't see anything anyway, the lights are so blinding. But there was a moment tonight, when the lights went down and I felt this..." She hunched her shoulders with a shiver. "And there you were."

He couldn't speak. Was this really happening? Right now? He honestly wasn't sure. But it seemed right. It seemed...perfect.

HIDING IN HIBBING

Janey stepped down the three concrete stairs from the stage entrance, pausing no more than five feet from Ziggy.

"I'm so glad you came to see me."

"I wouldn't have missed it," he said, instantly wincing at the glib triteness of his own words, wishing he could suck them back and swallow them. He wanted to turn away, feeling the sharp sting of her sincere gratitude.

"I can't lie to you again," he said, becoming weightless now, shedding the burden of deceit. "I didn't even know you were in the play until I got here."

She struck an adorable pose, one hand raised, palm open, a foot cocked jauntily — flirtatiously? — ankle turned, toe down and heel up. "Surprise."

"It really was. The best surprise ever."

Her gaze flitted across the ring on his left hand, then quickly drifted off, searching to focus somewhere else while she gathered her thoughts. Her pose deflated.

Finally she managed, "So are you...?"

"Married?"

"I was going to say 'happy'."

"Yes." he said. "Both. Married and happy." There was no point dancing around it. "She's here... with me tonight. Her name is Susan."

"Susan," she said in a hushed whisper, then smiled bravely. "I'm sure she's wonderful."

"Yes, she is." He let it go at that, allowing Janey to fill in the rest. A gaping silence swept between them.

"Are you...?" he began.

"Oh yes. I am. I truly am," she said with bubbly enthusiasm. "It's such an awesome thrill to be up on stage." She stopped, recognizing the look in his eyes.

"I was going to say..."

"Oh... Married," she said, realizing now, chagrined. "No." She allowed the tiny word—tiny yet so incredibly potent—to float out on a pensive breath. "With all the traveling, and the craziness; the life of an actor, you know."

"But you finally got to be a hippy."

"Ah, yes...that. Ha! Well, a make-believe hippy. It's fun, for a few hours each night. I guess now I can be all the things I never thought I could. You opened that door for me."

"The door was there all the time. You opened it. I just rang the bell."

"Are we engaged in a game of ridiculous metaphors now?"

He chuckled stiffly, the way he often did when at a loss for a clever rejoinder.

Janey fell silent. She pressed her open hands together in contemplation, two fingertips lightly touching her lips, thumbs gently braced under her chin, as if praying. She seemed adrift, unsure whether to speak her thoughts.

"The time we had together...it was so short..."

"I wouldn't change it in any way."

She gazed off, at something distant. "Do you...ever wonder...?" Her eyes came back to his, "What if...?"

"Of course. But I try not to."

He couldn't let her go on, afraid where it might lead.

"You were so damned impressive up there tonight," he said, thrusting their conversation in a safer direction. "It's obviously where you belong. Up there on the stage, in the spotlight."

"It's where I feel most comfortable." She laughed at the irony. "Hard to believe, isn't it?"

"No. Not at all."

"You recognized who I was long before I did."

"That was easy. Anyone could tell you were amazingly talented. And that you would become an incredible woman."

Janey shrugged demurely. "I'm just a little girl from Hibbing, Minnesota who still believes in her dreams." Then tilted her head with a sweetly generous smile. "Because of you."

"I didn't do anything."

"You changed my life."

"I still regret that I ever lied to you."

"Regret is a waste of time," she said, brushing a wisp of hair back from her face. "I seem to recall someone telling me that."

She had him there. He looked askance at her, trying to shrug it off with a wry smirk. "And I suppose you believed him?"

She nodded. "I've never forgotten it."

"So, here we are... and now you're telling me."

She nodded again, very slowly, smiling with certainty. "I guess that's the gift we gave each other, isn't it?"

When Ziggy returned to the front of the theater, Susan was waiting patiently near the curb. Her eyebrows arched in expectation.

"So? Was it who you thought it was?"

He glanced back toward the alley, an oddly wistful grin on his face.

"Yes."

She waited a few moments, giving him a chance to continue. But he didn't. "So who was it?"

"Someone I knew a long time ago."

When he didn't go on, she leaned forward, invading his vacant stare. He saw the sly crinkly smile she always gave him whenever he tossed out some bad pun or a strangely disconnected remark. "Are you going to tell me about her?"

He couldn't resist grinning at Susan's impish tenacity.

"Yes. Yes, I will." He turned toward her, no longer avoiding her persistent inquiry. "But tonight is all about us. Everything else can wait."

"Good," she said. She hooked his arm with hers, tossed her scarf back over her shoulder. "Come on, Arthur. Let's go check out our fancy hotel room."

Five weeks later, Susan announced she was pregnant. This prompted Ziggy to proudly proclaim that if she gave birth to a boy they should name him Joe, Ray or Tony. Susan smiled serenely at his exuberant declaration, confident that a darling little girl stirred within her.

Eight months later, Emma was born. Once Ziggy saw her wispy mop of tiny blond ringlets and radiant blue eyes, all thoughts of little boys evaporated from his mind. She was his angel.

He had fleetingly contemplated suggesting they call her Janey, but instantly rejected the idea as totally inappropriate; it would be strikingly insulting to Susan as well as unfair to both their child and Janey. In his mind, there was, and would always be, only one Janey. This strange compartmentalizing of logic, emotion and memories seemed terribly iniquitous to Ziggy so he scrubbed all remnants of it from his mind, never thinking of it again.

A week after Emma's first birthday they moved out north to Buffalo Grove, taking up residence in one of the trendy new suburban tract rentals neatly tucked side-by-side amid a smattering of newly-planted spindly saplings that would eventually grow into bowers of sprawling leafy elms.

As from the beginning, Susan continued to call Ziggy by his given name, Arthur, never acquiescing to the peculiarly unfamiliar nickname that everyone else preferred. Ziggy enjoyed the unique singularity she alone conferred on him, never even suggesting otherwise. He had taken on several identities over the years: Artie Zigmond—until after 2nd grade —then "Ziggy" Zigmond through high school, and, of course, the bogus alias Ziggy Jett, rock star, in Hibbing, Minnesota. But Arthur was his absolute favorite and it proved to be where he found his greatest comfort.

HIDING IN HIBBING

January 1995

The daily train ride in from Buffalo Grove was a pleasant diversion for Ziggy, giving him a chance to read the Trib front to back, occasionally gazing out the grime spackled window at the incongruent structures flashing by outside—ramshackle beside sturdy, derelict thrust upon tidy, darkly sinister gnashing its teeth into the buoyantly vivid and charming—neighborhoods of divergence and distinction clustered together with haphazard grace, inhabited by souls all possessing the same jumble of discordant attributes, dissonant notes out of tune with each other, but hallowed and whole when taken alone.

This dazzling visual fusion always stimulated the hushed places in Ziggy's mind, sending his thoughts spiraling into a creative tailspin that inevitably led to a wacky new idea for the next day's column. At the very least it would reveal a path to some disconnected source of inquiry, prompting research that would guide him to one new discovery upon another.

On the return trip in mid-winter he would stare, mesmerized, at the icy rime pasted on the window that framed a darkening mosaic of white rooftops and blurry snow. In the spiky spires of creeping frost he envisioned the microchips of the digital revolution that was now upon them, imagining ones and zeroes buried invisibly in the frozen patterns, pointing the way to fresh revelations. The computer age had presented a billion new doors for him to open and explore, allowing the breadth and reach of his speculative technology column to swell far beyond its original humble beginnings.

On January 6th he arrived home to find a plain white envelope in his stack of mail. There was no return address in the upper left corner, just the neatly printed name—Joe Studebaker.

He stared at it for a long moment, a flood of unexpected emotions washing through him, then tore it open with the dull edge of his finger leaving the flap ragged and frayed. Inside he found only a single piece of paper, folded in half. On it, in neat block letters: *YOU WERE RIGHT.*

Nothing else. Just those three words.

He turned it over, finding the flip side blank.

Maybe he had missed something. Peered into the envelope. It was clearly empty. He studied the outside for some clue, some further telltale note or scribble. But all he found was a thirty-two cent stamp, a Chicago postmark and yesterday's date.

You were right. He let the words march through his mind while, on the periphery of his awareness, Emma's tiny voice drifted faintly from the kitchen, chattering softly while Susan prepared dinner, accompanied by the clunking of pans and dull thudding of drawers and cupboard doors.

Right about what? He almost muttered it allowed. Maybe he did. He wasn't sure.

He didn't mention the note to Susan. This was his mystery alone to solve. Besides, she didn't know who Joe was and any explanation of their quirky past experiences would have required the disclosure of endless details, layered with convoluted anecdotes that would likely strain credibility, easily encouraging bewilderment and misunderstanding.

It taunted him for days, turning his commutes to and from downtown Chicago into unfocused reminiscences of his escapades in Hibbing, replaying the erratic moments like a fuzzy dream, logic and plausible chronology taking a back seat to impressionistic chaos.

At night Ziggy lay awake haunted by Joe's words, unable to unlock their ambiguity. He couldn't have been referring to Ziggy's casual prediction of MTV; Ziggy had never even mentioned the concept to Joe. Moreover, its advent was now nearly fifteen years in the past. MTV had already become old school—as Ziggy had cogently predicted that it would to Chuck Walters—gradually evolving into a hapless conglomeration of cheap adolescent movies, gross-out cartoons and exploitative music star bios that wallowed in crash-and-burn rehab and career suicide. *It will change ...everything changes*, he had told Chuck.

He tossed and turned every night, punching his pillow into submission, searching vainly for peace in its puffy folds, constantly flipping to the cool side to refresh his cheek. But sleep wouldn't come. *Right about what?*

He considered tracking Joe down and just asking him point blank what he was referring to. It would be easy. Joe was now an established, well known personality in the world of television advertising. His production company was right downtown, somewhere on LaSalle. He knew that much because of the in-depth profile they ran on Joe in the Sunday Tribune a few years back.

But he was reluctant to ask, afraid he'd discover it was just something stupid that he wouldn't even remember. Something so trivial and inconsequential that when Joe told him what it was he'd have to lie through his teeth, pretending to recall it. And his bald prevarication would be so blatantly transparent Joe would call him on it, making him feel like an insignificant gnat, eminently squashable, disposable, easily flicked by a finger into obscurity.

He flipped his pillow. Punched it.

No. He would rather live within the evasive mystery, imagining it to be something quite spectacular and special, something that might actually demonstrate he is truly unique in this crazy world.

While he grappled nightly with his pillow, restlessly snarled in twisted sheets and blankets, unable to sleep, Susan lay beside him in twilight slumber, quietly fretting about her husband's twitchy unease.

DAVID O'MALLEY

On January 29th two of Ziggy's friends from the paper, Ken Smalls, who covered college sports, and Bill Krasean, the science and medical editor, came over to watch Super Bowl XXIX with Ziggy. They brought chips and beer so Susan wouldn't have to bother.

Emma, now seven, wasn't into football. Not yet anyway. That would come later. So Susan promised to take her to see a matinee of Disney's *The Jungle Book* in downtown Chicago and then out to get a Gihrardelli chocolate sundae afterward.

Both Susan and Emma gave Ziggy a quick peck on the cheek as they scurried out the door, telling him to have fun. He wished them the same, playfully wiggling Emma's tiny hand between his fingers.

The San Francisco 49ers were strongly favored to devastate the San Diego Chargers so expectations were high the game could be a real dud. Since the Bears weren't in the fray, nor the neighboring Lions or Packers, interest in the Chicago area was at low ebb.

But a quick interception following the kickoff led to 49er quarterback Steve Young throwing a 44-yard pass to Jerry Rice on the third play of the game, setting a record for the fastest touchdown in Super Bowl history. It was followed by another frenzied push downfield and at five-minutes into the first quarter San Francisco led 14-0. It looked like they were right on course to an expected easy victory. But in football, as in life, nothing is ever certain.

Susan and Emma just missed the express train, so they had to wait for the local. They chatted all the way in about dolls and Scooby Doo. But as they poked along, stopping at every station, Susan anxiously checked her watch more than once worried they might miss the beginning of the movie.

When they finally arrived, Susan hustled Emma along, walking as quickly as her short stride allowed on the slippery sidewalk, moving up LaSalle toward Michigan Avenue. She tugged her daughter past the distraction of brightly decorated store windows, promising they would take more time to look after the movie.

They paused at the corner of LaSalle and Michigan Avenue waiting for the light to change, shivering in the ruthless cold wind that swept up from the icy lake. When it finally flashed green, Emma stepped out first into the crosswalk.

Neither of them saw the huge city bus run the yellow light and barrel toward them. But Susan heard the whining roar in her left ear, sensing a giant wall closing in, spewing a huff of thunder, horn blowing like a raging bison. She grasped Emma's sleeve, fingers clutching viselike around her small wrist, wrenching her backward with a fierce explosion of maternal instinct. Both of them felt the blast of hot air from the bus exhaust panel as it swept past, the gritty metal brushing the soft fabric of their matching winter coats.

"Mommy," Emma said, her voice tiny and quivering. She hugged Susan, continuing to tremble in puzzled shock, not certain what had just happened. Susan hugged her daughter for several minutes, clutching her so tightly her muscles ached. She pulled back only to assure concerned bystanders that they were okay.

Once they had both recovered, they carefully crossed the street, looking back and forth several times before daring to venture out.

As it happened, the start of the movie had been delayed by a balky projector which, when finally made operable, presented numerous trailers for coming attractions, so they didn't miss a thing.

After the show, Susan and Emma took extra time to look at every single window display at Marshall Fields and then shared an extra-large chocolate sundae, giggling as they recalled highlights of the movie.

Susan vowed to herself she would never tell Ziggy about the scary incident with the bus. He was already having enough difficulty sleeping. It would serve no good purpose to plant another seed of trepidation in his soul.

At the half, the score was 49ers 18, Chargers 10. All the chips were gone and only half a bag of Cheetos remained.

"Told ya, it's gonna be a massacre," Ken said. He popped the cap off another beer.

"Ehhhhh, don't count the Chargers out yet." Bill was originally from San Diego—well, San Juan Capistrano, but close enough—so he felt compelled to profess his loyalty to the home team.

Ken pulled his wallet out with a grandiose gesture, cracking it open and digging around inside. "Hundred bucks says they get their asses kicked." Slapped some bills on the oak coffee table between the empty Lays bag and scattered Cheetos.

"You're on," Bill said, taking the bait. Dug into his pocket, but left his hand there. "I've got it, but I'm not laying it down for you to steal. You're gonna lose anyway."

They both laughed, clinking their beer bottles together to seal the bet, chortling as they drank to it.

Beer was a magic elixir. It turned men into boys, instilling them with all kinds of foolishness.

Ziggy smiled, pleased to see his friends having fun. He loved journalists; eloquent on the page, coarse as back road dirt when off the clock.

"What'dya say, Zig, we get a pizza?" Ken said.

"Sure."

"We'll buy," Bill offered, "you're the host. We'll get it."

"Even better."

"Dominos?" Ken said.

"Naaaah. That crap?" Bill made a face. "Little Caesars."

They both roared. Neither of them would ever touch anything but true Chicago-style, thick crust, baked by a fourth-generation Italian.

HIDING IN HIBBING

"Where's your phone book, Zig? We'll call Giordano's, order a large."

"In the kitchen, counter by the fridge."

Ken and Bill grabbed their beer bottles, trotted off to the kitchen.

Ziggy gazed at the TV screen. The half-time analysis was wrapping up.

"Pepperoni okay?" Bill called from the other room.

"I'm good with whatever you guys want," Ziggy hollered back.

The television fell silent; the screen grew dark, pulling Ziggy's attention to it. A murky swamp lit by a full moon materialized. Crickets chirped in the night. It was so vivid you could feel the dank humidity. A big ugly frog on a rock rhythmically croaked *"bud"* several times.

Drawn by the odd sound, Ken and Bill stepped back into the room, staring at the screen with mute curiosity.

Two more nearby frogs on lily pads joined in, randomly croaking what sounded like *"weis"* and *"er."*

Ziggy leaned forward, elbows resting on his knees.

Ken and Bill both sputtered laughs, stepping closer.

The three frogs croaked in sequence, over and over, *"bud"...."weis"...."er"...."bud"...."weis"...."er"...."bud-weis-er"*

The camera tilted up to a big neon sign on a swamp shack. Budweiser!

Bill and Ken doubled over in hysterical laughter, stumbling around helplessly, mimicking the talking frogs.

Joe's cryptic note suddenly came crystal clear.

Ziggy *had* been right. You *can* sell beer with a talking frog. Talking frogs *are* funny. Way funnier than talking fish.

Ziggy sank into the soft caress of the leather cushions, arms stretched out wide across the back of the couch, feet up on the coffee table, a grin on his face broad enough to crack his skull.

He was inexorably happy in his special domain.

His bailiwick.

DAVID O'MALLEY

HIDING IN HIBBING

That night, thanks to Joe and Susan,
Ziggy slept like a baby, without a care in the world.

But things change. They always do. You can count on it.

DAVID O'MALLEY

HIDING IN HIBBING

By the way...
San Francisco beat San Diego, 49 to 26.

Sometimes there are no surprises.

Acknowledgements

Many thanks to my circle of close friends and fellow-authors who provided their support, especially those who offered to read a seemingly endless number of drafts and revisions, generously giving their advice, good natured criticism and many creative ideas that I readily and happily appropriated as my very own. *Hiding in Hibbing* would not have come into being without your benevolence, encouragement and insight. In particular: James L. Conway, Julie Staheli, Pierce Gardner, Jeffrey Conlon, Carl Reiner, Barry Livingston, April Kelly, Brent Maddock, Michael Spence, Marion Draugalis, Sue Mansfield and Patricia Heath.

I owe a special debt of gratitude to Jerry Bowles for making sure I interpreted the world of *The Ed Sullivan Show* accurately. My sincere appreciation to Judge Gary Allen and his wife, Pat, who generously let me disappear into their lake cabin to begin my literary trek. Also to Bernie and Audrey Toutant for granting me unlimited use of their tranquil wooded hideaway in Port Austin, Michigan while I struggled to put the characters and plot into focus.

A monumental vote of thanks to Arthur Pembleton who actually experienced that incredibly brutal Minnesota blizzard and lived to tell about it. I was fortunate enough to hear him recount his amazing true tale and he generously granted me the opportunity to twist and pummel it into existence, first as a screenplay, then as this novel.

A very special thank you to Caitlin... who never lets me get away with a single error.

And most of all, I want to extend the warmest acknowledgement of eternal gratitude to my incredible editor, creative spirit and adorable muse, Karen Conlon O'Malley. I couldn't do any of this without you. And I wouldn't want to.

Made in the USA
Lexington, KY
01 April 2015